Praise for...

Tears of Min Brock

Some of the best stories I can remember are those that take me out of my own existence and insert me into a world I have never known. I get to become a part of the story and the adventure and excitement also becomes a part of my own. In *Tears of Min Brock* by J. E. Lowder, I have again found one of those fascinating epic fantasy worlds that are daunting and dangerous, yet broodingly beautiful as well.

- BlogCritics Books

Lowder pulls you into a world of chaos and hope. You can almost feel the breeze and smell the foliage as you walk with the main characters through this well written story. I give it far more than the usual five stars!

- Opus 'N' Pen

Not too many books can truly be described as epic. Narnia, Lord of the Rings, Pullman's Dark Materials...and now *Tears of Min Brock*. This is one book that clearly deserves the 'epic' description.

- Book Lovers Paradise

Lowder has created an intricate fantasy world full of despair and darkness as well as hope and luminous beauty.

- Examiner.com

Tears of Min Brock is a heartfelt story of epic proportions with two loveable characters. It is an epic in every sense: a myriad of characters, a war of worlds, and a healthy dose of mysticism.

- Sift Book Reviews

I haven't read a lot of fantasy this year. I'm not a particularly huge fan of the genre, so a book has to sound really good for me to be interested in reading it. Let me say this: reading a book as good as Tears of Min Brock is making me want to grab every single fantasy book I possibly can and devour them. This book gripped me right from the very beginning, and when I wasn't reading it, I was thinking about it.

- Music, Books and Tea

TEARS OF MIN BROCK

TEARS OF MIN BROCK

J.E. LOWDER

WordCrafts

Published by WordCrafts Press
Tullahoma, TN 37388
www.wordcrafts.net

**To Laura, whose gentle words always
shoo away the vul jens roosting within.**

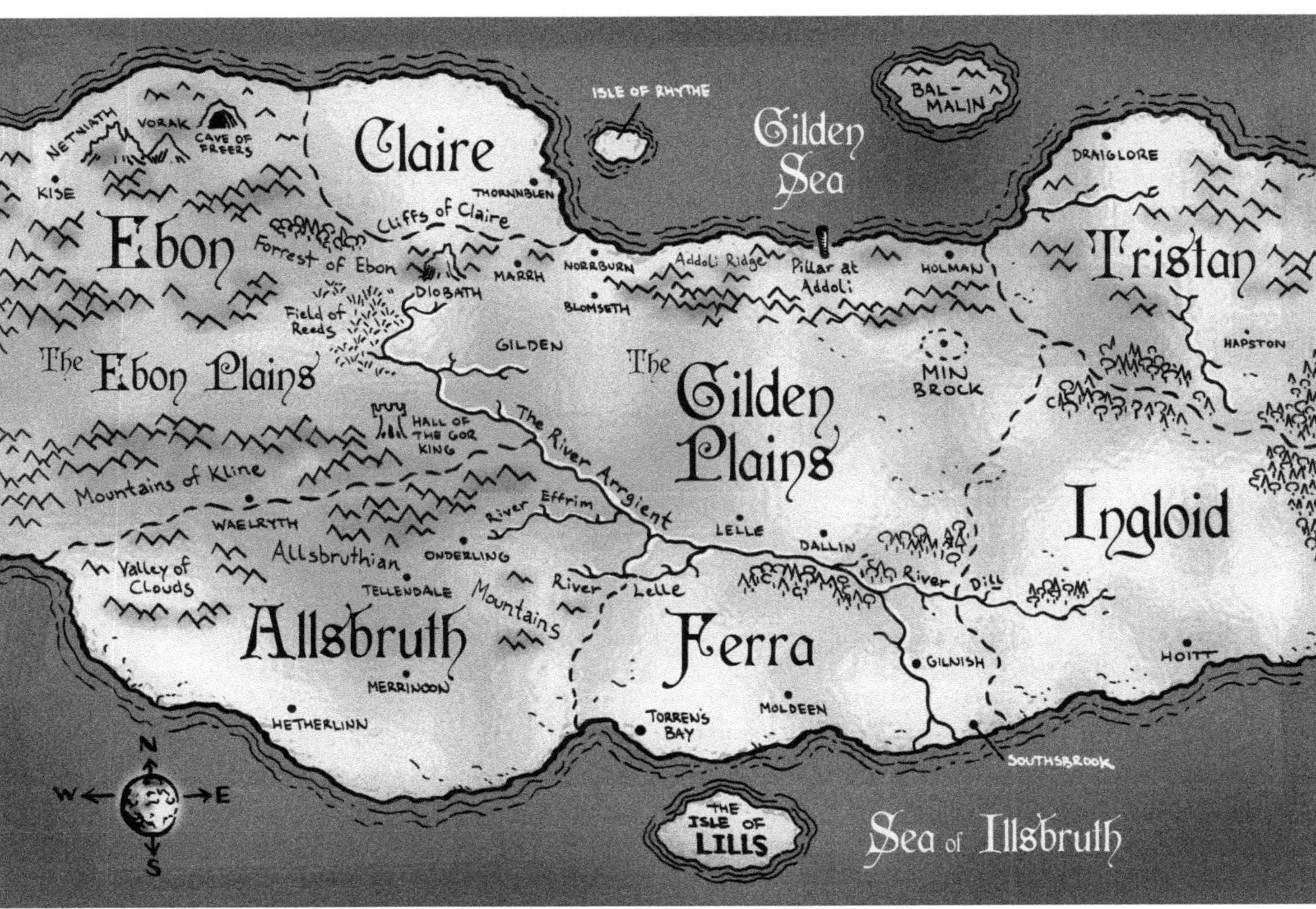

ISLE OF RHYTHE
Gilden Sea
BAL-MALIN
Claire
DRAIGLORE
NETNIATH
VORAK
CAVE OF FREERS
KISE
THORNNBLEN
Cliffs of Claire
Ebon
Forrest of Ebon
NORRBURN
Addoli Ridge
Pillar at Addoli
HOLMAN
Tristan
MARRH
DIOBATH
BLOMSETH
Field of Reeds
GILDEN
The Ebon Plains
The Gilden Plains
MIN BROCK
HAPSTON
HALL OF THE GOR KING
The River Arrgient
Mountains of Kline
River Effrim
Ingloid
WAELRYTH
Allsbruthian
ONDERLING
LELLE
DALLIN
Fish River
DILL
Valley of Clouds
TELLENDALE
Mountains
River Lelle
Allsbruth
Ferra
GILNISH
HOITT
MERRINOON
MOLDEEN
HETHERLINN
TORREN'S BAY
SOUTHSBROOK
N
W
E
S
THE ISLE OF LILLS
Sea of Illsbruth

Prologue

The winter moon glowed ominously. Unusually large and ghostly blue, its sapphire beams dotted the landscape while long shadows crisscrossed the nations.

Despite midnight's stillness, despite the frigid night, something wonderful - perhaps even magical - stirred.

A breeze.

Leafless trees swayed to its touch, awakening from a dream, and yet, the breeze did not bring a snowstorm or even clouds for that matter.

It simply carried the subtle scent of a flower.

A tulip.

The great oak took note of the phenomenon from atop its knoll, straining with all its might to turn into the wind. Unlike the other trees that encountered the warm breeze, the oak's sweeping branches danced in the moonlight, for it had been waiting patiently for this moment for many summers.

The breeze became a zephyr and the oak bowed to its might, all the while searching the midnight sky for his anticipated return.

High above in the northern hemisphere, a thread of silver coursed the blackness, and the oak knew this was not a comet or even a falling star. It watched the argent light fly southward before falling from the sky, knowing it had disappeared for a reason. It was on a mission of secrecy, and none of the nations, especially Ebon, could know of its arrival.

Nevertheless, the oak knew the course it would take, and imagined it zipping over the Gilden Sea whose cresting waves were but a blur of sapphire. Next, the tree pictured the silver beam zooming inland and racing across the vast Gilden Plains.

Nearing the border of Allsbruth, the nation the oak called home, it descended to the treetops. Swooping around mountains, darting over the River Arrgient, and twisting along winding roads, the silvery beam flew for the rendezvous with the oak. Approaching the hamlet of Hetherlinn, it slowed to a stop and hovered above the knoll.

The oak stretched its long limbs toward the mighty warrior and his mount, and it swayed in the wind, cheering their arrival. Both warrior and steed glowed as if a full moon resided within, while streams of blue light fell like shooting stars from his flowing cape, and a long sword was strapped to his side. The warrior's face was his most captivating feature, ablaze with color like fire in a wintry sky.

The warrior, in turn, gave the regal tree a formal bow, acknowledging that their reunion had been long overdue. He admired the tree's far-reaching branches and towering height, recalling a distant time - as if in a dream - when the children of Allsbruth climbed it in hope of hearing a whisper.

Defeat in the Dark War with Ebon and the Cauldron changed all of that. Now, villagers of Hetherlinn avoided the oak and even banned their children from it as well.

After all, swirling within the whispers were stories from the nation of Claire. Even though such tales could lead to freedom, the price was more than they were willing to pay. So they accepted the restraints of the Cauldron's Oracles, bowed beneath Ebon's military rule, and vowed to never listen to the whisper again.

The enigmatic warrior turned his gaze toward the sleeping village of Hetherlinn. Their tiny cottages sat in the shape of a crescent moon around the town's communal fire that, at this time of night, was just a faint glow. Despite the hamlet's small size, it was the epicenter of defeat in the Dark War. Sleeping inside cottages Number 17 and 7 were the men whose actions at the Battle of Min Brock continued to shadow the nations with despair. The warrior let his gaze wander from their homes, for he was not sent to question their allegiance or even punish their failures.

His was an altogether different mission.

Retrieving his crossbow from his back, he noched one of his bolts. Wrapping a white parchment around the clear crystal shaft, he secured the message with a thin strip of leather. Raising the weapon to his shoulder, he aimed and sent the bolt zipping through the air. Seeing that it struck its mark, he repeated the process again and again. Satisfied that he had accomplished his task, he darted through Hetherlinn, blue-silver beams disappearing into the deepest of shade.

Chapter 1

The Moon King

Thud.

Elabea was startled awake.

"Who's there?" she gasped as she pulled her covers close.

Although only fourteen summers of age, Elabea had seen her share of Ebonite night raids. Even so, she would never get used to warriors barging in while her family slept. Herded gruffly out into the night, they would be led to the communal fire with the other villagers. While Ebonite commanders took roll call, the warriors harassed them: spittle and curses flew; blades threatened children and women; kicks and punches landed on the men. Elabea quickly learned that the census was merely an excuse for Ebon to flex its military muscle.

She scanned her attic bedroom's shadows for any sign of a warrior.

Nothing.

If not a raid, she wondered with a sigh of relief, *perhaps it was my father downstairs.*

Quinn often drank wildeberry wine well into the night, and in his inebriated state, sometimes hurled objects across the room followed by a string of curses.

Thud.

This time, Elabea recognized the sound as coming from outside. Gathering her courage, she peeked through a crack in her shuttered window.

Lances of silver-blue moonbeams crisscrossed Hetherlinn while the trees strained against the windstorm and hindered her vision. Suddenly, the trees parted, as if sensing her need for an unencumbered view.

Floating above the communal fire was a warrior and his mount that glowed like the moon. He turned and looked at her cottage, Number 17. Elabea gasped and jerked back into the safety of the shadows.

Did he see me?

Fearing the worst, she pulled her quilt close and sat perfectly still, hoping the ghost-warrior would soon be on his way. She tried not to worry, but worry she did.

He's definitely not an Ebonite. So where's he from?

She fretted, straining to hear any more sounds, wondering most of all.

Why is he here?

She jumped to the only logical conclusion her mind could comprehend, and that conclusion made her eyes bulge with fear.

He must be a monster from the Cauldron.

Flashbacks from her countless trips to the oak with her friend, Galadin, began to fill her with panic. *The Oracles,* she worried as she bit her lip. *He's come to punish us for climbing the oak.*

As quickly as that notion lit her anxiety on fire, another took its place, and cooled her like water. *We've played in the oak since we were five summers of age. Surely we would have been caught before now.*

She relaxed her grip on the quilt, but remained fearful of the creature looming beyond her cottage. She tried to push his image out of her thoughts, but her will was not up to the task. The harder she strained, the more engraved his face became.

And what a face. Like dancing fire in a wintry sky.

Her curiosity, a trait that got her into trouble more often than not, joined her inner fray, and soon, her fears were overruled by a desire to take another peek.

She pushed away her blankets and found herself once more at the crack, staring out into the moonlight. The hovering warrior had not moved, but instead of fear the sight of him sent peace coursing through her veins.

His steed rose and boxed the air with his front appendages. Then, in a silvery flash, they were gone; disappeared into the deeper shades of the night. It was as if they had never existed at all.

Elabea stared, mesmerized by their flight.

She laid back down, but she knew that sleep was out of the question - not because she feared his return, but because her imagination simply could not leave him be. Throughout the night, she pondered every possibility as to his identity.

Being restricted to her village by the Oracles, she was limited to information from beyond its borders. He was not from any of the surrounding nations, she reasoned. She had already ruled out the possibility that he was Ebon, nor was he a creation of the Cauldron. She tested another theory, one that went against the teaching of the Oracles.

Could he be from Claire?

The idea stirred her fantasies to the wind. High within her imagination they swirled, like snow on a zephyr.

Exhaustion finally took its toll, but before she drifted off to sleep, she felt the need to bestow him with a title.

The Moon King, she murmured. *He's the Moon King.*

Morning came too soon, and Elabea stumbled out of bed. She tiptoed quickly across the cold planks and threw on her brown tunic. Woven from a thick cloth, it resembled a floppy bag more than a dress. It was the required outfit of Hetherlinn, as ordered by the Oracles, creating uniformity and squelching individualism. She often wondered if the other nations had to dress the same.

She pulled her wavy cinnamon-colored hair out from beneath her tunic and it fell past her shoulders. Her eyes were morsels of dark chocolate reflecting a fiery heart, and her smile - when she thought to smile - was inviting. A few freckles, sprinkled like nutmeg, adorned her creamy cheeks. Elabea was an attractive girl on the cusp of womanhood, but she did not consider herself pretty. Aside from an occasional compliment dropped by her mother, all she heard were insults. The residents of her tiny community seemed to hold a personal grudge against her, and many in Hetherlinn, especially the ancient widow, Mithe, castigated her on a daily basis. With nothing else to counter the poison, she accepted their demeaning comments as the truth.

Elabea slipped on warm wool stockings and boots, then strapped a thick leather belt around her waist. The belt, snug about her, accentuated her developing figure, and gave her the sensation of wearing something slightly more attractive than a sack.

She stepped to the square opening in her floor. The warmth from the kitchen fire below embraced her while the aroma of breakfast porridge made her stomach rumble. She descended the rickety ladder, the rungs creaking beneath her weight.

"Mother," she asked as she dragged herself to the table near the fire. "Did you see anything...odd...last night?"

"No," Areall answered. Her tone was as dull and flavorless as the porridge she scooped from the large black pot that hung over the fire. Like everything else in their cottage, the fireplace was simple and primitive, by order of the Oracles. Rough in places, with some cracks here and there, it was anything but elegant. Black soot covered the stones, rising up to the thatched roof.

"Last night, I saw something...or someone...riding out of Hetherlinn."

"Probably just an Ebonite warrior on a night patrol," Areall sighed as she plopped the bowl of gruel down in front of Elabea.

"I *know* what they look like, and he was definitely not one of them." Elabea snatched up a wooden spoon. "He was larger than any man I've ever seen, and he glowed blue like the moon." She dug into the creamy broth.

"You must have been dreaming." Areall's voice was overly tired for so early in the morning.

"I'm *not* a child," Elabea snapped back. "I've seen fourteen summers and in another four, I'll be permitted to marry..." In a more sullen tone she continued, "If anyone will have me."

"Perhaps the moon was playing tricks on you," Areall yawned, not the least bit interested in the conversation. She knew Elabea's curiosity could be relentless, like a wolf in winter, desperate for a meal, and she was in no mood for it.

"At first, I was frightened, but soon..." Elabea's thoughts drifted to the events of the previous night. She let the conversation fade for a moment, then with the spontaneity of youth she exclaimed, "Whatever he was, he was magnificent."

Elabea twirled her spoon as her imagination began to work. "Is there a Moon King," she asked.

"Moon King?" Areall chortled. "There hasn't been a king other than Brairtok *anywhere* since the Dark War and..." Her rosy cheeks faded to white as if death had touched her flesh. In a serious tone, she abruptly added, "Let's talk of different matters."

"Could he have been something of old, something from the Dark War?"

Elabea's spoon stopped twirling as she pondered the next question, one she was certain would get her into trouble for asking.

"Mother, could he be from Claire?"

Areall's eyes widened. "*Never* mention that nation again. You know the Cauldron's Oracles ban discussions of things that might be...or might have been."

"I know," Elabea persisted, her spoon spinning in her fingers. "But do you really think the Cauldron can hear inside our cottage?"

"Yes."

"Then why hasn't it seen me at the oak, or heard Galadin and me talking about Claire..."

Areall clasped her hand over Elabea's mouth. "Hush, child."

Elabea looked into her mother's buggy eyes. She had seen that look before; more times than she could count. It came with every question she asked about the Cauldron, Ebon, the Dark War and the forgotten land known as Claire. It was the look of fear.

"The vapors from the Cauldron of Ebon travel far and hear much," Areall whispered. *"You must respect the Oracles, my daughter."*

Areall did not remove her hand until she was convinced Elabea would humble her tongue. Finally, she dropped her hand and returned to her chores, as though nothing out of the ordinary had happened.

Elabea stared at her mother. "Aren't you the least bit curious?"

"No," she replied.

"Well, I am," Elabea snipped, her curiosity piqued. "Nothing happens in Hetherlinn, or in all of Allsbruth for that matter."

Areall spun around. Her eyes narrowed. "*Nothing* is good, Elabea. *Nothing* means no more war. *Nothing* is a blessing to life."

Elabea thumped her spoon against the table with a petulant pout. "If this is life, then life stinks."

Areall sighed and decided upon a different tactic. Pulling up a chair, she sat across from Elabea, hoping a calm discussion would end this battle of wills.

"Do you remember the stories of your youth," Areall gently asked.

"Yes," Elabea moaned, still beating out a rhythmic cadence with her spoon.

"Then you remember that the Dark War ended the tyranny of the King of Claire. Since that day, the Ebonites and the Cauldron have guarded and guided us. The Cauldron's drone is a gracious reminder of all we've been blessed with."

Elabea stopped the thump, thump, thump of her spoon and listened. She had become so accustomed to the drone's perpetual presence that she no longer actually heard it, but she knew it was always there, just like the air that she breathed, as constant as day and night, winter and spring. Its tone conjured images in her mind of the wind howling through the hollow of a dead tree, low in pitch, monotonous. Ominous.

"That's why," Areall continued, "we must try our best to obey the Oracles of the Cauldron."

"And what of their night raids?" Elabea huffed. "What have we done to deserve those?"

"It's for our own protection. They simply need to tally us to make sure no one has..."

"Listen to you," Elabea interrupted. "Can't you see that we're prisoners in our own village?"

"Oh, Elabea," her mother sighed. "I wish you could see life through my eyes."

"And I wish you could see through mine."

Silence.

"I suppose," Areall conceded, "we've lost some liberties; but those are but inconveniences compared to the peace and prosperity we now have."

"Peace and prosperity?" Elabea shot back. "*The Oracles decree* we can only travel five arrow shots from our village. *The Oracles determine* what we can and can't talk about. *The Oracles forbid* you to teach us how to read. *The Oracles demand...*"

"Enough," Areall interrupted, her voice almost a whisper. "Such curiosity leads to a rebellious heart, and a rebellious heart leads too..."

Elabea rolled her eyes and began banging her spoon against the bowl again. Areall gently laid her hand on top of her daughter's to stop the incessant drumming, then, with a patronizing smile, returned to her chores.

The conversation was over.

After a moment of silence, Areall asked, "Would you like to continue learning how to knit?"

Elabea let out a dramatic sigh. "You *know* I hate to knit. And why aren't you willing to discuss this? Why do you pretend all is well? Do you really enjoy the night raids...and wearing *this?*"

Elabea yanked at her tunic.

Areall smiled, but it hung broken and crooked on her attractive face, beaten down by war and the oppressiveness of the Oracles.

Quinn, Elabea's father, picked that moment to stumble out of his bedroom. Bumping his forehead against the low threshold, he mumbled something that sounded like a curse, rubbed his sore head and staggered toward the fireplace. There, he fell into a wooden chair to begin another day, sitting and staring into the glowing embers that held no answers to his misery. Like all the days before, Quinn would slip further into despair, an occasional grunt about Min Brock the only thing that shattered his silence.

"Father," Elabea announced, "I'm going to the meadow."

Like the other children of Hetherlinn, Elabea was banned by her parents from visiting the meadow and climbing the ancient oak that grew in its midst. Despite their commands, threats and subsequent punishments, Elabea continued to visit what she called, *her meadow.* Overcome with their own personal pains, Quinn and Areall resigned themselves to defeat, and Quinn waved a rubbery arm while Areall huffed disapprovingly.

Elabea threw open the door and the cold breeze took her breath away. She pulled her shawl closer. A rustling sound near her ear made her turn to inspect. There, embedded in the doorpost's rough planking was an arrow. And not *just* an arrow. The shaft was clear, glistening like dew, while the fletchings were unique colors: the cock feather was yellow while the hen feathers were orange.

Wrapped about the arrow's shaft and secured with a leather strip was a parchment that twitched with the breeze.

The thud I heard last night must have come from this arrow.

This isn't an Ebonite arrow, she noted. *Their shafts are wooden and the feathers black and white. More proof that the Moon King isn't from Ebon.*

Before her thoughts could fade, his mystical face flashed in her imagination. *I didn't see him shoot this, but who else could have done so?*

The rustling paper stirred her curiosity.

If I take it, I risk violating the Oracles, but this wouldn't be the first time. Elabea glanced furtively back at her parents. *Besides, I've been going to the oak for most of my life. Nothing has ever happened, even when Galadin and I dared to ask to hear a whisper.*

Stepping outside, Elabea closed the door behind her, then stretched her fingers toward the shimmering shaft. Flesh touched parchment and tingles raced up her arm. Startled, she jerked her hand away.

The Cauldron's never known about us at the oak. How will it know now? What harm could come?

She stretched out her hand again, and this time yanked the arrow free.

Nothing happened.

She untied the leather and unrolled the parchment. Even as a simple girl from Allsbruth, she knew that the paper's thickness and weight were proof it was an expensive quality. Exquisite black etchings were on one side, except for six characters that were gold.

I wish I could read, she bemoaned.

Drawn to the golden letters, she ran her finger across the marks. Suddenly, a whisper pierced the winds.

"Elabea."

She shuddered and withdrew her finger.

"Galadin?" she demanded, looking this way and that for her best friend, who was noted for playing practical jokes. Only the wind answered.

Armed with the proof she previously lacked, Elabea went back inside.

"I told you I saw something last night," Elabea crowed, holding both the parchment and arrow high.

Areall's eyes widened as if seeing a poisonous snake about to strike. She sprang toward her daughter and snatched the offending items from Elabea's hands.

"What have you done?" Areall scolded as she raced to the door. "What have you *done?*"

She heaved the arrow outside and slammed the door shut. "Your curiosity will bring death to us." She darted to the fireplace.

Startled by her mother's erratic behavior, Elabea stammered, "What are you doing?"

"This is a curse," Areall shouted, crumpling the parchment into a ball. "It violates the teachings of the Oracles." She tossed it into the flames. "I must destroy it before…"

She let her sentence fade, as if satisfied that the fire would quell any uprising their daughter had instigated, then returned to her chores as if nothing had happened.

Quinn lifted his throbbing head and glared at the women. "Why must you two be so *loud?*" he thundered.

Elabea remembered a time many summers ago when his eyes sparkled with life, but that was before he went off to fight in the Dark War. Now they were opaque and lifeless. Quinn's eyes drifted to the parchment in the fire. Even in his hung-over state he recognized it.

His eyes became icy. "Where did you get *that?*"

Backing away, Elabea answered truthfully, "It was attached to an arrow that was stuck in our door. Why? What is it?"

"*It* is from the land of lies," he slurred.

"*Claire,*" Elabea whispered. She realized that despite the flames, the parchment was not burning.

"Don't say the word," Areall yelled, her placid expression replaced by churning rapids. Turning her fury on Quinn, she shouted, "Your night of drink is making you talk too much."

"I'll talk when and *how* I like," he yelled back.

While they argued, Elabea saw her chance. Darting to the fireplace, she grabbed a small stick on the hearth and plunged it into the coals.

"Stop," Quinn roared as he struggled to rise from his chair. "Leave it." Becoming dizzy, he slumped back down.

"Amazing," Elabea muttered as she dragged the parchment onto the cool hearth. "It's not burnt and is even free of soot. It's so…*beautiful.*"

"Beautiful?" Areall snorted. She crept toward the parchment as if an evil spirit possessed it. "Its beauty is its deception," she whispered. "Burn it, child. Destroy it or you will curse us. The Cauldron will know and see. They will come."

Elabea calmly lifted the parchment from the hearth. "They've never come before. Besides, how can something so beautiful be evil?"

Without another word, Elabea raced out the door.

Chapter 2

Forged Friendship

Elabea darted away from her home, longing to escape her parents and more importantly, the shackles of the Oracles. She did not consider herself a rebel, or one brave enough to defy Ebon's might. She simply hungered for two qualities her home and village could not provide: love and acceptance.

She glanced at the parchment clutched in her hand. The tingling sensation was gone, but the thought that it had been delivered from Claire sent goose bumps racing over her back. She had been taught that Claire was destroyed in the Dark War, and that it was a land of death and deception. The parchment and the Moon King were proof otherwise.

As she ran, she took in the cottages of Hetherlinn. Constructed from planed boards, they were stained white while the windows, of which there were only two, were sealed with dark green shutters. Thatched roofs sloped off the quaint two story dwellings and nearly touched the ground. Their most notable feature was the numbers above the unpainted doors. Black stain, sloppily brushed by Ebonite warriors, numbered each cottage.

Another requirement from the Oracles so Ebon can tally us like cows.

Hers was Number 17 and sat at a distance from the other cottages. She liked being far away from the others, especially when her father had had too much wildeberry wine.

Another glance. Another painted number.

14.

She recalled seeing a young boy, Phinnton, peering at her from his bedroom window. She would wave, but he was too shy, and would dart back into the shades.

At night, the sweet refrains sung by Phinnton's mother floated like a dream into her bedroom. She would open her shutters and rest on her window frame, soaking up the musical serenade. Every now and then, when the wind was blowing her way, she would catch some of the lyrics.

The Singing Stones of Addoli, she reflected. *How I wish I knew what that meant…*

Several summers past, the singing simply stopped. Elabea assumed the boy was older and grew tired of bedtime lullabies. A rumor spread that Phinnton's mother had been whisked away one night by the Ebonites for violating an Oracle. From that day forth, Phinnton and his father became hermits.

The sight of crystal arrows stuck in the door of each house in the village jolted Elabea from her reverie. The parchments, attached to each shaft, rustled in the wind like dried corn stalks. Curious, she slowed her pace.

I'm the only one who's removed the arrow and untied the parchment.

She suppressed her fears until, nearing the communal fire, she heard her neighbors whispering and saw them pointing at the arrows. Anxiety and fear sparked within Elabea's thoughts.

Mithe, the old widow, spied Elabea and the parchment she clutched in her hand.

"Look," she hissed to the assembled families. "Here comes Quinn's only child. Behold what the homely girl is holding."

The whispers stopped. Eyes stared at her parchment. Children hid behind their parents. Elabea froze in her tracks.

Mithe wobbled toward her, leaning heavily upon her thick, twisted cane. Wrapped about her head and shoulders was a dark tattered blanket; a few long, gray hairs protruded out.

Peering from the shadows was a round face whose flesh no longer fit the bone. Seventy summers had covered it with large, thick wrinkles, some of which cascaded off her high cheekbones like floppy saddlebags. A furrowed brow, wrinkled by bitterness, concealed her pain-filled eyes. The one feature that made Elabea cringe was her voice - steam hissing out of a pot that had been on the coals too long.

Mithe raised a long, bony, accusing finger at Elabea.

"Destroy that invitation before it destroys us."

"So it's an invitation," Elabea cooed, delighted to finally know the note's contents.

Mithe's eyes narrowed, angry with herself for inadvertently revealing the parchment's nature. Regaining her composure, she continued her tirade.

"Do you wish to curse us? I command you to destroy it."

"Why is everyone so afraid of it? What's it an invitation to?"

Silence.

Elabea searched their faces. "It's from Claire, isn't it?"

The crowd pressed toward her.

"Silence," one man shouted. "The Oracles forbid you to speak the name."

"Death will come. We'll be cursed," yet another threatened.

"Take your parchment and leave us. *Now*," a woman boomed.

"I don't believe the Cauldron can hear," Elabea countered. A corporate gasp erupted from the crowd. Undeterred, Elabea continued. "What if the Ebonites tell us such tales in order to control us with our own fears?"

"Stupid waif," Mithe hissed. "You know *nothing* of such things."

"You're right," Elabea replied in defense, "I'm ignorant because no one has taught me such things. You refuse to teach us how to read. How can I know if I cannot read for myself?"

The crowd stepped closer, but all eyes were on the parchment, as if it held unspeakable powers.

Or unspeakable evil.

"Can't you see?" Elabea said, her voice full of emotion. "If we cannot read, how can we discern true stories from false? You've taught us that Claire was destroyed in the war. But doesn't this parchment tell otherwise?"

Mithe stepped between Elabea and the mob.

"Then allow me to tell you a short story," Mithe countered, her saggy cheeks wobbling back and forth. "Long ago, during the Dark War, we received parchments just like the one you're holding. My husband and two sons journeyed to Claire to answer the invitation, as did your father. They were made warriors and began to fight along side the King of Claire.

"In the great battle at Min Brock, the men of Allsbruth were trapped and outnumbered. The Ebonites destroyed them with no mercy, butchering them upon the Gilden Plains. My husband. My sons. Killed. And for what? For a parchment from the..." She stopped before her tongue spoke the forbidden name. "He, the one who sent the parchments, did nothing to help, and they died like dogs."

Mithe enjoyed the pain and distress her words were causing Elabea. She continued her story.

"Your father has never told you his tale?"

Elabea shook her head.

Mithe snickered.

"Quinn, the mighty leader of Hetherlinn, has never told you why he and Gundin were the only survivors of Min Brock?"

Elabea's eyes became as big the moon. She bit her lip to quell the tears.

"Ah," Mithe gloated. "Evidently not. Then here is the truth: Your father is a coward. He betrayed us all. Your father and Gundin should be dead. Not our men. Not *my* men.

"Now get rid of that cursed parchment before we do it for you."

The mob rushed forward.

"Stop."

The voice came from the shadow of a tree behind cottage Number 7.

Galadin emerged from the shade and stood beside Elabea.

"Look at this," the widow snapped, her long finger wiggling at Galadin like a serpent. "Behold the son of Gundin. The greatest warrior to ever walk Hetherlinn. Where is your father now, boy?"

Galadin stiffened his back and glared at her. "Leave Elabea alone. Go back to your worries, old woman."

Mithe continued undeterred. "I'll tell you where your father is. Mad he is, lost in his old dreams. You're the son of a madman, Galadin. One day, you'll join his insanity."

Galadin's eyes became slits of rage but he held his tongue. He leaned close to Elabea and whispered, "Let's get out of here before they charge us."

She took his hand and he led her toward his cottage, all the while keeping an eye on the unruly crowd that continued to hurl threats, curses, and even stones at the two young people.

"Guess I showed them who is the boss," Galadin said, his eyes twinkling with confidence. Elabea, however, wondered if her parchment was what had protected them; almost like an invisible shield.

Galadin, like his father, was barrel-chested and tall. His strength and size made strenuous, tasks like chopping wood or hauling water, look like child's play. His eyes he got from his mother. They shone like black pearls when he was captured by joy, as when he pursued a deer in the forest; but when he became angry, they clouded over like thunderheads.

Yet, despite his strong physique and towering size, within him was a weakness. Mithe was correct: His father was going mad, and he feared he would follow in his father's footsteps. Galadin had been successful in concealing this shame from everyone in the village. All, that is, except one.

Elabea.

She was glad Min Brock had forged them together, even though she had not known the reason until now, and even if they were outcasts in their own village. They were identical in age, and even in their younger summers, sensed they were different from the other children. Neighbors' foreign looks made them feel on edge. Huddled friends' chilling whispers isolated them even more.

So they formed a secret pact, an unspoken allegiance, in order to weather the storm. At the heart of their friendship was a deep understanding that no one else in Hetherlinn could offer, not even their parents. Galadin understood why she needed to escape to the meadow and climb the oak, despite the Oracles, and he listened to her stories, even when they were wilder than anything he had ever hunted.

Likewise, Elabea comprehended why he fled cottage Number 7 and explored the woods, and why she was the one he shared his hunting tales with. Simply put, they knew what it felt like to live in homes full of shame. More importantly, they had learned how to survive despite it.

Nearing cottage Number 7, Elabea asked, "Did you see or hear anything odd last night?"

"No, just my father snoring. Why?"

"Well, last night, I saw an amazing creature." Elabea became animated as she talked. "Only it wasn't an animal." Her words came faster, spilling over each other. "It, I mean *he*, looked like a man - only not like us - so I gave him a name…the Moon King, and…"

"Slow down. What are you talking about?"

"Late last night," she said, focusing on a slower delivery, "I saw a mysterious rider on a flying horse; they both glowed like the moon. I wish you could have seen them. I'm positive the Moon King is the one responsible for shooting the invitations into our doors."

Galadin tried not to snicker, but this was not the first time he had heard one of her amazing stories. All were fashioned into fantastic proportions.

"Look," he said, "I've hunted through every thicket and meadow the Oracles will allow. Let me assure you that there is no one like the Moon King. The only odd thing I've witnessed is a bald hermit. I've only gotten a glimpse of him, and I've nicknamed him the Wizard of the Wood. But trust me, he's anything but mystical. Gone are the days of strange beings, magical creatures and mighty warriors."

Flustered, Elabea snapped, "I know what I saw."

"Are you sure? The moon can play tricks on your eyes. I have often mistaken things late at night in a full moon. Elabea, there is nothing out there except bears, wild cats, boars, deer and birds." He paused. "Although, I did see a gor once."

Elabea cocked her head to the side.

"You've seen a gor?"

"Yes," he answered, his smile as radiant as the sun.

"But gors don't live in Allsbruth."

"I *know* that," Galadin huffed as his smile fell. "I was atop a high cliff and saw them far off in a valley. They were enormous."

"Did they fly and glow like the moon?"

"No. They were hairy and walked on all fours, occasionally standing on their hind legs to reach branches…"

"Trust me, Galadin. What I saw was not a gor."

Elabea turned her thoughts to the parchment.

"Did you get one of these," she asked, holding it up for him to see.

"Yes. I pulled it off too, but my mother took it and threw it in the fire. If what Mithe is saying is true, then you need to burn yours too, and fast."

"Are your parents home," she asked.

"Why?" he answered, raising an eyebrow.

Elabea didn't reply but merely smiled.

Galadin rolled his eyes. "My father is still asleep. Mother went out to inspect the crops."

"Good. We can go check on your invitation without them knowing about it."

"Weren't you listening?" he said as he folded his arms across his chest. "I just told you my mother destroyed it."

"Sorry I'm so curious," she said, her mischievous smile still firmly in place, "but may I go look, anyway?"

Unfolding his arms, Galadin gave in. He knew how stubborn she could be. Reluctantly, he led her inside.

Walking to the fireplace, Elabea picked up a poker and began fishing among the hot coals. Beneath the embers, a bright glimmer of gold caught her attention. She pulled the parchment out, blew off the ashes and gingerly held it up for Galadin to inspect.

"That's impossible," he gasped. "It's not burned; not even singed. I saw her throw it into the flames."

"Now aren't you the least bit curious?" she teased, wagging the parchment in front of his face.

She placed their parchments side by side on the table and examined them.

"They're identical," Galadin observed.

"Except yours has seven gold emblems while mine only has six. I wonder what they say?"

"I don't know, and to be honest, I don't care. Let's get out of here. Let's go to the meadow. We need to let the villagers calm down."

Elabea remained fixated with the parchments. "You heard Mithe. She said these are invitations from the Only, from the land of Claire. This proves that the stories we've been taught aren't true. Claire wasn't destroyed after all."

"This proves nothing," Galadin argued from the door, looking this way and that for a surprise attack.

She set her hands on her hips. "Then tell me who shot the arrows in our doors?"

He shrugged while keeping guard. "I have no idea. Maybe you're right. Maybe Claire really does exist. I still don't care."

"Why not?"

Another shrug. "Mithe was right. My father is going mad. So when I hear him babbling nonsense about Claire..."

"Really?" she interrupted. Her arms relaxed and she stepped toward him. "He talks about Claire? What did he say?"

"That it was the most beautiful land..."

"Beautiful?" Elabea breathed. "Tell me everything."

"Not now," Galadin warned. "If we discuss this any more, that mob by the fire will come get us. Or the Cauldron will hear and Ebonites will come"

"That's another thing," she huffed, her hands once more finding her hips. "How do we know it hears all? We've been going to the oak for a long time and nothing has happened to us. Not a raid; not even a single rider. I doubt anyone is going to get hurt if we simply *talk* about such things."

Galadin turned his gaze to her. He knew how she could be when she wanted to argue a point. Normally he wouldn't mind, but this time she was challenging the authority of the Oracles along with Ebon's military might. He was not afraid of a fight, or even of going to war. But now was not the time.

Resting his hands on her shoulders, he said, "Let's just leave the parchments and forget about all of this. Besides, life is better than it used to be."

Elabea turned away and stared into the fire. "The way it *used* to be?" she pouted. "We've never known anything *but* this life."

"True, but I hear the old ones say that it's better to surrender our freedom for peace than to..."

She spun on her heals and glared at him. "Peace? My life is anything but peaceful. You know what my father is like when he drinks, and Mithe torments me daily, and your father..."

A deep voice from the adjoining bedroom called out, "Galadin? Who's there?"

"Just Elabea, Father. Go back to sleep. We're leaving."

"Did Quinn send her? You know we both fought in the Dark War? I, the Great Gundin, battled many a foe..."

"Yes, Father," Galadin replied as his shoulders slumped. "We all know. Please go back to sleep."

Galadin whispered to Elabea. "Now's not the time to discuss such matters. Let's go to the meadow. I need to get far away from..."

Gundin emitted another loud cry.

Elabea gave Galadin a sympathetic nod. She scooped up the parchments as they raced out the door.

Chapter 3

Oracles Revealed

Mithe spied them racing from cottage Number 7, heading for the thicket nestled beside the meadow.

"Yes, run away," she hissed. "Run to your oak. Go climb into its forbidden branches and take your parchments with you. The Cauldron will find you. You'll see. *You will see.*"

Galadin glanced at Elabea without breaking his stride.

She's sad…again, he noted. *I wish Mithe would leave her alone.*

Flashing his mischievous grin while dodging a tree limb, he said, "They say Mithe is so ugly that she scares death away."

Elabea chuckled. Galadin was relieved to see her eyes sparkle, even if only for a moment.

Sprinting downhill toward the creek, they hopped over the gurgling water and then trudged up the opposite side to the meadow.

The blanket of clouds parted and sunbeams flooded a lone oak atop the knoll. They stood in awe of the majestic tree that, even in winter, was magnificent to behold.

Monstrous gray limbs stretched skyward. Spaced apart like stairs, they were perfect for climbing. The trunk was so large it would require four grown men holding hands to encircle it. The meadow's tall, brown grass rolled away from the oak like a king's robe.

"Let's go climb it," Elabea said.

"We're too old to play in trees."

"Too old?" she snickered. "Where in the Oracles is *that* stated?"

Galadin smiled. Like Elabea, he too loathed the restrictions of the Oracles, and savored the opportunity to rebel against them.

"Remember the first time we climbed?"

She reflected. "I think we were five summers of age."

"Seven," he corrected. "It was winter, when all the leaves are off the trees, and you can see the oak clearly from Hetherlinn. Was I the one who challenged you to go to it?" he said with a smirk.

"Yes," she scowled, "and I remember getting in big trouble that day, too."

"Yeah," he nodded, relishing the punishment as a sort of badge of honor. "Did you know that when our parents were children, they played in the oak all the time, even with the Dark War raging? Some even say they heard whispers."

Galadin looked about, as if to see if anyone was listening or watching. Elabea gave him an incredulous look. Satisfied they were alone, he asked, "I know we've toyed with asking to hear a whisper when in the tree, but..." he gave another quick glance about them. "Have you heard one?"

Elabea considered telling him about the whisper that called her name, but unsure as to what it was or who had whispered it, decided against it.

"No," she replied.

Her answer satisfied him and he nodded.

"Not too long ago," Elabea confessed, "my mother told me a similar story about her childhood visits to the tree. Even though she told me to never visit it, I could tell she missed those days. She even said the meadow used to be full of giggling, playing children."

They took in the winter grass swaying in the wind.

"Well, not any more," Galadin observed.

Elabea focused her attention on the tree. "In many ways, we're just like the oak."

Galadin tried to comprehend what she was implying but was unable to make the connection.

She explained. "Like the oak, we're shunned by our village. We suffer because of our father's shame; the oak suffers because whispers were heard."

Looking into his face, she asked, "Do you ever wish you could hear a whisper in the tree...just once?"

He nodded. "Do you?"

"Yes. I'd love to hear tales of what might have been and what might possibly be."

She paused to reflect and then continued to reminisce. "Remember when we climbed all the way to the top?"

"Do I? You could see the forever snow on the Mountains of Allsbruth. No matter the season, it's always there. And on a clear day, you could see the River Arrgient glistening in the distance." Then more softly, as if to himself, "I'd love to explore and hunt beyond the marker. I can only imagine what creatures live out there."

"Maybe one day," she whispered.

Galadin saw her tell-tale smile. "Oh no. I know what that look means."

"Race you," she blurted as she took off for the oak.

"Hey," he shouted after her, "That's *cheating*."

He gave pursuit, but like all the other times they raced, even with a fair start, he knew he would never catch her.

Reaching the trunk, Elabea gazed up at its branches.

"I've spent most of my life up there," she said as Galadin arrived, holding his sides and gasping for air.

She continued her soliloquy. "Even from my cottage, the oak beckons me to come play in its branches. I know this will sound crazy, but it seems to listen to my dreams."

Her eyes found Galadin's and her voice became maudlin. "If I tell you something, do promise not to laugh?"

"Sure," he answered, preparing to bite his lip should he feel the urge to snicker.

"When my father's moods made me cry, the oak somehow comforted me. It was almost as if it hugged me."

He gave her a sympathetic nod and she was thankful to have a friend who understood.

"When I'm hunting," he confessed, "it feels like the woods are cheering me onward. Does that make sense?"

She smiled and nodded.

Gazing back up at its crest, Elabea added, "I used to pretend I was holding onto a ship's mast as the winds rocked me to and fro. I'd dream of being anywhere but Hetherlinn." Her voice softened. "I'd dream of being anyone but Elabea."

With a sigh, she grabbed the lowest limb and began to ascend. Galadin followed, and together, they climbed to the top.

"Look," Galadin pointed at their village. "There's Mithe hobbling about the fire. She's still ugly, even from way up here."

Elabea giggled. Sharing the view from the oak with Galadin made her pain-filled life seem far away, almost as if it were someone else's.

Her eyes swept beyond the Allsbruthian Mountains.

"Just think," she said. "Somewhere out there is Claire, the most beautiful land anyone's ever seen." As her imagination sparked, her speech became faster and faster. "Imagine, meadows twice the size of ours. Mountains that are huge - no, behemoths; and covered in forever snow. And the sky..."

"Elabea," Galadin interrupted. "You're doing it again: making up stories you know nothing about."

Her expression grew somber. "Do you think he's alive?"

"Who?"

"The King of Claire. The Only."

Hearing her say the forbidden name made Galadin shudder. "Don't say the *name*," he scolded. "The Cauldron will hear."

Elabea rolled her eyes at him. "That's my point. If he was killed during the Dark War, then why can't we say his name? But if he's alive, then these invitations are proof of so much more."

Galadin, who did not entertain logic as readily as Elabea, merely shrugged. "Well," he interjected, "if he *is* alive, then why haven't we seen or heard from him?"

"We have," she fired back. "He sent *these*."

She pulled out her invitation.

"That doesn't prove he lives," Galadin replied as movement far beyond the meadow caught his attention.

Cantering toward Hetherlinn was an Ebonite patrol. Elabea saw them as well. Her face turned white with fear.

"I was wrong," she whispered in horror. "The Cauldron did hear."

"Settle down," Galadin reassured her. "They're probably out just checking on our numbers. Strictly routine." But deep inside, he too feared the worst.

Ten riders approached the town's communal fire. The villagers huddled together as one rider peeled away and systematically went from dwelling to dwelling removing the arrows.

"If that's the case," Elabea questioned, "then why did that rider immediately go retrieve the parchments? It's as if he knew they were here."

The Ebonite stopped in front of cottage Number 17. Not finding an arrow, they heard him shout, albeit faintly, back to his commander. Cottage Number 7 evoked the same response.

Galadin and Elabea stared at their parchments and then at each other. And as only close friends could do, they silently voiced their concerns and fears with facial expressions.

The warrior trotted back to his comrades. The commander shouted an order and the patrol encircled the people. Long, two-handed swords were unsheathed.

"What are they doing," Elabea asked as she clung tighter to the tree.

"This isn't good," Galadin said between clinched teeth. "They've never drawn their weapons before, even on night patrols."

The warriors held their blades upright, the tips pointing skyward. Then in unison, the ten warhorses moved as one. Right legs were raised and then slammed to the ground followed by the left. This sequence was repeated, and like a rope tightening around one's neck, the cavalry squeezed toward the terrified villagers.

"They're going to trample them to death," Elabea exclaimed, realizing her curiosity with the parchment had cursed her hamlet, just as her parents and Mithe predicted.

Galadin shook his head in disbelief. "My father told me about this Ebonite formation, but I just assumed it was his mindless babble."

She looked into his face for the answer.

"He called it a March of Reeds," Galadin explained, his gaze fixated on the warhorses' pounding hooves. "It happened after the defeat at Min Brock. All the storytellers of Claire were rounded up and led to a marshy field where they were trampled to death by Ebonite cavalry."

As the circle of death closed, two men approached the Ebonite leader. Galadin and Elabea glanced at each other in disbelief.

"Our fathers?" they mouthed to each other.

The Ebonite commander lowered his blade.

The March of Reeds halted.

A dialogue, although faint, ensued between the two men and the commander. With no warning, he swung his blade at the helpless men. One fell to the ground wounded.

"Father," Elabea shouted.

Mithe stumbled forward and pointed in their direction.

The commander looked over his shoulder and spotted the knoll. Spurring his warhorse, he galloped toward the meadow while the other warriors trotted out of Hetherlinn.

"They must be going to get reinforcements," Galadin surmised, "or maybe they are trying to encircle us. Either way, we've gotta go."

Galadin descended as quickly as a squirrel.

Elabea stared at the wounded man. "But my father..."

"There's no time. Hurry."

For the first time in her life, Elabea did not argue with him. When they reached the lower branches, they jumped to the ground and sprinted away from Hetherlinn, but the tall grass made running difficult for two young people on foot. It wasn't such a challenge for a warrior on a warhorse.

Spurred by fear and the sound of thundering hooves, they increased their speed. Elabea raced past Galadin and reached the safety of the woods. Galadin tripped and fell headlong into the field.

"Get up," Elabea screamed. "He's close."

Galadin rose, but it was obvious he was hurt. As he tried to put weight on his ankle he fell again.

"Galadin," she cried as she ran back up the incline to help.

"No," he ordered. "Run!"

The commander stopped within a stone's throw of Galadin, and Elabea covered her mouth with her hands to stifle a scream.

The Ebonite's long, curly, black hair and beard, trademarks of Ebon's warrior caste, flapped tauntingly from beneath his open-faced helmet. Like most Ebonites, he was large and powerful. His saddle was covered with etchings that told tales of the Cauldron. Dark armor, fused with pieces of leather, covered him from his neck down to boots like lizard scales.

His warhorse was just as intimidating, standing a good head taller any horse in Allsbruth. Armor covered its head and snout and bore the pouncing lion crest of Ebon. Thick, dark leather covered the horse's front and rear flanks.

The commander glared at the helpless boy while his warhorse snorted in anticipation of the kill. An evil smile crossed his face as he raised his sword's tip skyward.

"Dog from cottage Number 7," he snarled, his deep voice sending a chill down Elabea's spine, "the Oracles forbid you touching contraband beyond your markers. The Cauldron knows you have the parchment. The penalty is death."

Spurs drove into his horse's flanks. Hooves ripped open the field. Leather and armor creaked and rattled.

"First blood," the warrior cried.

Galadin scrambled on his hands and knees, desperate to reach the woods. Elabea screamed and started to run to help him.

"Get out of here," Galadin ordered her. "Now!"

She stopped, fear paralyzing her as she watched him retreat like a field mouse from a lion. Suddenly, she felt a hand rest upon her shoulder. She gasped, fearing one of the other Ebonites had caught her. Instead, she was surprised to see an odd-looking man standing beside her.

He was bald, and had a purple birthmark in the shape of a flower on the top of his forehead. Clothed in a magnificent, dark green robe and holding a staff, his touch quelled her curiosity and fears. Riding on his shoulder was a brown creature the size of a squirrel.

He pointed his staff at the Ebonite. The animal unfurled bat-like wings and darted for the commander's head. The animal struck the Ebonite in the face with its long, mouse-like tail. The warrior shrieked in pain, dropped his weapon and covered his face with his hands.

Spooked by his master's cry, the warhorse galloped recklessly toward the oak. With hands still on his face, the warrior rode blindly, unable to see the danger looming. A low limb moved, as if suddenly shoved by a giant, invisible hand, and snagged his long hair. Yanked from his saddle, the commander's lifeless body swung back and forth as his horse galloped away.

"Rise," the stranger commanded Galadin.

Galadin stood as ordered, amazed that his ankle no longer hurt. He stared at the stranger as the brown creature flew back and landed upon his shoulder.

"I know you," Galadin declared. "You're the Wizard of the Wood."

"Hurry," the wizard replied as turned on his heel. "More warriors will come."

"You healed my foot," Galadin exclaimed.

"I did no such thing," he shouted over his shoulder. "I simply enabled you to see that you had been bewitched."

"Bewitched? By who?"

"By the vapors of the Cauldron. They convinced you to trip and that you had hurt your ankle. You felt pain when there was no pain to feel. Come, hurry. Talk is dangerous."

Chapter 4

Forbidden Stories

The Wizard of the Wood led them to a hidden trail not far from the meadow. Galadin eyed it suspiciously.

"I hunt this area often, so why haven't I seen this path before," he asked the wizard as they entered the foliage.

"Perhaps you've never needed to see it until now," the old man replied as he hopped over a log. The wizard's pace was swift as he led them away from danger.

Once they reached a shadowy valley with cool, damp air, the wizard stopped. His eyes swept the area, his ears attentive to the slightest sound of their enemy in pursuit. He glanced at the animal perched on his shoulder and studied its demeanor. The creature calmly chattered, and Elabea assumed it was how he communicated with its master. The wizard scratched some tufts of fur near its wings, and said to the children, "We're lucky. We haven't been followed."

"But you've led us past the marker," Galadin pressed.

The wizard smirked. "Going beyond the Oracles' marker is the least of your worries now."

He pushed aside some saplings and ushered Elabea and Galadin into a dark world.

Stepping into the thicket, they discovered a narrow hidden cave. The wizard motioned for them to follow and he led them inside.

Due to its width, they had to walk single file. The walls were damp and a musky scent hung in the air. As the light from the outside faded, they blindly followed the wizard, his muffled footsteps the only sign that he was leading the way. Elabea and Galadin extended their hands to feel along the passage and they shuffled feet to avoid stumbling. Galadin was about to ask about their whereabouts when a faint glow from up ahead told him they were nearing their destination.

The corridor emptied into a cavern the size of two Hetherlinn cottages. It had a low ceiling that was void of rocks jutting down like dragon's teeth typically found in a caves. A fireplace filled the room with eerie shadows and the scent of roasted meats and exotic spices.

"Wow," Galadin said as he admired the wizard's home. "It must have taken forever to carve out the fireplace." He ran a hand along its smooth surface. Chiseled on each side of the wood mantel were nooks that held lit candles. Pots and pans, blackened from the flame, were stacked in an orderly fashion on the hearth. "So where does the smoke go," Galadin asked as his eyes searched the cave's wall. "Won't it alert the Ebonites to our whereabouts?"

The wizard ignored his questions, and instead, scurried about, tidying up his dwelling for his guests. Elabea, still overcome with shock from the Ebonite attack, stared about the room. A simple bed fashioned from unwhittled tree limbs sat off in the shadows. Thick, dark blankets covered the bed and were neatly tucked and smoothed so that not a wrinkle could be found. A robe, identical to the one the wizard wore, was folded on top of a mound of clothing heaped by the foot of the bed.

What captured her imagination was the vast display of oddly bound objects. Stacked along one wall and covered with what appeared to be leather, they were stuffed with parchment. Some were fat while others were quite slim. Some looked older than the mountains, yet others looked brand new. Judging by the amount, Elabea concluded they were of great importance to the mage.

The wizard led Elabea to a chair beside the fire, then retreated to a far wall where drying herbs were hung, their various shades of green appearing black in the dim light.

He broke off a small twig, returned, and squeezed it into Elabea's hand. He whispered into her ear, "Chew this. The sweet sap will ease your fears." She began nibbling while staring blankly into the coals.

Turning his attention to Galadin, the wizard swept his arm toward the table and chairs in the center of the room.

"Please sit down," he invited. "Time is one commodity we do not have in abundance."

Next, he instructed his animal with words Galadin did not recognize. The obedient creature at once flew and perched on the bed frame.

Galadin, who was not as trusting as Elabea, stepped cautiously toward the chairs, his hand resting upon his dagger. His keen eyes, trained from many seasons hunting, examined the wizard's cave. He too noted the odd stack of leather bound parchments, but something in the shadows made him gasp. Leaning against the wall, hidden, yet plainly visible for the scrutinizing eye, was the silhouette of a large sword.

But swords have been banished by the Cauldron, he wondered. *How did this wizard get one?*

He continued toward the table, thankful the mage had his back turned and hadn't seen his alarmed expression.

The wizard, who was gathering things from a large wooden cupboard, said over his shoulder, "To answer your prior question, the chimney flows deep within the hill. No one will ever smell my fire.”

He turned around holding a pewter plate full of smoked pheasant. Gliding to the table, he slid the platter into the center. Galadin stood behind one of the chairs and stared at the mound of food.

The wizard looked Galadin over, then with a smile said, “Fighting for one’s life is hungry work, is it not?”

Galadin’s stomach rumbled, but he eyed the food apprehensively for fear the wizard had poisoned it. Before long his insatiable appetite overruled his better sense of judgment. He plopped down and began devouring food.

“My name is Il-Lilliad,” the wizard informed him.

Galadin simply nodded as he stuffed more food into his mouth.

“I am *not* a wizard.”

Galadin mumbled something unintelligible around a mouthful of smoked pheasant.

“I’m a storyteller.”

The pheasant turned to ash in Galadin’s mouth.

“So you have heard of storytellers.”

Galadin looked down at his half-eaten meal.

As if reading his mind, the stranger reached over and grabbed a piece of pheasant. “Do not fret,” he said as he took a bite. “I have not poisoned you.”

“You...are a storyteller,” Galadin said, half in fear and half in disbelief.

Il-Lilliad nodded.

“I thought they were all killed in the Dark War.”

“No, I am very much alive,” he chuckled, patting his chest as if to prove he was not a ghost.

Galadin’s eyes swept the room, looking for an avenue of escape. *Why did I take the chair farthest from the cave’s entrance?* He glanced at Elabea. *She seems fine; she’s still chewing on the twig.* His gaze found Il-Lilliad’s staff resting against the mantel. On top was a beautifully carved feminine face. It turned toward him and whispered...*“Flee the Oracles.”*

“Your staff,” he exclaimed, nearly falling off his chair. “It’s alive.”

“Yes,” countered Il-Lilliad, “but she is a lady, not an *it*.”

Galadin stumbled to his feet and drew his dagger.

“You have powers that are unlike the Cauldron’s,” he challenged, slowly scooting protectively toward Elabea. “I know your ways, storyteller. I don’t want to hurt you, so just let us go.”

Galadin waved the blade to frighten Il-Lilliad.

The storyteller leaned back in his chair. “I do not think you can hurt me with such a weapon," Il-Lilliad chuckled as he reached for some meat. "But I am curious. Please tell me, what is it you think you know about storytellers?"

Galadin stared at Il-Lilliad's purple birthmark. "My father warned me of men like you. I thought his madness had conjured such things. Now I see he's not as mad as I imagined."

"Go on," Il-Lilliad urged, taking another bite.

"At birth, a purple birthmark appears on the heads of those who are to become storytellers. They spend their lives telling the dark stories of the King of Claire; stories of what could be, and what must never be. More powerful than a legion of warriors, their tales can alter the course of men, nations and battles. Our defeat in the Dark War ended the rule of storytellers and the Only. Peace and prosperity now reign because your stories of lies and evil are gone forever."

"Lies and evil, you say," Il-Lilliad replied as he pulled a leg from the pheasant's carcass. "Curious. Very well, continue."

"Stories from the dark days have been banned by the Council of Ebon. As the Oracles say, 'Death visits all who utter the name of the dark king of Claire.'"

"Really. And what, dear boy, happens to those who hear such a story?"

"They too...are executed."

A wry smile crossed Il-Lilliad's lips. He leaned forward, his eyes locking on Galadin's. "Would you care to hear...*a story?*"

Galadin tightened his grip and thrust the dagger at Il-Lilliad.

"Never," he fired. "You're a curse. The Cauldron will track us no matter where we go or where we hide."

Il-Lilliad smiled, enjoying the game. Leaning back once more, he continued his questions.

"What happened after the war?"

"The storytellers were captured and destroyed in what is called a March of Reeds. Many summers later, a legend spread that the most evil storyteller of all miraculously survived."

Il-Lilliad raised an eyebrow and pointed to himself. Galadin nodded.

"Lucky for you, Galadin, that I arrived and being full of *evil*, decided to rescue you and Elabea."

"How did you know my name," Galadin inquired, taking a step backward.

"Simple. Elabea called you in the meadow, remember?"

He's right, Galadin thought. *But, I don't recall calling out hers.*

"Very well," Galadin said, hoping to catch him in a lie. "That explains how you know mine, but how did you know hers?" He pointed his dagger at Elabea.

"That too is easy. You called her name as well."

"You *are* a liar," Galadin gloated with a thrust of his blade. "I never called her name. Your tongue has exposed you for the evil that you are."

"Very well," Il-Lilliad replied, studying the boy to see if he was worthy enough to hear the answer. "I will tell you the truth, but it will be much harder to accept."

"Try me," Galadin commanded through clinched teeth.

"I heard the King of Claire, the Only, whisper her name the morning she discovered the parchment."

"A whisper?" he chortled. "Once more you're lying. She never heard a whisper."

"Yes I did," Elabea said as she rose from her chair. "I heard it when I found the parchment. At first I thought it was someone playing a trick on me, or perhaps just the wind."

Galadin's dagger arm dropped to his side. "Then why did you tell me otherwise?"

She shrugged. "I wasn't sure myself. Honest."

"Tell me," Il-Lilliad asked Elabea, "what did the whisper sound like?"

She reflected for a moment, then said, "It was gentle and elegant...like a lark's song in spring."

Galadin, overcome with questions, raised his dagger to a threatening position.

Il-Lilliad walked over to him and gently lowered the blade.

"Please put that away before you hurt someone...perhaps yourself."

Once the dagger was sheathed, Il-Lilliad paced about the room, his great robe flowing with every turn. Stopping, he asked Elabea, "Did you see anything unique the night before?"

"Yes, a mystical rider... the Moon King."

"Moon King?" Il-Lilliad chuckled. "That was Manno Vox, the King of Claire's greatest warrior."

Galadin and Elabea looked dumbfounded at each other.

Il-Lilliad, perplexed by their confused expressions, exclaimed, "You have never heard stories of Claire?"

"Just what we've been taught, that the king ruled with terror and force."

"Terror and force?" Il-Lilliad sighed and shook his head. "Impossible. Those, young children, are the lies."

"What about this," Elabea asked as she pulled out her invitation. "Is this evil?"

Il-Lilliad's brow furrowed with frustration. "What makes you ask such a thing?"

"Because everyone in Hetherlinn told us so. They even threatened us."

Il-Lilliad paced once again.

"Who do you suppose told them," he asked, hoping to unravel their thoughts like a thick knot in a length of rope. Galadin and Elabea said nothing - not because they were being insolent, they simply did not know.

"I shall tell you," Il-Lilliad chimed as he thrust an arm upward. "The dark whispers from the Cauldron, that is who."

Turning on his heel, he stopped and looked intently into Elabea's face. "When you heard the whisper, were you frightened?"

Elabea reflected on that morning: the cool breeze, the flapping parchment, the whisper floating with the grace of a butterfly.

"At first, yes, but then I felt...excited, full of joy."

"Exactly." Il-Lilliad shot his arm into the air to accent the point. "How could something evil conjure such feelings?"

"That is the power of its deception," Galadin argued.

"Deception?" Il-Lilliad countered. "Why do you think those Ebonite warriors came to Hetherlinn? Was it coincidence? Perhaps chance? No. The Cauldron knew Manno Vox had delivered the parchments the night before and that the King of Claire was whispering once more. When you took the parchments, you unwittingly informed the Cauldron that you heard his whisper. That is why the Cauldron hunts for you."

Il-Lilliad searched their curious faces. "You've no doubt read your invitations, haven't you?"

"No," they answered.

"And why not?"

"Because...we cannot read," Elabea replied, embarrassed.

Il-Lilliad sank into a chair.

"Then the Oracle of the Cauldron has come to pass," he said in a disturbed voice. *"They will turn from the stories and hide them from their children. The stories will fade, lost forever within the shadows of their darkest dreams. With such passing, the King of Claire will live no more."*

Il-Lilliad shook his head in disbelief. "The Cauldron detests the stories of the Only. When the last storyteller dies, when the last tale of Claire fades like a winter sunset, darkness will rule your lands forever. Now do you understand? Are your eyes open to the importance of this day?"

Still perplexed, they shook their heads.

With great patience, the old storyteller explained. "The land of Claire whispers a story. From this story, one gets an idea, a thought and a glimmer of hope. This idea grows and creates a dream...and this dream blossoms into a way of life. It is this way of life that the Cauldron detests more than anything."

Il-Lilliad flashed them a smile. "Allow me to tell you a story."

"Never!" Galadin leapt to his feet and pressed his dagger against Il-Lilliad's throat. "Didn't you hear what she said? The Oracles of the Cauldron forbid such stories. We'll be killed. Now just answer our question, what do these say?"

Il-Lilliad searched Galadin's eyes. *Naïve to think his little dagger and brawn can defeat me. With but a tale, and a miniscule one at that, I could rend him to pieces. But now that the whisper is calling again, I'll not battle an ally.*

Il-Lilliad used his storytelling abilities to read the stories written on Galadin's heart.

You'll no doubt be a great warrior, just like your father. Yet I wonder: will you fall prey to the Cauldron's trickery as I saw Gundin do at Min Brock?

Il-Lilliad drew in a deep breath in an attempt to relax Galadin, and answered. "That is what I wish to do. My story will tell you what they say, but if a story is still too much for you to bear, then I propose this: Allow me to tell a tale. Surely the Oracles allow a harmless tale?"

Not sure how tales were different from stories, Galadin looked to Elabea for guidance. She glanced at Il-Lilliad who gave her a secret wink. Despite his shrewdness, she found herself trusting him. She gave Galadin an approving nod.

Galadin sheathed his dagger and Il-Lilliad stood back up.

"Now, before I begin," Il-Lilliad said after retrieving his staff, "please have a seat and close your eyes."

Feeling threatened, Galadin challenged him once more, "If you so much as try and turn the tale into a story, I'll cut your throat."

"I vow to only tell a tale," he reassured with a kind smile and raised hand as if taking an oath. "Now please, have a seat and close your eyes."

As the children settled back to hear the tale, they noticed how the orange and black shadows from the fire danced wildly about the cave, making Il-Lilliad appear mysterious and somewhat dangerous. With racing hearts, they closed their eyes.

Il-Lilliad began the tale with words from a forgotten land. They flowed like a warm breeze and wooed them into a peaceful sleep. Before dozing off, Elabea cautiously snuck a peek. She thought she saw Il-Lilliad floating in mid-air, his dark green cloak sparkling like a rainbow, and his physique appearing much larger. What surprised her most was his smile. It was radiant, making his face glow as if on fire. A sudden memory came unbidden to her mind.

Was it a forgotten dream or had father once smiled in such a manner? Unable to keep her eyes open, she followed his tale into a dream.

Chapter 5

Sevritts of Ebon

Gundin did not remember how he got to the middle of Hetherlinn. Nor did he recall Quinn yanking him from cottage Number 7 or how they made their way past screaming women and terrified children. Even the thundering hooves of their enemy entering Hetherlinn did not stir him from his delusions.

It was no wonder that he stared glassy-eyed at the Ebonite cavalry that encircled the villagers. Within his mind, he was back in the Dark War, leading a charge of men toward an Ebonite stronghold. This dissolved into a vignette in which he sat with his men around a campfire sharing pipes and stories.

Amidst his fantasy, he felt the ground shake. He tried to make sense of it, but could not, for the rumbling was coming from somewhere beyond his illusions.

The ground shook again followed by what sounded like a thunderclap. The foreign effects became shards of recall that pierced his fantasy-world like lances.

He battled to discern fact from myth, truth from fantasy. He fought to regain control of his thoughts and center them once again in reality, something he had not done since the Dark War.

As if awakening from a dream, he found that he was with the other villagers near the fire. Some were ghostly pale, others wept, but he had no idea why.

Gundin continued to piece his strange experience together, trying to make sense of the earthquake and thunder. Memories flashed like lightning, and within the heat of its light, he remembered the March of Reeds shaking the ground, followed by the Ebonite cavalry thundering out of Hetherlinn.

A man moaned. A quick glance at the ground revealed Quinn wounded.

How did this happen? Followed by the truth, albeit foggy. *Yes. I remember. It was as if I was in a dream. Together, we confronted the Ebonites...just like in the old days. How we found such courage, I don't know.*

Gundin helped Quinn to his feet and scanned the faces of his neighbors with the eyes of a seasoned warrior.

"I need two volunteers," he announced.

No one moved. No one said a word. Not only were they still in shock from the Ebonite attack, but Gundin -who normally only mumbled or grunted undiscernibly -seemed to be normal.

Two boys, who looked to be in their sixteenth summer, stared with mouths agape at Gundin - spooked by his sudden transformation.

"No volunteers?" Gundin asked the villagers. "Very well, I choose you two."

The boys exchanged bamboozled looks.

"Yes, you both just volunteered," Gundin commanded. "Journey down the road and hide in the brush. Should they return with more men, alert us."

The boys nodded but remained frozen in place.

"What are you waiting for?" Gundin boomed. "Hurry."

They sprinted down the road.

Gundin pulled back Quinn's tunic to examine the wound.

"You're lucky. That little wound will heal in no time."

"Quinn," Areall exclaimed as she ran to his side. "I feared they'd killed you."

She touched his cheek and reminisced of their time as a couple before he had gone off to war, back when their love flourished, as did Allsbruth. His quiet disposition, as well as his ability to inspire others to greatness, were the traits that had attracted her to him; and his eyes that danced with life, and could with but a glance make her heart race.

Leaving her memories, Areall studied Quinn in hope of seeing those familiar eyes. Instead, she felt as if she were staring into bottomless pits. His passion for both her and life had perished at Min Brock.

Anger sparked and burned hot in her heart. She hated Quinn's choice to numb his shame with wine, and she loathed the disparaging comments made by her neighbors. Spinning away, she marched toward the primary culprit.

Mithe was easy to spot. She stood apart from the others and stared through the leafless trees at the nearby meadow.

"You hag," Areall spat. "You brought this upon us. When will you leave us alone?"

"When?" she replied, her eyes fixated on the dead Ebonite hanging from the oak, "When your family's blood spills just as my men's blood did at Min Brock."

Areall spun her around. Mithe's cane went flying, and she fell to the ground. Areall straddled her and glared down at her. "What has Elabea ever done to you? *We* are to blame, not *her*."

"She is a continuing reminder of Quinn's shame and betrayal."

Before Areall could reply, the sentries ran back shouting an alert.

"Ebonites," the boys shouted. "Coming this way…with…a wagon."

Areall left Mithe and rejoined Quinn as the Ebonite patrol, escorting a large wagon with tall sides, galloped past.

Raising his right arm, the commander signaled the entourage to stop. Their warhorses snorted in anticipation of a March of Reeds, and the villagers shuddered with fear. From within the wagon came the sound of rattling chains and deep barks and grunts from what sounded to be large animals.

The commander's beard and hair were peppered with gray, a sign that he had seen many campaigns during the Dark War.

"I'm Commander Hinnmith," he announced with head held high. "My scouting party has reported that all of Hetherlinn received parchments from the King of Claire. In accordance with the Oracles of the Cauldron, everyone must die."

The townspeople screamed. Some dropped to their knees and pleaded for mercy. Hinnmith and his warriors sat motionless, unmoved by their plight. A voice that sounded like hissing steam cut through the villager's wails. Hinnmith raised his arm. The crowd fell silent. He beckoned for the widow to come near.

"Commander," Mithe gave an awkward curtsy, "we did not touch the forbidden parchments. Your scouts can confirm this, for they didn't find any on cottages Number 7 and 17."

Hinnmith's eyes narrowed. "Is this correct," he asked one of his officers over his shoulder.

"Yes, sir."

"So tell me, soldier, why must an old Allsbruthian woman add information to your report?"

The soldier did not reply, for it was not meant as a question, but was an Ebonite rebuke.

Mithe continued. "Commander, you seek the children that took the invitations, and who have climbed the oak to listen for whispers, but they have fled. And behold. They have murdered one of your own."

She pointed to the swinging corpse.

Hinnmith's eyes burned with rage. He turned in his saddle to address his officer. "You forgot to mention *this* in your report."

"Commander," the officer replied, "after we attempted a March of Reeds, Commander Thull sent us back to get reinforcements to chase the rebels. He, in turn, gave pursuit. I didn't know he was killed."

Hinnmith arched his back and stared at the officer. "Why did Commander Thull give the order to perform a March of Reeds?"

"Sir, with all due respect, the entire village received the invitations."

"Yes, but only *two* children violated the Oracles."

Hinnmith drew in deep breaths in an effort to control his emotions. He disliked the younger leaders under his command. They were too smug and too quick to draw first blood. He needed to discipline them for their breach in military protocol, but this would have to wait until they were well beyond Allsbruth.

Mithe wobbled closer to Hinnmith. "As you are well aware, commander, the Oracles state: *'The faithful should never be punished for the rebellion of a few.'*"

"Please," Areall shouted as she pushed her way through the crowd. "Commander, don't listen to her. It wasn't their fault."

"Oh, but it was, Areall," Mithe hissed like a viper. "And it is *your* fault as her mother for not having more control over her. This all began when you let her climb the oak."

"Then kill us," Areall pleaded of Hinnmith, "but leave our children be."

Hinnmith stared at Commander Thull's corpse. Without taking his eyes off the swinging body, he ordered: "Old woman, go bring me some of their clothing so we can get their scent."

"No," Areall screamed. Facing her neighbors, she begged, "Please help us. They're so young. Don't do this."

"So you would have the faithful die for Elabea's rebelliousness?" Mithe countered.

Galadin's mother, Daryess, joined Areall. The mothers looked longingly at their neighbors, but the only response was heads dropped down or eyes glaring back at them.

"See?" Mithe said. "They too know what must be done."

Areall looked to Quinn for help, but aside from his wound, she could tell there was no fight in him at all. Areall fell sobbing into Daryess' arms.

Mithe sent her granddaughter to gather the clothes. The girl ran to cottage Number 7, entered and soon emerged with a cloak.

"Gundin, stop her," Daryess pleaded, but the Cauldron had discovered his rejuvenated spirit. Focusing the drone on him, it smothered his senses the moment Hinnmith's entourage arrived. Once more, Gundin was back in his fantasy world.

The girl darted into cottage Number 17 and returned waving Elabea's shawl. She sprinted back and handed her grandmother the clothing. Mithe patted her on the head and then presented the clothes to Hinnmith as a sacrifice for their survival. He snatched them from her grip.

"Release them," Hinnmith ordered.

Iron squealed upon iron as the wagon's rear door crashed to the ground, the reverberations making the citizens shudder. Frantic, animalistic grunts came from within the wagon, followed by the sound of chains clanking and rattling together. Horrific barks filled the air. The villagers stared at the dirt as shame snaked through them all.

Two enormous creatures emerged from the wagon's shadows. Walking on all fours, they pulled hard upon the chains the Ebonites desperately held in check. Long, quill-like hair, mottled black, gray and white, covered their torsos. Broad shoulders supported thick, short necks and their wide heads peered this way and that with eyes dark and sinister. Long, bear-like claws studded each paw and clawed the dirt in anticipation of hunting, killing and eating. Snarling, the creature revealed sharp teeth, and powerful jaws capable of ripping apart flesh and bone.

One beast sniffed the air and emitted a sharp bark. Rearing on its hind legs, he towered over the villagers as the warriors strained on the chains to maintain control.

"These are sevritts," Hinnmith announced. "They are faster than a horse and can follow a trail that has been cold for days. Once the boy and girl are found and executed, then your village will be spared further reprisals."

He tossed the clothing at their feet.

The sevritts sniffed the pile and pushed it to and fro with their snouts, periodic guttural grunts piercing the silence. They stopped sniffing, then raising their heads skyward, they sounded a high-pitched bay that diminished to a low growl.

Hinnmith shouted the Ebonite battle cry. "First blood."

Chains were dropped and the beasts lunged toward the huddled people. Screams filled the air, but the sevritts were on the trail of Elabea and Galadin. They leapt over the crowd and sprinted toward the meadow.

Areall and Daryess dropped to their knees sobbing while Gundin helped Quinn toward cottage Number 17.

Hinnmith gave his officer a final order. "Retrieve Commander Thull's body."

"Will we burn him here?"

"*Never*. There has been enough disgrace here already. We'll give him a military burning once we cross into Ebon."

As the officer galloped off, Hinnmith gave Mithe a contemptuous look. Although he despised the Allsbruthians, he had even more disgust for anyone who would betray their own people in order to survive.

"The Oracles also state," he offered her, his voice icy cold, *"Beware the smile from a traitor."*

The officer returned with his grisly burden. Thull's corpse was placed inside the wagon, and the heavy door raised and latched into place.

Mithe stood alone, and leaned on her cane as she watched Hinnmith's entourage ride away.

The villagers stood lifeless, emotionless eyes fixated on the ground. Despite their zeal to shed blood to appease Ebon and the Cauldron, they were too ashamed to look at Areall and Daryess.

The wind swirled dead leaves aimlessly about Hetherlinn, and the villagers scattered one-by-one to their numbered cottages, leaving Areall and Daryess alone in the dust. Doors were quietly shut and the wind scattered the leaves into the darkening sky.

Chapter 6

The Day of Reckoning

Il-Lilliad's tale flowed like a spring breeze over Elabea and Galadin.

"Long ago, there was a great and wise king who ruled Allsbruth. His name was Simeion, and he aligned himself with the King of Claire who was called the Only. Storytellers roamed the lands freely, telling all who would listen the grand stories of Claire. Prosperity and peace flowed like rivers of honey through Allsbruth for more than one hundred summers.

"Borders could not contain the tales of Claire, so they flew north to Ebon. The Ebonites feasted upon the stories, growing more and more enchanted with the King of Claire. All, that is, except for a handful of men who were jealous of their neighbors, blaming the King of Claire for what they had not. Calling themselves the Council, they met every night in secret within the dark halls of Netniath. There they poured the longings of their hearts and souls into a small fire that burned with a black flame.

"Unbeknownst to the Council, the black fire fed upon their passions, and over the cycle of many summers, began to grow in size and power. It discovered its voice, *a whisper,* and the Council learned its name, *the Cauldron.*

"The Cauldron had an insatiable appetite that the Council could not appease. So its invisible vapors soared beyond Netniath, to consume the hearts of those willing to listen to a foreign whisper. Over the Mountains of Kline and the Allsbruthian Mountains it flew, into the land of Allsbruth to prey upon the weak. The storytellers were wise to its deviousness, and with the power from Claire, battled the vapors back to Ebon. Caged within Netniath like a wild lion, the dark fires of the Cauldron burned bitter with hatred for the King of Claire, his stories and his storytellers.

"The cycle of summers paraded by, and the Cauldron continued to grow. It whispered to the Council of a day of reckoning - a day when it would have enough power to destroy anyone aligned with Claire. The Council vowed uncompromising allegiance to the Dark Flame, and a plan came to life. It was insidious, simple and involved a young boy in Allsbruth, whose name was Friarlinn. He was the younger of King Simeion's two sons.

"When Friarlinn was of eight summers, he heard a whisper he thought was from Claire. It flew upon the night wind and sounded like a lark in spring. Night after night, Friarlinn entertained the whisper. One night, it posed a question...

Why is your brother, Culdean, to be king?

"Friarlinn embraced the question. The black vapors pushed aside the stories from Claire in his heart, and with its one question, jealousy was birthed.

"Time passed. He was a young man of twenty summers when his father passed into forever, and Culdean became king. Jealousy filled Friarlinn with rage. The whisper came bearing another question.

Why is the King of Claire restraining you from what is rightfully yours? Are you not deserving?

"Friarlinn finally asked the question the whisper had been patiently awaiting.

What must I do to become king?

"The whisper was filled with delight and replied that all he had to do was continue to listen. Obediently, Friarlinn bowed before his open window in anticipation of the whisper's promises and power. As the nights passed, two things occurred: His jealousy grew like a wildfire, and his desire waned for the stories and the true whisper of Claire.

"On one such night, the whisper invited Friarlinn to journey to Ebon and meet their leader. Friarlinn complied. He met with Brairtok, who promised his hordes of warriors would rise up against Culdean, but only on two conditions: Friarlinn would have to kill his brother with his own hands, and Ebon would be allowed to conquer all the surrounding nations.

"The pact was signed in blood, and Friarlinn rode back to Allsbruth to consecrate the deal. On a moonless night, with the vapors from the Cauldron roaming freely in his mind, he fell upon his sleeping brother and stabbed him in the heart. The whisper breathed deep the aroma of first blood, delighting that the day of reckoning was to begin. Ebonite drums beat out their war cadence. From the halls of Netniath a drone was released, flooding the lands and holding at bay the stories of Claire. Next, the Cauldron cast forth the power it had been storing up for many winters into the Mountains of Kline. The ground rumbled. The mountain was split. And the passage known as Waelryth was formed.

"One night, Ebonite warhorses stormed into Allsbruth. Without a king to lead them, the armies of Allsbruth were crushed. Blood flowed like a river in the once-peaceful land. The Dark War had begun.

"As the battles unfurled, Friarlinn became king and rose to greatness and power, just as the whisper had promised. The fumes of the Cauldron seeped into every culture like a deadly fog, suffocating the stories of the Only and filling all with its own twisted tales and myths.

"Satisfied that victory was in hand, the whisper turned on the one who had given so much. Brairtok entered Friarlinn's chamber, and while the king slept, the warlord slit his throat. The whisper delighted that all was going as planned. Darkness and lies took root and flourished, disguised as stories from the King of Claire.

"Nevertheless, the nations continued to fight, and the Dark War was passed to the next generation. The Cauldron took note of his warlord, Brairtok: Although others throughout the lands had come and gone, he did not age.

"Desperate for an answer to this phenomenon, the Cauldron drew all tales and stories about the Only into its dark fires. Relentlessly it searched, until finally, a story hidden from all was uncovered. It was so simple and plain that it had gone unnoticed. The tale disclosed that with the death of all the storytellers, the stories of Claire would exist no more, and the King of Claire would pass into forever. Furthermore, whoever was king at the time would have life immortal.

"Elated with its discovery, it shared the tale with Brairtok, who vowed undying allegiance to the Cauldron, covetous to share life immortal with the Dark Flame. The Cauldron gave Brairtok his next mission: March to Allsbruth's remaining stronghold - Min Brock—and destroy them all.

"Brairtok's forces flooded the Gilden Plains and surrounded Min Brock. They laid siege while the Cauldron's whisper lulled Min Brock's leaders into a dangerous pact: Surrender all the storytellers and their lives would be spared. The leaders agreed to the terms, and the storytellers were handed over to the army of Ebon. All was going as planned until a renegade force from Min Brock attacked the Ebonites. Although only a suicide mission at best, the Cauldron was outraged at such rebellion. Brairtok launched a full-scale attack on Min Brock and killed every last warrior...except the leaders who had signed the pact. These he released, and they fled home, branded forever as traitors and cowards.

"With the demise of Min Brock, the Cauldron turned its fury upon the storytellers. Men, women and children were herded into the Valley of Reeds like cattle. Ebonite warhorses lined up at each end of the Valley. A lonely drumbeat sounded. The drone intensified. In unison, the warhorses lifted one leg at a time and brought them down hard, smashing the reeds before them. The drumbeat quickened. The horses pummeled another row of reeds. Again the tempo increased, as did the cheers from the spectators. With heads held high, the storytellers knelt and called out to the King of Claire, but the Cauldron had anticipated this. The drone intensified and drowned out their cries.

"Powerless, the storytellers huddled together. They humbly bowed their heads in honor to their king as the merciless wave of warhorses crushed them. Martyred blood splattered upon their silver armor, causing it to tarnish. Drunk with power, Brairtok ordered his warriors to immerse their armor in the blood. Silver armor transformed to black-red and remains as such to this day.

"As the life of each storyteller passed into forever, the Cauldron burned with increasing energy. It cast its despairing fumes further and further. Brairtok felt his life being extended, power surging through him as never before.

"But their confidence was short-lived. The next summer, the Cauldron discovered a new story. It started as a myth across the Sea of Illsbruth. From Torrens Bay, it grew from myth to tale. By the time it was drawn into the Dark Flames, it had blossomed into a story. It told of a storyteller, one who had survived the March of Reeds. He had fallen wounded and lay beneath the bodies of his dying friends. Under this blanket of death he survived. Later that night, he escaped by pushing his way through the sea of bodies. Finding refuge in a hidden cave far, far away, he was nursed back to health by a rusk.

"The Cauldron was furious. One life stood in the way of its glory. It searched for this storyteller, but he was much too cunning and eluded capture. Patiently this storyteller waited in his cave, longing for the day when his stories would be needed once more - a day when the Only would break his silence, ushering in the War of Whispers.

"I am that storyteller. That time is now."

As Il-Lilliad's story unfolded, Elabea found herself sitting high in the branches of her oak. Everything was dream-like, and Il-Lilliad sat on a branch across from her. In this dreamworld Il-Lilliad spoke.

"I knew you had heard his whisper. I saw it in your eyes. Even the Ebonite warrior could not dispel its purpose."

"Yes, but you said the Cauldron whispers too. How do I know I heard the Only?"

"The true whisper gives life. The Cauldron's whisper mimics and only offers questions. That is why you must hear the stories. You must learn to listen with ears that thirst for the stories of life."

Elabea's brow furrowed. "I don't understand."

"You have heard the whisper of the King of Claire. You have been awakened from the vapors of the Cauldron." He leaned forward, his eyes found hers, and he delivered his next words with light-filled eyes. "Elabea, you are to be a storyteller."

Elabea gasped and covered her mouth. She knew that the Oracles not only forbade the stories from Claire, but promised horrible consequences for those who became storytellers. "No, I...I don't want to."

"You can no more *not be* than you can decide *to be*."

"I just want to remain in my meadow."

"Do you?" he asked as he leaned back against the oak's trunk. "The King of Claire has heard your dreams from this tree, and he has whispered them to me as well. You have longed to leave Hetherlinn and be someone besides Elabea. Now is your chance."

"Yes, but it was not to be like this. It was to be..."

"Peaceful?" he finished for her. "Easy?"

She nodded.

"Elabea, nothing of worth is easy; and the only peace you can hope to find is beyond your meadow."

The thought of becoming a storyteller unnerved her. "The Oracles promise death to anyone who tells such stories."

"The King of Claire has whispered to you. He will not let you face this alone."

Overwhelmed, she shook her head. "I'm only fourteen summers of age. How am I to do this?"

"You will always be asked to do the impossible against impossible odds. That is the mystery of being a storyteller. Remember, a storyteller is never alone; your heart is now the Only's. Listen and learn the stories of life."

Her mind overflowed with countless questions and scenarios, but before she could ask another question, the oak began to spin around and around. She clutched the trunk for fear of falling. She was spinning so fast that she could not discern sky from ground. As quickly as it had started, it was over.

She opened her eyes and was once more sitting in Il-Lilliad's cave.

"Amazing," Galadin exclaimed after opening his eyes. A glance at Il-Lilliad stirred his mistrust and Galadin's joy-filled face clouded with doubt. "Are you *sure* that wasn't a story?" he asked with a thrust of his dagger.

"I promise you," Il-Lilliad answered as he gently lowered Galadin's blade, "it was just a tale."

Il-Lilliad flashed Elabea another secret wink.

She gave a meek smile followed by one of her many questions. "Was what I just experienced...in the oak...with you...a dream?"

"No, that was not a dream. You have heard the whisper of the Only."

Galadin's face wrinkled in confusion. "What are you talking about?"

"While he was telling us the tale about the Dark War," Elabea explained, "he was telling me a separate one."

"I don't remember hearing it," Galadin replied.

"That's because," Il-Lilliad offered, "it was not your tale."

Galadin's expression contorted even more. "So what did he tell you?" he asked Elabea.

She looked into his eyes. "That I'm to be a storyteller."

"How?" he asked her. "Everyone says that storytellers have a birthmark. You have no such marking."

She was about to agree with him when a childhood memory flashed before her eyes like lightning.

I was in my seventh summer, she reflected. *Mother was brushing my hair, but on this particular morning, I remember her suddenly stopping. I could feel her fingers searching my scalp. I thought she had found an insect or perhaps a scar...*

Elabea froze at the memory. *And then, as quickly as she stopped to look she began brushing again, only this time her efforts were frantic, as if trying to hide...*

Elabea gasped. Her eyes widened with fear.

She parted her hair to reveal as much of her scalp as possible. Galadin moved closer to inspect. Hidden beneath her locks was the distinct purple birthmark.

"Has that always been there?"

Elabea nodded, wishing it were not, and wondering why her mother never spoke to her about it.

"You both must hurry," Il-Lilliad interrupted. "Now that Elabea has heard the whisper, the Cauldron has too. You both will be hunted."

"I still don't understand," she stammered. "What about the parchments?"

"They are invitations from the Only to all his people," he replied while searching among his vast collection of leather-clad parchments. "Each parchment was personally addressed and signed with gold letters. They spell your names. You were the only ones in Hetherlinn to answer."

Finding what he was looking for, Il-Lilliad let out a loud "Aha." Spinning on his heel, he rejoined them. "You will need this in order to survive your journey," he said handing it to her.

"Journey?" Elabea replied as she took it, bewildered by the thought of such an undertaking. "Why can't we go back home?"

"Your way of life is forever gone, Elabea. You must travel to Claire, for it is there you will become a storyteller."

More and more questions flooded her, and the more she tried to make sense of them, the more confused and anxious she became. "That's impossible. Claire was destroyed by the Ebonites."

Il-Lilliad's eyes softened as he read the story on her heart. *Poor child, you've been fed lies and told they're truth. Those you love and trust have wounded you with their words and stories. No wonder you are so frightened.*

With a gentle hand to her shoulder, he answered, "My dear Elabea. You must begin to learn the stories of the Only in order to see what is true and what is not. The Cauldron has hidden its tales amongst the words of Claire, masking itself within such wonder. Your father never meant to hurt you, but his shame and stories have. And your mother hid the birthmark from you not out of spite, but in order to protect you."

His gaze hopped from Elabea's face to Galadin's. "Despite what you have been taught and what your senses now tell you, you must believe me when I say that Claire is still there."

Elabea studied the leather bound object she was holding. Although extremely old and weathered, it felt so comfortable and inviting to the touch. She brought it close to her nose. Despite its age, it smelled like freshly tanned leather.

She flashed Il-Lilliad a curious look.

He smiled, and with a nod, encouraged her to continue to explore it.

The top piece of leather was covered with mysterious etchings and pictures. She traced them with her index finger. Goosebumps raced up and down her back. A deep longing began to fill her, begging her to discover the stories within. She opened the cover. Neatly trimmed parchment papers were inside. Flipping through them, her eyes drank in the wonderment of the many words and illustrations. As the pages turned, they cast a scent that was sweet and pleasant, reminding her of spring flowers.

"What is it?" Galadin asked.

"Why, it's a book," Il-Lilliad answered, stunned at such a question. "It is a living, breathing creature filled to the brim with endless stories. Stories about questions and stories with answers to questions."

Their faces clouded with confusion.

Il-Lilliad's joyful expression fell. "Oh yes, the Oracle," he said sadly. "I forgot. You've never seen a book before, and you are unable to read."

Il-Lilliad lightly clapped his hands. The brown animal flew from its roost and landed in his open palms.

"This is a rusk," Il-Lilliad said as the animal fluttered its thin wings that were covered with brown fuzz. "Most were destroyed with their storyteller masters in the March of Reeds."

The rusk sat on his rear haunches with his front appendages tucked, but they could see that he had what appeared to be black, human-like hands instead of paws. Il-Lilliad continued, gently rubbing the down-like fur behind the animal's cheeks.

"My rusk knows all of the stories in the book you now hold. He will instruct you and be your teacher."

The rusk turned his round face toward Elabea. He blinked his large dark eyes and studied her, as if to see whether she would be as good a master as Il-Lilliad. His small nose sniffed her scent while his cat-like whiskers flickered. His fur looked silky, glistening in the firelight, and she noted a ridgeline of stiff hair that ran from his head all the way down to his long tail.

"Do not lose him," Il-Lilliad advised Galadin, "or let harm come to him. For without the rusk, you will be lost in a strange land."

The rusk scampered up Elabea's arm and sat on her shoulder. It pressed its wet nose to her neck, its whiskers tickling her. Much like the calming effect from the herb twig, she felt great peace from its presence.

"Are you *sure* you want to go through with this?" Galadin asked as she giggled from the rusk's playful antics.

"What do we have here in Hetherlinn?" she answered, rubbing the animal's tufts of fur like she had seen Il-Lilliad doing. "My father's a drunk, and yours is mad. Besides, haven't we always dreamed of doing something daring like this?"

"True," he answered, becoming annoyed at how playful she was with the rusk despite the harrowing journey that lay before them. "But aren't you forgetting that as a storyteller, you'll be hunted by the Ebonites for the rest of your life."

The rusk fluttered its wings and Elabea's face glowed with excitement, her fears diminishing with every beat of his wings. "I know. But would you rather stay in Hetherlinn and be a farmer for the rest of your life, or try and become the warrior you've always dreamed of being?"

Galadin pondered the thought as Elabea continued.

"Just think, Galadin, this could be the beginning of something very special. Something…very exciting."

Galadin sighed. He knew she was right. He wanted to get as far away from his father and become anything but a farmer.

"So be it. We journey to Claire," he answered as he reached out to stroke the rusk's long tail.

"Never touch the tip," Il-Lilliad warned. "There is enough poison within to kill ten Ebonites."

"That may be," Galadin replied, unimpressed with the creature's capabilities, "but I've got *this*."

He proudly held up his dagger.

"Oh yes," Il-Lilliad huffed, *"that."* He walked to his bed and retrieved something from the shadows.

"Where you are going," Il-Lilliad said as he returned, "you will need *this.*"

"Your sword?" Galadin exclaimed.

Wrapping his fingers tightly around the sword's sheath, he marveled at the polished leather. Bands of silver graced its tip and top, and detailed etchings encircled the upper band. The guard was also silver and curved toward the weapon's tip. The hilt matched the sheath, but was not polished, and a silver pommel with an engraved tulip on one side, capped its top.

Galadin gripped the hilt and withdrew the blade halfway. It slid so smoothly that barely a sound could be heard. Despite the dim light of the cave, the metal reflected his face with great brilliance.

"Swords are forbidden by the Oracles," Galadin said as he admired the blade.

"So I hear. I, however, am a storyteller and do not follow such Oracles."

"But there isn't a weapon like this in all the lands," Galadin said as he continued admiring the weapon. "So how did *you* get one?"

"After surviving the March of Reeds, I discovered it lying nearby. How it got there has always been a mystery to me. That is, until now. Look on the backside."

Galadin flipped it over and saw more etchings in the top silver band.

"They look familiar…"

"Hand me your invitation."

Galadin pulled it out and gave it to Il-Lilliad. The storyteller held it next to the etchings. Galadin's eyes widened.

"They spell your name," Il-Lilliad explained.

"How can that be? I wasn't alive when the March of Reeds happened," he countered. "This must be for another Galadin."

"Do you truly believe that on a dark night, after surviving a massacre, I just happened to find a sword with *your* name on it?"

"There must be another explanation…" Galadin stammered.

"Galadin," Il-Lilliad fired, irritated by the boy's stubborn doubtfulness. "This is not from Ebon, and storytellers do not carry swords. So tell me, how did a weapon from Claire, with your name etched upon it, end up beside me in *Ebon?*"

"This is from Claire?" Galadin said, his admiration for the blade battling with the doubts of his past. "I find that impossible to believe."

"Your doubt, my dear Galadin, will be your greatest foe."

"My greatest foe? I don't understand."

Placing his hands on Galadin's shoulders, Il-Lilliad looked deeply into his eyes.

"In time, you will understand my words. For now, dedicate your heart to what I am about to ask of you. This sword comes with a price: You must get Elabea to Claire at all costs. Do you understand? At all costs. The War of Whispers has begun. Only storytellers can turn the tide in such a war. That is why Elabea must get to Claire. Protect the rusk. Guard the book. Without them you are doomed."

The reality of the adventure sank into Galadin's mind. Fear tugged at him. He shook it off as if it were a cold wind. He solemnly nodded.

Il-Lilliad led them out of the corridor to the cave's entrance. Resting upon his staff, he studied the surrounding woods.

"Galadin," Il-Lilliad said as his eyes swept the shadows beyond, "much will be asked of you. In fact, if you could see all that lies before you, you would not have the courage to leave my cave."

Galadin drew in a deep breath. He slowly donned his sword.

"Storytellers," Il-Lilliad continued, "also have the ability to read stories being written within another's heart. I have read your tale. So has the Only. You will be the warrior you long to become."

Facing Elabea, Il-Lilliad smiled as she stroked the rusk's silky, brown fur. "Look out into the woods," he instructed her, "and tell me: Do you see or hear anything unusual? Perhaps something fresh or alarming?"

Elabea looked, listened and sniffed. She shook her head.

Il-Lilliad draped his arm over her shoulder and pointed out into the lush forest.

"The whisper has not only awakened you, Elabea, but also the woods and the lands beyond. It is a world that has been asleep ever since the Dark War ended. You and Galadin will see things, hear things and feel things that will make your hearts leap for joy."

He studied both sets of eyes, a teacher longing for his students to grasp the deeper meaning to his lesson. "At the same time, the Cauldron will intensify its efforts to find you, summoning creatures neither of you have encountered before."

And then to Galadin, "There is more than bear and deer in those woods."

"I know," he replied as he stiffened his back. "I've seen the gors."

"Gors?" Il-Lilliad snapped. "They are the least of your concerns. The creatures I am referring to only frequent one's nightmares. You must never let your guard down. *Never.* Do you understand?"

Galadin rested his palm upon his sword's pommel and nodded.

"Why aren't you coming with us?" Elabea asked.

"I must go to Hetherlinn. Something tells me some old acquaintances of mine are in need of a good story."

Chapter 7

Remnant Whisper

Long before there were kings in Allsbruth, there flowed a serene river, but it was not an ordinary stream like that of air or water. This river was a supernatural force containing all that was good, noble and powerful from the surrounding nations. Flowing high above the clouds, beyond where eagles soar, it flowed into Claire as it was intended to. There, the King of Claire observed the watercourse, listening to the stories within with great interest. Then he added his stories and sent the river racing back from whence it came.

But that all changed when Ebon became victorious in the Dark War.

Discovering the currents, the Cauldron drew the river toward its citadel, Netniath. Pouring through a tower window, the river churned along the ceiling toward the Council's chamber.

Glacial winds swirled within the chamber, tapestries and curtains billowed like sails of ships lost at sea. Ice covered the architectural features of the room and either dangled as icicles from the ceiling or gathered in large heaps along the walls. Torches, lit upon Min Brock's demise, burned with a blue flame, making the chamber glow ice-blue like the glacier caps atop the Mountains of Kline.

In the center of the room sat the Cauldron; a large, round iron encased the black flames that leapt panther-like into the frigid air. Before the Dark War, it was an architectural masterpiece of silver, glimmering like a king's signet ring. When Brairtok had his men immerse their armor in the martyrs' blood, the Cauldron was so delighted by the armor's transformation that it decided to do the same to every building and architectural element in Kise. Now the Cauldron was coated in soot and grime and muck, all of which bubbled on its sides like tar. Despite the fire's intensity, it did not radiate heat, but instead, blasted icy winds throughout Ebon.

Sitting about the Dark Flame, with covered heads humbly bowed, was the Council of Ebon. Exhaled breaths became vaporous clouds that dissipated into the winds. Although the air was frigid, they sat comfortably upon their chairs, letting the wintry atmosphere invigorate them through and through.

The river's swirling currents exploded overhead, and they raised their shrouded heads from their meditations. Lifeless eyes peered from beneath gray cloth at the watery wonder. Gaunt frames became energized and wrinkled flesh radiated with the river's rainbow of colors. Awestruck, their ashen faces followed the river's course as it oozed over the Cauldron's sides, sizzling like bacon over an open fire.

The Dark Flame gorged itself upon the river from morning to dusk, dusk to dawn. Unable to satisfy its appetite for power, the Cauldron enslaved the river, feasting upon the river, vowing to never release it until it had served its purpose - until the day it made a startling discovery, and stopped its consumption.

At first, the Cauldron was alarmed, for its dark flames shot to great heights only to die to a glowing black ember. Finding the source of the problem, the Cauldron flung the indigestible thing onto the floor of the chamber.

The Council stared in horror at what lay at their feet. Silvery, sleek and glistening like a fish out of water was a remnant tale from Claire. They gagged from its sweet scent and smothered it with a blanket to conceal its grotesque beauty.

The Cauldron felt otherwise, and gloated over such a finding, for now it knew that their enemy's stories and whispers could be discovered within the river. Once discovered, it could retrace the river's course to find the source of such rebellion against its Oracles.

So it was that the Cauldron and the Council first learned of Elabea's whisper.

"Behold," the Cauldron whispered to the Council. *"I have discovered the remnant of a whisper to a girl - Elabea. Our enemy hails her to journey to Claire and become a storyteller."*

The Council moaned, for their hatred for anything from Claire awakened their wrath. With voices like stone sliding upon stone, they each spoke a collective plan of action.

"So the King of Claire lives."

"He has found the courage to whisper again."

"Did defeat at Min Brock not teach him enough humility?"

"The whisper speaks of a young girl."

"Elabea is her name."

"She is to be a storyteller."

"Fear not, brothers. What can one girl do to us?"

"True. The Only is desperate, choosing one so small."

"Despair has captured his mind."

"Do not sing of glory yet. For just one story can spark hope."

"She must die before her whisper becomes her story. Before she realizes all that she can do."

"Destroy her with her own dreams."

And then in unison...

"Death begets death."

Bowing their heads, they gazed into the Cauldron's blackness. With clasped hands, they sang the drone's pitch, their voices becoming louder and louder. At the climax of their volume, they cast their monotone song beyond Netniath. Far away, within the Caves of Freers, four vul jens awakened to the Council's song and took to wing.

Bird-like, with dark purple plumage, their black eyes blinked and glowed within deep sockets like the Cauldron's Dark Flames. Long appendages dangled beneath, ready to snatch or tear their prey, and a triangular piece of bone sat upon their heads like a grotesque crown. In place of a beak was a long snout, the top overlapping the bottom that held two fangs that jutted upwards. They descended into Netniath and circled the Cauldron, paying homage for being summoned into service once more.

"Our enemy has summoned a storyteller," the Cauldron advised them, *"an Allsbruthian girl named Elabea."*

The vul jens shrieked with delight. How many winters had passed since they had feasted upon their favorite prey - storytellers?

During the Dark War, they tracked the scent from Claire's stories back to the storytellers' camps. In the shadows of night, they roosted nearby, waiting patiently until their hapless prey fell fast asleep.

When the time came, they glided like dark shrouds down upon a victim's chest.

Vigilant they sat, riding the rise and fall of torsos, like gulls upon a darkened sea. Poised with wings outstretched, they watched for the storyteller's one moment of weakness - a dreambreath: The magical moment when sleep faded into a dreamworld and Claire's goodness was ushered in.

Like a rogue wave across a moonlit bay it came: The storyteller's chest rose higher and higher to drink in the nocturnal air.

At its zenith, the vul jens attacked. Purple plumage transformed into vapor, dreambreath inhaled vul jen mist, and darkened haze flew unchallenged into the storyteller's dreams to become a Dreamhunter.

There, the Dreamhunter attacked, injecting the Cauldron's poison deep into the storyteller's dreams. Where hope and peace had once flourished, despair and dismay blossomed. Where tales of Claire had flowed like mountain streams, rot and filth swelled upon blackened eddies. Where sweet dreams had danced with delight, nightmares rose like ghouls from shallow graves.

"She does not travel alone," the Cauldron added. *"A boy accompanies her,*

but fear not, for he is powerless to stop you. Nevertheless, be on your guard for our enemy, the inept king of Claire, has whispered again. He is most cunning and will use anyone or anything to stop you.

"*Now go. Fly fast and far. Listen for the whisper from Claire. Listen for our enemy's stories. They will lead you to her.*"

The vul jens soared out of Netniath and into Ebon's dark sky. They ascended to the invisible river, and once within, they discovered the residue of a whisper from Claire.

Dark wings flapped against the cold winds as the vul jens changed course. Although muffled, their feathers seemed to beat out the name of a girl.

Elabea.

Chapter 8

The Pilgrimage

There was a saying throughout the lands: "Anything for a price in Torrens Bay."

Nestled south of Allsbruth and cradling the Sea of Illsbruth was the nation of Farra. At its southernmost point was Torrens Bay, a large port town that relied on the importing and exporting of goods for its daily survival. Along with attracting commodities from other ports, it was a city where fortunes were quickly made and lost, where immigrants could start anew and felons could escape capture.

Torrens Bay was exquisite.

Torrens Bay was repugnant.

A man who carried the weight of fifty summers on his shoulders wove through the busy market streets of Torrens Bay. Walking beside him, and a step or two behind, was a handsome boy of sixteen summers. They both wore simple attire woven from dark brown cloth to go unnoticed, or to be viewed as poor pilgrims.

The street was constructed of smooth, large river stones laid side by side. Horse-drawn wagons rumbled up and down, the *clunk-clunk* sound of their hooves echoing over the noise of the bustling shopping district. Shops lined the street, each one unique in color, size and architecture. Vendors stood in the doorways shouting over the raucous street sounds, bartering for patrons to buy their wares. Customers poured in and out of doorways like bees from a hive.

Although early in the morning, the man of fifty summers watched as men and women, possessed by strong drink, sang raunchy songs from a balcony overhead. He passed one shop that offered fine clothing woven from colorful silks and linens. Beside it was a shop that sold trinkets fashioned from gold and what appeared to be human bones. Disgusted with what he saw, he turned away.

"Torrens Bay," he muttered to himself. "How can such decadence dance beside such beauty? Evil meshes with goodness."

As he walked, he scrutinized every face for any hidden intent or malice. Thieves, mercenaries, pilgrims, and refugees were the general populace, and he wished he could have avoided Torrens Bay. Danger lurked within every shadow, every doorframe. The very air oppressed him, as if the hands of the Council pressed down upon him.

The boy, on the other hand, spun around in awe, enjoying the tantalizing aromas and the orchestra of sounds. From his left he was courted with purchasing weapons of all shapes and sizes. A vendor on his right pushed delicious smelling sweetbreads his way. From a nearby balcony four women of questionable character called to him.

"Newcomb," the boy shouted to the older man as he returned their wave, "see how friendly everyone is?" The women on the balcony cackled at his naiveté.

"Torrens Bay is *extravagant*," the boy exclaimed.

"Yes," the older replied. "A wonderful place...if one desires to be robbed, cheated or murdered."

"Newcomb, do you know what your problem is," the boy asked while street gymnasts performed in an adjacent courtyard. "You don't know how to have fun."

"Lassiter, my life is not about pursuing fun. It is about protecting and educating you, but I fear our walk through Torrens Bay will be counterproductive to such training."

Newcomb's face looked younger than most men his age, and his gait - when not encumbered by the haunts of Torrens Bay - was quick, decisive and energetic. A life filled with studying the tales of Claire had furrowed thin lines across his forehead, as if plowed by a farmer of great dedication. Beneath his loose-fitting garb was a slender, athletic frame that he carried confidently.

A slender nose led to his forehead that ascended gracefully like a hill. His thick, white hair glistened like silver dew upon a spider's web and nestled beside his ears like the wings of a dove.

His eyes set him apart. Jade green, they could be as formidable as the cliffs of Ebon or as gentle as a breeze from Claire.

Newcomb was a man of mystery and great wisdom.

Reaching a less crowded portion of the street, Lassiter reiterated, "But you *never* have fun."

Newcomb stopped and gave him a stern look. "Perhaps if you were easier to manage, I could."

Lassiter stared back, dumbfounded for a brief moment. A smile broke across his handsome features. "I get it," he fired. "You were making a joke. You were trying to be funny."

Newcomb shook his head. *Was I as exasperating when I was sixteen summers in age?*

"So Newcomb, why are we here?"

"Do you mean that in the immediate sense, or in the philosophical sense? 'Why am I here in the physical realm?' or 'What is my purpose in life?'"

The boy cocked his head. "You are definitely irritable today."

"Must everything be a joke to you? You seem to think that life is just one big carnival."

"Isn't it?"

Agitated by the Lassiter's silliness, Newcomb pulled him into a dark alley and made sure no one was watching. His jade-green eyes studied the boy. Lassiter was slender and wiry, and one day would fill out to be a man of good size and strength. Fluffs of golden hair, like a field of fall wheat, rolled in thick waves down to the collar of his brown tunic. His face held rich blue eyes that twinkled, untainted and untarnished by the harshness of life.

But it was the boy's heart that concerned Newcomb. The potential for greatness lay within like a champion stallion waiting to be bridled and raced across the plains. Lassiter too often ignored this side of his nature, choosing instead to dance with folly. He seemed bent on seeking a life full of comfort and ease.

"Let me see it," Newcomb whispered.

Lassiter reached into his tunic and produced a parchment. It was white and covered with words written in black ink, all except for one written in gold.

"I have taught you this foreign tongue," Newcomb said. "Read it to me."

Lassiter stared at the parchment. He marveled at both its beauty and its strange delivery - wrapped around the shaft of a crystal arrow that was fired into his door. He rubbed his index finger over the gold letters that spelled his name and read...

"Lassiter."

Next, he read the black letters.

> *Whisper ride spring's scent to woo wayward love with tale,*
> *Parchments white like doves take flight and soar beyond the veil.*
> *Melody of Addoli one day must squelch Dark Flame's dire drone,*
> *Then return to me, sweet melody, but dare not come alone."*

He looked at Newcomb. "So?"

"So?" Newcomb repeated, crossing his arms. "That's all you have to say about a personal invitation from the King of Claire? Have you forgotten all your studies and readings from the parchments? Have you forgotten the stories I've taught you about the Only?"

"No, your tutoring has not been wasted. I simply don't think it's that important."

Newcomb pulled him close and pressed his nose to the boy's.

"I vowed upon your mother's deathbed to keep a promise she asked of me. To my dying *breath* I will keep that promise. Although right now, I almost wish I'd never made such a vow."

Lassiter's back stiffened and he pushed away from Newcomb. "Do you think I enjoy you following me around, making everything into a story?"

"That is because everything *is* a story."

"But you have been with me since..."

"Since your father died?"

"Exactly, and that was when I was of two summers."

"Your father was a great man."

"Yes, I believe the stories you've told me of him, but now that I'm older, I want to discover life on my own. I may not wish to see the Only, if he even exists."

"He does."

"I'm not so sure. Where is the proof? Is he walking the streets of Torrens Bay? I don't think so."

"You must go to Claire," Newcomb pressed, his voice as firm as stone. "You have an invitation."

"Only if I wish to go."

Newcomb's eyes flared. "I promised your mother, and I'm a man of my word. You *are* going to Claire."

"Then you must carry me, for I don't wish to go."

With that, Lassiter darted back into the street. Newcomb shook his head, pulled his resolve together and dashed after the boy.

They walked in silence; each hoping time would change the other's stubborn mind. Neither yielded.

As they neared the edge of town, and the streets gave way to broader landscapes, they spotted three tents. Long poles supported the centers while smaller poles circumvented the outer edge. Ropes were tied to the pole tops and stretched in taut lines to the ground where they were staked. Inside vendors sold animals of all shapes and sizes.

They entered the closest tent. A mass of men and women bartered for animals for consumption, labor or pets. From the next tent they heard a horse whinny. Curious, they entered and were greeted by a myriad of sounds: The low grunt of pigs, the caws of wild birds and the roar of a large cat. The scent of rotting straw, human sweat and manure hung thick in the air. Lassiter covered his nose.

A vendor barked his rehearsed sales pitch to every passing customers. He spied Newcomb and Lassiter. Desperate to make a sale, he gruffly pushed his way toward them through the crowded tent.

"Greetings," he hailed with much bravado.

Newcomb gave a slight nod.

"What a handsome son you have." He gave Lassiter a firm pat on the head. Lassiter jerked away.

Undeterred, the vendor continued. "May I interest you in a pet for your boy? These are very tame creatures."

Newcomb studied the array of animals. To his left was an old horse. The animal chewed listlessly and did not appear to have the strength to stand, let alone carry anyone or anything. Tethered nearby was an Ebonite tiger. The once-great animal sat docile in the dust, whip scars marked his face and sides. Perched above the vendor's table were exotic birds. Their once-radiant plumage dull and thin, their once-joyful calls dormant. In a corner of the tent sat several white goats, so malnourished that their hides looked to be too small for their bones.

Newcomb was about to give the vendor a verbal lashing when something behind the goats caught his eye. A small animal with its back turned cowered in the shadows. Tethered to a stake by a leather leash, its little body shivered either from fear or starvation.

"You are torturing these animals," Newcomb roared.

"Not me," the vendor protested, holding his hands up as if to push away Newcomb's accusation. "I'm at the mercy of the merchants from other ports."

"Mercy?" Newcomb fired. "These animals need mercy from *you*."

Desperate to make a sale, the vendor continued his pitch, this time in a singsong voice as he feigned compassion. "I do what I can for these lovely creatures. I'm sure if they had a good home and love…" he gave Lassiter the most pathetic, sad look he had ever seen. Lassiter chuckled at the man's horrible acting abilities. "…that they would spring back to good health in no time."

Newcomb remained focused on the tethered animal in the shadows. "How much for that one?"

"You have exceptional taste, sir. He is rare; rare indeed."

"Perhaps, but see how he is shivering? He is dying."

"Then make him a home. Help him to live once more."

"How much?"

The vendor studied Newcomb's face and drab garments to measure his worth. "Twenty-two gilns."

"Twenty-two?" Newcomb chortled. "Perhaps if he were fit. I will give you five."

"Five? I paid double that for him."

"Very well then. You shall receive ten."

The vendor's mouth went agape as he realized Newcomb had out-smarted him, but with only one coin left in his purse, he nodded to the agreement.

Turning to retrieve the animal, he mumbled obscenities about how a street beggar had outwitted him. When he tried to scoop up the animal, the creature spun, unfurled his wings and snapped at his fingers.

The vendor jerked his hands away. With a nervous laugh, for fear Newcomb would walk away from the deal, he shouted, "Nothing to fear. He always does that. It's his way of…showing love."

Newcomb whispered into Lassiter's ear, "I only wish he'd bitten him."

The vendor untied the leash from the stake and cautiously led the animal to Newcomb. Placing ten gilns into the man's outstretched palm, Newcomb took the leash and began untying it.

"Be careful," the vendor warned, taking a step backward. "Although small, he will bite."

"Now that's odd," Newcomb countered as he threw the leash at the vendor. "You just told me that was his way of showing love." He knelt and held out both hands for the animal to sniff and explore.

"Did I say that?" the vendor snipped as he pocketed the gilns. "Either way, a deal is a deal. He's yours now. No refunds." He spun on his heels and sped to a new customer.

The animal trusted Newcomb's scent and weakly climbed into his palms. Newcomb drew the animal close to his face as he stood back up. "Do not fret, little one," he whispered. "You're free from his tortures. We will nurse you back to health."

Leaving the tent, they continued their journey. Every now and then, the animal fluttered its wings, but Newcomb could tell the effort was painful.

"What kind of animal is it?" Lassiter asked. "It's not really a bird, but neither is it really a beast."

"I haven't seen one of these in a long time," Newcomb replied as he rubbed under the animal's chin. "I assumed they were all killed in the Dark War."

Newcomb's jade eyes sparkled with excitement. "Lassiter, this is a good omen."

"This?" Lassiter snickered as he pointed to the scrawny brown animal. "I think your good omen is almost dead."

"When it's healthy, it'll be our ally, as well as another set of eyes and ears." Newcomb flashed Lassiter a rare smile. "This, Lassiter, is a rusk."

Chapter 9

First Blood

Galadin's sword rattled as they sprinted away from Il-Lilliad's cave.

"Why do we have to run?" Elabea asked as the rusk flew beside her.

Galadin led her down an incline and merely answered with, "Because."

His curt reply only infuriated her. "Because why?"

"Claire is a long way away," he told her as they maneuvered around a thicket of wildeberries. "Plus, Ebonites could attack at any moment."

She caught up and said, "I know Claire is far away, but we can't run the entire way. Besides, aren't we making a lot of noise running like this?"

Galadin slowed to a stop. The rusk landed on Elabea's shoulder.

"I suppose you're right," he admitted. He did not like the fact that she pointed out a flaw to his running strategy.

Starting again at a fast walk, Galadin led them deeper into the woods. Reaching a hill, they trudged to its summit where he pulled her behind a tree to hide.

"Up ahead," he half-whispered, "is the road into Hetherlinn. Our journey will go much quicker if we travel on it instead of the woods. Since Ebonites patrol on horseback, we'll hear them coming in plenty of time to dart into the woods to hide. Agreed?"

Elabea nodded.

Knowing that once they set foot on the dusty trail they would be easy to spot, they watched and listened for a long time. Convinced it was safe, at least for the time being, they stepped out into the open.

They kept to one side and used the trees' shadows to aid their concealment. Although their pace was brisk, it was not frantic. They spoke little, afraid their voices would carry and alert beasts or Ebonites.

At sunset, the woods quickly cooled and deeper shadows crisscrossed the road. The day's remnant light surrendered to night, and blue moonbeams dotted the road here and there. Elabea held onto Galadin's arm as her eyes swept the dark for any sign of their enemy.

With no warning, Galadin stopped.

"What's wrong?" Elabea whispered.

"Nothing. We're simply nearing the marker." He pointed to the wooden post glowing in the moonlight.

"That's it? I thought it would be bigger, or more intimidating."

"No, that's all it is - just a white post with the seal of Ebon."

"Have you ever journeyed beyond?" she asked.

"You know the Oracles forbid me to."

"I know, but haven't you at least jumped across then back to see what would happen?"

"No," he answered. Realizing she might interpret this as fear, he quickly added: "I wasn't afraid to cross. I simply couldn't risk the chance that the Cauldron would retaliate and harm my family." He caught her shadowed face, and in a quieter voice added, "Or you."

Elabea hoped he did not see her blushing in the moonlight.

"Maybe you're right," she said, steering the conversation away from the awkward moment. "Although we did go to the oak countless times and even asked to hear a whisper, and nothing happened."

"Well, that changed when we took the invitations."

They stared at the marker. Could it magically alert the Cauldron to their whereabouts? Did it possess the ability to kill them on the spot?

Elabea searched Galadin's face, longing to see his expression, but the shadows hid him well. "I'm frightened," she said. She squeezed Il-Lilliad's book for comfort. "Are you?"

Galadin stared at the post. Unlike Elabea, he had often journeyed to the marker while hunting and sometimes sat for half the day wondering what was beyond or what would happen if he crossed. Every time he did, a nagging question loomed: *Would he have the courage to find out?*

"Not tonight," he finally answered as he walked to the post. He rested his palm on its top, took a deep breath, and gave Elabea a parting look. Without another word, he marched into the forbidden zone.

He waited and Elabea searched the road, but nothing happened.

"Well," he called to her, "I'm safe for now. Hurry. Either way, we need to be on our way."

Elabea stared at the post's seal. The black iron disk with the emblem of a pouncing lion looked all the more ominous up close. Like Galadin, she took a deep breath, held it and darted past.

Once more, nothing happened.

Relieved, she released her breath. As soon as she did, the wind whistled through the trees. She darted to his side.

"The wind," she said. "It got stronger when I passed the marker."

"Merely coincidence," he encouraged, his senses focused on the road ahead. "It's nothing to fret about. Besides, if it did sound an alarm, we'll be ready." He patted his sword.

However confident his answer was, Elabea felt otherwise. She began to see things in the shadows and hear things in the wind. Her breath quickened. Her mouth went dry from worry. She pondered what might be ahead, or worse, what crept up from behind. A low-pitched moan made her jump.

"Did you hear that?" she whispered.

"It's just the wind," he reassured, "rubbing tree limbs together."

"But it sounds so..."

"Scary?"

"Yes."

"It used to frighten me too until I heard it during the day. Now I simply don't think of it as something wild in the darkness. Try thinking about it like that."

They continued walking. When Elabea heard another sound she dismissed it as just the wind in the trees, until she noticed Galadin. He had stopped and was staring back down the road.

"What's wrong?"

"Shh. I thought I heard something."

Knowing how he liked to tease, she cocked her head to the side and fired: "If you're trying to frighten me..."

The sound came once more. It was a deep, dark tone that stabbed at their marrow.

"Please tell me those are tree limbs," Elabea begged.

The sound came again. This time, it was much closer.

"Whatever it is," he answered, "it's coming fast."

Again it sounded, as if the dead were crying out to the living.

Galadin drew his sword. He focused his eyes down the road. The trees swayed in the wind, like spectators in anticipation of a nocturnal game of carnage.

In the distance, colossal beasts charged out of the purple and blue shadows. Reflecting the moonlight, their eyes glowed an incandescent orange. Claws tore at the road while snarls revealed large, sharp teeth.

Elabea screamed. "What are they?"

"I don't know. Run. Climb a tree. Quickly."

"But what of you?"

"There's no time to argue. Run." He pushed her toward the woods.

"I'm not going to leave you. I can help."

"With what? That book? Run."

"No."

As they argued, the moonlight became brighter, as if the clouds had parted, but they knew it was a cloudless night. Despite the charging beasts, they looked up to investigate the new light. Hovering high above was a magnificent warrior and stallion that were translucent and glowed.

"Galadin, look. It's the Moon King - Manno Vox. He's here to help."

"A little help would be greatly appreciated."

Manno Vox raised his crossbow to his shoulder. Galadin snapped his gaze back to the creatures. They were almost upon them. He raised his sword and squared himself for battle.

Suddenly, a great flash of light, like lightning, struck the base of a hollow tree beside the road in front of the beasts.

"How could he be that bad of a shot?" Galadin criticized.

The massive tree crashed across the road. Undeterred, the creatures pawed and climbed their way through the thick branches.

From the hollow of the tree a new sound entered the battlefield. It was a rumble that grew in volume and shook the ground beneath their feet. A swarm of small, flying creatures exploded out of the trunk and into the night sky.

The swarm darted through the moon's rays near Manno Vox. He raised his right arm and, like a general ordering his cavalry to charge, pointed toward the beasts below.

The flying animals dove from the sky and engulfed the nearest tracker. The beast fell to the road and pawed and bayed.

The remaining tracker leapt for Galadin, but the young warrior had not taken his eyes off the beast. At the last possible moment, Galadin dove forward with his blade pointed skyward. The sword tip slashed open the stomach, and the beast howled in pain. It crashed to the ground, regained its feet and turned to attack again. Once more, Galadin was one step faster.

He swung his blade with all his might.

The beast's head rolled across the road.

With the battle over, Elabea studied the mysterious creatures that completely covered the other tracker. Their bodies, which were scaled like the lizards from her meadow, had a soft sheen that reflected the moonlight's glow. Membrane-like wings were folded inward, enabling them to use the claws at the top to rip and tear. Although difficult to see, their rear legs appeared short and stumpy, like a hawk's, and gripped tenaciously to the beast's body.

Their scaly heads were oval, and a flattened skirt of darker scales wrapped around their necks. Every now and then, one of the creatures would flex this skirt and it would stand up as stiff as a collar. Long, spines ran through it and emerged as sharpened points that fanned out all around the neck. When flexed, the animal's appearance became all the more sinister.

Triangular tails, which were stubby like their rear legs, were pulled underneath to protect their vulnerable bellies. They emitted tiny squeaks and groans as they ravaged the sevritt with vicious, rapid bites.

One of the animals stared at her and flickered its yellow reptilian tongue. Elabea stared spellbound into its azure blue eyes that glowed like fire.

They lured her closer.

"They wish to be friends," she said dreamily.

The creature shrieked, revealing rows of sharp teeth.

Galadin grabbed her.

"What are you doing?" he asked, but he too made the mistake of looking into their blue eyes. He felt light-headed and his will and battle senses weakened. Realizing the danger he was in, he pulled away from the creature's mesmerizing gaze.

"Elabea, don't look into their eyes."

"So beautiful," she mumbled sleepily as she reached her hand for them.

Galadin grabbed her around the waist and pulled her away.

"They're so beautiful," she slurred as she tried to get one last look at their charming eyes.

Once he had her clear of the swarm, and her mind began to clear from the enchantment, Galadin led her past the fallen tree. Smoke spiraled into the night. Manno Vox's bolt was completely intact, despite the flames it had produced. A great heat poured out of the crystal shaft.

They marveled at the bolt's magnificence and then looked up at Manno Vox overhead. He spurred his stallion and zipped across the sky like a shooting star.

"I assumed he was aiming at the beasts," Galadin noted, "but he meant to hit this tree. Somehow he knew those creatures lived inside its hollow. It's as if he wanted to see if I could protect you."

"Well, what did he see?" she asked.

"He saw," he answered as a smile tugged at his mouth, "that I could."

"And what do you see?" she asked, already knowing the answer.

"I see…that I can."

As they watched Manno Vox's light dissipate, Galadin said, "Il-Lilliad was right; the woods are awakening. Who knows what other creatures surround us. It's foolish to walk so openly down the road. I know it's dark and spooky, but we must enter the woods."

"If they're awakening," she asked, "won't the woods be more dangerous?"

"Possibly. But I know my way through the woods better than I know this road."

With that, he led her boldly into the forest, his sword held at the ready.

Chapter 10

The Visitor from Claire

Hetherlinn was unusually still. Cottage doors were barred, fires were lit, and families huddled together inside, certain that the Cauldron would retaliate with its whisper or warhorses.

Even the communal fire glowed eerily, either from the lack of attention to its dying coals, or because it too sensed the stirring of something great throughout the lands.

The anomaly to the quiet was cottage Number 17. It was abuzz with activity and light. With every candle lit so they could see Quinn's wound, Areall and Daryess rushed about tending to his injury. Gundin sat by the fire, his voice unusually loud.

"That's not a wound," he huffed, once more back in time when he was greater than the sum of his current summers. "During the Battle of Tellendale, I saw men lose an arm and continue to fight. Swinging, lunging with their swords, taking down ten men before dying."

The women ignored his ramblings and wrapped the wound in gauze.

"It takes more than an Ebonite blade to drop Quinn. Side by side we battled for the King of Claire, fighting the Ebonites. What glory we brought to Min Brock. Champions. Victors."

Daryess shook her head as she continued to nurse. *I miss the man who once fought for my heart,* she mused. *Now, he's adrift in a sea of illusion in which the Battle of Min Brock was a victory and not a...*

A knock at the door startled her from her thoughts. Gundin sprang from the chair with dagger drawn.

"Who's there?" he shouted, his mind flitting between reality and fantasy.

"Linwith," came the muffled answer from the other side.

Gundin cracked opened the door. Seeing that Quinn's older brother was alone, he swung the door open and Linwith darted in

"A stranger is in town calling for you two," Linwith reported.

"Ebonite?" Gundin asked while shutting the door.

"No, worse. A *storyteller.*"

"A storyteller?" Quinn muttered as he tried to sit up. "Impossible. They were all butchered after the defeat at Min Brock."

"I fought at Min Brock too, brother. I know a storyteller when I see one."

Quinn pushed the women aside and swung his feet out of bed. Gundin helped him up and the trio returned to the village fire.

It was late in the afternoon and long shadows fell about the village, but even their dark shades could not hide Il-Lilliad's identity. He stood tall and leaned on his staff, calling aloud two names: Quinn's and Gundin's. Neighbors peered out from cracked doors.

"I'm Quinn. What's your business?"

The storyteller studied the men. "The summers have not been kind to you," he stated.

Puzzled expressions covered their faces.

"You don't recognize me, do you?" Il-Lilliad asked.

They shook their heads.

"Pity. I recall you three all too well."

"Then tell us," Quinn ordered. "Your very presence is in violation of the Oracles. You could bring destruction to us all."

"Judging by your appearance and your village, I'd say that I'm too late for that."

"Riddles," Gundin thundered between lapses of fancy. "Just like a storyteller. Answer the man."

"Very well," Il-Lilliad replied. "Before I do, I thought that you would want to first learn about your children's whereabouts."

"Our children?" Quinn asked wide-eyed. "What have you done with them?"

"Nothing, except help them on their way," Il-Lilliad answered.

"More riddles. What are you talking about?" Gundin said with a threatening step toward Il-Lilliad.

"I met them recently," Il-Lilliad replied as he let his staff rest in the crook of his arm. "They allowed me tell them..." he held onto his next words and savored their worried expressions, "... a story."

Upon hearing the word "story," the onlookers slammed their doors.

"You fool," Quinn shouted. "The Cauldron will hear it and destroy them."

"Don't worry, my cave is safe from the probings of the Cauldron."

Il-Lilliad shifted the staff to his other arm. "As you are well aware, as a storyteller, I am capable of reading the stories being written on someone's heart."

Leaning toward the fathers, he said, "I read Galadin's and Elabea's."

Their faces paled.

Il-Lilliad leaned back. "Within those tales I discovered your names amidst all of their thoughts and feelings. That, gentlemen, is why I am here."

"They're alive?" Daryess asked as she and Areall pushed their way through the men.

"Are they safe?" Areall begged.

"They are in very capable hands," he said with a smile. "They have accepted the invitations and are on their way to Claire."

The women gasped in horror.

"Elabea has heard the whisper," Il-Lilliad continued. "You all know what that means. Surely you remember your childhood days playing in the oak…listening for the whisper…hearing the stories of Claire…"

Collectively, they reflected on their youth and the seasons spent climbing the magnificent tree. Despite the Oracles shackles and their despair, a forgotten memory glimmered and sparked. It involved a whisper that flitted through the branches, seemingly dancing from limb to limb as it told tale and story. How they loved to listen, entranced in dreams, pondering this or wondering that.

As quickly as the childhood memory appeared, Min Brock's defeat shrouded it with blackness. They once more felt the weight of the drone and the restrictions of the Oracles. A whisper, identical in tone to the one they heard as children, stirred their fears with a question - *"Aren't your children following the same reckless course you did? Did this not lead to death? Despair? Defeat?"*

The whisper darted away before Il-Lilliad could react, but it was satisfied with the results: The parents' stared glassy-eyed at the ground.

Il-Lilliad realized what had just happened, and focused on the men's inner world. *At the heart of your pain is your betrayal at Min Brock, and despite our days together, you still don't recognize me. So I shall begin our new story with a reintroduction. Perhaps the way to turn this horrid defeat into victory is to battle it out in the open, heart to heart.*

"When we last met," Il-Lilliad began as he looked the men over, "I had long hair and was apprenticing with an older storyteller."

The men left their concerns for Elabea and Galadin and instead, tried to remember such a distant time. As if a secret door was flung open, they each remembered, and the blood drained from their faces.

"You were led away from Min Brock with the other storytellers," Linwith recalled. "So how did you…"

Il-Lilliad raised a hand. "Now is not the time for such tales."

"You've hunted us down to seek revenge," Quinn gasped.

Il-Lilliad chortled. "There is no need for retribution from me; you wage such a war on yourselves. Based upon the stories I just read on your hearts, you all have been doing so for some time."

The group tried to comprehend it all, but it was too much to take in all at once. The whispers. The invitations. The children. Now a storyteller had arrived, but instead of revenge for the crimes of their past, he seemed to be offering a bridge over the Oracles...or if nothing else, a means to escape their shame.

Still, they feared the worst.

"The King of Claire is not whispering once more to seek retribution," Il-Lilliad explained, "but to bring liberation from the tears of Min Brock."

"You don't understand," Quinn answered reflectively. "Even if we were to believe you, what could we possibly do? We're not young men anymore. We have no weapons. The drone smothers every nation while the Cauldron knows when an Oracle is violated. We can never change. It's impossible."

Il-Lilliad smiled. "Then it is time for a story. Only a great story can change the impossible."

"Don't," Gundin shouted with arms held high as if to stop a runaway horse. "Stories are banned by the Oracles. Death will come to us all."

"You still don't understand, do you?" Il-Lilliad asserted as his eyes jumped from face to face. "The whisper from the Only has already been heard by the Cauldron. The invitations *have* already been accepted by your children."

He turned and held Areall in his gaze. "As her mother, you've known for many a summer that she bore the birthmark of a storyteller."

Areall's eyes watered as she looked at Quinn who, up until now, had no idea about the birthmark. His expression of shock was more than she could bear.

"Yes," she whimpered, "but I was only trying to protect her. We've been through so much."

"I know," he soothed. "While we have been standing here, I've read your tales."

Looking directly at Areall and Daryess, he added, "You two have endured more than enough heartache."

Addressing the group, he said, "Story or not, no matter what you decide here and now, your enemy will return to destroy you."

"All we want," Quinn interjected, "is the Cauldron's peace and..."

Il-Lilliad cut him off by thumping the ground with his staff. "The peace the Cauldron offers is an illusion. Look about Hetherlinn. Your homes are numbered for tallying purposes. The Oracles bind your lives and minds like steel shackles."

Their shoulders slumped as the truth of Il-Lilliad's words struck home. At last Quinn found the courage to speak for everyone. "Very well. Tell your story."

Il-Lilliad's eyes appeared to radiate light. He raised his arms in celebration, for he had dreamed of this day within the confines of his cave. *"Fly, unfettered hearts, upon the winds of Claire..."*

The head on his staff began to inhale the mystic effects of the Cauldron.

"Gird loin and arms amidst the Cauldron's gales."

The pure air from the mountains of Claire cleansed their senses as it had before defeat in the Dark War.

"Languish rewards when worms leave their lair..."

Music of magnificent beauty suppressed the rumble from the drone.

"When whispers birth stories, and lore begets tales."

Il-Lilliad rose high into the air, his cloak dancing with rainbow colors.

"Your pyres of anguish, your hearts black as night.
Shall bloom like a tulip amidst Allsbruth's throng.
Justice I send upon moon's bluest light,
Shout 'Death begets life.' Claire's purest song."

Il-Lilliad's story was like froth from a waterfall, drenching the cottages with living waters. Villagers ventured outside, hope filled them once more as they gazed upon beautiful images of their future that floated above Hetherlinn.

Husbands and wives looked at each other with the longing of young lovers. Children ran excitedly toward the hovering Il-Lilliad and marveled at the sights and sounds that swirled about him. A warm spring breeze pushed aside the cold Ebonite air, and a miraculous sign appeared: A red tulip pushed its way out of the cold, gray soil and stood bold by the edge of the village.

Il-Lilliad floated back to the ground, and, as the last refrain from his story faded, so did the spring air and music from Claire. The cold winds of Ebon swirled about once more, and the Cauldron's drone fell oppressively upon Hetherlinn. The tulip, however, remained poised as if spring were in the air.

"This flower," Il-Lilliad said as he let his fingers trail off its red petals, "is a gift from the Only."

"A tulip can't defeat Ebonite swords and warhorses." Gundin challenged with arms crossed.

"Gundin's right," Linwith interjected. "This may be a sign, but what we need is an army. We need a miracle."

"The tulip *is* your miracle," Il-Lilliad exclaimed as he walked briskly toward the men. "Come to it daily and breathe deeply. Over time, its aroma will purge your minds of the poisons from the Cauldron and remind you of the story you heard today."

"Even if we are faithful," Quinn argued, still too ashamed of his past to look Il-Lilliad in the face, "how could this defeat our enemy?"

Il-Lilliad began to pace. "The tulip offers you a chance to start over. It marks the dawn of a new day, giving you a reason to live, to fight and perhaps even to die. It is your awakening."

The men nodded in agreement, but Il-Lilliad knew they still lacked the conviction necessary for such an undertaking.

Quick steps brought him close to the men. "The figurine on my staff will disperse my story before the Cauldron hears it," Il-Lilliad explained. "Which will give us time to tackle our next job."

The men stared at him, dumbfounded.

"Together," Il-Lilliad continued, "we must form a plan."

"And that plan must include rescuing our children," Areall demanded.

"Yes," Daryess added.

Il-Lilliad took in their troubled expressions. His heart ached for their anguish at not only losing their children, but of being married to men with tainted pasts. Yet, he had to tell them the truth.

"Quinn and Gundin are not strong enough yet. There will come a time for them to fight, but today is not that day."

Tears rolled down the women's cheeks. "Our children," Areall said between sobs, "Are alone in the wilderness…journeying…to Claire."

"If it even exists," Daryess chimed in.

"They are children no more," Il-Lilliad replied. "They are well armed and watched over by Manno Vox. Try not to worry."

Addressing the men, Il-Lilliad said, "As the creatures from Bal-Malin declare, 'Together, all. Alone, nothing.' Gentlemen, it is time for us to prepare for war."

He spun around and his cape sent a dust cloud into the air. Without so much as a glance back at the men, he marched to cottage Number 17.

The trio remained frozen. They knew that one step forward would alter their lives forever. Yet despite the odds and the memory of Min Brock, a vibrant tulip growing on a winter day gave them hope.

They exchanged glances, and as only men who have shared war together can do, read each other's expressions.

Without a word, they made their decision.

They followed.

Chapter 11

A Worthy Ally

After a cold night's sleep in the woods, Galadin and Elabea continued north toward Claire. Galadin glanced at his sword as it swung in time with his gait. When he touched the hilt, sparks of courage rifled through him. Elabea followed close behind carrying a bag on her back that held Il-Lilliad's book and the provisions he had given them. Cradled in her hands was the rusk.

"He's so adorable," she said to no one in particular.

Galadin said nothing, but instead focused on navigating the forest.

"Look at his eyes."

She stared into the rusk's round face that was covered with very short, tan hair. Its dark eyes sat nestled like two walnuts in a fold of brown moss.

"I wonder what he eats," she asked Galadin.

Galadin, who was consumed with their dangerous journey, simply gave a disapproving huff.

"He probably eats nuts and wildeberries," she answered herself as she rubbed its short snout.

"Why not ask it?" Galadin joked.

"You're absolutely right. Il-Lilliad said he could tell us about the book so he must be able to talk."

Elabea stopped and brought the rusk close to her face. His cat-like whiskers tickled her cheek. "What do you like to eat?"

The animal merely nudged her face with his small black nose.

"My name is Elabea. Sounds like *Ella-bay*, which is Allsbruthian for *dreamer of days*. His name is Galadin which means *boy warrior* and…"

"Both our names will be *dead* if we don't keep moving," Galadin interrupted.

Elabea rolled her eyes and once more kept pace.

"Why doesn't he talk to me?" she asked.

Galadin shrugged, not the least bit interested or concerned.

The rusk scampered up her arm and sat on her shoulder. With his tiny, human-like hands, he clung tightly to her cloak and curled up into a ball. Even asleep, his deadly tail was ready to strike should danger arise.

"Isn't the rusk cute," she asked.

"If you think flying rats are attractive," he snapped.

"My, your mood is foul this morning."

Galadin stopped, planted his hands on his hips, and glowered at her. "Maybe, but we're traveling to Claire and are being hunted by the Cauldron and the nation of Ebon. Ancient creatures are awakening all around us. We have only the provisions Il-Lilliad gave us, and I don't have a map. Not to mention the fact that Claire may have been destroyed in the Dark War. So if my mood is *foul*, it is only because I'm concerned for our wellbeing. Now, may we please continue on, or must we continue to talk?"

"See, rusk," she said as she scratched the rusk's neck. "Sir Galadin's mood is sour."

Galadin blew out an exasperated breathe and stormed away.

"I'm sorry," Elabea said when she caught up with him. "I'm just so excited. We're going to new places and we are going to see things no one else in our village has seen. What do you imagine Claire to look like?"

"Honestly?" he asked as he scanned the woods for any signs of danger.

"Yes."

"All I've heard is that Claire was destroyed in the Dark War."

"Well, I don't believe that."

"Then what do you believe?"

"I believe it's there. After all, I did see Manno Vox and hear a whisper."

"Who knows what you heard," he said as he scooted over a fallen tree. "That whisper could have just been your imagination. You're putting your hope and faith in the words of an old storyteller."

"Perhaps, but I know what I saw, and I know what I heard."

"Fine. You believe Il-Lilliad. I'll trust the facts and what I can see."

"Then how do you explain your sword?"

"What do you mean?" he asked as he helped her up a slippery incline.

"It bears your name, remember? Mysteriously discovered by Il-Lilliad after he survived the March of Reeds."

Galadin's face remained stoic. He fingered the etchings. "I'm sure there's an explanation; I just don't know what it is."

"Well then, if you don't believe Claire exists, why are you accompanying me?"

Galadin caressed the sword's hilt as he pondered her question. He had always enjoyed her company, but something was changing. Whenever she looked at him, her dark eyes seemed to dance on his heart. The way her body swayed when she walked made his mouth go dry. Even the way she talked captivated his imagination. He was not sure what to do with these new feelings, but one thing was certain: He was not about to share them with her until he mastered them.

"Well," he replied, "I want to discover what's beyond Allsbruth. If we can never go home again, I might as well find a new home. Besides, I thought you might want the company."

Elabea smiled, and Galadin felt his heart rise into his throat. He turned his concentration back on their path and let their conversation die. Galadin pushed through the dark foliage while Elabea followed. Without warning, she screamed. Galadin turned, his hand ready to draw his sword.

"What's wrong?" He searched this way and that for what had scared her.

"The rusk bit my ear," she answered as she massaged the bite.

Galadin relaxed his hand. "Serves you right," he snapped. "Rats, even flying ones, bite."

The rusk's tail began to flap rapidly on Elabea's cloak, while the ridgeline of hairs stood erect.

"Something's wrong," Elabea whispered. "He did the same thing back on the road...right before those beasts attacked. I think he's trying to warn us."

The rusk began flapping his bat-like wings with the speed of a hummingbird. He darted off her shoulder and hovered with his poisonous tail poised to strike.

"Hide behind this tree," Galadin ordered. "I'll go take a look. Probably just a bear."

Galadin drew his sword and searched the woods. The sun was still rising over the hills and shadows stretched eerily across the forest floor. He scrutinized every shadow, every tree, for anything that did not belong.

Elabea screamed again, and this time there was panic in her cry.

He sprinted back and found three men surrounding her.

Wurmlins. The name flitted through Galadin's consciousness. *Nomadic thieves.*

One Wurmlin grabbed Elabea by the shoulder. Her backpack fell, and the book spilled out, its pages open to the wind.

Galadin charged forward with sword in hand.

The second Wurmlin searched her backpack while the third threatened her with a dagger.

A brown flash zoomed toward the Wurmlin that held Elabea. The rusk's poisonous tail struck his face. He dropped to the ground, convulsing in the dry leaves.

The brown blur flitted toward the Wurmlin that was rummaging through her backpack and struck home again, leaving the man writhing on the ground.

"Run, Elabea," Galadin ordered. "Run for your life."

Free from her attackers, Elabea sprinted away. The rusk, concerned only for Elabea's wellbeing, abandoned his attack and escorted her to safety.

Galadin swung his blade at the remaining thief's exposed belly. As he braced himself for the impact, a brilliant flash of white light shot out of the blade, and he sliced through nothing. The force of his powerful swing caused Galadin to lose his balance, and he spun to the ground.

"What happened?" he stammered while scrambling to regain his footing. "How did I miss?"

"Now waif," the Wurmlin snarled, twirling his wicked dagger. "Tis my turn."

As if spooked by a foreign sound, the Wurmlin stopped his attack and stared at his exposed stomach. A thin, red line appeared, as if drawn by an invisible hand, and slid across his torso. When it reached his other side, the thief's eyes rolled back, and life fled from his face.

Like a felled tree, the upper half of his torso toppled off and rolled to a rest beside the other dead men. The lower half of his body continued standing erect. The sight made Galadin shudder.

He crept toward the eerie half-corpse, half expecting it to fall; or worse, run away.

"How can there be no blood?" he wondered as he examined the body parts. His eyes jumped to his sword. The blade glowed orange, like a length of iron in a blacksmith's furnace. The answer popped into his head.

The sword must be magical, and its heat cauterized the wound.

He drew the enchanted sword that bore his name close.

And yet, it doesn't give off any heat. In fact...

He wet his finger in his mouth and gingerly touched the glowing steel with his fingertip, as if snuffing the flame on a candle.

...Stone cold.

Elabea ran back with the rusk fluttering protectively overhead. Greeted by the macabre scene of death and dismemberment, chills ran through her body, and she suddenly felt sick to her stomach. Turning away so she would not get sick, she asked him, "Did you do *this.*"

"Yes. Well, actually the sword did. Look. It's enchanted."

They watched as the glowing orange blade faded back to its normal silver color.

Elabea's brow furrowed. "It didn't glow like that the other night when you killed that beast."

Galadin nodded. "I know."

"So what did you do or say to make it charmed?"

"Nothing," he shrugged as he sheathed his sword. "I'm as baffled as you are."

Elabea stared at the severed body and then let her eyes wander about the woods. "Il-Lilliad was right. We've entered a very strange world."

Chapter 12

Dawn of the Awakening

Before leaving Hetherlinn, Commander Hinnmith sent a scout to follow the trail of the sevritts while he and his men headed north toward Ebon with the wagon carrying Thull's corpse.

Early on the second day, the scout approached the patrol at full gallop.

Hinnmith ordered his entourage to halt.

"I found them," the scout blurted as he came along side Hinnmith. "They're all dead."

"Excellent," Hinnmith replied, taking note of the scout's wild-eyed expression.

"With all due respect, sir, it's not the children who are dead but the sevritts."

Hinnmith snickered. "Sevritts...dead? You probably mistook dead gors for the..."

"No, sir," the scout interrupted, "I know what I saw."

"Did you just interrupt me?"

"With all due respect, sir, permission to show you something?"

Hinnmith's eyes narrowed. He gave a subtle nod. The scout retrieved something from his saddlebag.

"I found this arrow," he said as he handed it to Hinnmith. "I'm not familiar with the markings. Are you, commander?"

Hinnmith ran a gloved finger over the yellow and orange fletchings, mystified by the crystal shaft. His gaze rested on the nock. "This isn't an arrow. It's a crossbow bolt."

The scout's eyes widened. "Commander, that's impossible. That would mean that whoever shot this is bigger than..."

Hinnmith raised his hand to cut off the scout. He then turned to address his men.

"Listen up. We're riding further down the road to investigate the sevritts' status. There is a new enemy on the prowl." He thrust the bolt overhead for them to examine. "I want two patrols to flank our perimeter - one on the left, the other on the right. Be alert. First blood."

The two patrols fanned out into the woods while Hinnmith, the scout, and several soldiers escorted the wagon down the road.

When they came to a tree that blocked the road, the scout maneuvered to the other side. "Commander, come see for yourself."

Hinnmith rode to inspect and upon seeing the bodies, jerked back on the reins. His combat experience took over; trained eyes surveyed the surrounding woods, looking for any sign of an ambush.

"Did you investigate the surrounding area first?" he asked the scout as he continued his surveillance.

"Yes, sir. The perimeter is secure," the scout replied. "Aside from the children's footprints, there were no other tracks on the road or in the woods."

Hinnmith nodded, somewhat relieved since he had no idea who or what fired the massive bolt.

The sound of two patrols maneuvering through the brush relaxed his mind.

Good, he thought as he watched their shadows glide through pockets of light to his left and right. *They ride at a slow cadence, no urgency; no sounds of combat.*

To those nearby he said, "Our patrols are in position. Nevertheless, be alert."

The warriors drew their swords.

Hinnmith's eyes wandered back to the sevritts' dead bodies.

One was beheaded; clean cut as if by a sword. But there are no swords in the region - other than those held by my men. All have been confiscated by order of the Oracles, so how was this possible? Could the bolt truly be from a giant? How? All nations bow before Ebon. The Cauldron sees all.

He pondered the fate of the second sevritt. The only proof that it had ever lived was its skeletal frame.

This defies logic.

"Commander," the scout interjected as he too tried to piece together what happened, "perhaps the tree fell and killed them, and then some gors consumed this sevritt's remains."

Hinnmith fidgeted in his saddle. Although he felt safe from an ambush, there was something vaguely familiar about the battleground that set his teeth on edge.

"No," he answered, "that couldn't be. See how their bodies are out in the open and not trapped beneath the branches? Besides, gors can't devour a carcass like this...every bit of flesh has been eaten off."

His eyes wandered from the white bones and found the tree. Unable to take his eyes off it, his thoughts spiraled out of control as if he were under a spell. The uneasy feeling settled over him again. A chill arced down his back. For a moment, he thought he was losing his battle senses, until he remembered a tale from thirty winters ago.

On his first assignment as a warrior, he was stationed at one of Ebon's outposts. It was late at night, and he had just returned from a long reconnaissance mission. Numb with cold, he entered a tavern for fire and a warm meal. Aside from the owner, cleaning mugs behind the counter, the small room was empty except for two old veterans sitting in the corner, their tales swirling amidst their pipe smoke. Hinnmith warmed himself by the fire and tried not to listen, but their voices carried, and their tales stirred his imagination.

They spoke of a time in their youth when Claire awakened creatures greater than the sum of their blades. The karshe—a silver-plated dragon, laired in the Sea of Illsbruth—that could capsize a boat with a swish of its tale. The la-zeer, whose home was the frigid waters of the Gilden Sea, which struck without warning with teeth sharper than Tristan steel.

When their stories shifted to land creatures, their voices faded to half-whispers, their memories stemming from first hand horrors. Hinnmith trained his ears their way, not wanting to miss one nuance of their tales.

"Commander," the scout blurted, interrupting Hinnmith's flashback. "Are you alright?"

Hinnmith ignored him; the story was coming back in quick succession. *Hollow trees. Tiny dragons. Mystical blue eyes.*

"Commander?" the scout interrupted again, as the wagon driver dismounted and climbed over the tree trunk to survey the carnage.

Hinnmith recalled more of the story from that frosty night long ago.

Flying dragons. No larger than bats. Swarming as one with eyes that glow blue like a fire's flame. Captivating gaze, luring prey close. Awakened by the Only from lairs deep within…

"Dead trees," Hinnmith finished aloud.

"Dead trees, sir?"

The driver gazed into the black abyss where the tree once stood.

"This can't be happening," Hinnmith said to no one in particular. "That story came from a time long ago when the King of Claire was alive, when he was mighty and strong. He's been dead now for many winters. The woods and seas have been silent of anything mysterious."

"Commander, what are you talking about?"

Hinnmith snapped out of his daze and spotted the driver hunched over the hole.

"Move away from there, soldier," Hinnmith barked.

The scent of charred wood and damp soil welcomed the driver. Deep in the darkness, countless blue lights blinked and beckoned him to draw closer.

"That was an order," Hinnmith shouted, but the driver was already entranced. He reached for the sapphire lights that twinkled like thousands of stars.

The ground rumbled just as Hinnmith's memory cleared, and the name the two old veterans spoke rested on his tongue.

"Fea dracas," he announced. His back stiffened as he cried out, "Retreat. Fall back. *Fea dracas.*"

"Retreat?" the scout asked, perplexed why his battle-tested leader had ordered a command forbidden by the Cauldron. "And sir, what are fea dracas?"

He was answered by an explosion out of the hole. Fea dracas swarmed about the driver, then engulfed him. Squeals from the tiny dragons united with the man's screams.

"Fall back," Hinnmith barked. "Now."

Stunned by the attacking horde, the men sat frozen. Hinnmith slapped the scout across the face to bring him back to his senses. "Now, soldier."

Hinnmith spurred his steed to a gallop, and as his warriors came to their senses they followed suite.

The scout rode beside Hinnmith, but dared a glance back. The driver was motionless beneath the swarm.

"What about the bodies of Commander Thull and the driver?" the scout yelled over the pounding of their horses' hooves.

"Leave them," Hinnmith replied, digging his spurs deeper into his animal's flanks.

"Sir," the scout shouted as the patrols joined them in their mad dash, "every Ebonite warrior is to be burned with full military honors."

"Soldier, there'll be nothing left of them to burn."

Hinnmith never looked back.

The scout, angered by such cowardice from his commander, shouted: "With all due respect sir, we should fight these creatures. The Oracles of the Cauldron command it. Warriors of Ebon do not retreat."

Hinnmith glared at his zealous scout. "You know *nothing* of such stories, do you? If you did, you would race ahead of me."

Hinnmith's eyes swept the woods ahead and behind them, convinced they were surrounded by thousands of unknown and unseen enemies. The scout and remaining warriors shook their heads in disgust.

A bolt of lightning struck up ahead and a tall tree toppled across their path.

"Hurry," Hinnmith ordered, spurring his horse to even greater speed. "That tree just unearthed another lair of fea dracas."

Hinnmith and his men forced their steeds to leap over the trunk.

Thunder struck.

"Did you hear that?" the scout asked as they galloped off. "Lightning and thunder and not a cloud in the sky."

Before Hinnmith could answer, a horse whinnied followed by a man's terrified scream. The scout glanced over his shoulder. A fellow warrior and his warhorse were blanketed with fea dracas. The horse bucked crazily while the rider thrashed wildly in his saddle, but fea dracas never let go once they latch onto warm flesh.

Witnessing another attack by the fea dracas, the surviving warriors let their skepticism about Hinnmith's courage fly. Some even darted past their commander.

"Next time," Hinnmith shouted after them, "I won't wait."

Manno Vox hovered high above the forest and watched Hinnmith's entourage retreat. He noched one of his crystal bolts, raised it and aimed at another tree concealing a horde of fea dracas.

"Let them go," the whisper from Claire commanded. *"Escort Hinnmith and his men safely to Ebon. I wish them to tell Brairtok and the Cauldron that I have awakened the world around them with a whisper. The time has come."*

Manno Vox nodded at the order and relaxed his trigger finger. He glided down to the treetops, just above and ahead of the fleeing Ebonites. When the fear-crazed warriors caught a glimpse of him, their eyes popped even wider with fright, and their mouths flew open in shock. Manno Vox savored Hinnmith's reaction most of all, for the Commander's countenance expressed an emotion rare amongst brave Ebonites.

Awe.

Chapter 13

The MerriNoons

As dusk approached, Galadin looked for a safe place on the mountain for them to sleep. Up ahead he spied a rock overhang and led them toward it.

Peering into its depths, he said, "Look, Elabea, a tiny cave. Rest here. I'll return shortly."

"Where are you going?" she asked, fearing his zeal for adventure would keep him out all night.

"We need some supplies. I won't be gone long. You'll be safe."

"And what of you?" She looked past him out into the darkening woods.

Galadin patted his sword, smiled and darted off.

Elabea sat on the cave's dirt floor. The valley's breeze rushed in and she pulled her shawl close while the cave's dampness made her sneeze.

Sleep tugged at her relentlessly. Her eyelids became heavy. A twig snapped and her eyes flew open.

The cave was pitch black, as were the woods beyond.

How did it get so dark, she wondered. *Am I dreaming? If I'm dreaming, then I'm asleep, but I don't remember closing my...*

Crack.

The sound was closer and made her jump. Her imagination went to work, creating Wurmlins, Ebonites, or worse - heinous creatures from the Awakening.

She risked a whispered, "Galadin?"

Silence.

She felt in the darkness for Il-Lilliad's book. Her fingertips encountered soft leather. Relieved, at least for the moment, she clutched the book to her chest. Sensing her alarm, the rusk landed on her shoulder, but even his presence could not appease her growing fears.

Another twig snapped. Her heart raced. She pressed back against the cave's wall. A silhouette appeared in the entrance. Her mouth went dry. The figure approached. She tried to scream but could not find her voice.

The shadow whispered, *"Are you asleep?"*

Recognizing his voice, she huffed and thought about throwing the book at him. "Galadin, don't *ever* do that to me again."

"Do what?" he asked as he dropped an arm full of firewood to the cave's floor.

"Frighten me. I thought you were a Wurmlin or an Ebonite."

The darkness concealed his face, but she was positive he was smirking.

"And don't smile like that," she fired.

Galadin stammered, "How do you know I'm..."

"Because I've known you all my life. You always get that sassy smile whenever you tease me."

"I didn't mean to alarm you," he chuckled. "Please, relax and get some sleep. We've had a difficult day." He pulled berries and roots from his pockets and set them beside the firewood. "Besides, who knows what tomorrow holds?"

"How long were you gone?"

"I'm not sure. Why?"

"It seemed very short and yet, it became dark so suddenly. I must have fallen asleep."

Galadin sat down, his outline filling the overhang's entrance. She could see him fiddling in the dark with his fresh supplies.

"Galadin," she ventured. "I was very frightened."

"Well, you're safe now," he replied while sorting the wood. "To keep you from worrying, I'll sleep by the entrance." He reclined upon the cave's dirt floor, withdrew his sword and with its hilt within grasp, relaxed and closed his weary eyes.

Elabea sighed, frustrated that he did not seem to comprehend all that she was trying to express. She thought about leaving the matter alone, but instead, braved a deeper explanation.

"What I mean...well, what I feared most...I mean I was afraid that you wouldn't return; that you had run back home."

Dripping water echoed from deep within the cave.

"Did you hear me?" she asked him.

A soft snore answered.

She sighed and pulled her shawl closer. Resting her head upon the book, she began dreaming of summer days sitting in her oak.

Elabea woke to a familiar smell. She sat up and rubbed the sleep from her eyes.

"A fire?" she mumbled.

"I thought you were going to sleep all day," Galadin said, squatting by the tiny fire beneath the overhang. He fed another twig into the hungry flames.

Watching the smoke rise lazily into the air, another fear gripped her. "Won't the fire give away our location?"

"No," he answered, pointing to the overhang. "The cave is pulling all the smoke inside. It must go deep within the mountain. Besides, I'm using balmwood which doesn't create as much smoke as oak or hickory."

He stirred the contents of an odd-looking container that rested on the coals.

"What are you doing," she asked.

Satisfied that it was finished cooking, he lifted the container from the fire, careful not to spill its contents or burn his flesh.

"Brewing my lady some mint tea."

The tea's fragrance floated upon the breeze, its aroma transporting her to happier days. Galadin handed it to her as if he were handing her a newborn child.

"Careful. It's hot, and the container is fragile."

"You made this?"

Elabea cradled the delicate, make-shift teapot, turned it about, admiring its craftsmanship.

"Yes, from balmwood bark. As long as the liquid within is higher than the flames, it won't burn."

She took a sip.

Galadin watched, hoping his gift would be well received.

The hot tea soothed Elabea's throat that was raw from the night's cold air, and the mint calmed her troubled spirit. Closing her eyes, she savored the moment.

Galadin smiled. "I'm glad you like it. Here, eat these."

He handed her a large ivy leaf that was wrapped around some small objects. Placing her teapot on the dirt floor, she unfolded the leaf and discovered wildeberries, nuts and roots. She began to devour them, but then stopped.

"Forgive me, Galadin. I was rude." She raised the delicacies up to him. "Would you care for some?"

"I've already eaten," he said while stomping out the fire with his boot. "We'd best be on our way."

She stepped to the mouth of the cave, took another sip of mint tea, and surveyed the woods below. Despite how she had always yearned to leave Hetherlinn, she found herself missing the communal fire, the numbered cottages, and the mundane routine of her village life.

Maybe Mother was right. The Oracles do offer peace. All we've found so far is trouble.

At the center of her longings was a desire she could not make sense of.

Despite her horrid home life, she missed her parents.

"Do you think my father is alive," she asked.

"Yes," Galadin replied as he scattered the coals so there would be no trace of their fire. "He's strong and the attack was not a death blow."

"Do you think our parents miss us?"

Galadin recognized a familiar tenderness in her voice. It often came when they sat atop the oak together and she reflected on her life in Hetherlinn. He always wanted to show his concern, but as hard as he tried, he could never find the right words to speak. Sometimes, he felt a strong urge to hug her or take her by the hand. Instead, he sat beside her, like a bump on the tree.

This morning was no different.

At a loss of what to say or do, he did what came naturally to him: he tried to make her laugh. He hobbled about, using his stir stick as a cane.

"The children," he hissed, imitating Mithe's voice. "Where are the waifs of Hetherlinn? I miss hurling my ignorance at them. Where, oh, where are they? My life is empty without them."

Elabea giggled, then downed the remainder of her tea.

"It's time for us to go," Galadin said as he tossed the stick deep into the cave.

Retrieving her pack, Elabea stowed the teapot within, keeping it for sentimental reasons rather than for practical ones.

The rusk landed on her shoulder. She looked into his face and felt her homesick feelings fade. "I'm glad you're with me, rusk."

He chattered as if he understood and was trying to console her.

"I only wish I could understand you," she said as she tossed the pack over her shoulder and raced after Galadin.

In order to stay ahead of their enemy, Galadin kept their pace fast. The day was uneventful until they spooked a flock of quail nesting on the ground. The birds exploded into the air with a boom. Elabea squealed and even Galadin, the experienced woodsman, jumped. By late afternoon, their growling stomachs reminded them they had skipped lunch.

"I'm hungry," Elabea said as they climbed a steep grade.

"Grab some wildeberries," he advised, continuing his brisk pace. "They grow everywhere."

"I'm tired of berries and roots," she complained. "I want meat cooked over a fire with potatoes. When will we eat *those* again?"

Galadin was about to fire off a sarcastic reply when he caught the scent of tantalizing aromas.

"Do you smell that," he asked as he stopped and sniffed the air.

"Yes. Food, and it smells wonderful."

"We must be in magical woods. You asked for meat and potatoes and now I smell them cooking."

"No, it's not meat and potatoes," she countered. "That's yeast bread I smell."

Galadin, whose appetite was stronger than his apprehensions, broke into a run in pursuit of the meal. Elabea, and the rusk who flew overhead, came alongside him, matching his pace. He flashed her a smirk and then sprinted. She caught up and with a burst of speed, whizzed past. As he watched her long hair wave good-bye through the trees, a troubling thought came to mind.

"Elabea, stop," he cried between gasps. "This could be a trap."

"Nice try," she fired over her shoulder. "I won't fall for *that* old trick."

She disappeared over the ridge.

Galadin quickened his pace, his hand ready to draw his blade. He reached the summit, then raced down the other side, fearing the worst for her safety. Nearing the bottom of the hill, he was relieved to find her peering around a large pine with the rusk perched on her shoulder.

"A clearing," she whispered as he came alongside her. "And look what sits on its edge."

A small cottage sat in the shade of large cedars. Made of sun-dried clay and painted white, it had a wooden door with windows on either side. The roof was covered with variegated moss that was rich and wild, but the chimney, constructed from river stones, was void of smoke.

"It looks deserted," Galadin whispered.

"Yes, but someone, somewhere, is cooking yeast breads."

He sniffed the air. "Yes, but I also smell fire, and meats being cooked. Don't you?"

She nodded. "But why isn't there smoke coming from the chimney?"

The door opened and a bald, plump man stepped outside. He wore a white vest that hung loosely over his belly and a pair of white baggy trousers. A wooden ladle was clutched in his hand and dripped what appeared to be broth.

"He looks harmless," Elabea whispered.

"You're too trusting. He could be an Ebonite assassin."

The idea that this fellow could possibly be dangerous made Elabea giggle.

"Your tongue talk is funny," the rotund man said as he stared straight at their hiding place. "Now please tell me why you hide behind trees and whisper?"

Their mouths fell open.

"How could he hear us? We're too far away," Galadin whispered even softer.

"Simple," came the stranger's reply. "Although small, our ears are very big."

Elabea studied her rusk and was relieved that his fur was not standing up on end.

"Stay here," Galadin advised as he rested his palm on his sword's pommel. "I'll investigate."

He stepped into the clearing. "My name's Galadin," he informed the stranger. "We're from Allsbruth."

"I am Digri," the man answered, unruffled by neither Galadin's approach nor his sword. "Welcome to MerriNoon."

As Galadin neared the cottage, he scrutinized the plump man and realized a feature that had previously gone unnoticed. He was no taller than a child of five summers.

Galadin stopped far enough away from the cottage to retreat, if necessary, or to have time to draw his sword and attack. "We couldn't help but smell the delicious aromas," he informed the bald MerriNoon. "Are you the one cooking?"

Digri beamed. "Yes. MerriNoons are master cooks; artisans of culinary delights."

The wonderful scents caused Galadin's mouth to water and set his stomach to rumbling. He was dying for a taste. Then a thought crossed his mind.

"You don't say," Galadin replied with a quick glance back at Elabea. She spotted his mischievous grin and as her eyes widened, shook her head to try and stop whatever he was planning.

Galadin brushed her warning aside, and addressed Digri. "Some say Allsbruthians are the best cooks."

Digri's smile fell. He scowled. "Allsbruth?" he snapped, marching briskly toward Galadin.

Galadin, who hadn't expected the MerriNoon to respond in such an aggressive manner, stumbled backward as he looked around for any signs of an ambush. The woods were empty.

"Allsbruthians know *nothing* of cooking," Digri fired, swinging his ladle wildly as he stormed closer. "Too much fire. Too little spice."

Elabea darted to Galadin's side. "What are you doing," she scolded. "You're making him angry."

Galadin held up his hands in an attempt to appease the little man. The MerriNoon stopped and glowered at them.

"Since I've only dined upon Allsbruthian food," Galadin said, making sure to keep his tone pleasant so as not to further agitate the tiny chef. "I'm unable to decide if what you're saying is true."

Digri stroked his chin, pondering the dilemma. Seizing upon an idea, his eyes ignited with excitement.

"A solution I have," Digri announced. "We will cook for you so you can decide."

"Really?" Galadin replied feigning surprise and flashing Elabea a smirk. She rolled her eyes. Galadin continued to barter with Digri. "We would be honored. Once we eat your food, we'll decide if MerriNoons are the best chefs."

"Minimal cost, great value. You do have money?"

Elabea and Galadin exchanged glances. In their haste to flee Hetherlinn, neither had had time to bring even the smallest of coins.

Galadin shook his head.

Digri's smile faded to a frown. "MerriNoon law forbids us to cook for no compensation. I am troubled that our disagreement will not be overcome."

Elabea broke the awkward silence. "What if we work for food? We could clean the dishes after our meal."

Digri's face beamed once more. "Work for food. Yes, *yes*. Very acceptable conditions. Please, come inside."

Digri spun around and reentered his cottage, but Elabea and Galadin stopped at the door.

"We're too big," she exclaimed, staring at the door that was half their size.

"Of course you are," Digri said from within. "To the back go. I shall meet you there."

Making their way past a thick hedgerow and ducking beneath limbs, they emerged into Digri's backyard. It was a large garden full of mature trees, green grass and beds of freshly turned soil where flowers of every shape and color grew.

Scattered about the yard were cooking fires. One MerriNoon was holding a white crystal close to a stack of unlit wood. The crystal glowed bright, and without even a single spark, the wood caught fire.

"Wow," Galadin marveled. "That sure is easier than striking steel and flint."

Large black pots of stews were being stirred while spits holding meats from a half-dozen different animals were slowly turned. The air was filled with the fragrance of hickory-smoked meats, yeast breads, rich spices and fresh herbs. The MerriNoons, who watched them with great curiosity, were identical in every way except for their height.

"Welcome to MerriNoon," Digri exclaimed as he arced his arms overhead. Lowering them again, he added, "Allsbruth is very far away. You must be famished. Come."

He led them to a long table that was comparable in size to those used in Allsbruth. Digri climbed up into the oversized chair at the table's head while Galadin and Elabea sat across from each other on long wooden benches.

"Why aren't your table and chairs small?" Galadin asked.

"Simple. We have many guests to MerriNoon. All are bigger than us. How would they eat at a MerriNoon-sized table?"

Digri clapped his palms. The food was served. Plates of yeast breads, bowls of stews and chowders, platters of deer and boar were promptly brought to their table.

Raising his hands in the air, Digri proclaimed, "MerriNoons are a people of peace and welcome all to our table that savor fine food. No one has ever been turned away.

"During the Dark War, we chose neutrality and thus continued to serve our delicacies. Storytellers, Ebonites, mercenaries, Tristanites and even royalty enjoyed a respite here. Today, my fellow MerriNoons, is no exception, for sitting before you are a husband and wife..."

Elabea gasped.

"We're *not* married," Galadin stammered.

Digri's brow furrowed, then glowed again. "Correction. Sitting before you are a brother and sister from..."

"No," Elabea interrupted. "We are simply friends traveling together."

Digri's face twisted about as he pondered the news. He leaned in and spoke to them with a softer voice.

"But the Oracles forbid traveling so far from..."

He stopped himself, leaned back and smiled. "Forgive me. This is MerriNoon. What you have done in violation of the Oracles is of no consequence here."

Projecting his voice once more to the throng, he continued. "As I was saying, sitting before you are two friends who have journeyed all the way from Allsbruth. Let us prepare to dine."

Digri grabbed a piece of roasted fowl. Galadin and Elabea filled their plates and began feasting upon the delicacies. When one platter was empty, a MerriNoon swiftly served another. Elabea finished eating first and waited, with some impatience, for Galadin to finish. He consumed several more rolls and handfuls of meat before pushing away his plate.

"Digri," he stated as he leaned back and wiped his mouth on the sleeve of his tunic. "I was wrong. MerriNoons *are* the greatest cooks anywhere."

Digri nodded, grateful that his confidence was once again restored.

"Now it is time for us to repay you," Elabea added.

Leading them to a small grove of pine trees, Digri pulled back some branches. Galadin and Elabea stared at each other in disbelief.

"MerriNoons may be great chefs," Elabea said, staring at the mounds of dirty dishes and pots, "but they must hate to wash dishes."

"Clean these," Digri said.

"All of them?" Galadin replied.

Digri looked at the large array of dishes. "Is it too little?" he asked.

"No," Galadin blurted. "It's too *much*. We will be cleaning for..."

Elabea elbowed him in the ribs.

"What Galadin is trying to say," she explained, "is that we presumed we would wash what was used for preparing our meal."

Digri brought his palm to his round chin. His index finger tapped a cadence on his cheek as he considered Elabea's request.

"This is how it is done in Allsbruth?" he asked.

"Yes," Elabea replied.

"Then it is good. You do."

The MerriNoons watched curiously as the two Allsbruthians began cleaning the pots, pans and platters from their meal. They whispered about how anyone could be so uncivilized as to clean such filth.

"Tell me Digri, how far away is Claire," Elabea questioned while scraping off a platter.

"Why are you going to Claire?"

"Because we have..."

Galadin nudged her in the side. Realizing she may have revealed too much, Elabea stopped talking.

"I don't need to know," Digri replied, "I am simply curious. You see, there is nothing in Claire."

"How do you know," Elabea asked. "Have you been there?"

"No. MerriNoons never travel far, but many from afar come to MerriNoon. All tell the same tale. There is nothing in Claire. Just sand."

Elabea's brow twisted with worry.

"Perhaps," Galadin countered, "but we desire to see for ourselves."

"Then you must hurry. Soon they will come. They love MerriNoon food and eat much. See?" he pointed to the mounds of dirty dishes behind the pines.

Galadin stopped scrapping. "Who comes," he asked as he wrapped his fingers around his sword's hilt.

"Ebonites," Digri answered in a jovial manner.

Elabea suddenly felt sick to her stomach as fear percolated through her veins. Galadin smiled at her but it was not his teasing smile. It was the grin he gave to help console her.

"We need to travel to Claire without being seen by the Ebonites," Galadin said. "What route should we take?"

Digri gave him a quizzical look. "Don't you have a map?"

"No," Galadin answered.

Digri turned and uttered something in his own tongue to one of his children. Running into the cottage, the child returned with a large folded parchment.

"Here," Digri said as he handed it to Galadin. "Take this. It is good."

Galadin unfolded the map. It was very old and was weathered on the folded edges. "Yes, it's *very* good. What amazing detail. Did you make this?"

Digri laughed. "No. MerriNoons cook. We cannot make maps. We traded food for it."

"Who made the trade?" Elabea asked.

"A tall man with no hair...like me." He rubbed his baldhead in a circular manner. "Funny purple mark here," he pointed to his forehead.

"Il-Lilliad," they said in unison.

"How long ago was this," Galadin asked.

"Long time. Three children ago."

Galadin studied the map for another moment before folding it up and putting it in his pack. "We thank you for the food, but we must be leaving."

Digri studied the setting sun to determine the time of day. "Yes, I agree. Their time is close. They prefer dining at dusk."

With that, the duo said good-bye and raced for higher ground.

Chapter 14

Hetherlinn's Council

The men sat around the table in cottage Number 17. They stared at each other as Areall served mugs of hot tea laced with honey. Il-Lilliad cradled his clay mug in both hands, enjoying the warmth as if it were a tiny kiln.

"Ahh," Il-Lilliad exclaimed while inhaling the tea's fruity aroma. "Allsbruthian tea. I believe the last time I partook of such a delicacy was before the Dark War. Thankfully, the Oracles haven't destroyed this too."

He gave Areall a grateful smile. She politely returned it, then stepped outside to leave them to the business at hand.

Linwith, whose mind was churning with questions, looked into Il-Lilliad's face.

"There's much I don't understand."

"In time you will," the storyteller said.

"Yes, but earlier, before you began your story by the fire," Linwith continued, "you mentioned an odd thing: *Languish rewards when worms leave their lair.* Worms? Lairs?"

"Why the Worms of Bal-Malin, of course," Il-Lilliad answered, as if it were the most obvious thing in the world.

The other men snickered.

Linwith continued. "You speak of these *worms* as if they are great creatures."

"Naturally, because they *are.*"

More laughter was followed by more sips of tea. A blanket of silence settled over the group, as Quinn addressed the issue he knew they all were pondering.

"So you were at Min Brock," Quinn ventured, still fearing revenge from the storyteller. "And you survived the March of Reeds. So much has passed since that day. Tell us your story."

Il-Lilliad set his mug down and nodded.

"As you know, after the defeat at Min Brock, I was led by the Ebonites back to Ebon. I fell wounded during the March of Reeds and lay hidden beneath my dying brothers and sisters. When I awoke, I fled back to Allsbruth and have lived as a hermit in a cave not too far from here. For many summers I have not been able to tell a story - or listen to one. I thought being unable to do what I was born to do was a fate worse than death, but over time, I began to understand. There was a reason I was spared. There was a purpose for the fires that burned deep within my heart. The cycle of summers passed. With each passing day, hope grew within me. I knew my task was to rest and to wait. Not an easy duty for a storyteller."

A faint smile pulled at his lips. He continued.

"Then I heard him. The thundering of his hooves across the night sky awoke me, just as it must have awakened Elabea. I ran out of my cave and looked to the starry sky. That is when I saw him through the trees. Manno Vox flying with great haste toward Hetherlinn. It was incredible to behold. I didn't presume to know all that this meant, but I was certain of one thing: my time in a cave was nearing an end.

"The following morning, I heard the whisper for Elabea. How overjoyed I was to hear the King of Claire's voice once more. Nevertheless, if I could hear the whisper, so could the Cauldron. I raced to the meadow to protect her."

"And what of us? What are we to do?" Gundin asked.

"Why, we prepare for war, of course," Il-Lilliad said with a pat on Gundin's back.

The men chuckled.

"With what?" Quinn argued. "We have already told you; we do not have a single sword. The army of Allsbruth is but a remnant of men that are too old, or boys who are too young. Besides...no one would follow us. No one would trust us. Our past is too much to overcome. The fact that you're here is a reminder of our shame at Min Brock."

Il-Lilliad nodded.

"The last thing I want to do is to dredge up such humiliation. But I can see that humiliation is entrenched in you both - much more than it is in Linwith. You Quinn, and you Gundin, must prepare yourselves before you can prepare anyone else. Once you are stronger, healthier, you can start training again. The other men will soon follow."

Gundin stood up to argue. "Exercise is not the same as training with a good sword or battle axe. Besides," he said as he patted his large chest and stomach, "this is all muscle. I'm fit and ready for battle now."

Linwith tugged on his sleeve and Gundin plopped back down into his seat.

"Every story has a beginning, and since ours must start somewhere, that somewhere is here," Il-Lilliad replied. "For now, we shall use wooden swords and..."

The men's laughter cut him off.

"You mean to say," Quinn asked between chuckles, "you expect us to train with sticks - like little boys?"

"Yes," Il-Lilliad answered. "But not as boys. As men in training."

Gundin shook his head as he laughed. "That is the most ridiculous idea I've ever heard."

Il-Lilliad continued, "It will take time to prepare for battle, perhaps even the cycle of many summers. You have an arduous task in simply preparing yourselves for war. Once that is complete, you will need time to prepare the men. Of course, all this must be done in secret. The Ebonites and the Cauldron must suspect nothing."

"So we joust with sticks," Quinn replied, his chuckles subsiding. "Very well. Let's say we agree to this. There's one detail you're forgetting. At best we can summon thirty boys and men here in Hetherlinn to fight. That's not much of an army."

"True. That is why we need to trust the Only."

Quinn shoved away from the table. "The Only?" he growled. "We've not seen or heard from him since the Dark War. You may have forgotten our stories, storyteller, but the King of Claire surely has not. We are the survivors of Min Brock. He will never let us forget."

"True. He has not forgotten Min Brock. I suspect he will deal with it in a manner neither of us expects. After all, if revenge is what he seeks, why did he send the tulip? Why the awakening?"

Quinn paced about. "A flower? A *flower*," he retorted, rubbing his hands together as if to keep warm. "A red tulip can't stop a March of Reeds. We need soldiers, weapons, alliances with other cities, with other nations..."

"Our faith is not as strong as yours, storyteller," Linwith interjected, hoping to quell his brother's emotions. Quinn snorted at his brother, then plopped back down at the table. "The odds against us are too great."

Il-Lilliad looked deeply into their troubled faces. He gave a solemn nod.

"I too am afraid," he confessed.

"But you're a storyteller," Quinn said. "I didn't think fear was an emotion you experienced?"

"Well, you're wrong," Il-Lilliad relied. "Only a fool claims to have no fear. But there is one thing that frightens me more than war. Dare to guess what it is?"

The men sat silent.

Il-Lilliad answered for them. "Hiding in my cave for another day."

Rising to his feet, he let his gaze wander up into the rafters as his thoughts drifted back in time to his early days as a storyteller.

"I was created to tell stories, just as you were fashioned to lead and fight."

Lowering his face to theirs, his eyes swelled with light as he voiced his rising emotions. "Gentlemen, the King of Claire *is* alive. He has whispered to us again. We were brought together for a reason, and we must draw together - or we shall perish."

He began to pace, accenting key words with an arm thrust upward. "The Cauldron fears only one thing: *stories* from the Only. It knows when people *taste* such tales, the Dark Flame can no longer *rule* their hearts."

Il-Lilliad stopped and took in their expressions. Although their faces still reflected doubt, his radiated assurance.

"I am confident," he said, his voice trumpeting his optimism, "that stories, not Tristan swords, will turn the tide in this war of whispers."

He slammed his fist down on the table to accent his declaration and the men jumped. The weight of his words stirred their darkened spirits, like a stick rousing dormant coals from a once great fire. With what little hope they possessed, they nodded in agreement.

Il-Lilliad looked into Quinn's eyes. "You speak with great honesty," Il-Lilliad said. "We most definitely will need help. That is why I must depart and journey to the Onderling."

"The Onderling?" Gundin roared. "That's suicide. Many have entered the underground world, but none have emerged."

"So the stories go," Il-Lilliad replied as he raised his mug for another sip.

Gundin's face reddened and his arms flayed about. "The Onderling is filled with nations of ruthless hordes. Cold-blooded. Ignorant as mules."

Il-Lilliad cocked an eyebrow. "If no one has survived the Onderling," he asked, setting his mug back down, "where do such stories come from?"

Gundin's face was now as red as the tulip growing in Hetherlinn. Unable to twist his way out of Il-Lilliad's logic, he grunted and crossed his arms over his thick chest.

"I may not know about *that*, but I do know the stories are true."

Il-Lilliad chuckled at Gundin's simple logic.

"What am *I* to do?" Linwith asked.

"You must journey to Tristan."

"Why?" Linwith objected. "Allsbruthians and Tristanites tend to quarrel a lot."

"Yes, but they possess something we desperately need. We in turn have something they desperately desire."

"What's that?"

"Tristan is rich in iron ore, and, despite their primitive demeanor, they are skilled blacksmiths. Some of the finest weapons in all the nations come from Tristan."

"Such weapons require golden gilns, of which we have very little," Linwith argued.

"True, but you possess something better than golden gilns...at least in the eyes of the Tristanites."

The men stared at Il-Lilliad, dumbfounded.

"Vegetables," Il-Lilliad said.

"Vegetables?" The men roared in disbelief.

"Tristanites love vegetables, but they are miners and smiths, not farmers. Since you had a good fall harvest, you can barter vegetables for a good cache of weapons."

The men filled the room with laughter.

"So, what you are telling us," Gundin snickered, "is that Linwith shall trade carrots for swords?"

"Precisely," Il-Lilliad replied.

The men continued to laugh in disbelief, but they soon realized Il-Lilliad was not sharing in their mirth.

"Wait. You're serious," Quinn said.

"Quite."

"Cabbages for axes?" Linwith retorted.

"Yes," Il-Lilliad answered with a firm nod. "It truly is a wonderful idea, if I do say so myself. Think about it."

He spun on his heel and started to pace again. "Should Linwith leave with a pocket full of golden gilns, any Ebonite warrior with half a brain would conclude he was on his way to purchase contraband forbidden by the Oracles. On the other hand, a wagon full of vegetables..."

"Would look like any other trade wagon leaving Hetherlinn," Gundin finished, the prospect of holding a sword once more making him come alive. "And since the Oracles allow trade wagons to travel beyond the marker during harvest season..." His smile widened. "Il-Lilliad, this just might work."

"A carrot for a sword?" Quinn asked, his shoulders still shaking from laughter. "If that happens, I'll truly believe the Only is alive."

Linwith, whose mind was busy analyzing countless scenarios to his trip, was fuming at the absurdity of his mission.

"This is all well and good," he snapped, "but how am I to get the weapons *back* to Allsbruth? The Oracles forbid weapons. I'll be spotted the moment I leave Tristan."

The room fell silent.

Quinn offered a solution. "We'll smuggle them inland."

Linwith had already pondered this and shook his head. "That'll take too long."

"There is another possibility," Il-Lilliad offered.

"What's that?" Linwith asked as he plopped down in a chair, overcome with the weight of his mission.

"Allow the King of Claire to reveal a way in his own time."

Linwith let his head fall and began mumbling something indiscernible.

As if that settled the matter, Il-Lilliad looked straight into Quinn's eyes. "There is, however, one last order of business that must be addressed. You must stop consuming drink, or you will ruin us all."

Quinn closed his eyes. His shoulders dropped. Wildeberry wine was the only delight he had left in his life.

"The King of Claire takes my daughter, and now he wants my drink?" he moaned.

"Listen to yourself," Il-Lilliad chastised. "Your love of wine is what chased her beyond your reach to begin with."

"If you say so," Quinn answered, his voice dull and filled with self-pity. "That was not my doing. It was the Dark War and..."

"Nonsense," Il-Lilliad pressed. "It was you, Quinn. The drink is deceiving you even as we speak. Fight it. Awaken."

Linwith rose and squeezed Quinn's shoulder. "He's right. The wine has been poisoning you, my brother."

"I know. I know," Quinn gasped, as the pain of his struggle and the loss of Elabea overwhelmed him. "But it's not as simple as you think. The shame of what I did at Min Brock is too great. Wildeberry wine is the only thing that helps me...forget."

Il-Lilliad grabbed his face and looked deeply into his eyes. "You must go to the tulip every morning," Il-Lilliad ordered. "Its scent will begin clearing your mind and awakening you. *That* will be the battle that will determine the war. Succeed in this and nothing can stop you."

Quinn closed his eyes. He thought of Min Brock. He thought of the tears shed by so many because of his actions. But it was the image of Elabea running for her life that shook him to his core. Despite his doubts and fears, he knew he could not let her down. Not again.

Quinn nodded in agreement.

"And Gundin," Il-Lilliad said as he released his hold on Quinn's face. "We need you to fight *this* fight, not battle in a war that has already been lost."

Gundin drew in a deep breath, blew it out and nodded his ascent.

"You must join Quinn at the tulip. This will be a hard battle for you, for your mind is overgrown with memories and guilt, like weeds in a garden. You must kill them, Gundin. You must kill them all.”

Il-Lilliad studied the men's forlorn faces.

And what of my faith, he wondered. *Am I to believe the King of Claire will use a drunk, a madman and a faint-hearted brother to wage war against Ebon and the Cauldron?*

He paused in hope of hearing a whisper from Claire, offering support or better yet, foretelling victories to come. He knew better than to expect such revelation. After all, he was a storyteller. It was his responsibility to tell such tales.

I know this isn't the season for such a tale. Just as in farming or hunting, timing must be perfect. It will mean the difference between success and failure.

“So be it,” he declared with a loud clap. “Linwith will prepare for his journey and must leave in the next day or two. I shall leave tomorrow at daybreak for The Onderling.”

“A wagon full of produce…” Gundin murmured as he pictured himself once more with a sword in his hand.

“For a wagon full of weapons,” Quinn finished. “Yes. This just might work.”

Chapter 15

The Dreamhunter

After racing up the steep hill outside MerriNoon, Galadin paused to get his bearings.

"The woods are casting long shadows," he observed, placing a hand on his hip as he caught his breath. "The sun will be setting soon."

Together, Galadin and Elabea gazed down at the clearing marking Digri's cottage. It was barely visible due to their elevation and the waning light.

A low, deep thud echoed from below.

"Thunder," Elabea asked, knowing full well there was not a cloud in the sky.

Galadin shook his head.

"Ebonite drums. Hurry. We must reach the ridge before they get to MerriNoon."

They once again charged up the incline. The drum cadence became clearer, its odd meter sending chills through Elabea. She pictured them marching in thick columns, their warhorses snorting and prancing about, longing to crush her bones with their hooves.

"They must be nearing the clearing," Galadin shouted over his shoulder as he grabbed a sapling to propel himself higher.

Their muscles burned and their lungs longed for a quick break to be replenished, but stopping meant death. With what little strength remained, they sprinted over the ridge and dove beneath a large pine. Wiping the streams of sweat off their faces, they were relieved to hear that the cadence was no more than a distant echo.

Galadin allowed them only a few moments of respite to catch their breaths. He rose to his feet and offered Elabea his hand. "Come on," he commanded. "We must get as far away as possible."

She was exhausted, but knew this was not the time to argue. Grabbing his hand, she pulled herself up and they were off again.

Galadin led the way along the ridgeline with long, brisk strides. His right hand rested upon his sword's pommel while his eyes scanned left and right for any sign of danger.

Elabea retrieved her book from her pack. She studied its pages as she walked. Even in the dim light, the pages aroused her curiosity and scattered her fears.

Almost like Il-Lilliad's herb twig did, back in his cave, she marveled.

She thought, perhaps, she was dreaming, but with every turn of the page she smelled wonderful fragrances; flowers in spring, the mountain air and sometimes even delicious foods cooked over a fire. The words on the pages were changing too, as she ran her index finger across the letters. They were no longer just black etchings upon white parchment. Now they were slightly raised and soft to the touch; soothing, like goose down.

But there were other mysterious qualities hidden within the pages that drew Elabea to the book like a thirsty doe to a stream. Sometimes, in the twinkle of an eye, she found she could see within each letter and the view was breathtaking. It was as if she were back in her meadow, watching the stars sparkle and dance, their light carrying her deep into the dark unknown.

She closed the book.

"Rusk, when will you tell me a tale?"

The rusk lighted on her shoulder and scampered down her arm to stand on the book. He began chattering to Elabea while moving his tiny black hands, as if trying to communicate to her.

Hearing the commotion, Galadin looked back at them. Despite his misgivings about the rusk, he no longer called it a flying rat and had begun to appreciate the creature's abilities to sense danger.

"So what did he say?"

"I don't know," Elabea sighed.

Then to the rusk: "You're *not* much help. I wish I knew what these words said."

"You're going to become a storyteller," Galadin said, "Shouldn't you be able to understand what it says?"

Elabea shrugged her shoulders. "I suppose that'll happen when I arrive in Claire," she said.

"I thought all storytellers had special powers."

"If I did," she answered, becoming flustered with his frustrating logic, "what would you want me to do?"

"Tell a story that gets us there right away."

She rolled her eyes at him. "I doubt it works like that. To be honest, I don't even know what a storyteller does. Il-Lilliad was the first one I've ever met."

Galadin gave a sympathetic nod, then dared a question. "Are you afraid?"

"Of the woods?"

"No," he replied as they rounded a jutting boulder. "Are you scared of becoming a storyteller? You do remember what Il-Lilliad said, don't you?"

Elabea looked away from the book and out into the darkening forest. She remembered his words all too well. They echoed about in her mind and swatted at her, like a wild cat. She whispered Il-Lilliad's words, "The Cauldron's lust for power will not be realized until all storytellers are destroyed."

Galadin recognized the anxiety in her voice and realized his curious probing had touched a sensitive part of her soul and stirred her fear.

"Sorry I asked," he fumbled to apologize. "I wasn't trying to be cruel or insensitive. I was simply..."

"Curious," she interrupted. "I know."

"Besides," he continued as they ducked under a leaning tree, "you have nothing to fear as long as I'm alive."

"Really?" she asked. "Why is that?"

"Simple. I'll hunt down the Ebonite's leader, Brairtok, and kill him," he answered with youthful bravado. "That way, you'll never need to fear anymore."

Elabea knew Galadin meant well. She knew he had the courage to execute such a heroic feat, but something deep inside warned her their battles would not be only with Ebon, but against the Cauldron and its drone. Even now, high upon a cold ridge far from Allsbruth, she could feel the drone beating down upon her like a hot summer sun.

They walked on in silence as the woods grew darker.

"Are we going to walk all night long?" she whined.

"No. I am searching for a place for us to sleep. I'm just being careful; I don't want to walk into a trap or stumble into any awakened creatures."

Spotting a grove of pines up ahead, he picked up his pace.

"Perfect," he exclaimed.

He led Elabea beneath the canopy of limbs where they gathered the brown needles together to form beds. They fell onto their pallets, and allowed the sweet-scented pines to lure them into a deep, exhausted sleep.

The rusk perched on Elabea with its tail coiled around his body. It too was asleep, but unlike Elabea and Galadin, its senses were attentive, probing the darkness for danger.

Its tail twitched once, then twitched again. Its eyes flew open and its ridge of fur stood erect.

Danger was imminent.

The rusk grabbed Elabea's tunic and shook, desperate to awaken her, but she was too exhausted to be aware its tiny attempts.

Sensing evil approaching his beloved storyteller, the rusk flew into the night sky. High atop a towering pine tree, lurking amidst the shadows, he came face to face with the predator.

"So, the Council has sent a vul jen," the rusk announced. "Too bad they did not know *this* rusk was still alive."

The vul jen sat silent in the darkness, for the night was his sanctuary, and his prey: the dreams of Elabea.

"Ahh, a rusk," it uttered in a flat, bored voice, as if annoyed by a pesky inconvenience. "Then it is true. She *is* to become a storyteller."

"Yes, and she will be a great one."

"Alas, she will soon be a dead one."

"Death for you is only a tail strike away, vul jen."

"Not if her dreambreath comes. Then all the poison in your little tail cannot save her."

The rusk looked at Elabea. She slept so peacefully, unaware of the danger high above. She rolled to her other side.

"Behold, her time draws near," the vul jen cried.

The rusk, knowing time was running out, darted for the vul jen and caught it off guard. It struck, but its lethal tail tip just missed its mark.

"So bold you are," the vul jen cackled. "Now be off. The night is mine and so are her dreams."

The vul jen spread its wings and swooped down from its perch. Landing upon Elabea's shoulder, it watched her rhythmic breathing, waiting for her dreambreath to arrive. Seeing her dreambreath nearing, the vul jen cawed with dark delight.

"Not this time," the rusk declared as it dove to attack. Watching Elabea's chest rise to draw in a deep gulp of night air, the rusk increased its speed to press the attack, but was too late. The vul jen transformed into a mist that Elabea inhaled by her dreambreath.

The rusk landed on Elabea and shook her with its tiny paws.

"Elabea. Wake up. Elabea. Awaken..."

The rusk called her name throughout the night, desperate to save her from the vul jen stalking her dreamworld. As valiant as his efforts were, they were in vain. All she could hear in her dreams were the drone, and a faint whisper...snickering.

Chapter 16

Mysterious Pilgrim

Newcomb sensed something was wrong.

"We're being followed," he whispered to Lassiter.

"How do you know?" Lassiter replied, casting about for any sinister looking characters. "This is Torrens Bay. Everyone looks suspicious."

"I've noticed the same man ducking into a doorway or alley every time I look back. Keep walking, I'll see who he is."

Newcomb ducked inside an alley and faded into the shadows. The rusk, sensing his master's alarm, tried beating its wings, longing to hover and protect.

"Not this time, little one," Newcomb cooed. "You are much too weak."

The rusk pulled in his wings and settled back down on Newcomb's shoulder.

Newcomb drew his dagger as he listened for approaching footsteps. The man in question came into view. Newcomb yanked him into the alley, slammed him against the wall and pressed his blade against the man's throat.

"Tell me why I shouldn't kill you," Newcomb seethed through clinched teeth while taking stock of the man's capabilities.

Fear-filled eyes that straddled a long, thin nose stared back at him. A scraggly beard covered his pointy chin and, judging by his frame, the stranger was thin and weak.

This is no assassin sent by Brairtok, Newcomb thought. *Nor is he a rogue warrior looking to collect a bounty.*

An odd sound drew his attention to the man's side. A lute that hung beside the stranger's waist, had banged against the wall and still reverberated from the impact.

"You're a minstrel," Newcomb spat.

"Please, don't kill me," the little man begged.

Newcomb pressed the blade deeper into his neck.

"Forgive me for following," the minstrel muttered, gasping against Newcomb's pressing blade. "I couldn't help but overhear you in the market."

Newcomb snarled at him. "Exactly what did you hear that compelled you to follow us?"

"You and your son have an invitation and are..."

Newcomb pressed his weight upon the minstrel, his blade on the verge of drawing blood.

"I can't tell you," the minstrel gasped, "if you keep…that blade…"

"Who's this," asked Lassiter, who had doubled back to see what was taking Newcomb so long. He was more intrigued by the minstrel's attire than by the fact that Newcomb held him cornered with a dagger.

"This?" Newcomb answered, his voice dripping with distain. "*This* is a minstrel."

Lassiter snickered. "Where did he purchase those funny-looking clothes?"

The minstrel wore a green hat whose brim formed a point that jutted out over his forehead. The top sloped upward to the back where it dropped sharply to the rear of his head. A hawk's tail feather jutted from the left side. His shirt, which was too big for his wiry frame, was tan, and covered with red, yellow and green cloth patches. Dark brown breeches hung loosely over his long legs, and were tucked into a pair of black leather boots of the type street gymnasts often wore.

"Please," the minstrel pleaded, the weight of the blade still making it difficult to breathe. "I can explain, but to do so, I must retrieve something from my pocket. Will you *please* allow me to do that?"

"Go ahead, Newcomb," Lassiter chuckled. "He looks harmless. But be careful. He might attack you with that lute."

Newcomb raised a warning finger in front of the minstrel's face, then took a half-step back.

The minstrel massaged his throat with one hand, and with the other reached into his shirt.

"Slowly," Newcomb cautioned, pressing the dagger's tip into his ribcage for emphasis. "I detest surprises."

The minstrel gulped and nodded. With slow, precise movements he pulled his hand from his shirt and held up his secret.

Newcomb's eyes widened. "Where did you get this," he demanded.

"It was given to me," the minstrel replied. "I couldn't help but see you both looking and talking about yours. I wondered if I might accompany you and…"

"Let me see it," Newcomb interrupted, unable to believe the King of Claire would whisper to a *minstrel*. He examined the parchment. There was no doubt it was authentic. He read aloud the engraved gold letters.

"Hanvil."

The minstrel flashed a nervous smile, clueless to what *Hanvil* meant and why Newcomb had uttered the word.

"Hanvil," Newcomb repeated. "That's your name?"

The minstrel's eyes widened with comprehension.

"Uhh…yes," he stammered. "That's my name. Hanvil. I've had it since birth."

"Most people do," Newcomb countered as he continued sizing up the minstrel. "You're positive your name is Hanvil," he demanded.

The minstrel huffed. "As I've already told you, yes."

"Interesting," Newcomb said.

"Why, interesting," the minstrel shot back.

"Hanvil is an Ingloid name. You're not Ingloid."

The minstrel gave a startled nod. "Of course I'm Ingloid. Born and raised," he protested.

"Your parents are Ingloid?"

The minstrel pumped his arms to accent his reply. "Yes, and proud of it too."

"Funny thing," Newcomb pressed his face close to the minstrel's. "All Ingloids have brown eyes. Yours are green."

The minstrel blinked his eyes, as if to try and alter their color. His smile quivered between a full laugh and a guilty grimace, but never left his face.

"I was…" he stammered, searching for a plausible answer. His smile broadened. "I was adopted."

Newcomb arched his eyebrows. "Really," he asked, feigning interest. "And your birth parents were from…?"

The minstrel shrugged. "I don't know. They died in the Dark War and…"

"You're *lying*," Newcomb barked, his sudden change of mood startled both the minstrel and Lassiter. "You'd better tell me the real story, before I end yours here and now."

"Alright, alright," he held up his hands as if to defend himself from Newcomb's verbal attack. "I'll tell you the truth." Feeling the dagger tip pressing into his ribs, he winced. "My name is DeMorley. I found the invitation."

Newcomb let out a wry chortle.

Relieved to see Newcomb smiling, the minstrel relaxed and his smirk returned. Just when he thought Newcomb was satisfied with his answer and would let him go, the bigger man's anger flared up like a wild fire.

"You don't walk down a street and find one of *these*," Newcomb rattled the parchment in front of the minstrel's face, and the blade once more pressed against his skinny throat.

"No, wait," the minstrel cried. "The truth. I'll tell the truth."

Newcomb stopped his attack and waited for the answer.

"I stole it. I saw it pinned to a door one morning and decided to take it. It looked to be of great value."

"You stole it from someone's home?" Newcomb glowered.

"Yes. This, I swear, is the truth."

"You insolent fool."

"Will I become rich," the minstrel asked, his greed making him oblivious to the trouble he was in. "I heard you talk of treasures."

Newcomb released him and backed away staring at the invitation. In a much calmer voice he said, "You must return this invitation to its owner."

The minstrel's money-hungry eyes filled with panic.

"I cannot."

"What do you mean you cannot?"

Newcomb's dislike for the musician grew by the minute. "You have legs and a will, do you not? Now go return this to its rightful owner."

"I cannot return to Ingloid. I *will* not return to Ingloid."

"Yes, you can," Newcomb replied, poking him in the chest with his index finger to accent his words, "and yes, you will. Now go to the docks and hire a boat to take you..."

"I don't have any money and..."

Newcomb fished out a small purse from his tunic and took out some coins.

Spying the money, the minstrel tried another angle. "No. You see, I can't go back because..."

"Because why?" Newcomb interrupted as he jingled the coins in his palm.

The minstrel's shoulders slumped along with his confident expression. His ruse was up. In a mousy voice he replied: "They'll kill me."

"Kill you?" Lassiter snickered. He had enjoyed their argument, but was at a loss at what such a spineless minstrel could have done to warrant a death threat. "What was your crime? Dressing poorly?"

"Funny," the minstrel feigned a wry smirk. "Let's just say I parted company with their money before delivering services I'd promised."

"Then it is only fair," Newcomb said as he began dragging the minstrel out of the alley, "that you should return for a special engagement."

He flung him into the street.

"You can't," the minstrel argued while flailing about in the dust. "You need me."

Newcomb sheathed his dagger, folded his arms and stared at the man lying in the muck.

"I need you," he laughed at the absurdity of the statement. "Do tell - why do I need you?"

"You need me because," the minstrel hesitated, his eyes darting about the street to make sure no one was within earshot. He continued in hushed tones, "Because I know you're going to Claire. I've traveled these parts and know the back ways. Plus, I speak several languages."

When it came to self-preservation, the minstrel was a master. His weapons of choice were not the blade or the fist, but lies, deceptions and bribes. An artisan of discerning others' weaknesses, he manipulated them to his gain.

"Besides," he continued, "you don't wish for me to reveal your secret identity and the nature of your journey, do you?"

Newcomb folded his arms across his chest. "Was that a threat?"

"Perhaps," he replied. He rose and dusted himself off, feeling his confidence soar. He knew a bluff when he heard one, and the man before him was bluffing. More importantly, he knew why.

Newcomb noted the change.

"Then you leave me no choice," Newcomb said as he slid his dagger back out. "I must kill you."

Instead of cowering in fear, as the minstrel had done before, he took a brazen step forward. "Ah, but there's the rub, isn't it? You can't."

"And why not," Newcomb asked, hoping the minstrel was bluffing and truly did not know his identity.

"Simple," the minstrel crooned, leaning close so only Newcomb and Lassiter could hear. He whispered, "Murder violates your oath as a storyteller."

Newcomb's heart raced.

Lassiter cocked his head and stared at Newcomb as if seeing him for the first time.

"A storyteller?" Newcomb chuckled, feigning surprise. "Do I look like one of those fools? They were all butchered in the Dark War."

"Really?" the minstrel countered, taking a step back. "I've performed the world over and have listened to the late night stories villagers tell. Your appearance, I will admit, is different than the tales depict, but your rusk..."

He gave a respectful nod to the animal perched on Newcomb's shoulder. "Well, he immediately caught my attention. But I needed more proof. I had to get closer in order to see if you had the birthmark."

It took all of Newcomb's will to keep his face emotionless.

"And just as I had hoped, you performed marvelously, pulling me into the alley to protect the boy. Such the storyteller. While you were busy threatening me with your dagger, I performed a masterful rendition of being the coward. That's when I saw it."

Lassiter's curiosity was piqued. "Saw what," he asked, looking from the minstrel to Newcomb.

Newcomb stood mute.

"Oh, my," the minstrel laughed, slapping his thighs. "Your son doesn't know your secret past."

Lassiter's brow wrinkled.

"Newcomb, what secret past?"

Newcomb's jaw tightened, his eyes narrowed. Grabbing the musician, he spun him around and pushed the tip of his dagger into his back. "Into the alley," he ordered. "Now."

Once safely within the shadows, Newcomb confronted the minstrel once more.

"I could kill you right now," he said between clinched teeth, "and no one would ever know."

The minstrel chuckled. He knew he held the upper hand and was enjoying the reversal of roles that were working in his favor.

"As I've already told you, storytellers can no more murder someone than a snake can fly. It goes against your vow as protégés. After all, what does your proud mantra from Claire proclaim?"

He thumped a finger against his chin as he thought. "Ah, yes," he recalled, "*Death begets life.*"

The two locked eyes.

Lassiter was befuddled. "What's this all about?"

"Yes, Newcomb," the minstrel taunted, "do tell your son what I'm talking about."

Newcomb kept his blade pressed against the minstrel's ribs and spoke. "Lassiter, as I've told you countless times, I am not your father."

"I know," Lassiter replied, "you're my uncle."

Newcomb shook his head. "That wasn't the truth. I'm a storyteller sent from the King of Claire to live with you on the Isle of Lills during the Dark War."

"A storyteller? But..."

"I'm sure your mind is full of questions, but now is not the time for such discussions," Newcomb gave the minstrel a hated look. *Nor is it good for this scoundrel to learn everything about us.*

"So," the minstrel interjected with a smirk, "since you can't murder me, and since you can't set me free for fear I will alert the Ebonites, it appears I will be joining you two after all."

With much reluctance, Newcomb nodded and lowered his dagger.

The minstrel pushed past Newcomb and strolled back into the street.

Lassiter's face contorted as he tried to digest all the new information, but it was too much. His mind was overwhelmed and a single emotion dominated his thoughts - anger.

"You deceived me," Lassiter shouted into Newcomb's face.

"My intent was to never harm you."

"How can I trust anything you've ever said," Lassiter asked, deeply hurt that the man he had trusted all these summers was nothing but a phony.

"How? Because everything else has been the truth."

"The truth? Even the stories from Claire?"

"Yes, especially those."

"I don't know," Lassiter said. "I'm not so certain anymore."

"Why? Because of the deceptive words of a minstrel?"

Grinding his teeth, Lassiter glared at Newcomb. "How are your words any different?"

He turned on his heel and followed after the minstrel.

Newcomb watched Lassiter catch up to the minstrel.

He had often dreamed of the day when he would explain everything to Lassiter. Never in his wildest dreams did he picture a minstrel manipulating the timeframe, or that such revelations would occur in a filthy alley in Torrens Bay.

"Lassiter," Newcomb hailed as he caught up. "I know you're frustrated, so let's discuss this later..."

"I don't trust you anymore," Lassiter blurted out, his attention captured by a seductive beauty flirting with him from the shadows.

"Please, listen to me. You've got to understand... "

"No, *you* need to understand," Lassiter yelled, his eyes now centered on Newcomb's. "I don't want to go to Claire. I wish to stay here." His gaze returned to the sultry woman with painted lips who was beckoning from the shadows. "Torrens Bay is gorgeous."

Newcomb blew out a frustrated breath and looked the other way.

"I've been to Claire," the minstrel said to Lassiter as he draped an arm over his shoulder. "Believe me, the women there are more beautiful than in any other land."

"Really?" Lassiter replied while giving the girl another flirtatious grin.

"Absolutely. Stunning. Like pearls, they are."

"Wasn't Claire destroyed in the Dark War?"

"If so," the minstrel said, giving Newcomb a reassuring wink, "then these invitations are worthless. Do you think I'd risk my life over something of no value?"

Thinking it over, Lassiter blew the woman a good-bye kiss before facing the two men.

"Then let us be on our way. Claire sounds absolutely wonderful."

Without another thought, Lassiter set out down the road with a spring in his step.

"You may thank me later," the minstrel quipped to Newcomb.

"Thank you?" Newcomb snarled. "You've only made things worse."

"Now *that* is a surprise. All you were doing was pushing him further and further from Claire. My logic, on the other hand, altered his thinking toward what *you* desired for him."

"Oh, you altered it. He mistrusts me, and you have him consumed with thoughts of maidens."

"I did no such thing. He is a young man. He is already consumed with thoughts of maidens. It is the nature of things. His true feelings were always present. I simply…redirected them."

"You manipulated him. You've never been to Claire."

"True. Nevertheless, it was *I* who convinced him to join us. Your line of reasoning was pushing him toward that lovely woman's embrace."

The minstrel also blew her a kiss. She waved him off and retreated into her dwelling.

Unaffected by her rejection, the minstrel leaned closer to Newcomb. "So tell me," he whispered. "Are they true?"

"Are what true?" Newcomb snapped.

"You know, the stories. Were Claire and the Only destroyed by the Ebonites?"

"You just told the boy they *weren't.*"

"That was said in order to…motivate him."

Newcomb shook his head, disgusted with the man's lack of scruples. "I guess you're just going to have to find out for yourself."

The minstrel pushed away from Newcomb. "So be it. But I hold the upper hand, storyteller. Don't ever forget."

The minstrel ran to catch up with Lassiter. With a playful pat on the boy's back, he looked back and flashed Newcomb a cocky grin.

Frustrated, Newcomb watched them joke and tease like the best of friends.

"A shallow boy, a conniving minstrel, and a storyteller," Newcomb pondered aloud. Then to his perched rusk, "Any words of wisdom?"

The rusk sat silent.

"I was afraid of that."

Chapter 17

Dangerous Dreams

Elabea approached her dreams as if drifting on a lazy river, unaware that danger lurked within the shadows. Walking unencumbered through her dreamworld, examining her thoughts for the one thing she feared the most, was the vul jen. Its teeth formed a feral smile.

"There you are," it snarled. "She has hidden you well, buried there beneath her hope. But you are very much alive in her. *Very* much alive."

It nudged the concealed emotion ever so gently. Elabea tossed in her sleep. It shrieked with delight.

"Your dread runs deep. Now, my sweet sleeping storyteller, it is time for it to awaken."

The vul jen clawed at Elabea's hope, exposing more of the tender area, then sank venomous fangs into her soft, vulnerable fear. The Cauldron's poison flowed into her veins and she tossed and turned. Satisfied, the vul jen withdrew his fangs and watched her dreamworld descend into a nightmare.

Elabea dreamed. She was walking toward cottage Number 17. An eerie, high-pitched tone surrounded her, filling her heart with feelings of doom and despair. Her neighbors lined the road, statuesque, eyes void of life, watching her return. Some hissed at her like angry cats. Others turned away in disgust. Her heart sank deeper into despair.

"Good, Elabea," the vul jen encouraged. "Embrace your new world."

She opened her front door. It was heavy and took all her strength to swing it wide. Inside a man sat, staring into the fire.

Father? she thought. *I never realized how much I've missed you.*

She longed to call to him. She began to open her mouth, but the vul jen clamped it shut.

She tried to walk toward him, but her feet floated off the ground.

Quinn held her invitation, but it was covered with blood. He turned to look at her. A tear rolled down his cheek.

"Elabea, why did you leave? Help me. Come home, please."

She floated dream-like to the kitchen table where a bucket of water sat.

I shall draw you a drink.

She looked into the water and caught her reflection. It dissolved into the visage of an Ebonite warrior. He bore a grotesque wound on his face.

She tried to scream, but the vul jen restrained her. She tried to flee, but the bucket of dark water grew and grew. It pulled at her, drawing her down against her will. Her heart raced, and she opened her mouth to cry. The vul jen laughed.

"Yes, dear storyteller. Call out to Claire. Call out to your king."

He released her mouth.

Elabea screamed, but her voice was mute. The water loomed closer. Distorted within its black recesses was the face of Il-Lilliad. He laughed at her as if she were a fool. Galadin's face materialized, as did Mithe's. They too were laughing. The water gurgled and boiled, and within every bubble another familiar face appeared, floating upward, popping as they neared her face, releasing another taunting laugh.

"Closer, dear Elabea, closer," the vul jen encouraged as he pushed her face toward the surface. Each exploding droplet stung like a whip lash. The eerie drone intensified. Ebonite drums boomed above the noise.

The vul jen spun her around; faster and faster, uncontrollably fast.

"Try calling out again," it urged. "Will no one save you?"

She screamed. Nothing. No sound. She fought with all of her will, but the vul jen was too strong. A thought, a flash of memory, gave her encouragement.

I'll do what I've done in the past when in a nightmare.

She bit her tongue.

The sharp pain threw the vul jen out of her nightmare and she woke up.

It was early in the morning, and Galadin was huddled over some kindling with the MerriNoon crystal. The wood burst into flame. Everything was normal...if anything about their adventure could be called normal.

Elabea was about to conclude that the whole ordeal had just been a dream - a horrible nightmare, to be sure, but still just a dream - when a sinister voice cursed her.

That voice did not come from the woods. It came from somewhere within.

"Well," Galadin said with a wry smile. "Somebody didn't sleep very well last night."

"What?" she snapped.

"You've been mumbling and thrashing about most of the night. Did you have a nightmare?"

"Perhaps," she grumbled.

The rusk, excited she was awake, hovered in front of her face, his wings flapping so fast they were but a blur. Agitated, Elabea swatted him away as if he were a bothersome mosquito.

"My," Galadin chastised. "Look who's grumpy this morning."

"Silence," she growled.

Galadin's smile faded. "Elabea, what's wrong with you?"

"Wrong? Let me tell you what's wrong. This whole journey to Claire is wrong. We need to return to Hetherlinn."

"We can't. They'll kill us."

"Who told us so? Il-Lilliad? Maybe he's the one lying to us. All I know is that my father is hurt and needs me. If I return, life will get back to normal."

The vul jen watched, delighted, from within her dreamworld.

Such victory with only one bite, he congratulated himself. *Only a few more nights and I shall transform her, destroying her with her own dreams.*

The rusk returned, fluttering before her eyes. The vul jen spied his archenemy. He hissed and began speaking through Elabea.

"Rusk, leave me be," she roared, trying to swat him away. This time, the rusk was too quick and avoided her attacks.

"Elabea, are you alright?" Galadin observed her more closely. "You're acting very strange. Yesterday the rusk was all you talked about. Now..."

"That was yesterday. Today I find it horribly annoying."

The rusk flew to the backpack leaning against the tree. It flapped about wildly, but Galadin and Elabea sat motionless. Frustrated, the rusk flew over to Galadin, grabbed him with his tiny black hands, and tried to pull him toward the bag.

"Playful creature," Galadin giggled while he kept his seat, oblivious to the danger within Elabea.

Undaunted, the rusk pulled with the intensity that marked him as a great protector, forcing Galadin to his feet.

"You're stronger than you look, little one," Galadin said as he let the rusk lead him to the backpack.

Realizing the rusk's tactics, the vul jen seethed with rage and spoke through Elabea. "Galadin, quit playing. We need to return to Hetherlinn. Now."

"Not so fast, Elabea. I think the rusk is trying to tell me something."

Galadin knelt beside the backpack. The rusk landed on top and pulled at the knot.

"Stop," Elabea roared as she stood. "Didn't you hear me?"

Galadin untied the knot and opened the bag. The rusk darted in and landed on Il-Lilliad's book. Curious, Galadin pulled it out. The vul jen cowered at the sight of it and bit deeper into Elabea's fear.

"We don't have time for books," she screeched. "Especially that one. Do you want to get us in more trouble with the Oracles?"

Galadin looked Elabea over. He had seen her frightened many times before, but never like this. Her eyes were wild, even a bit crazed, as if they were not her own. Instead of realizing the danger she was in, he assumed she was just overwhelmed by their journey.

"Elabea, you're not thinking clearly. You bear the mark of a storyteller. If you go back to Hetherlinn, the Ebonite warriors will execute you, and Brairtok will..."

"They will not. Those are the lies of Il-Lilliad's story. He is the one trying to destroy us."

Galadin looked down at the book, then up at the rusk hovering near his face, its fur standing on end.

"Something's wrong," Galadin noted. *"Danger looms. But where?"*

The rusk darted about the book. The vul jen's anxiety increased as he watched him flying over its cover.

"I think the rusk wants me to open it," he said to no one in particular.

Elabea took a cautious step toward him. "Put away that foolish book."

Galadin flipped open the cover. The vul jen's rage boiled over. It hissed and dug deeper into Elabea's fears. Oblivious to Elabea's plight, Galadin flipped through the pages.

"You never told me there were drawings. Look, here's an Ebonite warrior, and this one looks like a storyteller. But what's *this?*"

He held up the book for Elabea to see. The drawing depicted a bird-like creature covered with dark plumage, except for its bony head. In place of a beak was a snout, and it had long, curved, sharp teeth. The rusk landed and positioned his tail as if to strike the drawing.

Elabea hissed like a wild animal.

Galadin looked sideways at her. "What's wrong with you?"

"Close the book, and I'll tell you," she snarled.

"You're not yourself." With book in hand, Galadin stood. "I could understand if you're upset with me for all we've been through, but your anger toward the book...and the rusk? That's not like you."

"I am perfectly fine, boy."

"Boy?" Galadin repeated, so flummoxed that he took a step backwards. He studied her with the eyes of a hunter and approached her as if she were a wild beast. "You called me 'boy.' It's as if someone else is speaking through you."

With each step he took toward her, Elabea cowered back, her face contorting with rage. He stopped, and with a commanding voice demanded, "Who are you? Where is Elabea?"

With startling speed, Elabea kicked the book from his hand. It sailed through the air and landed with a thud.

The rusk swooped down and landed on the open pages, eager to join the battle with the vul jen. It stroked the black letters as if brushing its fingers atop flower petals. Another swish of its hand, and the letters rippled as if floating atop a pool of tranquil water. The rusk skimmed some of the letters up, and they solidified into a black ball that glistened in the morning light. With the black orb in hand, it flew toward Elabea.

"Get away from me" she shrieked with a wild swat at the rusk. "Galadin, he's trying to kill me. The black ball is poison."

Galadin no longer listened as Elabea's childhood friend. Instead, he observed her as the hunter facing a dangerous and unknown beast. His muscles were taut, ready to spring into action. "I'm coming, Elabea," he said as reached his hand out toward her. "Be strong."

She slashed his hand with her nails like a panther. "First blood," she snarled.

Galadin glanced at his wound, then at Elabea. A wicked smile creased the corners of her mouth, sending a shiver down his spine. His eyes narrowed.

"Kill the rusk," she demanded.

"No," he countered. "Whoever you are; whatever you are; we're coming to save Elabea."

Galadin lunged forward, tackling her to the ground. She fought back with an unnatural strength.

"I hate you," she spat back as she kicked and clawed at him. "*I hate you.*"

While Galadin did his best to keep her pinned down, the rusk flew toward her with his black orb. Elabea screamed. She spit in Galadin's face, and with the strength of the vul jen's poison, pushed against him.

"Hurry, rusk. I can't hold her much longer."

The rusk marked her forehead with a single stripe of black substance from the orb. It turned silver, appearing as molten metal on her flesh. Elabea shrieked as her skin absorbed it. As the substance faded, so did her strength. Her muscles relaxed, and she lay motionless beneath Galadin's frame. Alarmed, he stood up.

"Is she dead," he asked the rusk.

The rusk landed on Elabea's chest and began massaging her face with its tiny hands. Galadin watched, helpless, hoping he had done the right thing, unaware to the battle unfolding within her dreamworld.

The molten metal took form within her dreamworld. It emerged, human in appearance, but covered in shining silver. It was dazzling to behold, as if the sun burned within its chest. Two pairs of metallic wings beat on its back, propelling it up to soar through the dark winds of Elabea's nightmare. It carried a double-handed sword that glowed red, like lava.

With great speed it flew, following the scent of the vul jen. It flew to Elabea's hopes and dreams, piercing eyes scanning every shadow and crevice, until its eyes spied its prey.

It stopped.

Pointing the two-handed claymore at the cowering shadow-creature it demanded, "Surrender."

"Surrender?" The vul jen scoffed. "Ebon *never* surrenders."

The silver warrior dove upon his nemesis with the battle cry, "First blood."

The vul jen fled for its life, zigzagging through Elabea's dreamworld, attempting to throw the silver warrior off his tail.

"Death begets life," the warrior shouted in pursuit.

"Death begets death," the vul jen countered.

Zooming toward the border of her dreamworld, the vul jen was forced to make a decision: turn and fight an invincible foe, or return to the world of reality. It opted to take its chances with the rusk and darted for the boundary.

With a cleansing dreambreath, Elabea exhaled. The vul jen began to re-materialize from the vapors of her breath.

The rusk shot into the air to attack.

Galadin stared horrified at the apparition before him.

"How did *that* get inside her?"

Elabea started to stir. He ran and helped her to her feet.

Nearing the vul jen, the rusk challenged, "I told you that you would die."

"I outwitted that silver fool you sent. I can easily overcome a puny little rusk."

The vul jen attacked, its claws outstretched and razor sharp teeth exposed. At the last possible second, the rusk darted away, snapped its tail like a whip, and threw the vul jen into the side of a tree.

The rusk dove, his poisonous tip prepared to kill, but the vul jen caught him with its claws. Jaws snapped while the rusk held off the chomping teeth with his tiny arms. Intertwined, they both fell to the ground.

"Galadin," Elabea pleaded. "Do something."

"I can't. I might kill the rusk."

The ferocious combat continued as a ball of brown and dark purple rolled madly in the dust. The rusk's tail struck but missed. Vul jen teeth snapped, almost crushing the rusk. As bravely as the rusk fought, it lacked the physical strength of the larger vul jen. The rusk lost its grip and was thrown to the ground.

Elabea screamed.

"I shall savor this kill," the vul jen snarled. "And as life ebbs away, sickly rusk, take this one thought to the land of dormant shadows: Without you, I will enter her dreamworld again and again. Elabea will be *mine.*"

Stunned, the rusk rolled his head to the side as the vul jen flew higher to prepare its death dive. Spying the book nearby, hope returned to the rusk. With its remaining strength, the rusk flung itself onto the open pages and stroked the words.

The vul jen dove, screaming, "First blood."

The rusk scooped up the words and formed another black ball, and heaved it with all its might toward its enemy. The orb exploded in a shower of white and silver light, incinerating the diving vul jen. Its body, completely charred and unrecognizable, fell to the ground near Elabea's feet.

Exhausted, the rusk fell back onto the book. Elabea and Galadin rushed to its side.

"What have I done?" she scooped up the rusk in a gentle embrace. "I nearly got us killed."

She clutched the guardian creature to her chest. "I could see both of you trying to help," she explained as she relived the ordeal. "But I was unable to move. I couldn't say anything. It was as if I was in a living..."

"Nightmare?" Galadin finished.

She nodded. "Was this my fault," she asked.

The rusk, catching its second wind, perked up and lifted its head. It met her gaze and answered, "No, it wasn't your fault."

"I can understand you," Elabea exclaimed. She turned to Galadin: "Did you hear him? He talked to me."

Galadin answered with a smirk. "You're hearing things...again. It's simply chattering like it always does."

She lifted the rusk up to her face and peered into his round face. "Why is Galadin unable to understand you?"

"Only you can, understand me, Elabea. And I can only speak when the book is open. Even then I can only answer when you ask a question."

"Are you hurt?"

"No, but you nearly were. Another night in your dreamworld, and that vul jen would have destroyed you."

"But you killed him. I'm safe now, aren't I?"

"For now. Vul jens travel in fours. This one has three brothers that will surely seek to avenge his death."

"But you can stop them. Can't you?"

"Perhaps."

"Perhaps?"

"Vul jens are great hunters. I cannot kill all three if they attack as one."

"Then what am I to do?"

"Listen to the stories from the book. I will read them to you. Let them grow within your heart like the flowers from your meadow. They will guard the door to your dreamworld. Only the stories can stop the vul jens. Nothing else."

Elabea set the rusk on her shoulder and picked up the book. She held it open, studying the pages, eager to hear the stories within. Galadin, who stood bemused as the rusk and the girl chattered, came alongside and gazed at the pages.

"The rusk told me that he can only talk when this is open. From now on, I'll carry the book.

"Absolutely," he said with a nod. "And I'll carry your pack." He snatched it off the ground, heaved it over his shoulder and led the way from their campsite.

Elabea held the book open in her palms and the rusk began reading her the tales. She marveled at their endless depth, devouring every sentence, every nuance with a heart famished for the stories hidden from her for so long.

As the rusk read, she heard a familiar sound from afar. It reminded her of a lark circling her oak, singing its song. She knew it as the whisper that first called her that fateful morning when she found the parchment. Now, as then, the whisper chimed but a single word.

"Elabea."

Chapter 18

The Gwyr

The vul jen's smoke, along with the words the rusk had used from Il-Lilliad's book, snaked skyward. Drawn toward Ebon by the invisible river high overhead, they floated back to the Cauldron. As the words neared Netniath, they transformed into silver, reflecting everything with dazzling brilliance. It was for this very reason that the rusk had used them as a last resort; the words would alert the Cauldron to their whereabouts.

The argent streak floated with the other vapors down the cold, dark hallway. As it fell into the Cauldron's black flames, the Council spoke as one.

"Someone has used the words of the Only."

"Yes. And a vul jen is dead."

"The words speak of a whisper."

"The whisper calls Elabea. She still lives."

They let out a heinous cry that sounded like dying animals.

"We must act quickly. There will be other words."

"Yes. For those words always lead to a story."

"And when a new story begins, ours will end."

"Summon Brairtok."

Low lying clouds hovered like ghosts about Vorak, making the citadel drool dark sheets of water. Over the course of many winters, the incessant dripping had scratched away at the surface like the fingers of a drowning man clawing for air.

It was not always thus. In its infancy, the unique steel edifices, attached to the tan stone, glistened in the light, making Vorak a palace of radiant splendor. That all changed when the blood of the storytellers stained the reeds. As the silver armor of Ebon's warriors grew black with tarnish, so did the walls of Vorak. The once magnificent citadel degenerated into a darkened mass, as black as the loss of hope.

Yet, the Ebonites, with darkened hearts, hailed such corruption as beautiful.

Brairtok sat in the great room of Vorak dining with his generals. Along one of the long walls was an enormous fireplace that cast great heat and light into the room. On the opposite wall, three long tapestries hung over tall windows, blocking the blasts of cold mountain air. Images of Ebonite campaigns were woven into the dark fabric, commemorating Brairtok's victories and forever capturing the glories of his reign as King of Ebon.

In the middle of the room sat their table. Made of dark, heavy wood, it was long and set with the best Brairtok's conquests could provide: Allsbruthian vegetables and roasted ox, smoked fish from the Sea of Gilden, sweets from Torrens Bay, and the finest wines from the regions to the south where the hot sun made the grapes grow sweet.

The mood at the table was jovial. They were rulers of all and had nothing to fear.

Brairtok enjoyed their company, laughing at their jests as each tried to top the other's stories. As he reached for a platter of meat, the hall's doors banged open, the sound reverberating about the room. Conversation at the table died.

An officer accompanied by his scout entered and walked briskly toward the table. They stopped and bowed before Brairtok.

"Hinnmith," Brairtok exclaimed with a rare smile as he snatched up a hunk of roasted boar's meat. "It's good to see you back so soon from Allsbruth."

Hinnmith's face bore a serious expression. "We have urgent news."

Brairtok ripped off a huge bite. "Are the waifs of Hetherlinn dead?"

"No. They're alive, my lord."

Brairtok stopped chewing and stared at Hinnmith. "Guard your words, my friend. We have known each other for a long time and have even enjoyed first blood together. Failing a mission violates Ebonite military code. You and I both know what the penalty is for such treason."

Hinnmith's expression did not waver. "I speak with the utmost respect, and may you live forever, my lord. Nevertheless, I must speak honestly of what transpired in Allsbruth."

Brairtok studied Hinnmith's eyes. He detected a trace of fear; a sight that made his stomach turn.

"Very well. Speak."

Hinnmith gathered his courage, knowing full well his word could be used against him in a military trial; if Brairtok even granted him the honor of a trial. Without visible hesitation, he braved his reply.

"Manno Vox lives."

The generals gasped, though Brairtok appeared unimpressed.

"Impossible," he snorted, continuing to chew the meat in his mouth. "I personally destroyed him in the Dark War."

"And I witnessed it too, my lord, but I speak the truth. He is alive and…"

"And what?"

"He is…different."

"Different?" Brairtok chortled as he nibbled at another bit of roasted boar's meat. "How so?"

Hinnmith had dreaded this part of the report. They would either brand him as a lunatic or a coward. Either way, his career, and possibly his life, was in grave danger. Locking his gaze with Brairtok's, he delivered the full report. He left nothing out.

"He rides a flying horse and glows like a demon from the moon."

The Ebonite generals snickered. Brairtok held up a hand to silence them.

"Seeing ghosts on the frontier?" Brairtok raised his goblet and sniffed the wine. "Sounds like a commander who is nearing madness or…"

He took a long swig from his cup before finishing his thought. "…or has consumed too much wine."

Hinnmith's eyes narrowed. As a seasoned veteran, he had learned to restrain his emotions, particularly when in the company of powerful men.

"That is not all," he continued in his calm tone. "Allsbruth is awakening. Fea dracas attacked us. They killed several of my men, along with two sevritts."

Brairtok slammed his goblet down on the table.

"Enough," he thundered. "I could have you arrested for treason for uttering such words. An awakening cannot happen. The Only is dead. Claire was destroyed."

Hinnmith remained poised, despite the horrid memories of the fea dracas ever-present in his mind.

"My lord, I am well aware of the facts. I pillaged Claire at your side. But you must believe me when I tell you, we witnessed an awakening. You must order our forces to full-alert and attack before we lose Allsbruth."

Brairtok pushed himself away from the table. Seeing him rise, and knowing the excesses of his rage, the other generals stared down at their plates or directed disapproving stares toward Hinnmith. They knew all too well that when Brairtok, the Lion of Ebon, prowled wildly about the room, no one was safe.

Brairtok paced to regain control over his anger. His face softened, and he assumed the guise of a father having a discussion with an errant son.

"You are a great commander, my friend, but tonight, I fear for you. This story of Manno Vox, alive and riding a flying horse, his appearance like that of a moon phantom. You speak of an awakening, of sevritts killed by children? Your story is too incredible. It tells of a man needing a respite by the Gilden Sea."

The generals chuckled nervously to show Brairtok their allegiance.

Hinnmith motioned for his scout to approach. The scout presented Hinnmith a long, leather pack.

"Then tell me, my lord," Hinnmith said as he reached inside the satchel, "where did I get *this?*"

Pulling out the crystal bolt, he heaved it at the the roasted boar sitting in the middle of the table. The generals ducked, shouting expletives at Hinnmith, then stared flabbergasted at the crystal shaft jutting out of the meat.

Brairtok approached it cautiously. He gently ran his fingers up and over the orange and yellow fletchings as if caressing a lover's back. The firelight danced off the glistening shaft and cast eerie shadows about the hall.

Hinnmith continued his report. "Manno Vox followed us. He could have killed us at any time. Instead, he shot this over our heads as we entered Ebon. It is a warning, my lord."

Brairtok continued stroking the crystal shaft. "So he lives anew with a fancy arrow." His voice was as smooth as the arrow's shaft. "No concern. I destroyed him once. I shall do it again."

"That is not an arrow, my lord."

All eyes were on Hinnmith. The commander swallowed nervously, knowing he may be taking his report too far.

Brairtok gave him a sinister smile.

"Whatever do you mean, Hinnmith?"

"Study the nock."

Brairtok complied, but did so in a patronizing manner, as if to humor his friend who was obviously going mad.

"Do you see the difference? This did not come from a long bow. This is a crossbow bolt."

"A crossbow?" Brairtok blurted with a loud laugh. "How can that be? This is the size of an arrow. If what you are saying is true, then he would tower over us."

Hinnmith nodded to confirm Brairtok's observation.

The smile drained off Brairtok's face. Anger returned and his black eyes glowed as if on fire. Yanking the bolt from the boar, he heaved it into the fireplace where it exploded into a bright ball of light. The glowing orb swirled about the room, and everyone present heard the whisper: *"Brairtok. I come."*

With a thunderous *crack*, the ball cast millions of blue sparks everywhere, and as quickly as they appeared, they departed Vorak, returning to Claire.

The generals looked to Brairtok for direction. Hinnmith's story sounded incredible, but now they had witnessed evidence of an awakening with their own eyes.

Brairtok was at a loss for words. To deny what they all experienced would communicate weakness on his part. On the other hand, to acknowledge Hinnmith's story of an awakening would usher in the only possible explanation: the Only was still alive.

A whisper spoke within his mind.

Brairtok, come.

Regaining control of his emotions, he announced, "I've been summoned by the Cauldron and Council. They will know what must be done to stop this...annoyance."

Brairtok climbed Netniath's spiral staircase to the hall of the Council. He entered the room and bowed, his black armor glistening in the Cauldron's dark light.

"Brairtok," the Council said in unison. "We know of the news from Allsbruth."

"Then Hinnmith's story is true?"

"Yes, but fear not. We saw this day approaching and have prepared well for it. Come forward. Receive a gift from the Cauldron: The Gwyr."

Brairtok bowed his head, giddy with prospect of receiving their blessing.

The Council reached as one into the Cauldron and withdrew embers from the Dark Flame. The coals smoked and sizzled in their hands like pig fat in a hot pan.

"With these embers, we give you the power of all Ebonite warriors before you. Strength upon strength, power upon power, wisdom upon wisdom shall be yours by virtue of the Gwyr."

Brairtok raised his head, and they placed the coals upon his forehead. The black fire burned his flesh, the putrid smell filling the hall with his sacrificial scent. Dispersed by the Cauldron's drone, the odor swept across the lands, calling forth the Ebonite warriors killed in battle during the Dark War. Spirits rose from dark, cold graves and flew across mountains and valleys, rivers and seas; a ghastly vapor swimming with muted colors.

The Gwyr.

Converging as one on Netniath, the Gwyr descended into the great hall and swirled about Brairtok.

"It is beautiful," he exclaimed as he spun about to study the translucent swaths of green, yellow, orange and black that snaked overhead. "So beautiful."

"Go. Distribute the Gwyr to your warriors as you see fit, and make them even more powerful. As long as the Cauldron burns, the Gwyr will never cease."

A Councilman placed a smoldering ember in his hand. Brairtok squeezed it tightly. Shutting his eyes, he breathed the fumes of his own burning flesh, relishing the pain it caused him. "Death begets death," he muttered.

The Cauldron delighted in his sacrifice of pain.

Eyes flew open, and Brairtok vowed, "I will *crush* this awakening."

"Patience. Elabea is listening to the words from the book. She dines on the stories like a babe upon a mother's breast. She desires to tell all the secrets within. Destroy her, and the Only's plans will fall like thousands of stars. The night sky will be forever dark."

"She will not reach Claire. I will bring her head back as a prize for you all," Brairtok boasted.

"The King of Claire is not dead as we had presumed."

"He has shown himself," Brairtok asked, stunned he had survived the Dark War after Ebon sacked the nation of Claire.

"Yes," the Council hissed together. "Yet he cowers behind his veil."

Brairtok, the power and glory of the Gwyr running through his veins, spoke with deep conviction. "What cowardice; bewitching a girl to do his fighting."

"Never underestimate the Only. He is most cunning."

"With the Gwyr, I will crush him. I will destroy them all."

"And when you destroy the last of the storytellers, you will be rewarded greatly."

Brairtok bowed and exited. A feral smile fanned out across his face. Marching out of Netniath, he clutched the black ember, the sounds of his sizzling flesh wooing him with portents of glory to come.

Chapter 19

Death Begets Life

Galadin's legs dangled over edge of the cliff.

It was already half-day, and the gurgling sounds from his stomach reminded him it was time for lunch. Removing his pack, he pulled out the last piece of smoked meat Digri had given them as a parting gift.

"Would you care for some," he asked Elabea, who sat cross-legged behind him.

She shook her head, still captivated by the stories the rusk was whispering into her ear.

"Did you know the Only is very powerful?"

"I wouldn't know. I've never met him."

"Hearing these stories, I feel as if I've walked with him in Claire. Would you care to hear some?"

Galadin smirked. "Perhaps you heard the Only whisper to you in Hetherlinn; perhaps not. I still have my doubts. But all morning you've done nothing but listen to that chattering rusk. If you ask me, I think you're becoming obsessed with these stories."

"I wonder what he looks like," she continued as if she had not heard a word he said.

Galadin shook his head and tore off another bite, turning his attention to the valley below.

"Do you believe he lives?" she asked him.

He continued chewing, savoring both the taste of the meat and the spectacular panorama that spread out before him. He swallowed, then replied.

"Honestly?"

Elabea nodded.

"No."

Elabea's countenance fell. "Why not?"

"Think about it," he replied. "Why the secrecy with the invitations? If he truly wants to meet us, why didn't he personally knock on our doors?"

"Because of the Oracles and Ebon's army."

"But if he's as powerful as you say, then why should he care about Ebon or the Oracles?"

Elabea thought long and hard but was unable to find a plausible answer.

"I'm positive there's good reason," she finally answered.

"Personally, I believe the Only is an imaginary person created by storytellers. It makes them appear powerful and full of mystique. Without the Only in their stories, they would just be ordinary people, like you and me."

"Then how do you explain Manno Vox or Il-Lilliad rescuing us at the perfect time? And what about me hearing the Only's whisper, or your name etched upon a sword from Claire? Explain *those.*"

"I can't, but just because I don't have an explanation, doesn't mean the Only exists. I simply need more proof. You, on the other hand, have been making up incredible stories all your life. Remember when you were of five summers and you told me you could talk to animals?"

Elabea chuckled. "I did have you fooled a few times."

"Then there was the time you boasted that you could fly. I can still see you perched high in the oak preparing to jump. Lucky for you, I suggested you begin your flight at a lower level. Do you remember what happened?"

"Yes," she admitted. "I smashed my nose when I hit the ground."

"So there you have it. I think you've created similar stories; only this time it involves the Only. By dreaming of becoming his storyteller, you can leave behind plain-old-Elabea from Hetherlinn. I don't blame you. If my father was a drunk, I'd create stories about someone great, too."

His words, although true, stung.

Perhaps he's right, she mused. *Have I conjured up such tales simply to escape who I am? To justify my father's shame?*

"Well," she countered, her voice quivering, "perhaps that's the same reason you do *not* believe."

"What are you talking about?"

"You're afraid to believe in anything you can't see or touch. After all, your father is lost in his fantasies. If you believe in something that you can't see, touch or taste, you fear you'll become mad, just like him."

Galadin snapped away from her gaze and yanked off another bite of meat. He stared across the valley.

A painful and awkward silence fell between them.

"I'm sorry," Elabea ventured. "Please forgive me for hurting you, but your words hurt me, too. I was only trying to illustrate is that..."

"Will you stop trying to *illustrate.*"

"Why are you still angry? I said I was sorry."

Galadin turned to face her, his gaze hot. "I'm not like him. I'm not going to be like him. I'm *not.* Do you understand? Every day in Hetherlinn I heard people whisper, 'There goes Gundin's boy. Will he go mad too?' They talked about him as if he were already dead. I'll show them all."

"So that is why you're journeying with me. It's not that you actually care about me; you just want to show everyone that you're respectable."

Galadin was breathing heavily. He picked up a rock, heaved it off the cliff and watched it bounce down the precipice until it disappeared from sight.

"Yes," he replied, oblivious to the pain in her voice. He grabbed another rock. "I want my family name to be great again, just like you do."

Elabea sucked in a quick breath. *He knows me too well. I suppose we are not that different. I want to redeem my father's shame at Min Brock, too.*

"Perhaps we're both lost," she said with a heavy sigh.

He let the rock fly.

"Lost?" he chirped, relieved the topic of conversation had changed. "We're not lost, I know exactly where we are." He tapped the map tucked away in his pocket.

Elabea was about to correct him, pointing out she was just using a poetic expression, but decided against it. Instead, her heart began to swell with strange feelings she didn't understand. She had always liked Galadin as a friend, but something was changing. Something about the strain of his muscles beneath his shirt, and the glint in his eyes whenever he looked at her.

"Come what may," she said, her voice soft, shy and more vulnerable than she intended, "I'm happy you're with me."

Galadin looked away, equally bemused by the changes in their relationship that he felt, but could not explain. Tongue-tied, he kicked some pebbles off the cliff and fidgeted with his sword.

A noise from the valley caught his attention and saved him from having to make a reply he was unprepared to give.

Four bear-like creatures lumbered into the clearing. They stopped and sniffed about something lying in the grass, then dropped to the ground and began rolling on top of whatever it was. Their movements seemed ritualistic, even ceremonial. When they stood up, their long, golden-brown hair was mottled burgundy from the blood of the dead animal.

"Gors," Galadin exclaimed, intoxicated with the sight of the beasts. "Scavengers of the woods. According to the stories I've heard, their stench is so foul you'll smell them before you see them."

To prove his point he sniffed the air, but all he smelled was the fresh mountain pines.

"I'm going down to get closer."

"What," Elabea asked, stunned not only at his sudden desire to hunt, but at how quickly his mind could abandon a discussion about their relationship. "No. You can't. It's too dangerous. They're enormous."

"I have this to protect me," he grinned, patting his sword. "Remember the Wurmlin? Sliced in two. Besides, the stories say that gors are passive animals."

Galadin found a path and started down the side of the cliff.

"Galadin," Elabea called out as he disappeared from view, "there's no time for this. The valley isn't safe."

His head popped back up and he peered over the cliff's edge at her.

"You stay here. I'll be right back."

With that, he disappeared.

Elabea wrestled with what she should do. Against her better judgment, she ventured over to where Galadin had disappeared. She leaned out until she caught a glimpse of him descending. The steep slope didn't appear to hinder him at all. He used the heels of his boots to brake his descent while grabbing saplings to aid his balance.

She glanced at the rusk on her shoulder. His large round eyes blinked back at her.

"Well, you don't appear frightened. I suppose a little adventure is acceptable."

She started to lower herself over the cliff's ledge, then remembered the pack and the book.

"Should I go back for them," she wondered aloud. The rusk answered, but all she heard was his chatter.

"Of course," she sighed with a glance at the closed book. "I can't understand your words, but I understand your concerns. Don't fret, little one. The book will be safe here."

The rusk pulled frantically on her tunic.

"Relax, we won't be long. I promise."

She crept down the steep mountainside, and once she gained the valley floor, she ran to catch up with Galadin. Hearing her approach, he turned and motioned for her to walk quietly. His face was serious.

"We're lucky," he whispered when she arrived. "The wind is blowing in our favor. Can you smell them?"

Elabea sniffed the air, then wished she hadn't. She covered her nose in disgust.

"It smells like Hetherlinn's fertilizing pen."

Galadin nodded.

I detest that thing, she thought. *Piles of manure, rotting vegetables, discarded animal parts from a hunt...all rotting and stinking in that pen beside the vegetable fields. Planting season is the worst. They toss the foul-smelling stuff everywhere, covering the new seeds and freshly turned soil. Even at night I could smell it riding the winds. I tried to fall asleep, but the rot was everywhere in my room.*

Reaching the clearing, they marveled at the gors sitting in the tall grass. Larger than an Ebonite warhorse, they sat scattered about with their backs to one another. One stood up and charged the dead carcass. Snapping off a bite, he scampered back and plopped back down to eat.

"This is exciting," Galadin whispered.

Elabea's eyes glared at him above her hand-covered nose.

While they ate, the gors continually surveyed their surroundings for predators. Beneath their blood-matted golden fur were powerful muscles that rippled whenever they moved. Broad shoulders supported their tall, thick heads, and their flat faces were covered with short, black hair. Rather than snouts, the gors had fat noses with flared nostrils. Their black, fur-covered jaws jutted outward. Large ebony eyes glistened like black pearls resting on a pile of dark ash.

One gor looked their way.

Elabea crept closer to Galadin.

"I don't think he sees us," he whispered.

The animal looked away.

"Watch me. Here I go."

"No," she whispered through her covered hand. She clutched at his tunic with her free hand.

"Don't worry," he half-whispered. "The stories say that they're shy creatures and never attack."

"Who told you such tales?"

"I don't remember," he grinned back at her.

Springing from her grasp, he charged into the clearing. He withdrew his sword and thrust it toward the beasts.

"Ahhh..." he screamed as he plowed across the field.

The gors turned their heads toward the youth. Three fled for the woods with giant strides.

"Run, you foul-smelling beasts. Run," Galadin laughed.

The remaining gor, who was half-again as big as the other three, didn't run. It stood its ground and stared at the invader.

"What's this?" Galadin taunted to the lone scavenger. "Defending your territory, are you? You must be a bull gor."

As if in answer, the creature rose upon his hind legs and reached its full height. It was an impressive specimen.

"So you desire a fight," Galadin taunted. "Come on. I'll cut you in half."

The animal rolled back its head and emitted a short, but deafening roar that echoed about the clearing. It glared straight at Galadin and snarled, exposing sharp teeth stained with blood. Dropping to all fours, it charged.

I thought they're supposed to be passive.

The thought flickered through Galadin's brain. Panicking, he glanced back at Elabea, who was desperately waving for him to run back.

Galadin shook his head.

It's too far. Even it I made it I might endanger Elabea. I have no choice...

He raised his sword before his face, assumed a defensive posture and faced the charging beast.

The bull-gor's charge rattled the ground. Staccato snorts matched its cadence, and rage filled eyes loomed. Within paces of the boy, the animal lunged.

Galadin swung with all his might and struck the gor's left foreleg. There was no flash of light, nor was the animal split in half. Wounded and enraged, the bull-gor rose on its hind legs and emitted an anguished cry.

Galadin stared at his sword in dismay, as if betrayed by a close friend.

Why aren't you glowing?

There was no time to wait for an answer. Desperate for survival, Galadin struck hard at the animal's underbelly, but its fur was too thick. His blow left only another flesh wound.

The bull-gor charged back and struck with its right arm.

Galadin tumbled through the air, and landed senseless against the hard ground. His sword was jolted from his grip and disappeared in the tall grass.

The gor's loud grunts peppered the air. It grabbed its helpless prey in its forepaws and shook him violently overhead. Galadin's body ached; his mind reeled from the thrashing. When he thought he could endure no more, the gor hurled him through the air. Galadin tumbled head over heels. He started to lose consciousness.

As the blackness engulfed him, a single thought passed through his mind: He would die, not as a warrior, but as a fool.

Galadin's eyes popped open and he was startled by the bright blue sky. He shook the cobwebs from his head, and though the world was still spinning, his battle with the gor crept into his mind like a timid cat entering a foreign home.

"I'm...alive," he mumbled to himself in disbelief.

"Yes, but you should be dead," Elabea scolded as she helped him sit up.

Though he had no memory of the killing blow, he knew the only way he could possibly be alive was if he had killed the beast. His brazen spirit reasserted itself.

"I knew I could kill that gor," he bragged.

"*What?*" Elabea was flabbergasted.

Galadin rubbed his throbbing head. "I said, I knew I could kill him. How else do you explain my survival?"

As he rubbed the back of his head, Galadin realized he was no longer in the valley of the gors. His face wrinkled with bewilderment.

"How did you carry me back up to the cliff?"

"I didn't. *He* did."

Elabea pointed to someone, or something, behind him. Galadin stood on wobbly legs and turned to look. Sitting on his fiery stallion was Manno Vox. Despite seeing him in the night sky when the fea dracas swarmed, and knowing him for a friend, Galadin stepped back in fear.

"He destroyed the gor and saved your life," Elabea stated, awe tinging her voice.

Manno Vox's face rippled like white water and danced with beautiful colors, like flames across a wintery night sky. Though void of mouth, nose and ears, he did have eyes, and they blazed like a thousand suns. Galadin tried to look into them, but they were too bright and brought fear to his heart.

A great sword hung sheathed at the fiery warrior's left side, ready to be drawn for battle. Resting across his lap was his mighty crossbow that glistened like well-polished silver. Both rider and mount glowed like a translucent silver-blue moon.

"Didn't you see him while you were battling the gor," Elabea asked. "He fell from the sky like lightning and shot the beast. Before the gor fell dead, he changed flight and caught you before you crashed to the ground."

Stunned by the turn of events, Galadin searched the valley below. A single plume of smoke rose into the air. Following its trail, he discovered the charred body of the gor. Even from far away, the bolt's crystal shaft glistened in the sunlight.

Galadin's shoulders fell, as did his gaze. He knew he needed to say something, but even a simple thank-you would betray his foolishness and shame. Pride kept his mouth closed.

Manno Vox's voice emanated from all around them, piercing the very cliff they stood on. Hearing his mellifluous voice for the first time, Galadin and Elabea dropped to their knees in fear.

"Galadin," he thundered. "Bearer of the sword of Claire. Protector of Elabea. You must awaken."

"Awaken?" he asked, looking to Elabea for help. She could only shrug.

"Your folly nearly destroyed all that is to be. Awaken."

"This wouldn't have happened if the sword wasn't bewitched. It betrayed me," Galadin argued.

"You betrayed the sword," Manno Vox countered. "It is not a weapon for sport. It is a sword of honor. Its power is revealed only when Elabea opens the book, and you wield it on her behalf."

"I never knew..."

"You also betrayed the book of Il-Lilliad by leaving it on the cliff."

"That's Elabea's fault," Galadin sulked. "Il-Lilliad gave the book to her. She's the storyteller; not me."

"You were commanded to protect Elabea, the rusk *and* the book. *You* are responsible."

Galadin shuffled his feet. *Why am I the only one getting blamed? Why isn't Elabea getting a tongue lashing too?*

As if reading his thoughts, Manno Vox roared, "Do you not remember Il-Lilliad's words to you back in his cave? Much will be asked of you."

"How do you know what he said?"

"Awaken, Galadin, son of Gundin."

"Awaken? I don't understand. What do you want me to do? Say that I'm to blame? Very well, I accept the blame. But what's wrong about wanting some adventure?"

"If it is adventure and battle you long for, then behold; your adventure is already here."

Manno Vox spurred his stallion to one side, revealing four dead Ebonite warriors.

"While you were indulging yourself in an *adventure,* you left yourself vulnerable to attack. These Ebonites nearly captured Elabea. I not only had to save you, but her as well."

Galadin started to protest, but as the realization that his careless actions nearly resulted in Elabea's death, he was overcome with remorse. He felt like a fool. He felt like a child. He felt her eyes upon him, but could not bear to lift his eyes to hers.

When he finally found the courage he glanced at her with somber eyes and mouthed, *I'm sorry.*

With a smile, she mouthed back, *It's okay.*

Galadin surveyed the surrounding hills and valleys. It was as if his eyes were opened for the first time. The area teamed with unnamable creatures from the awakening. Countless Ebonite warriors combed the valley, no doubt searching for them. For the first time since leaving Hetherlinn, he doubted his ability to do what Il-Lilliad had asked of him. Yet despite such a realization, one last argument begged to be asked.

"Manno Vox, you will always be near. So why am I..."

"I cannot always rescue you."

Galadin paced like a captured panther. "Claire is so far away," he blurted, as the full weight of his responsibility crushed down upon him. "Even with my magical sword, I can't defeat all of the Ebonites. My mission is simply...impossible."

"Impossible? Good," Manno Vox replied as he rested his hands on his saddle horn. "You are awakening."

"Awakening? To what?"

"When you departed Hetherlinn, you knew no fear. Now, you do. Why? What has changed?"

"This," Galadin said pointing to the dead Ebonites. "I never imagined our trek to be so dangerous and...difficult."

"Difficulty is the dawn's light to awakening. In its light you see all that you can, and all that you cannot, do. Search your heart, Galadin. You know the truth. What is your purpose on this journey?"

"To escort Elabea to Claire."

"That is not your purpose. That is your mission. There is more. What is the meaning of your name? Speak its Allsbruthian meaning."

"Galadin means, *boy-warrior.*"

"Now awaken. Embrace your truth. You *will* become a great warrior, but this is impossible to accomplish as Galadin. Therefore, you need a new name; a name that will enable you to be the victor. That name - Romlin."

"Romlin?" Galadin stammered with a quick glance at Elabea's face. Judging by her bulging eyes, she too was stunned. "I'm not..."

"You know the meaning of this name?"

"Yes. It means *warrior-man.* But I'm not..."

"You become as you act. You *are* Romlin. Romlin, the warrior-man."

I've only dreamed of a name like this, Galadin pondered. *What honor it brings, and yet...*

He once more took in the perilous hills and valleys.

...It is a name that is overwhelming. It is too much to bear.

Catching Elabea's reassuring nod and smile eased his anxiety a bit, but his doubts lingered.

Romlin is an impossible name to live up to.

Manno Vox answered as if he were listening in on his thoughts.

"To be Romlin is not something to think or feel. It is simply something to be. One step, one heartbeat at a time."

Galadin shook his head. "I'm unworthy, and unable, to do all you require. This name... this undertaking... it's simply impossible."

Manno Vox leaned closer to him. His voice softened. "The Only dances with the impossible."

Elabea's eyes sparkle with hope, while Galadin's flooded with uncertainty.

"There is so much I need to learn," he argued.

"Listen to Elabea's stories," Manno Vox instructed as he returned to his upright position. "From the tales of Claire you will learn all that is necessary for you to succeed. Now come. Stand before me."

Galadin shuffled over to his side. Manno Vox unsheathed his massive sword and held it ceremoniously over the boy's head.

"Galadin. Will you accept the new name chosen for you?"

Galadin raised his head and looked into Manno Vox's surreal face. He wrestled with what to do and felt divided. Part of him feared the change with great trepidation, while the other yearned for it like a man in the desert desperate for a drop of water on his parched tongue. He took a deep breath and nodded his head.

"Then Galadin, the boy-warrior, must die."

With a lightning fast sword thrust, Manno Vox pierced him in the heart.

Elabea screamed in horror as Galadin fell to the ground clutching the wound in his chest.

Manno Vox sheathed his blade and jubilantly roared, "Death begets life. Let the world know that Galadin is dead. Behold. Romlin is born. Forever may he live."

Elabea ran to his side. She was about to start crying when Galadin's eyes popped open. Frightened, she squealed and scooted away.

The man who had been a boy warrior sat up. He pulled up his shirt, but instead of a bloody wound he discovered a purple scar in the shape of a budding tulip. He looked at Manno Vox, a thousand questions in his eyes.

"I have awakened your heart, Romlin. Whenever you hear Galadin calling to you, remember this wound. Touch it daily, and the boy-warrior, Galadin, will flee."

Romlin rose to his feet, a new sense of being and purpose flowed through his veins. He turned to address Manno Vox, but the mysterious champion of Claire was gone. In his place sat a magnificent shield, sword and sheath. He marveled at them. He reached out his fingers and caressed them. They were a man's weapons, and were too big for his frame.

He stood the shield up on its end. It was circular, stretching from the ground to his shoulders. Fashioned from burnished silver, it was emblazoned on its front with the emblem of a dragon with wings unfurled and teeth exposed.

The sword was similar to the one Il-Lilliad had given him, but longer and heavier. Along the sword's guard he noticed the familiar etchings had changed. The letters he knew spelled *Galadin* had changed. Though he could not read, he had no doubt the new letters proclaimed his new name - Romlin.

"Incredible. Look at these, Elabea."

He swung the large shield over his back, surprised by how lightweight it was. He strapped the sword about his waist. Although the weapon hung awkwardly on his young body, somehow it felt...right.

"Something tells me," Elabea said as her thirsty eyes drank his new look, "that you'll quickly grow into those."

This time as he surveyed the hills and valleys where danger and death hid, and his hand touched the blade's pommel, a new courage sparked, flaring through his marrow. It was unlike anything he had experienced as Galadin. This felt more like lightning striking on a clear day: powerful, dangerous, mysterious. He reached inside his shirt, and brushed the purple scar with his fingertips. His boyish fears dispersed like bats seeing the light of a new day.

He took a deep breath and gazed into Elabea's eyes.

"Are you ready to dare the impossible?"

Elabea studied his eyes; eyes that held a confidence and maturity she had not seen before.

"Are you?"

Romlin's eyes flashed the answer, and Elabea felt a smile crease her face, and the blood rise into her cheeks. Suddenly shy, she looked away.

Picking up the bags and book, he handed them to her before heading for the woods.

Elabea remained transfixed, awestruck by the whole ordeal. Romlin turned, but instead of beckoning her to follow, a pensive look clouded his face.

"Elabea, you asked earlier if I believed the Only was alive, remember?"

"Yes," she answered, afraid to hear the answer.

"Well," he glanced at his new weaponry, "I'm beginning to believe."

She smiled. She wanted to run to him, to hold him close, elated not only by his new name, but by the change in him she was witnessing. Her feet refused to move. Now was not the time.

"We need to go," he said as he turned back for the trail. "We have a long journey ahead of us."

"I'm coming...Romlin."

Saying his new name made her feel giddy, as if she were floating on air. Following, she kept repeating it to herself over and over and over.

Chapter 20

A Widow's Revenge

Areall rolled over in her bed. Instead of finding herself lying closer to Quinn, she felt an empty space. The linens were cool to the touch. Alarmed, she sat up and looked about their bedroom. It was empty.

"Quinn?"

She whispered to avoid waking Elabea. As sleep wore off, her memory returned like a sharp, nagging pain.

Elabea's gone.

Sadness filled her as she got out of bed and dressed. Walking into the main room, she was greeted by the dying embers in the fireplace.

"Quinn?"

No answer.

She grabbed her shawl and stepped outside. Pulling it close about her, she headed toward the village fire. It was early morning; very early. A quick glance up through the trees revealed stars still twinkling, though crimson, mandarin and gold seeped into the indigo sky to the east. Sunrise was coming.

No one else was awake. She was about to return home when she saw the silhouette of a man, kneeling, humbly sniffing the tulip. She did not move or say a word.

Faithful to Il-Lilliad's counsel, her husband frequented the flower every dawn. At first, Areall thought she was losing him to madness, but then she began to notice the change. She saw it first in his eyes. His glaze of self-defeat was fading, as if the dawn's rays were cutting away the night.

She even found him staring at her with passionate eyes, the same eyes he held her with before he went off to war. Occasionally, he would wrap his arms around her waist and pull her close. At first the memories of all the pain he had caused was too much, and she pushed him away. Over time she softened, and cuddled into his embrace. True to his word, Quinn stopped drinking and even had Gundin throw out all his wine to remove the temptation.

Areall remained motionless, not wanting to break the tulip's spell. She found herself once again admiring her husband. Quinn was fighting to become the man he used to be.

The village began to stir, and sleepy bodies trudged toward the communal fire. Although it would be warmer nestled beside fires inside their own cottages, the communal fire was where the villagers gathered to plan the day's work. For many, it was a means to forget, amidst their comrades, the Oracles and Ebon's ruling might. Mithe wobbled out of cottage Number 3. When she reached the fire, she spotted Quinn hunched over the tulip.

"Look," Mithe railed to the sleepy villagers. "Quinn is once again embracing the flower. Tell us," she shouted over to him, "are you breathing in the madness of your past, like Gundin?"

Areall restrained herself from running and kicking Mithe's cane away and pushing her into the flames. Instead, she watched Quinn rise and head toward the fire. Out of the corner of her eye, she saw Gundin approaching the flower with his staff. He too humbly knelt and began to inhale its cleansing fragrance.

"I desire change," Quinn answered Mithe. "I desire to lead once more."

Areall's heart beat with hope.

"Change? You'll never change. Your legacy is Min Brock," Mithe hissed.

Areall scrutinized her husband. Since his return from the Dark War, he had cowered under such accusations. His body would sag, and he would accept such condemnation like a knife to the gut. This morning, he absorbed her words with shoulders broad and head held high.

"Min Brock is my shame," he said, "and shall be with me forever. But I can honestly tell you that a change is growing deep within me. I desire to leave a legacy that far outshines the tears of Min Brock."

Gundin had left the tulip and now stood beside Quinn. Areall saw the change in Gundin as well. His eyes, once glazed with madness, were clear, hard, like impenetrable fortresses of stone.

"And I suppose that Quinn's mad friend desires change too?" Mithe nagged.

Gundin glowered at her.

"Would you care to strike her, or may I?" he asked Quinn with a thump of his staff.

Quinn drew his dagger. Mithe's eyes bulged within the shadows of her shawl.

"Murderer," she shouted, her bony finger wagging accusingly at the sharp blade. "The butcher of Min Brock comes for me. No change in him. Behold a coward. Behold a *murderer.*"

The years of abuse from the old woman bubbled to the surface of Areall's consciousness and spilled out between clenched teeth. "Strike her," she muttered. "Be done with her. She's tormented our family for too long."

Quinn slowly twirled the dagger, marveling at its simplistic beauty and the many choices it offered him. He stopped its rotations and stared at the bitter old woman. The villagers gasped, afraid they were about to witness a murder. Instead, Quinn knelt and offered Mithe the weapon hilt first.

Mithe's mouth fell open for but a moment, but was soon replaced as an evil smile pursed her prune-like face.

"No," Areall shouted as she ran toward her husband.

Quinn held up his hand in a silent command to halt. His gaze remained focused on Mithe's face. "Take it. Do what you will."

Mithe snatched the dagger and held it ready to strike.

Gundin raised his staff to defend his friend.

"No," Quinn ordered.

Gundin obeyed but bounced his staff between his palms, ready to fight should the moment arise.

"It is your right," Quinn addressed Mithe, but his words were meant for the whole village, "to remind me of my cowardice. I betrayed your men, our men, at Min Brock. Their deaths are forever branded upon my soul. I will always have to answer for their deaths. No change in me will wash away the blood that stains my heart with shame. I cannot give you back your husband or your children, but I can give you my blade. Widow Mithe, I have, perhaps, hurt you the most. The choice is yours. My fate, and the fate of our village, is in your hands."

Mithe tightened her grip and pressed the blade tight against Quinn's neck. Gasps arose from the villagers. It appeared they would witness a murder after all...just not the one they had expected. A tiny drop of blood ran down his neck.

"Cut his throat," one villager growled. "Blood for blood. Remember our men who died. Remember Min Brock."

"No. Let him live," Daryess strode into the mass of people and took her place beside Areall. "If you murder him, you will become a greater coward than Quinn ever was."

Areall covered her mouth in a vain attempt to keep the pain within from erupting. She caught Quinn's glance and saw the sincerity of his intentions. She fell into Daryess' arms, sobbing and they knelt to the ground.

Mithe glared at them. "Weep your bitter tears, Areall. 'Tis but a sampling of my sorrows."

Mithe prepared to slice Quinn's throat when a girl of seven summers wrapped her arms around Areall, pleading with her to not cry.

"What are you doing," Mithe asked the child. "This woman deserves no pity."

The little girl turned and cast her large, innocent eyes at her grandmother.

"Go back home," Mithe ordered the child.

The little girl said not a word, nor did she move to obey. Her innocent eyes pleaded with Mithe's grandmother heart; urging her to forsake hatred and rediscover the goodness and love she had known before Min Brock.

The dagger shook in Mithe's hands.

"Don't look at me in such a manner," she begged the child as she wrestled with right and wrong, vengeance and mercy.

Quinn spoke what he assumed to be his last words.

"People of Hetherlinn. Whether I live or die, know this: The Cauldron has heard the whisper of the Only. The Ebonites will return to destroy us all. My death now, in some ways, would be gracious. But I would rather fight than partake of this mercy. I desire to lead once more. I would rather die fighting for you, than to die a merciful death now."

"Words," one man cried out. "Empty words. How do we know that we can trust you?"

"You had your chance to lead and you failed," another argued. "What makes this time different?"

Quinn nodded. "These are honest questions; questions I have been asking myself. The only answer I can give is this: I must prove myself worthy again. I must earn your trust. At the same time, you must risk trusting again. Not just in my ability to lead, but in the stories from the King of Claire."

Mithe's arm shook and her face crinkled as her granddaughter continued to console Areall.

With a deep sob, Mithe dropped the weapon. It plopped into the soft dirt just as the sun's rays broke over the surrounding hills.

Quinn massaged his throat, amazed he had been spared a death that he more than deserved. Retrieving his dagger, he addressed the young boys and old men of Hetherlinn.

"Gundin and I are preparing for war. We'd be honored if you considered joining us. The work will be hard. It may even cost you your life, but this I promise: our blood will not fall to no avail as it did in the Dark War…as it did at Min Brock. This I swear to you."

Without another word, Quinn and Gundin marched toward the wood where they had stashed their wooden training weapons. The boys and men of Hetherlinn looked at each other, hoping the other would make a decision. They knew Quinn's words were true.

One step forward would signal a turn from the Cauldron and a step toward Claire. It would signal war. It would cost them everything.

They shuddered at the thought of dying for freedom, losing their lives for an impossible cause.

A young man stepped toward the woods. He cast a single glance back at the others, then turned and followed Quinn and Gundin into the thicket. Another followed. Then a few more.

Areall rose to her feet, wiped away her tears and embraced Daryess. As she looked around the communal fire she realized only women and children remained. The last man in Hetherlinn was disappearing into the woods.

She laughed, and a single tear of joy rolled down her cheek. Quinn, the warrior leader of Hetherlinn, the champion of her heart, had returned.

Chapter 21

The Minstrel's Truth

Nearing the outskirts of Torrens Bay, Newcomb, Lassiter and the minstrel heard lofting waves of music. Rounding a corner, they found a musician playing a mandola. His eyes were closed and his face expressed every note and phrase he performed.

Newcomb stopped to listen.

The music was upbeat and the hypnotic melody soothed his troubled mind. He closed his eyes and let the song transport him to the Sea of Illsbruth, back to a time when life was less complicated. He tapped his toes in time to the song.

"So," the minstrel noted, "you do appreciate music."

"Yes," Newcomb replied with eyes closed, his frame swaying to the song's tempo. "I wish I could play as masterfully as he."

"If you enjoy music, then why do you dislike me?"

Newcomb raised his face and let the warmth of the sun wash over him.

"What makes you think I dislike you?"

He was back on the Isle of Lills; could smell the sea, hear the gulls and relax as he had long ago.

"I've performed for people all of my life. I can read faces better than you can read stories. Yours tells me that you not only dislike me, you detest me."

"Very well," Newcomb admitted as he swayed, "you're correct. I detest you."

"Yet you care for him?" The minstrel pointed at the street musician.

"The difference between you two is quite simple: He has a gift and a talent. You have neither."

DeMorley snorted. "How do you know? You've never heard me perform."

Newcomb released his imagined respite by the sea, opened his eyes and lowered his face to meet the minstrel's eyes.

"I too have been around many varieties of people, and know something of reading their tales. I've read yours and have concluded that there is no need for me to hear you sing."

"That is the most ridiculous notion I've ever heard."

"Prove me wrong. Perform."

"Perform," he replied, as if Newcomb had asked him to undress in public. "You mean here? Right now?"

"If you are the master you claim to be, this should be as good a time as any."

"I can't sing anytime you ask," he argued. "My art, like a fine meal, requires time for me to prepare...to get myself ready."

"It's just as I thought. You're an amateur."

"*Amateur*?" The minstrel's eyes flared and his face flushed. "I'll have you know I've been successfully performing most of my life. It's just that my music requires a...different audience."

"Precisely. You are not a musician like this fellow," he motioned at the mandola player who, despite their debate, was still performing masterfully. "You are an entertainer. A jester."

"I may not be as skilled a performer," the minstrel fired back, "but I'm no jester. I have more dignity than that."

"Indeed?" Newcomb arched an eyebrow. "Look at how you dress. Your attire shouts, *Look at me, I'm a jester for fools*."

The minstrel's face reddened further and his cheeks puffed out as he drew in quick breaths.

"My gift is writing songs, telling stories with my music."

"Really? Then play one."

"Now?"

"Yes."

"I cannot."

"Why not? Must you change clothes?"

"No, it's just that..."

"Let me guess - they are not well crafted songs."

"I'll have you know that mine are some of the finest songs you'll ever hear."

"I have yet to meet a minstrel who did not claim his songs were masterpieces. But when examined in the light of public performance, one quickly discovers they are rubbish."

The minstrel folded his arms across his chest.

"I'd gladly perform one of my songs, but they cater to a more...mature audience." He nodded his head toward Lassiter.

"Ah, now I understand," Newcomb smirked. "If your music was pure and passionate, generated from a heart that longed to connect with others, you would be known and sought after by all. But that is not the case, is it? Your songs are drab and ordinary. In order to draw patrons to your craft, you smear bawdiness and vulgarities on your songs like a farmer heaves dung across his field."

Unfurling his arms, DeMorley let them fly skyward with his reply.

"Yes. I admit it. They are fashioned to draw a fast coin. But my craft gathers more gold and silver than this...this...'artist' performing for *fools* like you."

Newcomb kept his eyes on the minstrel while reaching into his tunic. Pulling out a silver giln, Newcomb studied the minstrel whose eyes bulged as he recognized its worth.

"Were you ever paid this much for your dung songs," Newcomb asked as he flipped it into the street musician's lap. "True art begets true worth."

DeMorley's face burned crimson. His cheeks pumped wildly, like a blacksmith's billows, but instead of a verbal retaliation, he stomped off down the road.

"Newcomb," Lassiter asked, "weren't you a bit too harsh?"

"Actually," Newcomb said with a twinkle in his eye, "I believe I restrained myself quite well."

"I think he looks like a very capable minstrel."

"Your discernment is spot on: He is a minstrel, *not* a musician. Minstrels are scoundrels that feed off society like leeches. Creators of dung songs. Masters of manipulation."

"I disagree," Lassiter interrupted.

"Really?" Newcomb asked as he rested his hands on his hips. "And why is that?"

"I believe there is a purpose for his joining us."

Newcomb shook his head in frustration. "He is a thief and a rascal. The only reason he is joining us is because he has threatened us."

"True, but is it possible that our meeting him was intended to happen? After all, the minstrel's tomfoolery did not catch the Only by surprise. I believe we are to assist him in getting to Claire."

"My, my," Newcomb said as he stroked his chin. He pondered his protégé's thesis. "Who educated you in such a manner to perceive such premises and tenets?"

"You."

Newcomb's eyes twinkled with delight.

"So I did. There is hope for you yet, Lassiter."

Lassiter lowered his voice and mimicked Newcomb.

"Remember, Lassiter. Everyone needs our assistance, even the fools of the world. For if it were not for the Only, we too would be just as foolish."

"Those were my words?"

Lassiter grinned and nodded.

"That was different. You quoted me out of context. What I was trying to say was..."

"Was that it only applied in our classroom? That it only applies when life is easy, or when we encounter those agreeable to our dispositions?"

Newcomb placed his hands on Lassiter's shoulders and looked into his face.

"You are conversing with me as a man, not as a boy."

Lassiter beamed. Although he had not quite forgiven Newcomb, he still loved him. After all, Newcomb had been part of his life for as long as he could remember.

"At least give him a chance," Lassiter asked.

"Very well," Newcomb removed his grip from the boy's shoulders. "Your arguments were well founded and structured with wisdom and truth from Claire. But keep your guard up. Until I read all of the stories within his heart, we must not trust him."

Catching up with the minstrel, Lassiter put a hand on his shoulder. "We've not been properly introduced. My name is Lassiter. It's a pleasure to have you along. And this is Newcomb."

"We've met," DeMorley sulked.

"I must insist," Newcomb added sternly, "that we get you new attire."

DeMorley, fed up with Newcomb's raillery, stopped and faced the storyteller.

"I'm not changing clothes. These are perfectly fine. I just purchased them some days ago."

"You mistake me, DeMorley. I'm not trying to ridicule you," Newcomb answered with a kind pat on his shoulder. "We simply need you to blend in with our surroundings. Your...clothes...attract every curious eye near and far."

DeMorley folded his arms over his chest.

"I'm a minstrel. Without standing out, no one would come to hear."

"Which is further proof you lack talent," Newcomb thought, a wry grin working the corners of his mouth.

"What Newcomb's trying to say," Lassiter interjected, desperate to bring peace to their squabble, "is that although you have a wonderful outfit, we must be as plain as possible. Ebonite warriors are very suspicious and will investigate someone who draws attention to himself."

"Let them come. It's not like I've never performed for the Ebonites before. Besides, what would they do to a minstrel anyway?"

"Well, for starters," Newcomb answered, "they would search you and discover your invitation. Purloined or not, it is a violation of the Oracles. They would make an example of you by first cutting out your tongue, then chopping off each of your fingers."

The color drained from DeMorley's face.

"You're bluffing," he challenged.

Newcomb shook his head.

"Would they truly do that," Lassiter asked.

Newcomb thought about it for a moment.

"No," he finally answered, and DeMorley sighed with relief.

"First, they would torture him for a few days. *Then* they would cut out his tongue and hack off his fingers."

"Very well," DeMorley's voice cracked and squeaked like that of a mouse. "I shall dress plainly. But I don't have money for such a purchase."

"I'll buy them," Newcomb said. "You may pay me back later...with interest."

Turning down the next street, they found a clothing shop, where the minstrel was transformed into a common street person.

"How do I look?" he asked as he spun around.

"Very common," Newcomb answered. "Next, is the instrument. It too must go."

DeMorley tightened his grip around the neck of the lute. "Never. Wherever I go, it goes."

"You can purchase another later," Newcomb reasoned.

DeMorley's mouth dropped open, flabbergasted at Newcomb's proposal.

"You have no idea what this is, do you?"

"Yes," Newcomb replied. "It is a lute."

"Yes, but it is not just *any* lute. This," he replied proudly as he cradled the instrument in his arm like a baby, "is a Bellini."

Newcomb and Lassiter shared a blank look at the minstrel.

"What's this?" DeMorley exclaimed. "The oh-so-wise Newcomb hasn't heard the stories of Master Bellini?"

Newcomb shook his head. DeMorley relished the moment before continuing.

"Legend has it that long before the Dark War, a man named Bellini grew up in Holman along the border of Tristan. Tired of making a living fishing from the Gilden Sea, he began handcrafting lutes. After much experimentation, he found that Allsbruthian wood, specifically balmwood, provided not only the best looking grain, but resonated best, too.

"Next was perhaps his grandest of ideas. Instead of using gut for strings, like all the other luthiers were doing, he devised strings made from Tristan steel. It was brilliant. His idea revolutionized his business, and Bellini's name spread far and wide. Yes, the strings are more expensive and difficult to acquire, but the tone..."

Noticing he still held their attention, DeMorley lightly strummed his lute. Even Newcomb noticed the difference in tone compared to the other lutes he had heard in his lifetime. DeMorley continued with a flourish.

"Unfortunately, Master Bellini died a tragic death. Rumor has it that other luthiers were jealous of his success and hired an assassin to poison him. Of course, this was never proven. When the Dark War came, many of his lutes were destroyed or taken by Ebonite warriors as the spoils of war. Only a few remain outside of Ebon.

"All that to say," DeMorley concluded, "this lute is an irreplaceable treasure. Priceless."

He turned the lute so they could look within.

"Can you see his name? Inscribed with black ink?"

They peered into the lute's shadows and found the faded outline of Bellini's signature.

"If your story is true," Newcomb said, "then how did you come upon such an instrument?"

DeMorley smiled a toothy grin. "I know what you're implying and you're wrong. I didn't steal it. Bellini himself gave it to me."

"Why? Did he feel sorry for you," Newcomb jabbed.

"No, he favored a love song I composed for him. It enabled him to marry the woman he fancied."

"Really?" Lassiter said, intrigued by anything involving love, romance and maidens.

"Yes," DeMorley answered, soaking up Lassiter's interest like a sponge in water. "It was a pretty little ballad if I do say so myself. A nice, tender introduction in a minor key, then a modulation into a major key of such beauty and purity..."

"Enough," Newcomb interrupted. "You may keep the lute. But hide it beneath your garments."

The trio of travelers walked out of town, following the steep road that led to the wilderness. When they reached the summit they stopped for one last look at Torrens Bay. As the sun slipped beyond the sea's horizon, orange and purple hues painted the city with beauty, despite its questionable reputation.

"Lead on, DeMorley," Newcomb ordered.

With a contemptuous bow, DeMorley mocked, "Yes, my royal storyteller. I am but your humble servant."

Lassiter covered his mouth to conceal his laugh.

Newcomb was not impressed and glared at the minstrel. "This is fair warning; any tricks on your part, and I will not hesitate to take action."

DeMorley stood erect from his bow and let his smile fade.

"I understand," he said, giving Newcomb an equal glare. "Then let us be going. Night is approaching and we don't want a band of Wurmlins to find us."

Following the minstrel's lead, Newcomb slid his hand beneath his tunic and withdrew his dagger just as the sun set on the Sea of Illsbruth.

Chapter 22

Kindred Spirits

As night fell upon the sojourners, Romlin kept a keen eye open for shelter. Without warning, he stopped and raised a warning hand toward Elabea.

"Do you hear that," he asked.

She strained to listen. The woods were quiet except for the occasional hoot of an owl. She was about to nudge him in the ribs for teasing her when she heard it.

"Voices," she whispered in fear.

"Yes, and they don't sound like Ebonites."

This bit of news made Elabea breathe a bit easier.

"Let's have a closer look," he said.

Elabea wasn't certain this was a great idea, and worried that the old Galadin spirit was reasserting itself, but she decided to trust anyway. She nodded.

They blended with the shadows of the woods and crept toward the mysterious sounds. Elabea was proud that Romlin never hushed her. His lesson on stealth prior to his incident with the gor was proving invaluable.

Ahead, an orange glow radiated through the branches. The dropped to all fours to remain undetected and crawled forward. They hid behind a large tree and Romlin peered around the trunk for a better look.

"What do you see," Elabea whispered from the shadows.

"A large group of people," he whispered back. "Men, women, children; judging by their attire, they appear to be from different nations."

Curious, Elabea spied a look. The adults were eating and laughing around the fire while the children played near the shadows. She too noted their different types of clothing. They appeared to be families, not unlike the ones she knew from Hetherlinn.

She breathed a sigh of relief and ducked back.

"Can we trust them?"

"Well, we need a place to rest for the night and they don't have appear to have any weapons. Besides, I have the sword and you have the book and the rusk. If things get out of hand, simply open the book and with the magical sword, I can fight off any attacks so we can escape."

With no further discussion, he strolled out from their hiding place.

"Hello there," he hailed as Elabea darted to his side, trying to look everywhere at once.

The group fell silent. Romlin saw that he was wrong about the lack of weapons. Every man held either a club, quarterstaff or dagger, and stood ready to fight. The mothers made frantic gestures for their children to gather near.

"What business do you have," one of the men challenged.

"Just some warmth from your fire and a little food," Romlin replied.

"Step into the light. We need to get a better look at you," the leader shouted back.

Two dark shadows emerged from the shadows into the edge of the firelight. Seeing that it was just a boy and a girl, the leader relaxed his grip on his staff.

"You gave us a scare," he exclaimed with a nervous chuckle. "These are dangerous times, you know. Come, join us."

As Romlin and Elabea drew closer, the large sword strapped to Romlin's side became obvious. Though no one spoke of it, all the men noted it. The children whispered and pointed at it.

Elabea and Romlin warmed themselves around the fire while some of the women offered them bread and smoked meats. The leader rested upon his staff, his eyes focused on Romlin's sword.

He braved a question. "What are young folks doing traveling in these woods late at night?"

Romlin was too busy devouring the smoked venison to talk, so Elabea answered.

"We're journeying to Claire."

Her words had an unexpected effect on the entire group. They became quiet and still; the only sound to be heard was the crackling fire.

Elabea's gaze hopped from face-to-face, desperate to discern their mood. She couldn't tell if they were angry, afraid or simply intrigued.

"Claire was destroyed in the Dark War," the leader countered.

Elabea could feel their eyes pressing in on her. She felt like she was back in Hetherlinn. Her stomach churned. Images of Mithe popped into her mind, her harsh words cutting like a whip.

Can I trust them with the truth, she wondered.

She looked to Romlin for help, but he was too busy eating to be concerned with her plight.

"Well," she said with a sigh, hoping for the best, "we received invitations."

The women quickly covered their mouths to conceal their surprise.

"Invitations?" The leader tossed a scowling look at the women who, in his estimation, had revealed too much by their actions. "What sort of invitations?"

Elabea trembled as she slid her hand inside her tunic.

Am I doing the right thing, she wondered, once again looking to Romlin for help. This time he caught her glance, but merely shrugged while yanking off another big bite.

You're not much help, she noted.

Pulling out the pristine parchment, she held it up for them to see. The gold letters sparkled in the firelight.

"She has a parchment, too," one woman gasped.

The leader flashed the woman a stern look to silence her.

"You have invitations," Romlin asked with his mouth full, suddenly interested in the conversation.

The leader frowned, sighed, then nodded to his group. One by one, they slowly pulled out their parchments, the golden letters glittering in the firelight.

"My name is Tannon," the leader said, his tone much more relaxed and friendly. "This is my wife and these are my children," he said, wrapping his arms around the woman and children by his side. "We're from the village of Gilden. That family over there," he said as he pointed across the fire, "is from the city of Starren in Tristan. That family next to you is from the city of Dunnlinn in Ingloid."

"How exciting," Elabea exclaimed as she took in their smiling faces. She had expected to be rejected and chastised, as if she were still in Hetherlinn. Renewed hope swirled through her. "So, Hetherlinn was not the only village to receive invitations or to have Manno Vox visit."

"Who," Tannon asked.

He looked to the others to see if they knew who Manno Vox was. They either shook their heads or shrugged.

"We've never heard of any Manno Vox. All we know is that one morning we found these attached to a crystal arrow and stuck in our doors."

"So you're traveling to Claire to receive a treasure, just as we are," Elabea continued.

Tannon nodded.

"This has been the first sign of hope we've seen since the Dark War."

"May we travel with you," she asked.

Romlin flashed her an astonished look, hurt that she felt his company was not sufficient, or that she thought he was incapable of getting her safely to Claire.

"Perhaps. First, you must answer something that puzzles me," Tannon asked. He leaned on his staff and directed his gaze toward Romlin. "Where did you get that sword?"

Romlin continued to eat as if he had not heard the question.

"Did you hear me, boy?"

Tannon's once-friendly voice became agitated.

"Where did you get that sword? No man outside of Ebon has had a sword since the Dark War, and here you are, a mere boy, wearing that great weapon."

Romlin stopped chewing. His eyes burned into Tannon's.

"A mere boy?" Romlin rose to his feet.

Elabea placed a reassuring hand upon Romlin's arm and answered, "It was a gift from a friend."

"A friend?" Tannon snickered. "What type of *friend* gives a boy a weapon that's banned by the Oracles?"

"Since we're talking about the Oracles," Romlin challenged, stepping between Elabea and Tannon, "why are you all traveling beyond your village boundaries as set by the Oracles? Looks like you're in as much trouble as we are."

"True," Tannon conceded. "We are both guilty of violating the Oracles. But that still doesn't explain your weapon."

"Why should it matter to you if I have a sword?"

Tannon scowled, something akin to fear evident in his expression. Romlin smiled, reveling in the thought that he appeared dangerous to Tannon. Elabea did not smile at all. She realized the group's friendly disposition had melted away. Desperate to change the tone and mood of the conversation, she decided to reveal more of their story.

"Have any of you heard the whisper," she asked.

"A whisper?"

"Yes, a whisper from the King of Claire."

The entourage looked at each other dumbfounded.

"You see," she continued, "I've heard the whisper of the Only. I'm to become a storyteller. Look."

Eager to win them over, she lowered her head, pulled back her hair, and revealed her purple birthmark.

They gasped in horror and backed away.

"I should have known," Tannon barked, pointing an incriminating finger at her. "Your animal. I recognize that animal now. It's a rusk. You *are* a storyteller."

"Yes but..." Elabea continued, hurt by their sudden hostility.

"Enough," Tannon roared as he raised his staff. "Whispers? Swords? Birthmarks? You both must leave. *Now*."

"But we need to work together. The Only has whispered to you too, and...Haven't you heard his whisper," she asked.

"No," Tannon licked his lips, his eyes shifting about the shadowed woods looking for any hint of danger. "The Only died in the Dark War."

Elabea's face scrunched with confusion.

"If you believe he's dead, then why violate the Oracles and risk your lives to journey to Claire?"

"Because of the promise of treasure," a man from the back of the crowd answered.

"That's why we must help each other..."

"Never," Tannon interrupted. Gesturing toward the dark woods, he added, "You both must leave at once."

"But the hour is late," she pleaded.

"You were cursed in your mother's womb with the mark of a storyteller. Your very presence will alert the Cauldron of our camp."

"What if I tell you a story," she begged as she pulled out the book. "They're so wonderful."

"Silence."

Startled by his outburst, Elabea dropped the pack to the ground. Tannon pointed his staff at her.

"Don't utter one *word* from those tales. We're familiar with the stories of old. They please the ear but their truth brings pain and suffering." He made sure his words were loud enough to reach the deep shadows. After all, if the Cauldron was indeed listening, then perhaps they would be spared being punished for the children's rebellion.

"You're wrong," Elabea countered as she bent to retrieve her pack. "The rusk tells them to me, and they're..."

"I said, silence. If you tell one tale, it will find its way back to the Cauldron and we'll be hunted down like dogs. Just like *you*." Tannon thrust his staff to accent his last word. "We're done talking. Depart from us."

Tannon pointed toward the darkness of the woods.

Tears welled up in Elabea's eyes.

Maybe he's right, she fretted. *I am cursed. Or maybe I'm lost in a deceitful nightmare that's leading me to madness. After all, I'm journeying to an unknown land simply because I heard a whisper from a forgotten king.*

Sensing her inner turmoil, Romlin put a consoling hand on her back.

"Come on, Elabea," he said as he guided her away. "We're not wanted here."

Romlin glared back at the group. Tannon and his followers returned the look.

He guided Elabea into the dark woods. He wanted to put as much distance between the group and themselves as possible.

Elabea dragged her feet and her shoulders slumped.

"There we were," she said more to herself than to Romlin, "enjoying the graciousness of shared food, fire, and fellowship. Then a moment later, they send us away because you had a sword and I'm to be a storyteller. Don't they know they're in as much trouble as we are for violating the Oracles?"

Romlin did not reply. He knew there was nothing to say that would comfort her. All he could do was to help her around some large trees.

"Another thing," she continued. "If they really believe Claire doesn't exist, then why do they think treasure will be there?"

Romlin rubbed her back when they took a moment's respite after hiking up a steep incline.

She panted, desperate to catch her breath.

"Why are there so many hills?" she whined.

Romlin knew her question was not directed at him, so he remained silent.

Further up another grade, she said, "I don't believe I have the heart or the strength to see this journey through."

"I know, Elabea. I know." His voice was tender.

"What did I ever do to them?" Sweat dotted her brow. "I only wanted to help. It's not my fault I was born with the mark of a storyteller."

They reached the top of the ridge and Romlin stopped so she could catch her breath. As they drank in the cool night air, they spotted the fires from Tannon's group, flickering in the valley below.

"This is my fault," Romlin said.

"How," she asked, truly perplexed.

"I wanted their help, too. When I walked toward their fire, it felt like a weight was lifted off me, like it was no longer just my responsibility to get you to Claire.

"When they became fickle, I realized I never should have surrendered my commission so quickly." He clinched his fists, angry with himself. "I never should have been so weak."

Romlin looked into Elabea's face. Although shadowed, he hoped she could at least sense his earnestness.

"When Tannon started arguing with me about being a boy with a sword, I was okay with his threats. But when he started on you…"

His voice trailed off and he looked back down at the campfire. Setting his jaw, he told her, "I'll never put you through that sort of ridicule again. Do you understand?"

She nodded, but realizing he could not see her in the dark, she found his hand and gently squeezed it. "I know," she whispered.

"Tonight, I'll find us a safe place to sleep," he said, his voice chipper once more. "Come morning, we'll continue on to Claire. I'll get you there. I promise."

"I don't doubt your ability to get me safely to Claire," she answered with a pensive glance back at the flickering campfire. "But I wonder if I'm willing to pay the price to become a storyteller."

Chapter 23

Fragrance of Hope

Morning fog shrouded Hetherlinn with an eerie mystique. Cottages lurked in the murkiness like sleeping beasts, and even the communal fire glowed ominously in the gloom.

All were asleep.

Except for two men.

Gundin slipped quietly from cottage Number 7 and headed for the tulip. He marveled how it flourished against all reason, bursting with life beneath the cedar tree, its crimson petals a beacon of light amidst Hetherlinn's drab existence.

As he neared, a silhouette materialized out of the fog. It was the second sleepless soul, and he was bent over the tulip.

Quinn, Gundin noted.

As Quinn rose, Gundin let out a satisfied sigh.

"Sniffing the tulip daily is…"

"Humbling?" Quinn finished.

"Yes. We're warriors, and yet here we are on our knees sniffing a flower…like women."

"We lost the honor of being called warriors at Min Brock. We're farmers now."

They stood in silence and let their gaze fall upon the red petals of the tulip.

"My hope," Quinn continued, "is that in bowing in humility, and with the magical help of the flower's aroma, we'll rise to become warriors once more."

"Only this time," Gundin added as he knelt, "we will be greater than our failures at Min Brock."

"Agreed," Quinn said with a nod as Gundin began sniffing the tulip.

"So tell me," Quinn asked once Gundin finished his ablutions. "Has the fragrance helped? You know, with how you think?"

Gundin pursed his lips as he thought about it. He had noticed a more focused shift in his mind, and his lapses into the past were not as long or as frequent.

"Yes, but I have my reservations. The tulip may clear my mind, but it is not much help when it comes to preparing men for war."

"What do you mean?"

"We've been training for weeks and yet…" Gundin thought about how slow their army was developing. The younger ones were in better shape, but lacked the savvy required to grasp military strategy. The older ones understood military strategy, but were too old to spar for long periods of time.

"Don't despair," Quinn reassured. "They're developing well."

Gundin spat in frustration.

"Well enough to fight against a legion of Ebonite warriors? Hardly. Even with the best blades available, we'll be slaughtered. We need more men, Quinn. We must seek alliances with other villages."

"And violate the Oracles?"

"Does that really matter now? The Cauldron already hunts our children. We are surely next. It's only a matter of time."

"I agree that we need allies in this war, but let's not do anything rash. If we're caught seeking weapons or alliances, all hope for Galadin and Elabea will be lost. Besides, Il-Lilliad will be in the Onderling soon. My hope is that he'll rally the nations to join our cause. Now *that* would be a force to reckon with."

Gundin leaned close to smell Quinn's breath.

"Have you been drinking?"

"No," Quinn chuckled.

Gundin shook his head in disbelief.

"Then you're talking foolishness. The nations in the Onderling remained isolated even during the Dark War. They covet their independence."

"True again. But what if an event came to pass that would unite us as one?"

"Now I do believe you've been drinking."

"Dare to dream, Gundin. What if a great leader came, one who would unite us all?"

Gundin's face wrinkled at the thought. He shifted his weight from one foot to the other as he looked Quinn over.

"Are you implying *you* are this great leader?"

Quinn flashed him an incredulous look.

"No, of course not," he answered, then added with a rush of excitement, "I'm talking about a king."

"A king? Where are we to find a king? The lineage to the throne of Allsbruth was severed by Friarlinn's treachery and Brairtok's betrayal. Personally, I doubt Il-Lilliad will convince the nations of the Onderling to assist us in this war. He'll be lucky to survive."

"Perhaps. But something is happening deep within me that gives me hope. I know at first glimpse this task appears difficult, but I'm starting to believe we can accomplish it."

"Difficult? It's impossible."

"Very well, impossible. I'm reminded every morning, when I kneel over a flower like a fool, that against all odds it grows, thrives and lives. Look at it. It is surrounded by the death of winter and yet it grows. Perhaps we can too."

"Quinn, you're talking like a mad storyteller."

"Perhaps that's what we both need to become: Mad."

Gundin leaned on his staff and gazed into his friend's eyes.

They gleam with life, just like they did when you led us victoriously during the Dark War. Has there been enough change to guard against what transpired at Min Brock? Has there been enough change in me too?

"Well," Gundin answered, "it's certainly madness to wage war with this sad excuse for an army."

"Then we must work diligently with all that has been given to us."

Gundin snickered and wagged his head.

"We hit trees with wooden swords and pretend we're in combat. What sort of training is this?"

Quinn let his gaze wonder from cottage to cottage, imagining the faces of the families that slept within.

"You're right, Gundin. We could fail, and the burden of this responsibility weighs heavy upon me. I know the pain such death would bring to their loved ones. But come what may, I'd rather be buried in the field of battle, attempting to redeem my name from the shame of Min Brock, than rot in a grave in our potato field as a farmer."

Quinn reflected on the memories of Min Brock. They came every morning, ghouls from the Dark Flame, drenching him with disgrace. He knew he had a choice to make: Stand fast and face them head on, or return to his drink and perish.

His eyes wandered to his cottage; Number 17. "I abandoned Areall for my love of drink, and I pushed Elabea out of my life, out of my home." His eyes misted. In a hushed breath he added, "I may never see her again."

Quinn wiped his eyes and faced Gundin.

"I know this to be true: I can no longer live as a coward within the tears of Min Brock. This is my last chance to find redemption, to become the man I long to be for Areall and Elabea. Every morning I must make a choice. Today I choose to fight."

Gundin nodded as his eyes strayed to the tulip.

"What about you," Quinn asked him. "Do you wish to be remembered as Gundin, the great cabbage farmer?"

Gundin snapped his gaze back to Quinn.

"No," he thundered. "I'd rather die as a warrior. But we're both so vulnerable. What if you start drinking again, or I slip back to my old ways? What if Il-Lilliad and Linwith fail?"

"Then to quote Il-Lilliad, we must awaken. Perhaps the King of Claire still lives and is empowering this uprising. I have my doubts, but seeing this flower every day makes me consider the possibility.

"So we must not only train with great diligence but also renew our trust with the King of Claire. It is the only chance we have, for it will take a miracle for an army of Allsbruth to rise to power."

"That may take endless summers. I'm ready for a good fight now."

Quinn smiled as he reflected on Gundin's courage. At the Battle of the Forest of Ebon, Quinn had fallen wounded and resigned himself to his fate. From his right flank came the sound of metal-upon-metal along with men's shouts. Gundin stormed single-handedly through the Ebonite line and saved Quinn's life.

During the Battle of Gilnish, their left flank, overcome by Ebonite cavalry, began to retreat. Quinn watched helplessly, knowing that if they continued to fall back, the other flank would be exposed. Gundin ran to the weakened flank and fought with such intensity that he halted the Ebonite advance. Witnessing Gundin's bravery, the men found their courage, and with a loud battle cry, rallied and pushed the Ebonites toward the Sea of Gilden.

But that was before Min Brock.

"In time," Quinn replied, "you'll have your chance to fight. Right now, patience is our ally. Weren't you just complaining about how you needed more time because your men weren't prepared? It appears to me that now you have ample time."

"But what of Elabea and Galadin? Shouldn't we go after them?"

Quinn sighed and turned away.

"When I rode off to war, Areall stood in the doorway holding Elabea. She reached out her tiny arms like she always did when she wanted me to hold her. I thought I'd have plenty of time to cuddle her when I returned, so I just waved good-bye."

The memory was still tender and his heart throbbed like a wound that refused to heal.

"The Dark War lasted longer than any of us could have imagined, and Min Brock cost me more than I fathomed."

He stole a glance at cottage Number 17. Emotions swelled. He found it hard to swallow.

"What I wouldn't give to go back in time to hold her."

Quinn wiped his eyes. He pressed on.

"Like you, I returned not as a conquering hero, but as a broken man. To quell my shame, I drank, but whenever I sobered up the guilt returned with renewed vigor and took more and more wine to silence. Over time, Areall lost hope and Elabea retreated to her meadow. My family became yet another casualty of the Dark War."

Quinn's eyes were moist when he looked into Gundin's face. He rested a hand on his friend's broad shoulder and added, "If we leave now, we'll fail. We're simply not strong enough. My hope is that one day, we'll be ready to fight for our children."

Gundin's forehead wrinkled and he stepped away from Quinn.

"Maybe for you, but I'm ready and able now."

"Gundin, I know you're a fighter, but..."

"But what?"

"You're not healthy yet."

Gundin leaned toward Quinn.

"I'm strong *enough*."

"Really?" Quinn replied as he crossed his arms. He knew how stubborn Gundin could be as well as how blind he was to his own flaws. Quinn prepared himself mentally for a tough fight. "So you riding off to war didn't impact Galadin or Daryess?"

Gundin looked away.

Quinn chose his next words carefully, like a warrior deciding which weapons to take into combat. He wielded these words masterfully, not in an effort to hurt Gundin out of vengeance, but in an effort to lance his festering wound so that he could heal.

"Everyone in Hetherlinn watched Galadin grow up. It was easy to tell he was your son. He used sticks for swords and even swaggered about like you. Do you remember what you promised him when you road off to war?"

Gundin scowled.

"I do. You told him you'd adorn him with trophies from your victories. What did you bring home?"

"That's enough, Quinn."

"No, my friend, you need to hear this. Now answer me: What did you bring home?"

Gundin cursed beneath his breath. Quinn continued his verbal attack.

"I'll tell you: nothing but pain and a burdened heart. You may have been courageous in battle, but at home, you became a coward."

Gundin spun quickly and grabbed Quinn by the shoulders.

"Stop it."

Quinn's eyes narrowed.

"I may have become a drunkard, but you created an imaginary world where you reigned as victor."

"Shut up," Gundin spat into Quinn's face.

"Why do you think Galadin hunted all the time?"

Gundin gave him a violent shake.

"Stop it, Quinn."

"Do you really think he's proud to be your son?"

"I said, *enough*."

"Does Daryess enjoy hearing what others say about you?"

Gundin threw Quinn to the ground and straddled him with fists clinched. Quinn stared into Gundin's reddened face. He was not afraid of a swift blow, but feared his attack had been in vain and that Gundin would refuse to see the truth: that he was too wounded to fight for Galadin.

Gundin let out a deep breath and unfurled his fists. Arms dropped lifeless to his side as he stepped away. He started for his cottage, then stopped. His shoulders quivered then heaved uncontrollably. He buckled as if struck by an invisible sword. He buried his face in his hands and rocked back and forth.

Quinn rose from the dust and walked over to Gundin. He knelt beside his friend and embraced him as the tears of their failures watered the tulip of hope.

Chapter 24

The Valley of Clouds

Romlin and Elabea stood atop the bluff and took in the vista of the vast frontier that lay before them. The Mountains of Kline rising before them were only a day's journey away, and their beauty was captivating. Forever snow glistened on the peaks outlined against the azure sky. For centuries the mountains had protected Allsbruth like a cordon of warriors. Granite cliffs and ledges acted as sword, shield and buttress. That all changed when a mysterious event created a gap through the mountains, and Ebonite warriors swarmed into Allsbruth.

Elabea's eyes were glued on the gap.

"Mother told me it was formed by the Cauldron," she said. "The drone made the boulders crumble and cut the rocky mountain in two, as if with an invisible sword. When the rumbling was but an echo, a new passageway emerged from the dust."

"Waelryth," Romlin muttered, intrigued yet dismayed by its sight.

Elabea let her gaze follow the flight of an eagle soaring over the forever snow.

"How beautiful."

"You're crazy," Romlin snapped, oblivious to the raptor's flight. "Waelryth is anything *but* beautiful. It's dangerous. We're not going to simply walk through waving our parchments for protection."

Taking her eyes off the bird, she focused on Waelryth and cocked her head to the side as she studied its features.

"How do you know?" she teased. "You've never been here before."

"No, I haven't." Romlin pointed to the valley that lay between them and the mountain pass. A dense fog concealed the treetops. "But before we even get to the pass, we must travel through *that*."

In awe of the ominous mists, Romlin asked her, "Have you heard the stories of the Valley of Clouds?"

"Only that it is a place of mystery."

"Mystery? Entire columns of men have disappeared into its mists, never to be seen again."

"Why?" Elabea asked, her doe-like eyes roaming across the gray haze. "It's not that large."

"There are great beasts in that fog that prey on anything that wanders in."

She searched his face for a hint of a jest.

"You're making this up."

Romlin shook his head.

"I wish I was. I listened to the stories the old men of Hetherlinn told around the communal fire at night."

She wagged her head and snickered.

"You know better than to trust those stories from the Dark War. Those old men make up incredible stories just like..."

"My father?"

"No...I didn't mean...I meant to say...well, he does..."

Romlin clinched his jaws. His eyes narrowed.

"I didn't hear such tales from *my father*. I heard it from other men, other soldiers."

Elabea was at a loss of what to say. An uncomfortable silence enveloped them.

Romlin turned his attention back to the Valley of Clouds.

"For our sake, I hope they were lying," he sighed.

Elabea doubted the stories were true, but knew Romlin needed to feel she trusted him, so she began asking him questions.

"What do these beasts look like?"

Romlin shrugged his shoulders.

"No one knows, since no one has ever lived to tell about it."

"Maybe those old men were just trying to frighten you."

"Perhaps," he said.

Without another word he began the descent to the valley.

"Where are you going," she asked, alarm tinging her voice.

He stopped and gave her a puzzled look.

"I'm heading for the Valley of Clouds. Where do you think?"

"We're not going through now, are we?"

She bit her lip and her eyes hopped from his face, down to the valley, and then back to his face.

"Why not? You're probably right. Those were probably just old soldier's tales, each trying to outdo the other. I've hunted in the fog plenty of times. What's the worst that could happen?"

"The sun will be setting soon," Elabea countered with a nervous glance skyward.

"All the more reason to get started as soon as possible," he replied. "We have plenty of time."

She crossed her arms.

"I think we should camp here, and wait until tomorrow morning. That would allow us a full day to journey through."

Romlin's mischievous grin flared across his face.

"You're scared," he teased.

"Yes," she said, putting her hands on her hips. "And you're not?"

Romlin skewed his mouth from one side to the other. He had his reservations, but his curiosity overruled such anxiety.

"No."

"No? Why not?"

"Because I have this," he said as he touched the large shield strapped to his back. "And I have this," he said as he touched his sword.

"You haven't used them yet."

"True, but I used Il-Lilliad's, didn't I? Besides, I have you, the book and the rusk. Watch his fur. If it stands on end, then sound an alarm. His senses are better than ours."

Romlin's respect for the rusk had grown since witnessing him battle the vul jen. He would never again call him a rat.

"I would still feel better if we waited," Elabea replied, as she watched him take a few more steps down the slope.

Romlin turned back to her, his mischievous grin fading as he realized how frightened she really was. "You're really scared, aren't you?"

She gave a weak nod.

"Very well. If waiting will help you face your fears, then we'll start in the morning," he said as he trudged back up.

Elabea breathed a sigh of relief.

A high-pitched cry emanating from the valley pierced the sudden silence and reverberated off the mountain walls.

Elabea jumped.

"What was that?"

"Just a bear," Romlin reassured her, knowing full well that no animal he had ever encountered made such a horrific sound. "Let's find a place to camp."

Hoping to take her mind, as well as his, off the valley and the creatures hidden within it fog-shrouded floor, Romlin set about locating a campsite. He found one in the middle of a nearby grove of cedars.

Romlin leaned his shield against a tree while Elabea opened the book. As they sat and rested, the rusk, responded to the sound of the ruffling pages, scampered up her arm and sat on her right shoulder.

"Is Romlin telling the truth about the Valley," she asked.

"I am afraid he is, Elabea," the rusk replied.

"It doesn't look that dangerous from up here. Its length is short, and the clouds don't appear that dense. Thicker fog has settled over Hetherlinn."

The rusk only looked at her, until Elabea remember he could only answer questions.

"What makes it so dangerous," she asked.

"That is the subtlety of the Valley of Clouds. From a distance it appears harmless, but the clouds are not like the mists of Allsbruth. They are formed from the remnant vapors of the Cauldron. As long as the Cauldron burns, the Valley of Clouds will continue to exist."

"What if we rush through? Will we be safe?"

"Unfortunately, no one can do such a thing. The Cauldron's vapors disorient and deceive the senses. Romlin was right. Warriors have wandered for days, lost within the mists, only to perish from starvation, madness or the ryators."

"Ryators?"

"Wingless dragons that stand a little taller than an Allsbruthian man. Hunched over with backbones that jut out like mountains, they drag their long tails behind them when they walk. Since sunlight never reaches the valley floor, their skin is translucent. Their short arms end in long, sharp talons that they use to hold and slash their victims. Their teeth are sharper than a lion's, and their bite can sever a man in two. Because the clouds make seeing nearly impossible, they no longer have eyes, just eye sockets. They rely on their sense of smell and hearing to track their victims and..."

"Stop," Elabea commanded. "Why are you telling me this?"

"Because you asked," the rusk answered.

Elabea glanced at Romlin, who was busy gathering wood for a small fire.

"He has new weapons," she whispered so only the rusk could hear. "Will he be able to destroy them?"

"Perhaps."

"Can you?"

"Perhaps. Some."

Her heart tried to beat its way out of her chest.

"Then it's settled," she said slamming the book closed and rising to her feet. "We must journey around the Valley of Clouds."

"What," Romlin asked as he realized she was talking to him and not the rusk.

"I said we must go around the Valley of Clouds."

"We can't."

"We must. The valley is too dangerous."

"How do you know? Did the rusk talk you into this?"

"No, but he confirmed your stories about the fog and the creatures within it. They are called ryators."

"Ryators?"

"Yes. They are horrible dragons; which is why we *must* go around."

"But, Elabea, look at the map."

Romlin pulled Digri's map out of the pack, opened it and set it on the forest floor.

"We're right about here, near the Valley of Clouds," he pointed with his index finger. "If we journey as you propose," he said tracing the map with his finger, "we would have to forge the River Arrgient, and then travel to the Gilden Sea. From there we would have to journey for days by boat. Do you know how to sail? I don't."

"Then we walk. I'd rather take my chances in a boat than in *there*," she said, pointing to the valley.

"It would take too long to get around. Are you forgetting about the Ebonite warriors who are patrolling these woods right now, looking for us? Besides, you said yourself, the valley is not very long."

"I know, but after hearing about the ryators from the rusk, I know that they're too much for us."

Romlin bit his lower lip and nodded his head.

"Oh, now I see," he said, the hurt in his voice obvious. "You don't believe I'm capable of protecting you."

"I know you want to, and I don't doubt your convictions. It's just… well… I'm not sure you're ready for the challenge of the valley."

He turned away.

"I didn't mean to hurt you," she pleaded.

Romlin grabbed his shield and threw it over his back. He picked up his sword and admired the craftsmanship that had forged such a weapon. It seemed to call to him, not with an audible voice but with a quiet portentousness. And when he wrapped his hands about its hilt, purpose shot through his marrow like light from Manno Vox's bolt.

He studied the Valley of Clouds. Despite his doubts and fears, he longed to be the man-warrior his name implied more than anything, even if it meant battling ryators in the mists below.

He looked squarely into Elabea's eyes.

"I will protect you, Elabea. I've made a vow, and by my blood and sword, I *will* see it through."

Elabea's heart softened as she marveled at his determination.

"I don't doubt your word. I just wish my mind would comply with my heart."

The rusk darted off her shoulder and hovered. He faced the top of the hill with tail poised and fur up on end.

Romlin pushed Elabea behind him.

"What is it," she whispered.

He scanned the hillside, his sword battle ready. Only an occasional bird chirp could be heard.

"There."

Romlin pointed to a man's silhouette hiding behind a tree. He pulled his shield from his back and held it with his left arm while his right arm wrestled under the full weight of the sword.

"Is it an Ebonite," Elabea asked.

"Ebonites don't hide."

"Then who is it?"

"I don't know, but he's alone."

Something whizzed past Romlin's head.

"Where did *that* come from," he wondered as he stared at the small battle axe impaled in a nearby tree. "It came from a different direction."

Protecting Elabea with the shield, he scanned the woods for the other attacker.

"There," he blurted. "Wurmlins. Start backing down the hill. I'll keep an eye on them."

Before they could retreat, another object sailed his way. He raised his shield, more by instinct than training, and heard a percussive "ding" as an arrow deflected into the woods.

"That's odd," Romlin noted as they backed away and arrows fell in increasing numbers.

"What?" Elabea asked, wincing with every *ding* and *tang* of arrow against shield.

"Wurmlins only travel in packs of three. There are more than three on the hill."

A sound like thunder rumbled from the hilltop. Elabea peered around the shield to see Ebonite warhorses sailing over the ridge at full gallop.

"Run!"

Romlin pushed her ahead of him, then followed behind, keeping his shield between Elabea on the onslaught.

They sprinted down the steep grade dodging trees and bushes. Feet slid on the wet leaves and topsoil. The rusk flew protectively behind Elabea as the snorting warhorses, clanking armor and creaking leather grew louder.

"They're gaining ground," Romlin yelled without taking his eyes off their descent.

Elabea studied the valley below.

"It's too far. We can't make it," she shouted as they jumped over a fallen tree.

"Keep running," Romlin ordered, looking skyward. "Manno Vox, where are you? This time it's not my fault."

Faster," they heard an Ebonite shout. "Crush them into the ground."

The noise from the warhorses was deafening. They knew they were losing the race, but a sudden flash of light in the sky caught their attention.

"There. Did you see Manno Vox?" Romlin shouted.

"Yes."

"We'll make it now. Just keep running."

The Ebonites had also seen the great warrior, but they refused to surrender their prey.

"Summon the Cauldron's power," a voice from behind cried out. "Invoke the Gwyr."

The Gwyr's invisible force struck Elabea and Romlin like an invisible wave. Both stumbled from the impact. Romlin glanced up at Manno Vox for any sign of hope. He merely raised his right hand and pointed at them.

The Ebonites summoned the Gwyr again, and this time, Elabea screamed as both she and Romlin flew head first into the air.

Manno Vox sent a force from his outstretched arm that ripped Romlin's shield from his grip and hurled it downhill. With the same power, he transported Romlin and Elabea onto the flying shield.

"Hold on," Romlin shouted back to Elabea.

She grabbed him with one hand, and clutched the book with the other. The shield soared at knee-height downhill, and Romlin found he could steer it by shifting his weight.

Despite their increasing speed, an Ebonite warhorse pulled up along their left flank. Romlin shifted his weight. The shield darted for the warrior.

Clang.

The Ebonite sailed off his horse.

"One down, three to go," Romlin roared as they zoomed down the hill.

They reached the bottom and soared across the valley floor like a giant bird. Up ahead, dead trees marked the entrance to the Valley of Clouds. Romlin peered over his shoulder. The remaining Ebonites had gained ground and were coming fast.

"There are too many to fight," he shouted above the wind whistling in their ears. "We must go into the fog."

This time, Elabea did not argue.

As they zipped past dead trees, Romlin gazed up through the mist and spied Manno Vox. He would have sworn the shining warrior gave him an approving nod, but as the valley's fog enveloped them, he disappeared.

The shield landed with a soft *thud and* they scampered off.

"What a ride," Romlin exclaimed as he picked up the magical shield. "What do you say we go back and do that again?"

Elabea rolled her eyes as the rusk landed on her shoulder. They turned about and took in their surroundings.

The Valley of Clouds was a shadow land, a vapor of a forgotten time. Large, dead trees with ashen trunks loomed ominously in the corridor of death. Rotting vegetation and damp soil filled the air with a pungent stench. The mystical mists affected their senses.

"Everything is spinning around," Elabea said, trying to maintain her balance.

"I know," Romlin replied. He braced himself with his shield.

A sharp cry came from the shadows.

"It's the same sound we heard from the hillside," Elabea gasped as she drew close to Romlin. "Ryators."

Another beast answered from behind them. As they spun around to face it, another one called to their right followed by a bark from their left.

The creatures' ghoulish cries and barks grew in rapid succession as they crept closer.

Elabea clutched Romlin's arm. Her worst fear had come to life. They were surrounded.

Chapter 25

The Hunted Found

Newcomb marveled at the River Effron's course as it flowed toward the River Arrgient. Far ahead, large boulders and a few trees dotted the landscape surrounded by tall, brown grasses.

We're nearing the Gilden Plains, he mused.

Despite their uneventful trip, Newcomb brooded over the budding relationship between Lassiter and DeMorley.

Look at him, he fumed as he watched the minstrel prance beside Lassiter. *Dancing about like a fool. The boy is so enamored with his tales, I am not sure which of the two I despair of the most. I must watch my words. I don't want to be the reason Lassiter abandons his invitation's wooing.*

Newcomb checked to make sure they were not being followed, then announced, "We will rest beside those boulders up ahead."

"Thank goodness," DeMorley chimed. "You've pushed our pace now for three days."

When they reached the outcrop of boulders, Newcomb and Lassiter sauntered down to the river's edge while DeMorley pulled himself up on a nearby rock.

Perched at the summit, he swung his lute from around his back, plucked the taut strings, then stopped and turned one of the tuning pegs to adjust its sound. More plucks, a dissatisfied scowl and another adjustment were followed by quick strums.

"What are you doing," Newcomb asked as he scooped up some cool water.

"I thought I'd entertain you," DeMorley answered as he continued to strum. "No offense to you, but this journey has been boring."

"None taken," Newcomb replied. "No offense to you, but this is not the time. We must leave soon."

"Please let him sing a song," Lassiter begged. "You've had us on edge with every step we've taken. I expect Ebonite warhorses to charge out at any second. I agree with DeMorley, we need some entertainment."

"Our journey is not intended as entertainment," Newcomb countered, submerging his hands for another drink. "Be thankful it *has* been dull. Such dullness keeps us alive."

"But we do need a rest. You, especially."

Newcomb raised his hands to his mouth and slurped up the water.

"Maybe you're right. A brief respite may reenergize us all." With a stern look at the minstrel, he added, "No tavern songs - and whatever you do, sing softly."

"Sing softly? I can't truly express the genuine feelings my songs convey without singing with great enthusiasm."

"Suit yourself," Newcomb answered with a wave of his hand. "Go ahead and sing as loudly as you wish. Invite every thief, assassin and Ebonite warrior in the area to come join us."

DeMorley pursed his lips and scowled.

"So be it. I will sing softly. But only because *I* choose to."

Newcomb perched himself on another boulder to distance himself from DeMorley. Lassiter, on the other hand, sat at the musician's feet, eagerly awaiting the song like a child expecting a surprise gift.

DeMorley began to strum his lute.

"Quietly," Newcomb demanded.

The minstrel glared back, but softened his strum.

"I've been writing this song since we left Torrens Bay," DeMorley announced with great pride.

Lassiter's eyes widened.

"You're able to compose music within your head without using your instrument?"

He looked at Newcomb to see if his mentor was equally amazed. Newcomb yawned.

"Yes," DeMorley replied with a smile as he soaked up the attention. "Amazing, isn't it?"

Lassiter nodded. DeMorley looked at Newcomb in hopes of receiving an approving nod. Instead, Newcomb mouthed, *jester*. Infuriated, DeMorley turned his attention squarely upon his audience of one.

"The song goes like this."

He closed his eyes, strummed his instrument and began to sing.

Three journey hard from Torrens Bay,
To battle what may come their way.
In search of gold and maidens fair,
So they travel on to Claire.

A parchment white with letters gold,
To heed an invite so I am told.
A handsome boy, an artist grand,
With a fool who's an old, old man.

Treasure, treasure,
Their fame awaits in Claire.
Glory, glory,
The trio journeys there.

Newcomb touts he is the best,
He doubts I can pass the test.
But closely look and you shall see,
He is dumb as dumb can be.

Newcomb, Newcomb,
Frightens maidens away,
Newcomb, Newcomb,
Like a mule that brays.

Two sets of eyes peered at the trio from behind a thicket. The song echoed to them from a small man perched on a boulder. Beneath him, a boy rolled on the ground in laughter. Sitting on a rock some distance away was an older man. His arms were crossed, and his back was to the pair.

"This will be easier than I'd hoped." The voice came from a man of twenty summers from Torrens Bay. He bore a small arsenal of weapons necessary for his newest profession: bounty hunter.

By his side stood his partner, a man of formidable size and strength who had survived forty-seven summers. Auburn hair plummeted down to his shoulders like a lion's mane. With eyes that appeared as cold as ice, he viewed life and death simply as business. His nose was long and straight and rose like a monolith upon his high cheekbones. A wicked scar ran from his left cheek down to the corner of his mouth.

The older man carried a crossbow, and had two thick, black leather straps that crisscrossed his burly chest. One strap held a black leather sheath that housed a large sword he wore on his back, the pommel and hilt angled up and away over his right shoulder. A small yet deadly-looking weapon made from white bone was secured to the other strap, and hung at his chest. On his left hip rested a short quiver of crossbow bolts, and hanging from his right hip was a dagger. A thick belt about his stomach held a sling made of brown leather, and next to it was a pouch full of steel orbs the size of small oranges.

His tan shirt and brown pants were snug, and black boots consumed his breeches all the way up to his knees. On the outside of his boots were two small sheaths that concealed knives to use as a last defense.

"Do not find comfort in the appearance of the moment, Paradin," the older man said, based on his experience tracking people for pay.

"I'm not finding comfort, Draemel. I'm simply excited about how rich I'll be."

"Whether we kill him or take him alive is only half the problem," Draemel answered. "We still have to return him to the magistrate in order to receive our reward."

"I say dead. Less problems traveling," Paradin snapped as he drew his favorite weapon; a sinister-looking dagger with a slight curve to its blade.

"Spoken like a novice hunter. Have you not smelled the stench of death? It'll draw every gor and fortune hunter in the region. I don't relish having to fight off either kind of scavenger."

Paradin snickered.

"I'm not afraid. Either way, let's take him. I want to see his face when I put this under his throat."

"Not yet."

"Why not? You and me against those three is hardly anything to fret over."

"The minstrel and the boy worry me not. It's the older one I must study."

"Him?" Paradin gave a derisive snort. "He's old and weak."

"Older, perhaps. Weak? I'm not so certain."

"You're getting too cautious in your old age. Women of Torrens Bay have more courage."

Draemel snatched Paradin by the shirt and pulled him close. With a speed that belied his bulk, he unsheathed his white-boned weapon and pressed it into Paradin's gullet.

Created from a single large gor bone, it was a wicked purveyor of death. Fixed into its handle were three blades. The first was long and thin; perfect for jabbing. A curved blade, jutting from the bottom was used for slicing. The third—protruding from the middle of the handle—was stocky and jagged, capable of ripping large chunks of flesh with one slash.

Paradin's eyes widened. He knew all too well the stories of Draemel torturing his victims with his gor weapon. It was said Draemel savored every scream and the sound of tearing flesh. He looked into Draemel's eyes. They were as gray and cold as a winter's day.

"Your tone of voice is beginning to annoy me," Draemel whispered. "Do you know what happens when I get annoyed?"

"Yes. Yes, I'm sorry, Draemel," Paradin licked his lips. "It's just that we've been tracking him for so long. Now he sits in the open like a fat cow."

Draemel released him, re-sheathed the gor blade then picked up the crossbow.

"We'll move closer," Draemel instructed. "Keep your eyes on the gray-haired one. Especially watch that animal on his shoulder."

"The squirrel? Why? What can *it* do?"

"Nothing. Unless the man is a storyteller."

"A storyteller?" Paradin chuckled. "They were destroyed in the Dark War."

"Perhaps. I've heard tavern tales that say otherwise. Since you're so confident, I'll let you handle him while I will get the other two."

Paradin took a harder look at the older man on the rock. He had heard about storytellers and their power, but had assumed they were simply tavern tales enlarged by too much drink. The man on the rock did not look like the wielder of incomprehensible power.

"Very well," Paradin said. "We'll do it your way."

The bounty hunters crept toward the trio.

Newcomb heard a slight scraping sound, and stood up on his rock to find its source. Lassiter continued to laugh while DeMorley performed.

"Quiet," Newcomb said. The music continued. "I said *quiet.*"

Lassiter tried to stifle his laughter and DeMorley let the song fade.

"What is it," Lassiter asked between chuckles.

"Something is out there."

"You're bluffing," DeMorley chirped. "You just don't like my song."

"Silence, fool," Newcomb snapped. "Look at the rusk."

Newcomb had nursed the animal with great care and his efforts were beginning to pay off. The rusk hovered in front of Newcomb, its fur standing up on end, and his tail underneath poised to strike.

"What's it doing?" Lassiter asked.

"It's doing what rusks do. Alerting us that danger is near and preparing to fight."

"Danger?"

DeMorley fumbled his lute only to snatch it again. Realizing he was an easy target sitting high upon the rock, he slid down to a safer position.

"No one followed us," he said while peering from behind the giant rock. "I may be a minstrel, but I know when I'm being followed."

Newcomb had also climbed down and had drawn his dagger. He kept his eyes glued in the direction the rusk faced but saw nothing.

"I don't see anyone," Lassiter said as he shielded his eyes and peered about. "Perhaps the rusk made a mistake."

"Rusks don't make mistakes. DeMorley, take the boy behind those rocks."

"Me? What am I to do?"

"Protect him."

"With what? I don't have a weapon?"

"Use that instrument you are unable to play as a weapon. Improvise. Just go. Now."

DeMorley did as Newcomb commanded. Feeling better that they were out of harm's way, Newcomb advanced in the direction the rusk was facing.

"Be my eyes, rusk. Be my ears, rusk," he whispered to the faithful animal.

The rusk fluttered forward. Newcomb tried to watch the horizon and the animal at the same time. A rustling came from his left. Newcomb started toward the sound, but stopped when he heard DeMorley scream. He turned to run back to their aid.

"One more step and I'll drop you."

Draemel stepped in front of him, his crossbow leveled at Newcomb's stomach.

Newcomb stopped.

Paradin, bearing a wicked smile, herded Lassiter and DeMorley out from the rocks.

"I told you it would be easy," he shouted to Draemel.

"Quiet," Draemel commanded. He turned his attention to Newcomb. "Order that animal down, *now.*"

Newcomb hesitated, hoping to stall long enough to allow the rusk to attack.

Draemel trained his crossbow on Lassiter. "Do it, or the boy dies."

Newcomb whistled, and the rusk landed on his shoulder.

"Now," Draemel said. "Drop your weapon, if you please."

Newcomb's dagger plopped into the tall grass.

"If nobody moves, then nobody dies," Draemel said.

Newcomb's mind raced as he considered his options.

"Let me kill him now," Paradin shouted.

"Shut up," Draemel barked. "We're not going to kill him. Not yet anyway."

Draemel was within a sword's strike away from Newcomb.

"Turn and walk back to your friends, but be very careful. One false step and it will be your last."

Newcomb considered lunging, but knew it was too risky. He turned and did as ordered.

"Paradin," Draemel said as he scooped up Newcomb's dagger. "Make them lie down, then come here."

Paradin did as ordered, his eyes dancing in anticipation of their reward and the possibility of slitting their throats.

"I was right, was I not," Paradin bragged. "Easiest money you ever made."

Draemel ignored him. He was still studying the situation. Finally, to Paradin he said, "We'll take him and kill the others."

Paradin's eyes danced madly.

"Where are you taking the boy?" Newcomb asked.

"The *boy?*" Paradin chortled. "We're not taking the *boy* anywhere. The *boy* is going to die with you."

"But..." Newcomb held his tongue, perplexed. He assumed the bounty hunters were after Lassiter. Realizing they did not know the boy's true identity, he not only had to plan their escape, but do so while maintaining their secret.

"But...what," Draemel asked.

"But... why do you want to kill us?" Newcomb answered.

"Because we can," Paradin snarled.

"Let's just say," Draemel answered, "that you had the misfortune of traveling with the wrong man."

Newcomb glanced at DeMorley. "You mean..."

"That's right. We want *this* one," Paradin gloated, pointing his blade at the minstrel.

Newcomb and Lassiter looked at DeMorley in disbelief.

"Why him," Lassiter asked. "He's just a minstrel."

"Didn't he tell you his story?" Draemel asked, then allowed himself the luxury of a good laugh.

"Go ahead, DeMorley, tell your friends why we're here. You at least owe them that before they die."

DeMorley flashed Newcomb and Lassiter a nervous smile.

"They're from Ingloid," he stammered. "Remember? I owe them some money."

Newcomb's brow wrinkled. The information did not add up to this result.

"You tracked DeMorley all the way from Ingloid, just because he did not perform some songs?"

"Is *that* your story?" Draemel chortled to DeMorley. "You're more of a weasel than I suspected. Come now; tell them the *real* story."

DeMorley's face drained of color. "I robbed someone," he stammered.

"Not just someone," Paradin added. "The Lord-Counselor of Ingloid."

"Yes, yes, very well. I stole the Lord-Counselor's parchment."

"And?"

"And his jewels, gold and coins."

"You're leaving out the best part of the story," Paradin interjected. "You remember, DeMorley; the part about where you murdered him in his sleep?"

DeMorley's mouth dropped open. "Wh-wh-what?"

"You stabbed him, right in the heart, while he slept," Paradin exclaimed, drunk with the thought of murder even if done by another's blade. "Stabbed him at least a dozen times. I congratulate you. I didn't think a skinny little weasel such as yourself would have it in you."

"What? No. I did no such thing. Yes, I stole his lute, and his money, and his invitation, but I didn't kill him. I'm not a murderer."

"There must be some sort of mistake," Newcomb interjected. "He may be guilty of being a cheat and a liar, but this man's not capable of murder. Surely you can see that."

"No mistake," Draemel replied. "There is a price on his head. And I didn't travel this far only to discover...a *mistake.*"

"What proof is there of his crime?"

"They found his hat by the bed, and the Lord-Counselor had a parchment crumpled in his hand. It was written by DeMorley."

"Yes," DeMorley exclaimed in defense. "That was the song I told you about, Newcomb. I composed a love song for a woman he was interested in. I must have left my hat there by mistake."

"Your guilt or innocence is not my concern," Draemel answered without a hint of the emotion that animated Paradin. "We'll let the courts decide that. Paradin, secure DeMorley. I'll go take care of these two."

"Why do you get all of the fun?" Paradin whined.

"Because you enjoy it too much."

Draemel motioned with his crossbow for Newcomb and Lassiter to move away from DeMorley.

"Please, Newcomb," DeMorley wept. "Don't let them take me away. I swear on all the tales of Claire; I did not commit murder."

"Does it really matter," Newcomb answered as they walked away. "Your lies have finally caught you. If you're telling the truth, the courts will find you innocent and you will live. We, on the other hand..."

DeMorley continued crying as Draemel led them away.

"You got what you were hunting for. Why not let us go," Newcomb asked Draemel.

"Sorry. The reason I've been successful for this many seasons is because I don't make careless, emotional decisions. With you both dead, I have less to worry about."

"That's too bad," Newcomb countered, baiting the hunter.

"Why," Draemel asked.

"You'll not receive the reward and treasure we are seeking in Claire."

Draemel stopped.

"Treasure? What treasure? Claire is nothing but a wasteland. The Ebonites destroyed it in the Dark War."

"Perhaps. Perhaps not. The truth is on a parchment inside my cloak. May I show it to you?"

Draemel cocked his left eyebrow as well as his weapon. Aiming it at Lassiter's chest, he said, "Yes, but any sudden moves or surprises and I'll kill the boy."

Newcomb pulled out the white parchment and held it out.

"Put it on the ground and back away," Draemel ordered.

Newcomb did as commanded.

With his eyes glued on Newcomb and his finger ready to squeeze the trigger, Draemel leaned down and retrieved the invitation. He studied it using quick glances. Although not an educated man, he had learned bits and pieces of different dialects while hunting throughout the nations. Reading only a few of the words confirmed enough of Newcomb's honesty to whet his appetite.

"So?" Draemel replied.

"So," Newcomb repeated. "How much are they paying you for DeMorley?"

"3,000 gilns alive. 1,500 if he is dead."

"That is fine pay, but *this* is from the King of Claire. He does exist, and I know for a fact that he rewards better than anyone from Torrens Bay or Ingloid. If you let us go, we will give you our reward. It will be more than three thousand gilns."

"I can take DeMorley back," Draemel replied, "then go to Claire myself."

"You do not simply walk into Claire and demand treasure from the Only. Besides, these are personalized. They can be used only by us."

"How do I know you won't double-cross me?"

Newcomb slowly reached back into his tunic and pulled out his coin purse. He tossed the bag at Draemel's feet.

"Allow me to make a down payment on what we will owe you later."

Draemel reached down and retrieved the purple cloth bag, without taking his eyes off of Newcomb. The bag's weight felt good in his palm. Using his teeth, he loosened the drawstring that secured the top and glanced inside. Even in the shadows, the jewels and golden coins glittered. He estimated the contents to be worth more than two thousand gilns. A wolfish grin split his face.

"That was foolish. Now I can kill you both and still take this."

"You would have done that anyway. By letting us live, you will receive more treasure than you can possibly carry. Did you know that DeMorley has an invitation, too?"

Draemel glanced back at the minstrel. He was pleading for mercy with Paradin who was toying him with his curved blade.

"Paradin," Draemel shouted.

The younger bounty hunter stopped his antics to look Draemel's way.

"See if the minstrel has an invitation, like this."

Draemel held up Newcomb's invitation. Paradin nodded and searched the musician's cloak. He pulled it out and held it high for Draemel to see.

"What does it say?" Paradin shouted back.

Draemel, thankful his young protégé never troubled with learning to read, shouted back, "It says there's been a mistake."

He motioned for Newcomb and Lassiter to head back toward Paradin and DeMorley, then ordered the trio to lie face down on the ground.

"What mistake?" Paradin asked. "I don't see no mistake."

"You," Draemel replied. "My mistake was, I brought you."

In a smooth, swift motion, Draemel leveled his crossbow at Paradin and squeezed the trigger. Paradin, eyes stunned, dropped to the ground like a sack of potatoes. Draemel dropped the crossbow and unsheathed his sword.

"Stay down," he ordered the trio. "Any sudden moves and I'll slice off an arm."

"What about him," Lassiter asked, nodding toward Paradin, who was moaning in pain, his bloody hands struggling to pull the crossbow bolt from his chest.

"He'll be dead when the sun sets tomorrow."

"You cannot do that," Newcomb interjected. "He needs our help."

"You're quite right," Draemel replied. Raising a warning finger he added. "You stay right here and don't do anything stupid. I'll go help him."

Draemel sheathed his sword and marched to Paradin. Yanking him up off the ground, he pulled out his gor blade. Paradin screamed as Draemel dragged him kicking to a tree.

Draemel threw him to the ground and retrieved a short length of rope from his pocket. Still keeping an eye on the trio, he tied his former partner to the tree.

"There," Draemel said with a firm yank on the knot, and a wicked smile on his face. "I've helped. Now the gors will have no problem finding him."

Draemel placed two fingers in his mouth and whistled. A horse whinnied in reply, and the sound of galloping hooves could be heard. From around an outcrop of boulders Draemel and Paradin's steeds appeared. Draemel gathered in the reins of his stallion, a black animal with matching saddle and saddlebags. A double-handed sword hung sheathed on the animal's left side.

He snatched up his crossbow, placed his boot in the weapon's stirrup and cocked the weapon. With a spring, he mounted his horse, noched a bolt and aimed it down at the trio.

"Now, slowly get up. Boy, take these and tie your friends' hands."

Some ropes landed at Lassiter's feet.

"Now, mount Paradin's horse."

Lassiter complied with Draemel's orders, feeling he had no choice. He tied his companions' hands together, then walked over and gathered the animal's reins. It was dark brown with black saddle and saddlebags. He looked for a weapon but found none. He mounted and Draemel ordered him to move in front of him.

"You two walk behind his horse. I'll follow. One false move and I'll kill the boy."

With Lassiter in the lead, the entourage started out across the Gilden Plains. When Draemel and his prisoners crossed the last high ridge, Lassiter took one last look back. Paradin, delirious from the pain, cursed them by all he considered holy.

"*Draemel,*" echoed the cry of the doomed man. "You'll never get away. I will find you. *I will...*"

Chapter 26

Battle Within

Elabea and Romlin stood back to back as the ryators' barks neared.

Beyond the Valley of Clouds echoed the taunts of the Ebonite warriors.

"The ryators will do our job for us," one shouted while the others laughed.

"What do we do," Elabea asked.

"We must get through this fog. Come on, this is the way out," Romlin said.

"No, it's not," Elabea countered, grabbing his cloak. "That's how we came in."

"No, I am positive that *this* is the way out."

As they argued the ryators closed in around them.

"Romlin, the fog is confusing us. We don't know which way to go."

Romlin nodded as he put his shield over his back. He drew his dagger and extended it, hilt-first, toward Elabea.

"Here. You're going to need this."

She took the dagger and looked at its blade. It did not bring her comfort.

"No," she said handing it back to him. "I wouldn't know what to do with it."

Romlin shook his head in frustration and sheathed the blade.

The rusk roosted on Elabea's right shoulder. Peace settled over her as she gazed into its black eyes. She drew in a deep breath, knelt on the valley floor and opened the book.

"What are you doing?" Romlin blurted. "Now's not the time for a story."

She ignored him and tried to shut out the horrible sounds encircling her.

"Rusk, what I am to do?"

"Read the words."

"I can't read."

"Touch the words, as you have before. They will speak. They will roar. Then repeat what they say."

Elabea stared at the open pages. The letters rose and fell, as if breathing deeply in anticipation of a great battle. She lowered her fingers toward them. Heat rose up from the page. Her fingers shrank back.

"Do not stop," the rusk ordered. "Touch them."

Her index finger continued once more.

"Elabea," Romlin commanded, "the ryators are here. Drop the book. Stand and fight."

She hesitated.

"No," the rusk argued. "*This* is your fight. Touch the words. Read them. Let them consume you."

She closed her eyes, and raucous sounds fell like wolves upon her senses. She felt the drone pull at her strength like a powerful ocean current, draining her energy, making her feel lethargic and weary. Horrid shrieks from the ryators restrained her finger from touching the words. A distant whisper swirled about this cacophony wooing her away from her troubles. She focused upon its tone and longed for it to whisk her away.

"Elabea. Ignore the whisper," the rusk commanded.

"But it is from Claire and…"

"No, it is the Cauldron. It is an imitation. Touch the words."

The sounds swirled, roaring like tempest winds.

The whisper called to her.

"Child, why do you fear? Would I allow harm to come to one as wondrous as you?"

The rusk scampered down her arm and stroked her hand.

"Fight, Elabea. Ignore the false whisper's lie. Touch the words."

"Fight?" the whisper soothed. *"For what? Only I can offer you what you truly desire - acceptance."*

Elabea fought through the clamorous sounds and with all her strength, pushed her hand toward the page. Her fingertips touched the ridge of a word and a sweet melody filled her troubled heart and battled the dark drone from Ebon. Warmth like the dawn's first rays filled her whole being. Whispers of an unknown origin flew about in her mind like eagles around a mountain's summit.

"Elabea," Romlin roared, his sword at the ready. "They're upon us."

Elabea's eyes flew open, expecting to see the ravenous jaws of an attacking ryator. Instead, she was engulfed in the book. The letters were no longer black, but ivory. They stood above the parchment pages like row upon row of warriors. She stroked them; they were no longer soft, but were smooth as polished brass and strong as Tristan steel. They tugged at her and she found herself wanting to immerse herself deep within.

A ryator's bark sent a chill through her. She stopped stroking the page.

"Elabea," the rusk pleaded. "Ignore the dragons. Listen to the words."

She closed her eyes once more. The simple melody continued to battle the drone and a new whisper pierced the battle of sounds like a clarion call.

"*Elabea,*" it called. "*My delight.*"

"The true whisper," the rusk announced. "Repeat what it says."

Elabea nodded, clinched her eyes shut and stuttered the whisper's words.

"From land immortal my stories fly; tales of light my battle cry. Return Dark Flame to endless despair, behold the whisper that hails from Claire."

"You are speaking from the head," the rusk instructed. "Announce them from the heart."

"But I'm frightened," Elabea cried out. "I can hear the ryators...the drone...the Cauldron."

"Elabea," Romlin's anxious shout pierced her heart. "It's time to stand and fight. Close that book. They come."

"Ignore him," the rusk ordered. "Listen only to the whisper. Shout the words."

The first whisper spoke again.

"*Why fight when those you love have hurt you the most? It is the stories of Claire that have cast you into this despair, have they not?*"

The whisper from Claire increased in volume, drowning out the false whisper. The Cauldron shook off the tender melody, abandoned its charm and returned with an icy whisper like cracking ice.

"*So be it, homely child.*"

The Cauldron's whisper urged the ryators forward.

"*Shriek for first blood, my beloved dragons. Let the world know the power within.*"

The ryators howled in response. Romlin scanned the dense fog. The outlines of the creatures were discernible. Even through the fog they looked more ferocious than he had imagined.

The war of whispers raged deep within Elabea, whisper against whisper, drone against melody and disdain against delight. She was frozen in fear when a vision appeared in her mind. Men and women of unknown origin stood on a mountain ridge, their faces radiant, with parchments clutched tightly in their hands. Behind them sat the massive countenance of Manno Vox, at the head of a legion of warriors of similar proportion. Rising high above them all was another whose form she had never seen before. She tried to discern his features, but it was like trying to look into the noonday sun. The vision disappeared, and the second whisper, the true whisper, roared.

"*Do not fear, my delight. You do not battle alone.*"

With all the courage she could muster, she spoke from the heart.

"From land immortal my stories fly; tales of light my battle cry. Return Dark Flame to endless despair, behold the whisper that hails from Claire."

"Good," the rusk urged, taking to the wind and hovering nearby. "Again. *Again.*"

"From land immortal my stories fly. Tales of light my battle cry. Return Dark Flame to endless despair, *behold the whisper that hails from Claire.*"

"Faster. Louder."

Each time Elabea repeated the phrase with more intensity and passion, she felt the fog's effects diminish, and the Cauldron's taunts fall away like the echo from distant thunder. As the drone's weightiness retreated, she felt light and free. She heard herself shout the words, but it was as if she were listening to someone else from atop her oak. Despite the ensuing attack, she felt safe.

Romlin took his eyes off his adversaries for a moment and glanced at Elabea. His mouth fell open.

She held the book open in her palms. Her eyes were closed. She hovered in the air out of reach of the ryators. Her entire body twinkled with light and sparks flew off her as if from a great fire. As her passion grew, so did her radiance, illuminating the fog's gloom.

A familiar voice interrupted Romlin's reverie.

"Romlin. Turn and fight."

Romlin spun around, looking for Manno Vox.

"I hear you, but I don't see you."

The great warrior spoke again.

"Gone is Galadin. Behold Romlin, warrior for the Only."

The ryators emerged from the shadow of the mist and into Elabea's light. Romlin prepared for battle. His blade glowed orange.

A loud, cry erupted from overhead. Instinctively, Romlin stepped to the side and thrust his sword into the air. The blade pierced the leaping ryator through the mid-section. He yanked his sword free and swung at the next attacker, slicing it in two.

The sounds of snapping jaws surrounded him. Struck in the back, he cried out in pain and spun around. The shield on his back saved his life. With a mighty swing, his glowing blade hacked off the attacking dragon's jaw. He charged the beast and slammed it to the ground with a sharp kick. Swinging his blade from overhead, he split it from head to sternum.

Romlin pulled off his shield and dropped it to the ground. It rose into the air, and he hopped aboard. Kneeling, he darted about the battleground. His senses were sharp and alive, and he attacked with a ferocity he had never known before.

A small ryator jumped from a nearby tree, knocked him off his shield and sent his sword flying out of his grip. The ryator pinned Romlin down. It opened its mouth and hissed, its reptilian tongue dodging about rows of sharp teeth. Romlin grabbed its neck to hold it at bay as it snapped its jaws and lunged at Romlin's head.

"Death comes for you, boy-warrior," the Cauldron barked through the voice of the ryator. "You shall die not as Romlin, but as Galadin, the son of a madman."

The ryator's tiny forearms slashed at his chest, but Romlin managed to wrap his legs around them and pinned them to its side. As they wrestled, Romlin's wound consumed his strength, his muscles weakened.

Sensing Romlin's dilemma, Manno Vox's voice thundered up and down the Valley of Clouds, "Behold the warrior, Romlin, Son of Gundin, Conqueror for the King of Claire."

Hearing his new name revived Romlin's tired muscles. With a loud grunt, he rolled and pushed the dragon to the ground. He whipped out his dagger and thrust it between the dragon's ribs.

Romlin hopped off the dragon and dove for his sword. The wounded ryator regained its feet and charged. Romlin hurled the weapon end-over-end and struck the beast square in the chest. Catapulted backward, the ryator was impaled to a tree. The beast's death scream rattled within Netniath's darkened halls.

Defeated, the Cauldron's whisper roared in rage and retreated from the fight.

Romlin approached the dead dragon, grabbed the sword's hilt, placed his foot on the creature's torso, and yanked it free with one swift jerk.

The rusk whispered into Elabea's ear, and she drifted back down to the valley floor. The light within her faded as she opened her eyes to behold the carnage in the Valley of Clouds. Lying all about her were dead and dying ryators, and standing in the midst of the carnage was Romlin. His shirt was ripped and bloody, but his face beamed.

"You're wounded," she exclaimed as she darted for him.

"It's not that bad," he grimaced as she touched his wound.

"You destroyed them single-handedly?"

She tore off a piece of her long tunic to bind up his wounded back.

"Yes," he said somewhat amazed himself. "But I couldn't have done it without you. You were amazing."

"Me? What did I do?"

She dabbed his wound with the cloth.

"You lit up this area like the communal fires from Hetherlinn. I could even hear you within my head, warning me when I was being attacked."

"I did?"

"You don't remember?"

"No. I just remember hearing their jaws snapping, the rusk's voice and...and..."

"And what?"

She stopped tending his wound to reflect.

"I think I saw him."

"Who?"

"The King of Claire. But it was like a dream, and it happened so fast. Then I heard a song; and the whisper. They were so beautiful and peaceful, and I felt like I was soaring over our meadow."

"Well, forget what I said about not being the right time for a story. Open the book *any* time trouble comes."

They looked at each other with something more than admiration. Their friendship was blossoming into something deeper and stronger than either could explain. Elabea started to say as much when a new sound interrupted her thoughts.

"More ryators?"

"No." A grim frown creased Romlin's face as he gripped his sword hilt tighter. "It's the Ebonite warriors. They're coming this way."

"Won't the fog disorient them?"

"I doubt it. The Cauldron empowers Ebonites. It doesn't confuse them."

Romlin picked up his shield that had come to rest atop of a dead ryator. He tried to make it hover, but it fell powerless to the valley floor.

"I suppose it only flies when I do battle," he said.

He slung it over his back and winced in pain when it struck his wound. He let his gaze find Elabea. There was still a soft glow about her, and the book remained open in her hands. The mist closed in about him again, corrupting his senses. He felt disoriented.

"Elabea," he said as he put a hand on his forehead in hope of easing the dizziness. "I need your help. Is this the correct way out?"

"Yes," she answered. "The fog is not affecting me as before. I suppose it has something to do with the stories I just read."

Side by side, they journeyed out of the Valley of Clouds toward Waelryth as the rusk few overhead.

Moments after they disappeared into the gathering fog, three Ebonites rode into the clearing full of the dismembered corpses of ryators.

"Impossible," one roared as he surveyed the battlefield. "A boy and girl could not have destroyed so many."

"I agree," the second replied. "They must have had help. But look. No blood."

"You've forgotten who she is," the third and oldest warrior explained. "She is to become a storyteller. Has it been so long that our youth don't remember the power of such?"

"With all due respect, commander, those are myths," the youngest of the three retorted.

"Does this look like the work of a myth," their commander countered.

The younger warriors surveyed the carnage, shaking their heads. They had no answer.

"Dismount," the commander ordered. "We'll track them on foot. The fog is thick. They will be disoriented. I'll not lose them now."

They dismounted. With reins in hand, the commander bent over and examined Romlin and Elabea's footprints.

"What's this?"

He dabbed at a small pool of dark liquid on the ground. He examined his gloved finger and smiled.

"Blood *was* spilt. One of them is wounded. Let's hurry. Death begets death."

With a quickened pace, he marched into the fog.

"Storytellers? Dead ryators? Whispers from Claire? What manner of tales are these," one warrior mused.

The other simply shook his head, and together they followed their commander into the fog. Using Ebonite logic and the wisdom of the Oracles they tried to answer such riddles. But as hard as they reasoned, their battle-hardened minds could not dismiss what their eyes beheld. Such revelation birthed a feeling neither had experienced before.

Fear.

Chapter 27

A Deadly Pact

Paradin's head drooped on his chest. Draemel's crossbow bolt protruded from his upper torso. With the metallic, salty tang of blood thick upon his tongue, his mind wandered close to death. Only one thought kept him alive: killing Draemel. It was his one hope.

A noise pierced his haggard senses, jerking him back from death's abyss like a taut rope. He struggled to raise his head. A pack of gors slipped from boulder to boulder, sniffing the wind, attracted to his dying flesh and precarious position.

Paradin's heart raced. His mouth dried up and his mind churned wildly. He tried to deny the fact that gors would soon be dining upon his flesh. He jerked at the ropes, but his desperate movements only managed to cut his wrists causing his blood to spill faster.

"Draemel, I'll kill you," he muttered in the direction his former partner had fled. "Whether as a man or as a spirit, I will find you!"

Paradin dropped his head, surrendering to the inevitability of death. Yet, a new scent; an acrid scent; the scent of hope wafted past his nostrils. He inhaled deeply; lungs pumping wildly. The Cauldron's vapor dispersed throughout his body, and he welcomed its effects: invigorating and purposeful. Had it always been so present, so powerful? Or was this something one only experienced nearing death?

A soft, gentle whisper called to him.

"Do you desire Draemel?"

"Yes. Yes."

"Then let go. Surrender."

"But what will happen?"

"All your dreams will come true."

"But I'm dying and..."

"Yield."

"But how..."

"Surrender all."

Paradin opened up the last chamber of his will. Within this sanctuary were the countless disappointments and pains from his life. They had fueled his beliefs, his values and his identity. The tiny vestige also held the only innocence he had ever known. The whisper surrounded it.

Paradin heard another whisper, similar to the first, yet somehow different.

"Fly to me, Paradin."

"Who are you?"

"The King of Claire."

"Ignore him, Paradin," the first whisper instructed. *"He desires to destroy you."*

"I offer life. Delight. The Cauldron offers only..."

"Revenge, Draemel. Can the King of Claire offer you revenge?"

Paradin pondered his decision as the two whispers warred against each other.

"Are you not deserving of such sweet, sweet vengeance?" the Cauldron whispered.

"Yes," Paradin muttered, "Yes. *Yes.*"

Paradin released his will and the Cauldron consumed what remained of his soul.

The whisper from Claire cried in anguish, but it was not out of self-pity at losing the fight. It wept for Paradin's choice.

The Ebonite commander watched his two scouts gallop back across the plain.

"Report," he snapped when they were close.

"He sits alone, tied to a tree," one stated.

"Why is he making all that racket," the commander asked as he studied the landscape before them.

Even from this distance the man's silhouette was plain against the horizon. He could hear him babbling, and see his head bobbing about.

"Sir, he's singing."

"Singing?"

"Yes sir," the second added. "He's badly wounded and yet sings."

"He must be drunk," the first concluded.

They listened to the distant melody.

"Draw your blades," the commander ordered. "We'll investigate. Be on your guard."

As they encircled him, the commander studied the dying man. Coagulated blood stained both his face and shirt. Despite the bolt in his chest, he sang with great gusto, and his head flipped about to his song's odd-metered cadence. The song was dark and brisk with a staccato refrain, but its words were strange, haunting, and barely intelligible.

"What tongue is that," one warrior asked. "He's obviously not Ebonite, and yet his words sound familiar."

Paradin continued to sing, oblivious to the circle of warriors.

"It is Ebonite," the commander answered, "but it's an ancient dialect. He's singing something about glory…honor…first blood…"

"Look, commander, he's drunk *and* blind. He doesn't see us."

Paradin took a break from his dark melody.

"Oh, blind I'm not." He gazed up at the men. "I see you all very well. You, warriors of Ebon, are the ones who are blind."

"Look at his eyes," one warrior muttered beneath his breath. "He's not drunk. He's mad."

Paradin's eyes moved independently of each other. One rolled about, focusing on nothing, while the other blinked bird-like and darted from warrior to warrior. The battle hardened Ebonites drew back from his evil, crazed gaze.

Paradin addressed the warriors in his mad, singsong manner.

"Set me free. Set me free, and I'll set you free."

The commander motioned for one of his men to cut him loose. Once the cord was severed, Paradin leapt to his feet, and before they could react, sprang like a mountain lion upon the back of the commanding officer's horse. In a flash, Paradin withdrew the officer's dagger and pressed it against his throat.

"I promise what I promise. See what I say? Set me free, and I'll set you free."

Hate danced in Paradin's eyes as he held the officer with unnatural strength. The warriors were about to attack when their commander motioned for them to stand down.

"What do you want," the commander asked, the blade pressed hard through his beard and against his flesh.

"What I want is what you want. I want Draemel."

"Who's Draemel?"

"The man you want you see, you see."

"You have the tongue of a madman. I don't know what you are talking about. The Cauldron has sent us in search of a man and boy."

"Find me Draemel, and you'll find the others."

"They were here? They did this to you?"

"Yes. Yes. Now you see. Blindness is leaving you." Paradin tapped the dagger tip beside the commander's eye.

"Then let me go," the commander demanded.

"Let you go? Let you go? Then poor Paradin to your blades will go. No. You follow their trail. Do this, do this and you shall live. Give me

Draemel. Give me Draemel. The others you may have."

The officer nodded.

"So be it, madman."

To his men, he ordered: "Scouts, move forward. We'll follow the trail of this…Draemel."

The patrol followed the scouts, while the commander rode at the rear. Paradin kept the blade tip pressed firmly against the officer's ribcage while he examined his own wound. With his free hand, he grabbed the bolt and yanked it out. Instead of a cry of pain, he smiled and watched as the Cauldron's power healed his bloody wound, leaving only a jagged scar surrounded by new, pink flesh as evidence of the wound.

Paradin resumed his eerie song and nodded his head to the meter. The tune echoed over the warriors who were unable to fully comprehend the meaning, but the Cauldron understood and delighted in such adoration. In response it delivered to Paradin his just reward: madness.

Chapter 28

The Worm Master

Linwith jumped at every sound as he drove the slow-moving wagon over the ruts that passed for roads in the backwoods of Allsbruth. Convinced the rhythmic rattles, thumps and creaks from his barrels would attract the attention of Ebonite patrols or thieves, he constantly glanced over his shoulder back down the road.

"Carrots for swords," he huffed with a slap of the reins onto the horses' rear flanks. "I'll be lucky to get there alive, let alone return with weapons."

He had insisted on another joining him for protection, but Il-Lilliad said that Gundin and Quinn needed every available man to train for battle. So Linwith journeyed alone, the wagon's incessant groans nagging his troubled mind.

"Yes, Linwith," he muttered, imitating Quinn's voice. "Travel alone and in a wagon that's loud and noisy. That way you're an easy target for prowling Wurmlins and Ebonites."

He recalled Il-Lilliad's parting words of encouragement. At the time, they sounded so warm. Now, they seemed trite, even ridiculous.

Trust the Only, Linwith. He knows you travel alone and knows the importance of getting to Tristan.

Linwith let out a short, sarcastic laugh.

"Then *you* should have taken this journey, Il-Lilliad," he shouted back toward Hetherlinn with another slap of the reins. "I would have preferred to stay and train."

He had left Hetherlinn days ago and followed the Allsbruthian Mountains east. When he reached the River Lelle, he followed it north through a gap in the Allsbruthian Mountains to the River Arrgient toward the Gilden Plains. In order to reach the vast plains, he would first have to cross a narrow bridge that traversed the wide river.

Linwith stared at the bridge off in the distance and pondered the rest of his journey.

Once he crossed the river, he would continue north across the Gilden Plains. He was familiar with the massive prairie from his time in the Dark War. Knowing its vastness, he fretted over it. There were no thickets or woods to hide in. He would be easy to spot and easier to ambush.

If that was not enough to worry about, there were the lions that prowled the tall grasses. The scent from his lumbering horses would surely attract prides near and far. He had witnessed a lion attack many summers ago. The thought still sent chills through him.

Once past the Gilden Plains he would reach the Addoli Ridge, nestled beside the Gilden Sea. He would follow the ridge east and navigate through the rolling hills to the coastal town of Holman. From there, he would follow the coastline into Tristan.

On horseback, Linwith knew the entire trip was at least a ten-day journey. With a wagon full of goods, it would take a month, maybe longer.

Linwith was so consumed with his thoughts that he was oblivious to the insect buzzing about his head. Annoyed by the bee-like creature, he swatted it away, but the insect returned and darted about his head. Linwith got so aggravated that he pulled the team to a stop.

"Trust the Only," he shouted as he swatted wildly at the creature buzzing about his head. "Marvelous."

Linwith took with another wild swing.

"As if ambushes aren't enough to worry about, I now must defend myself against this pesky bee."

The creature landed on the flank of one of his horses. With slow, measured movements Linwith pulled his hat off and leaned toward it. He swung his hat, but at the last possible moment, the creature flew away.

Smack.

The horses neighed and took off at full gallop. The wagon lurched forward, tossing Linwith backward into bed with the barrels of vegetables.

"*Stop.* Halt, you dumb animals," he shouted as he tried to regain his seat, but the horses' thunderous pace made standing too difficult a task.

"Stop. Whoa. Halt."

The barrels bounced about the wagon bed like excited children at a holiday fair. Linwith regained his balance long enough to take in a horrible sight. The wagon was racing full speed toward the bridge.

Linwith's thoughts raced. *We can't cross going this fast. The bridge is too narrow. We'll sail off into the River Arrgient.*

Frantic, he regained his seat, only to be confronted with the tiny winged creature that had started all of the trouble. It landed on the wagon's headboard in front of him.

"*You,*" he yelled at the bug as he grabbed the reins. "This is all *your* fault."

"No, I was sent to help."

Linwith screamed and almost lost the reins again.

"I'm going mad. Now I'm hearing bees talk."

"I am not a bee."

Linwith jerked back on the reins while he glanced at the creature. It was as big as his thumb. Its abdomen was a shiny emerald green and it had six legs, like an insect, but the similarity ended there. Its bottom two legs were bird-like, while the other two sets were black and long and ended in tiny, human-like hands.

Linwith's gaze alternated between the looming bridge and the strange, talking insect-creature.

"I don't care who you are, or what you are. Be gone. If I don't stop this wagon I'll drown."

"If you stop, you will surely die," the creature countered.

Linwith pulled back hard.

"Whoa. *Whoa.*"

The plow horses were too frightened and refused to yield.

"I implore you," the creature shouted, hovering near Linwith's face. "Do not stop."

"Away, you flying varmint."

"Linwith, I beg you. Do *not* stop."

"How do you know my name," Linwith asked as he continued to strain against the horses' wild gallop. He didn't have time to ponder that he was talking to a creature from a fairy tale.

"From the stories of Claire."

"Stories? Claire? What stories?"

He was running out of time.

"Tell me why I shouldn't stop," he barked while yanking on the reins.

"Look behind you."

Linwith glanced back. An Ebonite patrol was galloping after him.

"Wonderful," Linwith blurted. "So this is what trusting the Only gets you. Death by the March of Reeds or drowning in the River Arrgient."

"We'll help you over the bridge."

"You? How?"

"Alone, nothing. Together, all."

The creature pointed to Linwith's right. All he saw was a small black cloud hovering over the river. The creature pointed to Linwith's left. Again, all he saw was a small black cloud.

"How can rain clouds help?" Linwith shouted.

"Trust me. Do not stop."

Linwith studied the bridge. It was wooden, had no guard railings, and was barely wide enough for one wagon. His eyes jumped to the river. It was beryl green, deep, wide and had claimed many victims.

"I can't swim. I'd rather take my chances with the Ebonites," Linwith argued as he strained to stop his team.

"No."

The creature zoomed down upon the reins. With unnatural strength beyond its size, the tiny creature ripped the reins out of Linwith's hands and flew with them high out of his reach.

Linwith reached out to grab them back.

"Give me the reins, you fool. I'll drown."

The bridge loomed. Linwith stood, preparing to jump when one of the black rain clouds descended upon him. He realized it was not a cloud, but a swarm of the bee-like creatures as they forced him to sit back down.

The wagon slammed onto the bridge with the horses at full gallop. Hooves and wheels rumbled across wooden planks. More creatures descended, flew on each side of the wagon and kept it centered on the bridge.

Helpless to do anything else, Linwith spared a backward glance. The Ebonite patrol had reached the bridge. He turned back around and saw he was halfway across.

"We'll never make it. They'll catch us before we reach the other side," Linwith shouted.

The second cloud swarmed the Ebonites, grasping them and lifting them into the air. They zoomed up high over the water, then released their prey. Ebonite warriors and warhorses fell from the sky, clawing the empty air in terror.

Splash.

Riders and horses struggled to swim, but the current was too strong and their armor too heavy. Before the wagon reached the far bank, the last Ebonite disappeared beneath the river's surface.

Linwith's horses galloped off the bridge and onto the river's embankment. The creature that held the reins brought the wagon to a stop, while the others formed a giant cloud overhead. Linwith looked at the bridge, then back at the creature.

"I suppose I was wrong," Linwith admitted, breathing a sigh of relief. "I'm forever in your debt."

He jumped to the ground, and bowed low before the tiny bee-like creature that had stolen his reins.

"No," the creature shouted. "You cannot bow to us."

"I must. You saved my life and..."

"The blessing is ours. To escort one such as you, this we gladly do."

The leader landed at Linwith's feet. The cloud hovered en masse behind their leader. As one, they bowed.

"Please," Linwith said as he waved his hands in a futile attempt to stop their homage. "You can't honor me like this."

The leader rose and hovered in front of Linwith's face.

"My name is Rittmar, chancellor for the nation of Bal-Malin."

"Bal-Malin," Linwith asked. "Why does that name sound so familiar?"

"For centuries, our people have listened to an ancient story that hailed from the great days of Claire. Listen.

Dark winter's eternal frost lures all to deep sleep,
The Cauldron, like a viper, strikes venom to Claire's heart.
Hope is soon vanquished from soul's mighty keep,
And Ebon reigns the victor, dark nights ne'er to depart.
But lament not, Bal-Malin, for dawn's light will appear.
Awake, slumbering souls, from winter's ghastly spell.
Hear now sweet whisper, Your Worm Master draws near.
Hail Linwith from Hetherlinn. Victory I do foretell."

Linwith suppressed a chuckle.

"I believe you've been greatly misled," he stammered. "Men of greatness do not consider diving off a racing wagon to save their life."

"Everyone must face their dark tales. And so it is with you. The stories of old will come to pass as long as you have the courage to continue."

Linwith shook his head in disbelief.

"Do you know what my name means in Allsbruthian? Linwith means *quiet one.*"

"That may be, but in the tongue of Bal-Malin, Linwith means *Worm Master.*"

"Worm Master?" Linwith's eyes widened as he remembered where he had heard the name before. "Il-Lilliad talked about such things in his story."

"So you are familiar with the greatness of the worms?"

"With all due respect, Chancellor Rittmar, where I come from a worm is anything but great. It is the lowest of creatures."

"Ah, but you are not where we come from. The stories tell us that the Worm Master will return to Bal-Malin to tame the worms once more, binding them to his will. Together they will deliver the Tristan swords to the armies of Allsbruth."

This time Linwith chuckled out loud. "This sounds like a joke, not a story of destiny."

"This is no joke. The worms lived quietly in their lairs through the cycle of many a summer. Many have entered their caves to try and bridle them for their own bidding. All have perished."

"Killed by worms?"

"Yes. Their talons are sharper than a Tristan blade, and each possesses other...powers."

"Powers? What powers?"

"Powers capable of defeating any adversary. These are not simple beasts of the woods. No, they are extremely intelligent creatures, each with a colorful tail that glows like fire. And their wings..."

"Wings?" Linwith wagged his head in disbelief.

"They await your return."

"My return? I've never been to Bal-Malin, so how can I return?"

"Such are the mysteries of the stories of Claire."

"Your story is impossible for me to embrace."

"Linwith, the success of your mission, and the success of this war, must be settled today, not tomorrow. From this moment forth, you must choose to live as Linwith, the Worm Master...or all is lost."

Linwith studied the entourage from Bal-Malin, then glanced back at the River Arrgient that had swallowed the Ebonite patrol.

"My task is to get these barrels to Tristan. In that, I'll need your help."

"Alone, nothing. Together, all. We would be honored to escort you in your journey."

Linwith smiled. Although he was older than Quinn, he had always lived within the shadow of his brother's greatness and doubted he had anything of worth to offer. Now, by the banks of the River Arrgient, the army of Bal-Malin had given him a new identity.

"So be it," he answered as he faced Rittmar. "Although I have my doubts to being the Worm Master, and question the power of these worms you speak of, nevertheless, I'll accept your help...*and* this new title."

The army of Bal-Malin rose into the sky as one, the beating of their wings drowning out the sounds of the wind and the river. They fell upon Linwith and shrouded him in darkness. Within this flying cocoon of living dark, Linwith felt himself being lifted up. He peered down between the gaps in the swarm and saw that the wagon was growing smaller.

Linwith turned his attention to his tiny saviors and studied them in more detail. From a distance, they all looked the same, but now he could see their uniqueness. Tiny, dark eyes blinked rapidly from cat-like faces. Short, black fur covered their bodies and revealed startling brilliant color when the sunlight hit it. Sapphire, ruby, emerald, gold, amber, silver, and mandarin shimmered like burnished metal.

The creatures of Bal-Malin chanted the name of their new champion, and their voices echoed across the River Arrgient.

Hail, Linwith...Worm Master.

Chapter 29

Whispers

Romlin and Elabea marched out of the Valley of Clouds and pressed on toward Waelryth.

The gap loomed before them like the mouth of a hungry beast, and despite its ominous presence they marveled at the multitude of birds swooping about the entrance.

The cliffs of Waelryth shot straight up and ended near the mountain peaks where forever snow glistened. Sunlight never reached the foot of those cliffs, so it was always dark and cold, and the winds of Ebon had etched thousands of tiny crags and miniature caves into the cliff walls. Rain, tarnished by the Cauldron's vapor, stained Waelryth a dull rust color. Darker shades oozed down the cliff walls here and there, like dried blood on a corpse's face.

Elabea imagined Waelryth to be the lair for horrible creatures and wanted to avoid entering it at all cost. Her eyes wandered to Romlin's bloodied tunic, providing an excuse for delaying their journey.

"We need to rest so I can look at your wound," she said.

Romlin shook his head.

"We can't stop now. Those Ebonite warriors will be coming soon, and the sun is sinking rapidly. I'll be fine."

Elabea's eyes jumped back to the cliffs.

"Are you certain the map didn't show another way through or around the mountains?"

"I'm certain," he replied as he too took in the foreboding passageway. "Trust me, if it had, we'd take it."

Elabea gave a slight consenting nod.

Nearer to the gap, they were greeted by the cool wind that perpetually flowed out of Waelryth. The closer they approached, the stronger it grew until it reached gale force. They were forced to hold their garments close and lean into the roaring wind.

Waelryth was wide enough for ten columns of soldiers to march side by side. It explained how the Ebonites had quickly invaded their country. Likewise, there was no obstacle to interrupt the onslaught of the rushing wind.

"Are you ready?" Romlin shouted above the wind.

A sudden premonition chilled Elabea's spine more than the fierce winds of Waelryth, and she cast her gaze back toward the Valley of Clouds. The Ebonite patrol had cleared the mists and galloped toward them.

"We'll never make it in time," she shouted, pointing toward the pursuing enemy.

Romlin assessed their position.

"You're right. We'll have to fight them here. There are three of them, and including the rusk, there are three of us."

Elabea shook her head.

"I'm too tired to fight again."

"So am I, but what choice do we have? The rusk and book will help."

Romlin wrestled against the wind to pull his shield off his back. Seeing that she had yet opened the book, he was about to chastise her when he caught her eyes. They were bone weary, but not from fear. She was simply exhausted.

"Run to Waelryth," he ordered Elabea. "I'll fight them off and join you."

"But..."

"There's no time to argue. Once you're safe, you can open the book and help me fight, alright?"

She gave a weak nod and was about to kiss him on the cheek when he pushed her toward the gap.

"Go."

Elabea stumbled forward toward the relative safety of Waelryth.

Romlin paused long enough to see her struggle against the strong winds. Convinced she would make it there safely, he turned and faced the Ebonites.

The wind hammered against his shield like a hurricane ripping into the sails of a ship. He tried to resist, but the gale was too strong and drove him to the ground. With the Ebonites almost upon him Romlin managed to gain his feet. He held his shield sideways to reduce the drag against the wind, caught his balance and unsheathed his sword.

Elabea had reached the safety of the cliffs and watched as Romlin was buffeted about by the winds of Waelryth; the warriors of Ebon were only a stone's throw away from him.

"The winds are too strong," she whispered to the rusk, or Manno Vox, she wasn't sure which. "He's unable to fight. Please help him."

Her whisper grew into a prayer toward Claire, then into a shout to the sky.

"He's wounded. He needs your help."

A gentle whisper graced Romlin's ears.

"You have battled well, but will you truly become the warrior you long to be?"

"Who are you?" Romlin twisted his head to find the source of the whisper.

"One who is able to give you all your heart desires. After all, are you not deserving?"

The thunder of hooves drove the whisper from his thoughts. With the odds at three against one, he knew he had to take drastic measures. He dropped his shield and gripped his man-sized sword with both hands. The three warhorses stopped and formed a line. The warriors' black beards and hair blew madly in the winds. They raised their blades skyward as the warhorses slammed their hooves into the ground.

Romlin took a defensive step backward.

"Show us how you fight, boy," one of the younger warriors taunted, his words empowered by the Gwyr and cutting through the winds.

"You were brave against the ryators, boy, but ryators don't battle like Ebonite warriors," another shouted.

Romlin's eyes darted about, hoping to see Manno Vox close by, or at least the rusk.

"Your eyes do not betray you, but your friends have," the whisper said. *"You are alone. Abandoned. Just as your father forsook you after the Dark War."*

"Leave me be," Romlin shouted in reply.

"I would rather give you what you truly desire...and what you truly deserve."

"And what's that?" Romlin spat.

"A name that trumpets glory and power for all the nations to hear. A name that the weak will bow to."

"That is why we journey to Claire," he countered, "to receive such honors."

The whisper fell silent, the March of Reeds approached and Romlin prepared to defend himself. He knew he had little chance of success. He was weary, he had lost a lot of blood and the wind challenged his balance. He wasn't sure how much longer he could even hold up his weapon. It was, after all, made for a grown man.

"Let's see how you fight face-to-face," the youngest Ebonite warrior challenged as he halted his horse and dismounted.

"Stay in formation," the eldest ordered. "We don't know where the girl is. She has a rusk."

"You worry too much, old man," the second warrior countered as he too stopped and dismounted.

"You fools. Mount your horses."

"Look at the boy. He can't even hold his weapon up, let alone fight."

"Besides," the other argued, "the girl ran into Waelryth. There's no place to hide within. If bangaleers don't consume her, we can capture her after we kill the boy."

The pair of Ebonites strutted toward Romlin, eager for first blood.

"Look at his eyes," the first goaded. "I've seen that look before."

"As have I," his companion laughed. "Those are the eyes that see death approach."

Romlin's heart raced and his breathing was labored. His lungs felt as if they were on fire and the wound on his back raged for his attention. Against all hope, he slid a hand within his tunic and touched the scar given him by Manno Vox, and breathed a silent cry for help to the King of Claire.

The warriors were almost upon him when he heard the whisper. It cut through the wind and the Ebonite taunts like a battle trumpet.

"Lie on the ground. Cover yourself with your shield."

"I can fight them with your help," Romlin shouted into the wind.

"You are too weary from your wound. This battle is mine."

A second whisper entered the fray.

"Do not listen to such madness. Did I not promise you the desire of your heart? Are you not a warrior so deserving? Stand fast and fight."

"Quickly, Romlin," the first whisper commanded. *"Lie down. Cover up."*

"Nonsense," the second whisper reasoned. *"Only a weak boy would do such a thing. Do you not bear a new name?"*

"Yes, but..."

"Should you not live up to it?"

Romlin yanked his hand from his scar and gripped the sword tighter with both hands. The wind slammed into him and spun him about. The two Ebonites laughed at the spectacle as they continued to approach.

"Romlin," the first whisper urged. *"Do not listen to the one that imitates and mocks. It desires only your demise."*

"If so," the second reasoned, *"then why am I the one encouraging you to fight? Would not the false whisper beg you to lie down and hide? Is that not...suicide?"*

Romlin's mind spun in confusion.

"Romlin," the first called. *"Only the true whisper may call you by your new name. Trust. Hide quickly."*

The warriors were almost within striking distance. Smiles of utter contempt filled their faces, and their swords were prepared to strike.

Romlin shut his eyes and made his choice. He dropped to the ground, curled into a ball and pulled his shield over him.

"Look," the first warrior chuckled. "He's soiling himself beneath his shield and crying for his mother."

A blood-chilling cry from Waelryth's walls echoed throughout the valley, followed by more high-pitched wails, their rapid, staccato bursts sending a shiver down Romlin's spine. He pulled his shield closer and held on against the wind with all of his strength. Romlin peered from beneath and watched the Ebonites' black boots approach.

"Hear that, boy," the closest warrior asked. "Bangaleers. Their lairs are within Waelryth. They wait in silence for unwary prey, then launch into the wind and attach to their victim's face. Thin claws wrap around the head so they can feast upon the brains. Even as we speak, they dine upon the girl. You'll be next."

A second pair of boots appeared.

"No. First blood is an Ebonite warrior's right. The bangaleers can wait. The Cauldron has them under our control anyway. They obey *our* orders."

"Remount," the oldest warrior commanded from afar, but they were too intoxicated with the thought of first blood to heed his order.

Romlin prepared for their barrage of steel against his shield. Instead, he heard a deep, dark roar from above and a warrior cried out in pain.

Romlin raised his shield enough to see the warrior stumble away, coddling his right hand. Blood dripped from long gashes torn by the claws of some large animal. Romlin cast about for the mystery beast, but saw nothing.

"Death begets life."

"For now, but time is my ally," the other whisper threatened as it retreated.

Romlin pulled down his shield in anticipation of the second Ebonite's attack when agonizing screams made him dare another look.

Something hideous was attached to his attackers' faces.

"Bangaleers," he presumed.

Stone gray and glistening with slime, the creatures were oval, flat and had five long, jointed appendages like skeletal fingers. These were wrapped around the Ebonites' heads.

The warriors pulled with all their strength, but they fought in vain. The bangaleers long, black tongues flickered about to test the air. Without warning, they slithered up their victims' noses. The helpless warriors fell to the ground, thrashing about wildly.

Romlin shifted his attention to the remaining mounted Ebonite, who was fighting off several bangaleers with his sword.

"*Stand,*" the true whisper ordered Romlin. "*Run to Waelryth. At my command, throw your shield up and into the wind.*"

"I don't have the strength..."

"*You have my strength. Go. I will not let you fail.*"

Romlin pushed himself to his feet, held his shield sideways to cut through the wind and ran for his life. Despite his wound and the winds, his legs felt fresh and strong. A glance back revealed the remaining warrior in hot pursuit. Several bangaleers lay on the ground, hacked into pieces.

Romlin focused on his task and raced into Waelryth.

Hooves echoed behind him. Panic pushed Romlin onward. When he felt he could not take another step, the whisper commanded, "*Now.*"

Romlin hurled the shield into the air. The wind shifted, caught the shield in a mini-maelstrom and whirled it high above his head until it was a speck against the sky. The winds of Waelryth shifted again, hurling the shield back with incredible force.

The pursuing Ebonite never saw the spinning disc. It severed off his head. His headless torso continued riding, the sword still gripped in his lifeless hand. At last the body fell from the saddle, and the warhorse, as trained to do, slowed to a stop near its dead master's side.

Romlin took a moment to catch his breath, regain his composure and retrieve his shield before looking for Elabea.

She was nowhere in sight.

"Elabea, where are you?" he shouted as he jogged down the passageway, his pace slowed by the gale-force winds and his own exhaustion.

The legs of a young girl jutting out from a pile of rocks caught his eye.

"*No,*" he shouted as he continued to struggle forward, the thought of a bangaleer attached to her face enraging him.

"Elabea, I'm coming."

When he reached her side, his heart sank. There was no sign of a bangaleer, but her face was pale and the rusk hovered frantically about her. Romlin knelt beside her and felt her forehead. She was still warm and breathing.

Instinct took over. Romlin grabbed Il-Lilliad's book, and opened it.

The rusk's eyes widened with hope, and it began hopping up and down on Elabea's shoulder, chattering something only she could understand. Her eyes blinked once, then opened. She stared at Romlin, as if in a dream.

"You're alive," she stammered with a weak smile.

"Elabea. What happened?"

"I was so tired. I saw you fall. I heard the whisper. I tried, Romlin. I did the best I could…"

"You were great. I heard you whisper to me again along with a second whisper."

"Romlin, I never whispered. I simply called to the King of Claire."

Elabea shuttered as she recounted her experience.

"It was horrible," she recalled. "The rusk flew up into the cliffs, and drew the attention of those hideous creatures. They gave chase. At the last possible moment, the rusk swerved out of the way, and they latched upon the Ebonites."

"If it wasn't you that whispered to me, then who was it," Romlin wondered.

"One whisper was from the Cauldron. The other must have been from the King of Claire."

"Are you able to walk," he asked.

"I'll try," she answered, weariness evident in her voice. "Can you help me up?"

Romlin helped Elabea to her feet, and she leaned heavily upon him.

After a few labored steps, Romlin realized it was an impossible task.

"Sit here," he said as he helped her rest beside the cliff's wall.

"I'm sorry," she apologized again. "Fighting with stories takes all of my strength."

"Don't worry, Elabea. We'll get through this."

He leaned his shield near her for protection, and something about it caught her attention.

"What's that?"

A miniscule piece of glossy black leather dangled from the dragon's claw and flapped in the wind. Romlin touched it. It was cold and wet. They stared at the thick substance on the end of his finger.

"Blood," Elabea observed.

Romlin remembered the roar he had heard when he hid beneath his shield followed by the sight of the Ebonite warrior clutching his injured hand.

"But whose," she asked.

Romlin managed a weak smile, the thought of a headless warrior falling from his saddle intruding on his thought.

"That's a story for another day."

An idea entered his mind of how to help Elabea travel on.

"Stay here," he said. "I'll be right back with help."

Before she could argue, he sprinted back toward the entrance of the pass.

Chapter 30

A Tale of Exchange

As time passed, Elabea's anxiety mounted.

Why isn't he back yet, she wondered. *Did the Ebonites find him? Are bangaleers feasting on...*

She shuddered, and pushed that image out of her mind.

Whinnying horses echoed about Waelryth. Her heart raced as she pulled Romlin's shield close for protection. Panic stricken, she watched as a black snout emerged from around the bend. She clutched the book close. Fearing the worst, she was about to ask the rusk for help when she spotted him.

Riding high in the saddle, and beaming with pride, sat Romlin. In his left hand he held the reins of another Ebonite warhorse.

Romlin hopped off the massive animal, then drew Elabea to her feet.

"Do you think it's safe to ride them," she asked as her eyes ran over the warhorses.

"What do you mean," he asked, oblivious to the heart of her question. "You've ridden horses before."

"Yes, but not like these. Their hooves bear the stain of innocent blood. They've served the Cauldron and Ebon."

"It's the rider that determines the horse," Romlin replied. "If we ride them for good, won't their darkened past fade away? Besides, these are great animals. Just look at them. We'll do well to ride them."

Elabea approached one of the animals and looked up into its face. It was a magnificent steed, dressed from head to tail with black leather and armor. Reaching up with both hands, she patted its snout.

"I must admit," she said, "he is beautiful."

"Beautiful?" Romlin chuckled. "He's a warhorse, trained to ride fearlessly into battle and trample men to death."

"I know," she said, "but you said that he could be used for good and perhaps that's true. Or maybe his heart can change. Perhaps ours can, too."

"You're talking in circles," Romlin replied, "and it's making me dizzy."

"In the book Il-Lilliad gave us," she explained as she continued rubbing his nose, "one word repeats over and over. Do you know what that word is?"

"No, what?"

"*Delight*. The King of Claire *delights* in all people. He *delights* in all creatures. He *delights* in facing impossible odds."

She began reciting a passage from memory.

"*Delightful is the fruit that falls from the trees of Claire. For within their harvest is the wine of my delight. Come, all who are forgotten, all who listen not, all who have tasted bitter herbs. For the nectar of my bounty is sweet and flows like the River Arrgient.*"

"More circle talk," Romlin interjected.

"Don't you understand what the story is saying? The King of Claire delights in embracing forgotten lives and transforming them into something of great beauty and purpose."

"So," Romlin chuckled, "you believe the King of Claire can turn this warhorse into a plow horse?"

She flashed him an amused look.

"Yes, but that would be easy. What I wonder is: Would he delight in me when others have not? Would he delight in transforming a foolish girl from Hetherlinn into a storyteller? That, Romlin, would be a miracle."

She pulled the animal's head down, and rested her hands upon its armor, then jerked them away as if she had been burned.

"Did you *hear* that?"

"No, what?" Romlin whipped his sword to the ready and scanned Waelryth for signs of their enemy.

Elabea stretched fingertips toward the horse's armor once more. But when flesh touched metal, she again yanked them off.

"*That.* You don't hear them?"

Romlin lowered his sword and touched the armor. Stunned, he heard the cries of thousands of men and women. Their laments were full of anguish and yet, swirling like eagles around the pain, were songs of celebration. The songs did not praise their demise nor cry for revenge, but spoke of passion for the King of Claire, their delight.

Romlin jerked his hands away.

"Who are they?" he whispered.

Tears rolled from Elabea's eyes.

"Remember Il-Lilliad's story about the storytellers being murdered by the Ebonite cavalry in a March of Reeds? I believe we've heard their cries from that fateful day, forever sealed in this armor."

Her gaze shifted to Romlin's eyes.

"I could feel their pain. I could see everything they suffered. It was *horrible*. And yet..."

"They sang a song of such joy," he added, reflecting on their shared vision.

She scrubbed her tears with the back of her hand and nodded. Romlin's eyes fell to the ground, as if ashamed by a sudden thought.

"But why didn't I hear them when I first touched the armor?"

"Perhaps you were listening with different ears," Elabea replied. "Perhaps it wasn't time for you to hear them."

Another sound, a physical sound, emanated from deeper within the pass. It wove its way in and out of the whistling wind of Ebon. Although the sound was powerful, it did not sound threatening.

The sound piqued their curiosity and drew them onward. Holding their warhorses' reins, they walked deeper into the passage. Emerging from around a bend, they experienced the source of the sound – a waterfall of breathtaking beauty.

"Magnificent," Romlin exclaimed as his gaze followed the waterfall from the pool at the foot of the cliff up to its source, somewhere far above and out of sight.

Together they walked to the edge of the basin formed by the waterfall's power. It was worn smooth from ages of flowing water, and the crystal clear pool was icy cold and deep enough to bathe in. The overflow spilled out of the basin and formed a narrow stream, about ankle deep, which flowed to the canyon's wall and disappeared through a large crack into some cavernous world hidden beneath their feet.

As Romlin stood, transfixed by the sight, Elabea pulled the book from her pack.

"Where is that tale, rusk?"

She flipped through the pages of the book.

"I remember you reading it to me earlier...something about returning broken or evil to the Only."

"Do you mean the story of exchange," the rusk asked.

"Yes, that's the one."

"Elabea, why are you looking for a story," Romlin asked, still staring at the waterfall.

"These horses are magnificent, but riding them doesn't seem right. The cries of the martyrs are too real."

The rusk nodded his head, pointed out the story in the book and whispered the words in her ear.

When the rusk finished its tale, Elabea retrieved the reins of her warhorse and led him to the edge of the pool. Placing her hands on either side of the animal's head, being careful not to touch the armor, she repeated the tale.

"From Dark Flame you were born,
Death and pain you have sown.
Return. For the King of Claire is yours to adorn.
Return. Forever life and glory is yours to own."

Elabea lead the animal beneath the waterfall until both she and the horse were drenched by the flow. It whinnied as the water pelted it from head to tail, but it did not resist.

"Romlin, look," Elabea gasped, awestruck.

Rivulets of crimson grime trickled down the horse's armor as the water fell upon it. The waterfall was washing away the stains from the armor, drop by drop, until the pool where they stood ran blood red.

"Magic water," Romlin exclaimed, marveling at his reflection in the the newly silvered armor.

"The water's not magic," she said. "It was the power of the story. Take your horse to the pool and repeat the words."

Romlin led his animal to the water's edge but stopped.

"I'm not sure I want to do this."

"Why not?" she asked.

"It's not that I don't wish to honor those martyred by the March of Reeds. I do. But if I'm to be a warrior then I need a warhorse. I don't need him changed into a gentle beast. Do you understand?"

"He'll always be a warhorse," Elabea reassured him. "Perhaps now, he can be more bold and brave than he ever was serving Ebon."

Romlin nodded, then led his horse under the waterfall and recited the same tale. As he watched the transfiguration of the horse's armor, he pondered his own wounds and weariness.

"Do you think the water can heal my wound" he asked.

"I told you, the water's not magic," she sighed, as if explaining to a petulant child who refused to understand. "But maybe there's another tale that can help. Is there, rusk?"

The rusk chattered as she paged through the book. At last he came to the story she was looking for. Without taking her eyes off the page, she listened to the rusk, translating the words to Romlin and instructing him to repeat after her.

Romlin stepped into the cool spray and recited the story, word for word.

"Who will hear our tales?"

He jutted his shoulder into the torrent of water.

"Who will call us delight?"

Cold streams drenched his throbbing injury.

"Wash our wounds with tears, ransom lost years..."

His back tingled as if being tickled.

"In these days of deception."

Warmth spiraled outward from the gash he received from the ryator attack, fanning finger-like across his back. Despite the icy water that drenched him head to foot, he was soothed by the heat and even savored the experience.

The warmth soon faded, and the waterfall's natural iciness returned. Romlin figured the process was over and led his warhorse, washed clean of its past, out of the falls.

Elabea reached out to examine his injury. She pulled back his soaked tunic with tender fingers, trying to avoid further exacerbating his wound, but there was no need for such caution. The once gaping slash was now a thin seam of red against new, baby-pink flesh. It looked as if someone had stitched it together. She laid her fingers on his flesh near the wound and felt heat, as if he had a fever, radiate into her hand.

"What's it look like," he asked, trying in vain to peer over his shoulder.

Elabea lowered his sodden shirt.

"All you have is a scar. Does it still hurt?"

He shook his head.

"I'm so glad," she smiled. Then with a mischievous twitch at the corner of her mouth she added, "I can't believe you made such a big fuss over so small a wound."

Romlin's jaw dropped.

"Small? You call that small?"

Then he caught the mood of the moment and they both chuckled. It had been a long time since they had laughed. He spun around and looked into her face with a beaming smile. She smiled back, and for a moment, she thought he was about to express his feelings for her when a blast of cold wind broke the spell and they both shivered.

"We should be on our way," Romlin said, pulling away from her gaze. "Waelryth isn't safe. Who knows what lies around each bend?"

He helped her mount and side by side they rode toward the other side. Romlin glanced at Elabea as they rode, savoring the way the wind tossed her hair as if it didn't have a care in the world. He marveled at how she and her horse balanced each other so well. Just as the sword from Manno Vox fit perfectly into his hand, so she looked natural riding the stallion. Like her warhorse, Elabea had a resilient spirit that the bit could not tame nor the bridle completely control.

"I believe your miracle is coming to pass," he called to her.

"What," she asked, unable to hear above the wind and the thundering hooves.

"Your miracle. You're...*changing*."

"What?"

"The story. I believe the Only is changing you, like he did our horses."

"I can't hear you," she shouted back.

He smiled, shook his head and rode on in silence. As he gazed at the young girl he had grown up with, a smile unlike any he had ever seen before radiated across Elabea's face like the sun. It took his breath away.

She was captivating.

C h a p t e r 31

A Story Comes to Ebon

Brairtok, along with his commanders, sat on their warhorses atop a small knoll outside of the city.

"Isn't she magnificent," Brairtok boasted with a wave of his arm toward Kise. "What a formidable city. She sits upon the foothills like a god and rules over the nations with darkness.

"The spoils from our many victories are proof of our greatness. Gold, silver and precious gems overflow our treasury while the best wines and food are stockpiled for Ebon's pleasure. Every nation's greatest works of art, literature and music resides within *our* walls. Even the uniqueness of our architecture is evidence of our superiority."

The commanders did not reply. They had served Brairtok through the cycle of many winters and knew that to interrupt such reflections would only stir his anger, an anger that burned perpetually like the Cauldron's flames.

"Gaze upon Netniath and Vorak," Brairtok continued with a gesture toward the citadels perched atop twin peaks. "They rise through the gray mists with such defiance, evidence that the King of Claire could never subdue such majesty and splendor."

The officers took in the view and noted the dreary clouds wrapped about the two mountains that straddled Kise. Vorak and Netniath jutted out of the gray, appearing to float atop the mists like phantom ships on a restless sea.

"Commanders of Ebon," Brairtok offered a rare smile, "always remember the power that resides within Netniath and Kise. By such might we will war again. The Dark Flames of the Cauldron will not be deterred from letting us claim what is rightfully ours. Now, order your troops to attention."

The drum corps was signaled and Ebon's cadence - a methodical, odd-metered beat - boomed across the valley. At the base of the knoll, thousands upon thousands of Ebonite warriors snapped to attention.

"I bring you good news," Brairtok shouted to his assembled forces, his voice carried by the wind and amplified by the Gwyr. "War approaches. Battles for gold and glory will soon be yours."

A unified, chilling war cry erupted from the army.

"The King of Claire has dared whisper once again. He has emerged from his hiding place to finally face his demise. His army is no more. His storytellers are all gone. By the power of Kise and Netniath we will crush Claire. First blood!”

The army exploded with war cries of “First blood!” as swords beat against shields and fists were thrust into the air.

On the far horizon, Brairtok noticed a small cloud of dust approaching, evidence of someone galloping at breakneck speed.

“It’s about time,” Brairtok sighed as the rider raced past the columns of men. “A scout bringing news of the patrol I sent in pursuit of the boy and girl.”

The rider charged up the hill where Brairtok and the commanders waited. He stopped, saluted and without hesitation delivered his urgent message.

“I bring news from the wilderness.”

“Excellent. Did the patrol capture the boy and girl?”

“My lord, it appears that…”

“A simple mission with an obvious outcome does not require a lengthy explanation,” Brairtok interrupted.

The messenger saw the rage burning deep within Brairtok’s eyes. He fought through his fears and continued.

“They were found by another.”

“So it took *another* scouting party to find the Allsbruthian waifs?”

“No, sir. The second patrol found the first patrol that had been missing for days.”

“Missing? You mean to tell me they were lost like women in the woods?”

The messenger swallowed hard, then continued.

“No, sir. The second patrol found the bodies of the first patrol.”

Brairtok’s eyes narrowed and his nostrils flared. He delivered his next sentence methodically.

“So you’re telling me that a girl and a boy killed four of our seasoned warriors?”

The scout hesitated, knowing full well that an incorrect answer could lead to a court martial…or worse.

“We’re not sure what happened, sir. We have ascertained that one soldier broke his neck when he fell from his horse near the Valley of Clouds, and two were killed by bangaleers near Waelryth.”

Brairtok arched an eyebrow.

“So, let me get this straight: A veteran cavalryman fell off his horse while bangaleers killed two others.”

The scout gave a subtle nod of assent.

Brairtok exploded.

"Your report is a fabrication of lies! Ebonite warriors just don't fall off their horses in combat, and the Cauldron has rendered bangaleers powerless to attack us. They've not hunted Ebonite flesh since before the Dark War."

The scout did not reply. To do so when Brairtok was this enraged would only make matters worse.

Brairtok patted his steed's neck in an attempt to regain his composure.

"Tell me," he said as he stroked the horse's mane, "what of the fourth, their commander?"

"He was..." the scout mumbled.

Brairtok glared at the scout.

"Speak up."

"Beheaded."

Brairtok ground his teeth and fidgeted in his saddle as he wrestled with the news. He leaned toward the scout. His rant began as a low mutter between clinched teeth, then boiled over into a roar.

"Swords have been banned by the Oracles. Even if one had been smuggled into Allsbruth a mere boy could *not* cut off the head of an attacking warrior on horseback."

"I concur, sir, and yet the evidence bears witness..."

"Impossible," Brairtok roared, his anxiety causing his mount to shy and whinny.

"My lord," one officer interjected in hope of sparing the messenger Brairtok's wrath. "It's possible that the report may be flawed. After all, if there were no survivors to give an eyewitness..."

Brairtok raised a hand, cutting the officer off in mid-sentence, and continued his interrogation of the young scout.

"Is that all the news you bear?"

"No, sir."

The scout drew in a deep breath before delivering more of his disturbing report.

"Two of their horses are unaccounted for."

Brairtok closed his eyes, leaned his head back as if savoring a wonderful thought, and then slowly lowered it again. Dark eyes blinked open.

"Two warhorses vanished into thin air?"

"Sir, the report states that..."

"Ebonite warhorses *never* leave their masters' sides, even if they fall in battle."

"Yes sir, I know," the scout answered. "I'm simply stating that..."

"You're stating *lies*. You are dangerously close to committing treason. You're telling me that in our nation's greatest hour, at the summit of its glory, a boy and a girl alone have managed what armies of grown men have been unable to do?"

"If I may, sir," Hinnmith offered hoping to appease Brairtok's rage, "there is one possibility."

"And what might that be," Brairtok snapped.

"That this tragedy is the result of an awakening, empowered by the Only."

Brairtok shifted in his saddle. The creaking leather sent chills up his commanders' spines.

"Explain yourself," Brairtok whispered, the danger in his voice evident.

"It's the only logical answer to explain these discoveries: Bangaleers attacking our warriors; a boy overpowering one of our experienced commanders; my own encounter with the fea dracas; and Manno Vox..."

Brairtok whipped out his sword, and his warhorse pranced and whinnied at the prospect of first blood.

"Commander," Brairtok threatened. "I could have your head for uttering that name. He was defeated in the Dark War. His name is not to be spoken, ever again."

"My lord," the scout added, "with all due respect, the evidence at Waelryth speaks of a warrior greater than..."

Brairtok spun around to address the scout.

"Chose your next words carefully. It sounds like your allegiance to the Cauldron is waning. I'm hearing words of admiration for the stories and legends from Claire."

The messenger stiffened his back and snapped his arm up, fist to chest, to salute his leader.

"Brairtok," he barked, "may your name be greater than all other names. I would gladly offer my life to bring glory to Ebon and to Brairtok."

Brairtok reflected on the messenger's disturbing report. He had discounted Hinnmith's account from several nights before as a fluke, or from too much wine, or from old eyes playing tricks on an aging warrior. The scout's account, however, seemed to validate Hinnmith's story. It troubled him.

The Cauldron sensed his concern and whispered to his mind.

"Journey back to that great day of justice."

The memory of the battle returned with vivid realism as an evil smile pursed his lips.

It was a deliciously deceptive battle strategy. Outnumbered, Brairtok, accompanied by wagons full of wounded men, approached the Army of Claire waving the flag of surrender. In honor of the surrender, the Army of Claire lowered their weapons and let them pass through their lines.

Once they were in the heart of Claire's forces, Brairtok shouted the command and the trap was sprung. The wounded men had only been feigning injury. They stood to attack. They caught the Army of Claire off-guard and soon gained the advantage.

Brairtok stormed through a line of warriors on his warhorse and came up behind the Army of Claire's leader. He battled valiantly from atop his steed, his armor glistening like fire and his sword slashing great swaths of destruction through the Ebonite forces. Sensing danger from behind, he spun around.

"*Yes,*" the Cauldron hailed as Brairtok continued to recall the day from long ago. "*Drink deep your greatest victory.*"

Through the slits of their helmets their eyes locked. Brairtok remembered the look of shock in Manno Vox's eyes. Brairtok, drunk with zeal, raised his crossbow and fired point blank into Manno Vox's armored chest. The bolt pierced his heart and catapulted him backward off his horse. With Manno Vox's demise the battle was over. Brairtok further disgraced their fallen bodies with a March of Reeds.

Brairtok chuckled as he returned his thoughts to the present. He was about to address his commanders when another memory, like a simmering fire stoked to new life, whispered as it had when he led that fateful March of Reeds.

"*Manno Vox. My delight.*"

Brairtok covered his ears in an attempt to expel the memory of the whisper from his subconscious.

"*No,*" he shouted.

His commanders shared bewildered glances and eyed Briartok as if he was going mad.

"I'll *not* listen to you again. They're dead. He is dead. Do you hear me? Our March of Reeds left no man alive."

The memory of the whisper continued undaunted, and just as he was forced to listen on that fateful day, he once more took note of the forgotten childhood tale...

"*As the dawn chases the night, so will the lives of those destroyed by the Dark Flame be. Rising like tulips through winter's frost, death will beget life.*"

Brairtok pressed his hands tighter about his ears and cried out as if in physical pain.

The Cauldron's whisper rushed to his aid.

"*Ignore the ranting of the lost one.*"

Brairtok drank in the Cauldron's words and he felt soothing power of the Gwyr pulsate through his marrow. His rage subsided and his confidence swelled. He lowered his hands from his ears as if nothing had just transpired. He addressed the scout in a tranquil voice.

"I'm confident we'll find an answer to this puzzling dilemma. Manno Vox is dead, of that I am sure. Nevertheless, never utter that name in my presence again. Is that understood?"

The scout nodded, grateful that the conversation was nearing an end.

"Tell me," Brairtok asked, almost as an afterthought, "what news is there of the other vul jens?"

"As you are well aware, my lord, when the rusk killed their brother, the other three followed. Even as we speak, they are preparing a trap. The girl has not yet reached Claire to become a storyteller, so she is hardly a threat for three vul jens, but this ambush is not for her. It is for the rusk. You are well versed with the Oracle concerning them: *As the rusk goes, so goes the storyteller.*"

Brairtok's chest puffed out with satisfaction, and he nodded. Even if Manno Vox were alive, his life would be short and pointless. With the death of the rusk, Elabea would be defenseless, and even Manno Vox could not protect her from Brairtok's horde of warriors.

Sitting high in his saddle, Brairtok faced his army and thrust his sword proudly over his head. War drums resumed their haunting cadence.

"First blood," Brairtok cried.

In unison, his army unsheathed their weapons and thrust them high.

"First blood," they echoed with one voice.

Chapter 32

Repose for Two

Elabea and Romlin turned their horses northward and followed the Mountains of Kline toward Claire. As they rode, Romlin pulled out the map Digri had given him. Ever since leaving MerriNoon he studied the map religiously, committing much to memory, amazed at its detail and accuracy. He unfolded the map and stared at the outline of Claire like a hawk in search of prey.

His heart sank.

The map had changed somehow. It was different.

"Are we lost," Elabea inquired, taking in his altered countenance.

Romlin forced a smile. She had a right to know, but she was still exhausted from their battles with the ryators and Ebonites. He worried that his observations about the map would only weaken her more.

Besides, Il-Lilliad and Manno Vox had given him an order: *Protect Elabea at all cost.* Wouldn't telling her about his discovery be hurtful? He concluded that he alone would bear this burden, at least until he knew what was causing the map to change.

"Lost?" he answered as calmly as he could, trying his best to not reveal his own worries about the map. "No. We should reach Claire's border in a few days."

He turned away from her, so Elabea could not see how troubled he really was. Refolding the map, he returned it to his pocket while his thoughts churned with worry.

Claire's cities, rivers and mountains - all its features - were fading from the map, like the flames sputtering out from an unattended fire. Some details were no longer visible.

A soft, gentle whisper spoke within his mind.

"Is it possible that the Oracle is true? That Claire no longer exists? After all, doesn't the Oracle state: 'Upon a map blind eyes behold what was becomes no more...'"

As quickly as it came, it fled, but it accomplished its mission. The seed of doubt was planted in his mind.

Romlin looked over his shoulder. No one followed. He let out a deep sigh of relief. He glanced skyward, thankful that Manno Vox continued to protect them from above the clouds. An unexplainable peace subdued his fears, and his confidence returned, but the nagging doubt still lingered.

He glanced at Elabea. Her shoulders sagged and her head drooped. She was exhausted. Though it was too early to camp, he knew she was in no condition to continue. He turned his horse around.

"What's wrong," Elabea asked, stifling a yawn with the back of her hand, while fearing the worst.

"Nothing. Just follow me, and stay close."

He spurred his horse to a canter and they soon arrived back at a site that had caught his eye moments before. He dismounted and, leading his horse by the reins, pushed his way through a stand of tall saplings.

Elabea dismounted and followed.

"Where are we going," she asked as they trudged through the thick growth.

"If this leads to what I think, it will be perfect."

"For what?"

"You'll see."

As the underbrush thinned, Romlin increased their pace.

"Slow down," Elabea complained, trying to keep up.

Romlin stopped when they entered a small clearing about the the size of a Hetherlinn cottage.

"It's just as I'd hoped," he said. "It's a perfect place to rest. A waterfall was once here, see?"

Elabea looked up at the rocky cliff towering before them.

"An ancient waterfall etched out this huge basin from the rock," Romlin declared as he rubbed the stone. "Feel how smooth the walls are. Over time, the river must have changed course and the waterfall stopped, which explains the thick grove of saplings growing up around it now. We'll be safe here."

Elabea rubbed the dark gray mountain rock; it was as cold and smooth as ice on a pond. Rising straight up into the sky, it provided the backdrop to their sanctuary while the blue sky was their ceiling.

Moss and ferns grew in place of the waterfall's pool, and their sweet aroma and tantalizing thickness called to her. She lowered herself into the plush growth, leaned back against the stone wall and exhaustion took over.

"What if they track us with those beasts, and..." she yawned.

"That's not your concern," Romlin replied as he withdrew his sword. He tethered their horses, then went to stand by the entrance. "Rest. I'll stand watch."

Elabea's fears could not restrain the sleep that tugged at her. With a deep sigh, she rolled to her side amidst the ferns. The rusk curled up beside her, his watchful eyes searching high and low for any danger.

Elabea awoke with a disoriented gasp.

"Where am I?"

"We're on Ebon's frontier, resting, remember?"

"Not really. I just closed my eyes for a moment. It didn't feel like I was asleep."

"Oh, you definitely slept," he answered with mischievous grin. "And you snore, too!"

"I do *not* snore," Elabea sniffed.

"Perhaps you didn't used to, but you certainly do *now*," Romlin chuckled. "You were so loud I thought you were going to give away our hiding place! And I thought my father snored loudly."

Elabea flashed him a scowl as she stood and brushed herself off. She retrieved her bag and pulled out Il-Lilliad's book. The rusk scampered up her shoulder to roost.

"Why do you listen to those stories all the time," Romlin asked, the memory of Claire's features disappearing from the map starting to nibble at his resolve.

"The stories are so...so..."

She sank down into the grass to read.

"So *what?*"

"So...alive," she finished. "When the rusk reads to me, it's as if I'm in the story and can see and hear all that's happening."

She flipped through the pages and found the tale. Though she was still unable to read for herself, she began to narrate it word for word, relying upon her memory and the countless times the rusk had recited it to her.

"*Upon a map blind eyes behold what was becomes no more; a shimmering veil of fathomless depth becomes a timeless door. Sage and prophet have reasoned mad yet slaves are crowned king, for beyond the veil the lark hails, 'Drink from my deepest spring.'*"

She paused and stared at Romlin, her eyes dancing with light.

"Isn't that exciting," Elabea asked.

Romlin bit his tongue to maintain control over his emotions. He did not reply.

Why would a story from Claire contain an Oracle from Ebon, and which whisper can I trust?

Elabea continued reciting from the book.

"*Meadows sweep like eagle wings to mountain's purple hue, whose glistening peaks of pearl white snow, like flames kiss sky's royal blue. Spin your eyes 'round compass points, no border will come in view; endless prairie, glen and stream whisper, 'All is new!'*"

She stopped and closed her eye, envisioning the wonders of an unspoiled land.

"Oh, Claire sounds so beautiful," she sighed. "I can't wait to see those mountains, can you?"

"I suppose," he said as his concerns about the map increased. "Honestly, I think Claire sounds too good to be true."

Elabea seemed not to hear his concerns, and continued the tale.

"*Lion, lamb, hawk and dove together share the brook. Winter, spring, summer, fall circle for a look. Dawn, dusk, eve and morn' sing of timeless days. Blood, sweat, tears and pain are now but washed away.*

"*Nested high upon great peak, like falcon perched for flight, sits a castle bathed in light with turrets strong and white. Within these halls resides the king whose dream it is to share, all that is and all that was in the land you know as Claire.*"

Elabea looked at Romlin.

"Every time I recite this story, I get more and more excited."

Romlin just stared at the ground.

"What is more amazing is that this was written long before our time. The date on the page proves it."

Romlin shook his head, shaking Elabea from her daydream.

"What's wrong," she asked.

"Nothing."

Elabea crossed her arms beneath her breasts, cocked her head to the side and tapped her foot. She reminded him of the way his mother looked when she expected an answer. He wondered if this was a mannerism handed down from woman to woman, or if it was simply a trait every woman was born with.

"I've known you all my life," Elabea said. "I know when there's something wrong with you, even when you say there isn't."

He shrugged, fiddled with his sword and avoided her eyes.

"I would have thought," she said as she closed the book, "you'd be excited about the part that says he wants to share Claire with us."

"I am. But what if the story is nothing but a riddle?"

"A riddle? Are you still having doubts?"

"Yes. Aren't you?"

"I suppose. A little...some days. But when the rusk tells me more stories..."

Romlin turned his back to her to hide his darkening expression.

"The rusk telling you stories. But as far as we know, that's all they are...stories. We still don't know anything for certain. Why is Claire cloaked with such mystery? Why is it so hard just getting there?"

"Perhaps it's because the Cauldron hunts us, or because the storytellers are no more. Maybe it's because after the Dark War everyone stopped listening and asking."

"I wish I had your convictions," Romlin replied.

"But you've seen Manno Vox. Hasn't all that has unfolded on this journey convinced you of Claire's existence?"

"It simply proves that a mysterious warrior flies about. Nothing more; nothing less."

Frustrated with his sour mood, Elabea walked away to where their horses grazed.

Romlin reached inside his tunic and pulled out his invitation. Despite the attacks of their enemies and the frantic pace of their journey, their parchments remained perfect in every way. Not even the slightest crease could be found. He turned his invitation over and over in his hand, studying it, thankful that Elabea had taught him what the words meant. He was learning to read, and it excited him, yet his doubts lingered.

"The invitations tell of great riches awaiting us in Claire," he said. "But I think there is more at stake here than silver and gold."

Still upset by his mood, Elabea continued stroking her horse's mane and refused to acknowledge his statement.

Romlin continued anyway.

"I understand why it's so important for you to become a storyteller. If the stories are true, then imagine what would happen if you returned to tell such tales to all the lands?"

"You just said that you didn't believe them," she answered, still unwilling to look at his face.

"I have my doubts; I admit it. But those are my battles, not yours. Il-Lilliad and Manno Vox gave me an order: Get you to Claire. A good soldier always obeys his orders, even if he doubts the objective."

Elabea said nothing.

"Elabea, are you frightened?"

She pondered his question while patting the horse's neck. She stole a quick glance at his face and noted the concern etched across it.

"Yes, she answered. "Are you?"

Romlin considered telling her about the changes on the map; of his fear that Claire's disappearance from the map might reflect Claire's disappearance from the real world. Instead, he revealed only a portion of his fears.

"Yes, but I'm not afraid of fighting to defend you. I hope you know that by now."

She nodded a quick assent and he continued.

"I do worry that our quest may be in vain."

Elabea searched his eyes. Although she would not have the full powers of a storyteller until she reached Claire, she knew her gifts were growing. One such gift was the ability to read people's hearts. In that instant, she read his.

She spoke words to strengthen him.

"If it weren't for you, I would never have gotten this far."

"I'm not so sure." He toed the ground, kicking up some loose dirt with his boot. "I almost got us killed by hunting those gors."

They smiled. Time had drained the horror from the event and transformed it into a comedic story to share around campfires.

"Perhaps," she replied. "But who was it that killed the ryators?"

"I did but…"

"Who found these horses?"

"Me, but…"

"Who is always thinking about my needs, about what I will eat next, rather than his own wants and desires?"

"Yes, but…"

"When I needed to rest, who found this beautiful place in a land full of evil and terror?"

Romlin smiled. Despite his misgivings about the map and Claire, her words renewed what little faith he had.

"As you long to be a great storyteller," he said, "I suppose what keeps me going is my desire to be the warrior Manno Vox said I'd be. If I tell you a dream I've been having, will you promise not to laugh?"

She smiled and nodded, hoping that she shared a place inside such a dream.

"Ever since we left Il-Lilliad's cave, I've had this dream. Sometimes it comes at night and other times it comes during the day. In this dream, I'm a great leader; a mighty warrior with an army at my back."

"An army?"

"Yes, a massive, powerful army. I feel like, somehow, someday, I'm supposed to become this person. Is that foolish? Am I going mad?"

Without waiting for her reply, he unsheathed his sword and paced, practicing fighting postures with it as he walked. Sunlight reflected off the blade and cast twinkling lights across the darkening mountain wall.

"What I mean is, am I losing my mind like…"

"Your father?"

"Yes."

Romlin drove the sword deep into the ground.

"I, too, have had a dream," Elabea confessed. "I dream I'll tell stories and tales that will heal our world. Does this mean I'm losing my senses...like my father?"

"No," Romlin yanked his sword out of the ground. "I suppose not. But the thought of becoming like my father makes me...it just makes me so... *angry.*"

Elabea drew close and laid a comforting hand on his shoulder.

"Romlin, I doubt that'll come to pass."

"Why?"

"Because you are..."

Elabea bit her lip and looked away, suddenly shy.

"I'm what?"

"You're...changed," she breathed.

His transformation had begun with his first step away from Hetherlinn. She saw it in the way he helped her dismount; his strong arms making her feel secure. When she went to sleep, she marveled at his willingness to protect her despite his fatigue. When he looked into her eyes, she felt dizzy, as if she had spun about in her meadow. When he smiled she felt calm, as if she were sipping soothing Allsbruthian tea.

She didn't share with him her secret dream; the one where they would one day marry and live in a cottage nestled beside their meadow, hand in hand watching their children climb the oak, to play and listen for whispers.

She swallowed, regained control over her emotions then continued.

"You've become more like a Romlin, and less like a Galadin."

"Thank you," he answered, without catching the nuances of her words. "Do you know what else I dream?"

"No, what?"

Elabea's heart raced, anticipating that he too envisioned a life with her as his bride in Hetherlinn.

"Once I'm a great warrior with an army..."

"Yes?"

She leaned closer.

"I'd want you to join us. Just imagine. An army with a storyteller would be *unstoppable.*"

"Oh."

Her heart sank back into its normal rhythms, the dream of their future life together fading with her sigh.

Romlin sheathed his sword and marched toward their horses. He grabbed the reins and leapt into the saddle.

"Come on, sleepy head? I need to get you to Claire."

Elabea pasted on a smile to mask her disappointment. She took the reins from his hand and followed him out of their sanctuary.

Chapter 33

The Onderling

Deep within the Allsbruthian Mountains was a place of darkness and mystery, a remnant of the forest's deepest secrets. Only those well-versed in the lore of Claire even knew of its existence.

Il-Lilliad paused atop a ridge to survey the primeval forest, savoring the aromas of pine resin, rich soil and pungent mosses. His eyes took in the valley far below. Shadows crisscrossed its narrow width, and although it was windy on the summit not a leaf or a fern stirred below. A hush rose up from the gorge and pressed against his face like the hot breath from an invisible beast.

"The valley to the Onderling's entrance," he said aloud, though there was no one to hear but himself.

He drew in one last breath from the ridge, then began his descent into the unknown. He slid over a large boulder then hopped over a log while his mind was flooded with stories of the Onderling: forgotten vales, hidden passageways, mysterious nations.

A steep drop interrupted his pace until he found saplings to use as handholds, and he continued his descent as if walking down a steep flight of stairs.

As he approached the valley floor, a long forgotten story rose from his memory.

The King of Claire had once commissioned three storytellers to journey to the Onderling in hopes of establishing a peaceful relationship, he recalled. They were never seen or heard from again. That mission had occurred over a century ago. Was it just a forgotten fable, or was there more to the story?

Il-Lilliad leapt from a small overhang and landed in the soft, damp basin. The air was thick and cool. A tiny stream rushed over rocks and ledges, but instead of it gurgling or swishing, it made not a sound.

Il-Lilliad's curiosity got the better of him.

"Hello," he called out, but no sound came out of his mouth.

Though intrigued by the mysterious power of the soundless valley, he nonetheless turned his attention to the task at hand. According to legend, the three storytellers followed a gentle stream to the Onderling's entrance. Perhaps the silent stream would be his guide as well.

As the stream descended deeper into the valley, Il-Lilliad kept pace with its swift current. The farther he traveled, the darker his thoughts grew. He would have preferred open battle upon the Gilden Plains to journeying to the Onderling, but he knew they were in need of allies and that the nations within the Onderling were vulnerable to attacks from Ebon. They could no longer pretend that the Cauldron's fumes would not find them. After all, they were the last of the free nations. Once Ebon discovered their location, they would be conquered and set like jewels in their crown of conquest.

The stream disappeared beneath a pile of moss-covered stones, each one the size of a man's head. Il-Lilliad stopped and stared at the spot that marked the entrance into a world from which he might not return.

He shuddered.

He did not fear death. He had faced it many times before in the Dark War. But this time was different. If he died, all those he cared for would suffer. Allsbruth would be without key allies; the Onderling would be vulnerable to Ebon's might; Elabea and Galadin might even perish. He closed his eyes and wondered if there was another way, other than braving the Onderling.

As if in answer to his worrisome thoughts, the King of Claire allowed him to see through the eyes of an eagle as it soared over the forests of Ebon. The eagle cleared a ridge and swooped down upon an open range. There, it spied Romlin and Elabea on horseback pressing ahead despite the dangers surrounding them.

The eagle banked and rode the wind high into the sky. Pulling his wings close, it dove for the ground like a falling star. Seconds away from impact, it spread its wings and swooped over the treetops.

The vision shifted, and Il-Lilliad was in Allsbruth many summers before. The eagle let out a majestic cry as it swept down upon an unsuspecting boy. Hearing the bird, the boy shielded his eyes against the brightness of the day and stared at the eagle. Il-Lilliad recognized the boy's face.

That is me, he marveled. *I remember that day. I was five summers of age, and it was the first time I had heard the Only's whisper. It came when I saw the eagle and heard its cry.*

The eagle flew across time and space. Il-Lilliad was now fifteen-summers old as he began his journey to Claire to become a storyteller.

The vision calmed him, and he marveled at the King of Claire's ability to live and breathe in the past, the present and the future.

The eagle zoomed straight up into the azure sky of Allsbruth. The fifteen-summers old Il-Lilliad followed its path until it disappeared into the sun. The older Il-Lilliad opened his eyes, and was back in the valley at the entrance to the Onderling, reassured of his mission and purpose.

He used his staff to pry and push the mossy stones aside, clearing an opening large enough to enter the cavern. Without a moment of hesitation, he disappeared into the Onderling.

The air was much cooler and felt heavy upon Il-Lilliad's face. He stooped to avoid hitting his head in the shallow cave, and followed the stream's course over rocks as slick as ice. Now that the stream was beyond the mysterious valley, its gurgling sounds could be heard echoing about the chamber. In the diminishing light he saw the stream disappear through a darker space on the opposite end of the cave.

He paused at the darkness and gazed within. Despite the failing light, he could tell this new chamber was massive. Perhaps it was the entrance into another cave, he reasoned. Perhaps it was the entrance to the Onderling. There was no way to tell. In his haste he had neglected to bring materials to make a torch.

Mustering his courage, he entered the gloom.

He felt his way along, using his hands and his feet, but after only a few steps he stopped and clung to a large, cold stone to get his bearings. Unable to see anything, he relied upon his ears. The stream's gentle burbling sounded as if it had joined forces with a dozen other streams. It surged now with a loud, gushing roar. Somewhere in the distance, he could hear a waterfall splashing into what he presumed was a large pool.

His nose gave him more clues to the new environment. Gone was the musky, dampness of the first cave. Instead, he breathed dry, warm air that carried the faint scent of sulfur, water and earthen dust.

As he held onto the boulder and contemplated how he would descend through the blackness without falling, he remembered a short story from Claire. It was one of the first he had learned as a young storyteller. At the time, it made no sense, and he had concluded that it was simply a lovely but inconsequential poem. Now, he wondered if the words had a hidden meaning. He recited them aloud.

"Into my heart flow the stories of Claire. From within to without will shine great light."

Nothing changed, except his conviction of the story's weight and truth.

He repeated the phrase, louder.

"Into my heart flow the stories of Claire. From within to without will shine great light."

Orange and yellow light, like a crisp fall morn, poured out of him. The vista before him took his breath away.

The waterfall he had heard was a silver torrent that cascaded over rocks littered with gemstones and raw ore that glittered like the stars. Far below the fall was a magnificent pool, with ripples that radiated outward toward the cavern's floor.

He discovered he was standing on a ridge that hugged the cave's wall all the way to the bottom. If he had taken another step forward, instead of hugging the rock, he would have fallen to his death, and that would have been the end of his mission to the Onderling.

He began his descent down the narrow pathway and marveled at the multitude of small caves, ledges and cliffs that accented the environment.

A troubling thought made him pause in his descent. The light that emanated from within his body made it possible for him to see everything around him, but it also meant he could be clearly seen by anyone who cared to look.

He had to chuckle at the irony: He saved himself from falling from the ledge, only to be plunged into the Onderling's dark mysteries.

He tried to extinguish the light by recanting the story but there was no change. He even blew on his tunic as if to blow out a candle, but to no avail. He had no other option but to move forward as carefully as possible, searching out crevices and shadows that might shield his light from anyone who might be passing by.

Once at the bottom, another puzzle disturbed his calm and kindled his fears. Since no one had returned from the Onderling to tell stories of what it was like, he did not know what he was looking for. Were the inhabitants of the Onderling giants, or were they small like children. Were they perhaps invisible? Were they even human?

So far he had seen nothing to indicate they even existed. He even entertained the notion that the Onderling was void of man or beast.

He turned about to illuminate the vast darkness, and spied five passageways that radiated out from the cave like spokes of a wagon wheel. Before he could study them, he heard a noise; a horn blast that echoed above the din of the waterfall.

He tuned his ears to determine where the sound originated. When it sounded again he could tell it was coming from the cave directly in front of him.

He turned and ran for the passage farthest from the horn blasts. The corridor was wide and had a gentle slope. It did not meander as he had expected, but ran straight as an arrow. Even with the light from his body, he could not see the corridor's end. As he ran for his life, a spark-sized light appeared far away in front of him in the passageway. He stopped and watched it grow in size and brightness.

"Torches," he grumbled. "Hundreds of torches."

He turned and sprinted back the way he came. The horn blasts continued, but they were closer and trumpeted a different message.

Battle calls, he thought.

Joining the horns was a new sound. Rhythmic, thundering, increasing in volume as it approached, the sound rumbled out of the corridors and washed over him.

Cavalry. And judging by the sound they are coming fast. How could they have horses underground? Are they even horses?

As if in answer to his unspoken question, torchlight poured out of the five passageways.

And to think I was worried I might die of starvation, he thought, surprised he was making a joke during a dire time.

Il-Lilliad took a deep breath, rested upon his staff and spoke what he assumed would be his last words.

"With the stories from Claire as my shield and lance, I will face this battle. By the power of the Only, I will fight to either live another day or of seeing him only."

Il-Lilliad shielded his eyes from the torchlight as both cavalrymen and foot soldiers raced into the cavern. They quickly surrounded him and aimed arrows, swords and lances at him. He had to smile at the absurdity of such a magnificent force arrayed against one old man.

The warriors were fair skinned, handsome with straight hair that glistened like sun on honey. Armor, chased with gold and silver and adorned with gemstones that were no doubt mined from this cavern, protected their heads and chests and covered their horses as well.

Foot soldiers, carrying torches in one hand and swords in the other, formed the closest circle around Il-Lilliad. Beyond them was another circle of cavalry, armed with lances and crossbows, and beyond them was another circle of cavalry with longbows.

The circles parted wide enough to permit a warrior on a white horse to approach. His face told of a man who had seen at least fifty summers, and yet his hair was as golden as the youngest man present.

"So many warriors," Il-Lilliad said to the approaching commander, "for one who travels alone and in peace? Does an old one from the outer world really pose such a dire threat to so great a people as I see before me?"

The commander stopped in front of him.

"It only takes one pebble to start an avalanche," he replied. "Who are you and why are you here?"

"My name is Il-Lilliad. I am a storyteller, sent by the Only to seek your help...and to warn you of a great danger."

"What great danger," the commander asked.

"The power of the Cauldron grows daily. Its vapors will soon find a way into your world. Brairtok's supremacy also grows, fueled by his lust for life immortal. I fear his army will grow until it is unstoppable."

"Unstoppable?" The commander's face was void of any sign of worry. "Against this army that surrounds you and will soon determine your fate?"

"Yes. You must believe me. If our worlds unite, we could defeat them."

"Yours is a world of shadows and whispers, where death and despair hunt like ravenous lions. We are the Aggellons. Ours is a world where peace and prosperity flourish side by side. Your nations rise, and your nations fall. All are destined to fade away like the mist from the waterfall. Ours is destined to flourish forever. Besides, we have heard such rumors of war before."

"This time is different."

"How so?"

"The King of Claire is preparing for battle. Manno Vox lives. The awakening has begun."

"Mere talk. We are familiar with your stories from the land of Claire, but they are only stories."

As Il-Lilliad pondered his next words, he noticed the expressions of the soldiers. He scanned their stories and discovered a secret. He permitted himself a sly smile.

"Answer me one thing, commander. If my stories are but tales one would tell a child at bedtime, then why do your men fear me?"

"We fear no one," the commander barked.

"Come now, commander. We are both men of action. But unlike you, I've been in battle before. I've looked into the eyes of my enemy. I know fear when I see it."

The commander's face tightened with anger. He gave a quick signal to his men, and Il-Lilliad prepared for the worst. Several soldiers approached him with swords ready to kill. Instead of striking him, they grabbed him and tied his hands together. They pushed him out of the circle to a waiting wagon. He climbed into its bed, and awaited his fate.

The horns sounded another command, and each battalion departed down the corridor from whence it came. Il-Lilliad's wagon jerked into motion and flew down a passageway. He marveled at the horses' speed and the ability of the Aggellon foot soldiers to keep pace.

Far ahead he could see a light. As before, it was the size of a spark, but due to their swift pace the light soon grew in size and brightness. The light was an entrance through which Il-Lilliad was thrust into a bright new world.

"Aggellon," he exclaimed.

The air was rich with floral fragrances; sweet spring grass and fresh mountain air. As far as he could see in any direction were grass-covered hills, glistening streams and pockets of trees. Birds soared in graceful circles overhead. Scattered over this landscape Il-Lilliad could see villages connected by meandering dirt roads. The colors of Aggellon were sharp and distinct, appearing brighter and richer than any landscape he had ever witnessed. Above was a great source of light that was as warm and bright as the sun, yet somehow seemed unnatural. The deep blue sky, which was void of clouds, seemed surreal.

Aggellon was indeed a land of ineffable beauty.

Aggellon was paradise.

The army galloped toward a city that sat proudly upon a rise in the distance. As they neared their destination, Il-Lilliad noted the city itself appeared to be constructed from stone, embellished with gold and adorned with sparkling gems. Rising above all the other buildings was a glorious structure with sweeping arches, elongated windows and ornate flags that flapped in the breeze. Il-Lilliad concluded it must be the palace for whoever ruled Aggellon.

The city gates, overlaid with shining silver, swung open to allow the speeding column to enter. Their pace slowed to a fast walk. Citizens in the courtyard stopped and stared in disbelief at the prisoner in the wagon. Some held expressions of shock, others of dismay, but all expressed the same fear he had seen in the soldiers' eyes.

The column stopped in front of the palace entrance. Gold inlaid doors swung open and men of obvious wealth and prestige walked out, dressed in richly colored robes and wearing polished helmets. Il-Lilliad assumed they were the rulers of Aggellon.

Il-Lilliad was escorted from the wagon and led before the dignitaries. As he neared, he noticed that one of the men appeared different from the others. He was shorter, and his face was round, not long and straight. Wiry gray hair protruded from beneath his gem-encrusted silver helmet, which appeared crafted to accentuate the color of his hair. He looked to be a man of sixty summers, but Il-Lilliad wondered why his hair was not golden, like the others. The gray-haired leader motioned for Il-Lilliad to approach.

"Tell me your name," he commanded.

Il-Lilliad bowed with hands to heart.

"I am Il-Lilliad, one of the Only's last storytellers."

"A storyteller," the leader acknowledged with an honorable nod of his head. "My name is TyNorai. I am the chancellor of Aggellon, but let us dispense with such formalities. What brings a storyteller to Aggellon?"

"I've come to ask for your assistance, and to warn you of an impending war that will inevitably find its way to the Onderling and Aggellon."

Laughter ricocheted among the dignitaries. TyNorai smiled as if addressing a dimwitted child.

"My friend, I am sorry, but your journey has been in vain. We are familiar with storytellers and the tales of Claire, but the truth is, we have no need for you, your stories or your alliances."

"Why not?"

"Aggellon has not seen war or crime for centuries. We do not need assistance from your world, nor are we inclined to offer our assistance to a world that cannot keep its own peace."

"Yet you have amassed an impressive army."

TyNorai smiled and nodded, acknowledging the truth of Il-Lilliad's statement.

Il-Lilliad continued.

"Ebon is marching to war, and they will find you. The Cauldron's power will consume this... this..."

"Paradise?" TyNorai answered for him.

"Yes. Paradise."

TyNorai motioned for the soldiers to leave and for Il-Lilliad to follow him and the other dignitaries into the ornate palace. As he followed, Il-Lilliad attempted to read TyNorai's story. Normally an easy task, he was surprised to find his way blocked, as if the chancellor's heart and mind were surrounded by an impenetrable stone wall.

Il-Lilliad was dumbfounded. The only other time he had experienced such opposition was when the Cauldron's vapors were present in a person's mind. Since the vapors had not yet reached the nations of the Onderling, he concluded that TyNorai was as mysterious as Aggellon was beautiful.

They entered the palace and walked down a hallway with towering walls supporting an ornately painted arched ceiling. The scenes of pastoral settings and grand vistas of Aggellon were masterfully produced, appearing so lifelike that Il-Lilliad felt if a breeze passed by it would stir the leaves on the painted trees.

The hallway was well lit, but by what means Il-Lilliad could not discern, for the hall was void of torch or flame. Walls were hung with fabulous tapestries and works of art that rivaled anything he had ever seen. Even the floor was a thing of beauty. The tiles appeared to be constructed from pearls and ivory that had been polished to shimmer like water.

"Let me understand you completely," TyNorai said as they walked. "You risked your life journeying to Aggellon simply to ask for assistance?"

"And to warn you of the growing power of the Cauldron. Yes."

"Surely as a storyteller you must have heard the tales of the Onderling. No one returns who enters our world."

"I have heard such stories."

"And yet you came?"

"I have the courage from the King of Claire, and faith in two young ones who have received invitations from him. Their courage is inspiring."

"Indeed," TyNorai replied as he led the entourage to a set of towering golden doors.

"And I have seen Manno Vox."

TyNorai's hand froze on the door handle; his smile masked a deeper concern.

"Manno Vox, you say?"

"Yes, he lives."

"Impossible."

The quiver in TyNorai's voice was almost imperceptible, but it was there. He regained his composure immediately and pushed open the enormous doors with ease, and led the party through.

"We regularly send scouts to the entrance of your world and listen to the stories that fly upon the winds. It is common knowledge that Manno Vox was butchered by Brairtok in the Dark War."

"If that is the case," Il-Lilliad challenged, "then certainly you've heard the recent war of whispers, and tales of an awakening."

TyNorai stopped, turned and studied Il-Lilliad's face.

"Leave us," he commanded the others. "I must question this man in private."

Bowing their heads, TyNorai's attendants left, the golden doors closing behind them with a soft *thump*.

TyNorai moved to one of three tall windows in his chamber. He drew back the thick drapes and gazed out upon paradise.

"Manno Vox. Deep within my heart, I'd hoped I would never hear that name again. For countless summers I have lived here in peace and affluence. Now you bring me stories of an awakening...of Manno Vox back from the dead."

"Yes, but if you venture into our world and spy on us through our stories, you already know what I've said to be true. Why is this such a surprise?"

The chancellor ignored the question and continued his musing. A wry smile creased his lips.

"Have you not guessed? Well, no, I suppose you haven't."

TyNorai turned from the window and faced Il-Lilliad.

"Like you, I too was once sent to the Onderling. I journeyed with the same fear and misgivings as you, and I was captured in the great cavern by the pool just as you were. I expected death, but instead, I found life. The tranquility, peace and beauty of Aggellon captured my heart. All my life I have sought such things, and here they were, before our very eyes...within our grasp. We were given a choice: Stay and live forever...or perish."

"We," Il-Lilliad asked.

"Yes, me and several friends. The Aggellons had seen us glowing in the cavern, just as they must have found you. Despite the fact that I was from the outside, they held me in high esteem. I knew that in time I could become a great ruler in Aggellon. As you can see, all my dreams have come true."

TyNorai removed his helmet, parted his hair and lowered his head. Beneath the gray strands, Il-Lilliad discovered a purple birthmark.

"How could I have been so blind," Il-Lilliad fumed. "You are a..."

"Storyteller," TyNorai finished Il-Lilliad's thought.

"That explains why I was unable to read your stories."

TyNorai nodded.

"An easy task for even the youngest of the faithful, though I have not needed to use that skill in some time. I quite enjoyed it."

Il-Lilliad's mind raced for an explanation to this extraordinary turn of events, when it broke over like a bright flash of lightning in a midnight sky.

"You are one of the three sent to the Onderling by the Only."

TyNorai nodded.

"But that was over a century ago. How can you be so old and yet look so young? It is not possible."

"There is no death in Aggellon. Life does not change here. Time remains the same."

"But you are a storyteller. Storytellers are obligated to fulfill their orders. By choosing to remain in Aggellon, you betrayed your king."

"Think about the stories you tell, Il-Lilliad. Are they not stories of a world in harmony and peace, where no one dies and all tears are dried? Where the streets are paved with gold and wealth abounds? Look around you, Il-Lilliad. Aggellon *is* that world."

"Perhaps. But if Aggellon is paradise, then my original question still stands: why do you need an army?"

"Obviously, to be prepared should your world invade."

"Or not so obviously," Il-Lilliad ventured, "because the peace and prosperity you speak of are no more than an illusion."

TyNorai snickered.

"Perhaps, but surely you're not going to compare your world's crime, poverty and war to our...what did you call it...oh, yes...*illusion*."

"No. Our world surely suffers more than yours appears to. Nevertheless, I remind you of what you already know in your heart; that true peace will come when the Only returns to power and... "

"Listen to you," TyNorai cut him off with a wave of his hand. "How long have you been waiting? What has changed? Death, crime and war continue to be your way of life, and yet you still cling to a hope that the King of Claire will rise up to destroy the Cauldron. Why waste your life for something that will not happen?"

"But it *is* happening. Manno Vox is proof of that. Invitations are being received once more. Surely you're aware of such tales."

TyNorai pulled his gaze away from Il-Lilliad's perplexing, prying eyes.

The truth dawned on Il-Lilliad.

"You have never sent anyone beyond Aggellon to listen, have you?"

TyNorai turned his back to him.

Il-Lilliad continued.

"Of course not. The valley is void of wind and sound so there would be nothing to hear, even for a storyteller. If you sent them beyond the valley, they risk getting caught and divulging the secret of Aggellon's existence."

TyNorai spun around to face the accusation.

"That valley used to be the gathering place for all the stories of the world. At the end of the Dark War, the Cauldron cursed it with silence, but before it fell silent, I learned of the destruction of Claire."

"Perhaps Claire was destroyed by Ebon; perhaps not. That is open to debate. Yet you continued this charade of being the all-knowing storyteller. My appearance was a surprise to you, and you were unaware of Manno Vox's reappearance. You have no idea what is transpiring in our world. I wonder what the Aggellons would think if they knew their leader was a fraud?"

If TyNorai was concerned by Il-Lilliad's implied threat, he did not show it. Instead he chuckled.

"You are indeed an insightful man, Il-Lilliad. Perhaps I am a bit of a fraud. Even so, my stories are far better than any tale you may have, and Aggellon's paradise is beyond compare."

"So, what has been the price of paradise?"

"What do you mean?"

"You yourself said that no one returns who enters Aggellon."

"Surely you can see that we can't allow anyone to return after witnessing this splendor. However pure their intentions, others would come, and they would bring crime and war to us."

"So what happened to the other two storytellers?"

"They were offered sanctuary."

"Did they accept?"

TyNorai walked to the window and allowed the view of breathtaking beauty to sooth his soul.

"No," he whispered as the memory crashed in.

"What happens to those that refuse sanctuary in Aggellon?" Il-Lilliad asked, his voice tinged with emotion, sensing where their conversation was going.

"The needs of the many outweigh the needs of the few. Their deaths were for the well being of the many."

"Their deaths?" Il-Lilliad repeated in shock. "Surely a nation of peace does not execute innocent men?"

TyNorai stared motionless out the window.

"They would not listen to reason. They refused to acknowledge the beauty and potential in themselves and in Aggellon. They were idealists...just like you."

"So you bowed to Aggellon's...*peace*...and watched your friends be executed?"

"The needs of the many outweigh the needs of the few."

"Your army isn't for protection from our world, is it?" Il-Lilliad shouted.

TyNorai spun around. "Dreamers, both of them," he spat as he marched to where Il-Lilliad stood. "They could have had it all. Just like you."

Il-Lilliad shoved him away.

"You swore an oath. Storytellers are not permitted to murder, nor to stand by while murder is committed. You were a passive participant. You are as guilty of their deaths as if you had shed their blood yourself."

TyNorai's face flushed red with rage.

"Enough of your babbling. You face the same choice as they: Sanctuary or death? Choose!"

The two storytellers locked eyes and Il-Lilliad spoke from his deepest convictions.

"The fruit of your life is like the landscape of your paradise, an illusion.

You have no future, and you cling to the hope within your own stories and myths. So, my brother, I choose life in death, and although my story may be silenced, hear this: The Cauldron will come. Ebon will invade your paradise. And when the Only returns, you will be found wanting."

"You have chosen. So be it. Guards!"

The golden doors flew open. Four warriors entered with drawn swords and took position around Il-Lilliad.

"Take our distinguished *guest* and prepare him for his execution."

The warriors gruffly grabbed Il-Lilliad, but before they marched him out, he offered a parting word to the fallen storyteller.

"During our...chat, you dropped your guard. I read a portion of your story, and discovered the tale you secretly hope will come to pass."

"And what is this *secret story?*" TyNorai retorted.

"You hope Manno Vox *is* alive, and you desire to ride beneath his banner once again. You are correct about the world above: Death, war and crime rage across the lands like wild rivers after the spring rains. But you also know that the true peace and purpose you thirst for will only come when you fight the Cauldron. War will come, TyNorai. So I leave you with this question: Who will *you* fight for?"

TyNorai clinched his jaw and pointed toward a doorway on the opposite wall.

"Take him away."

The guards led Il-Lilliad through the door and down the hallway to a circular staircase that disappeared beneath the opulent splendor of Aggellon. The world below was dimly lit by smoky torches that filled the air with sputtering bursts of warmth and the acrid scent of burning pitch.

Led through a narrow rocky corridor, he passed door after door of what he assumed to be the prison cells of Aggellon. Made of wood, they were stained dark from seeping moisture and black rot. He shook his head in disgust, for these cells were proof that Aggellon's prosperity was not a natural outpouring of its people, but was maintained and manipulated by a select few.

They stopped while a guard unlocked a cell door. Rusty hinges squealed like a pig being slaughtered as the door swung open. A torch attached to the wall was lit and shadows flickered and flitted about the cell like ghosts. Dripping water echoed somewhere beyond. A damp chill pierced him to the marrow.

The soldiers shoved him down onto a moldy bed of rancid burlap and marched out. The door slammed shut and the key turned in the lock with the finality of a coffin lid closing.

Il-Lilliad surveyed his temporary quarters by the light of the flickering torch. Despite his impending execution and dire conditions, he felt serene and tranquil.

As he rested on his bed, the stories from Claire flooded his mind, carried on the wings of beautiful melodies he had not heard in many a summer. Sleep came to him like a swan gliding across a tranquil pond. Floating away in a blissful dream, he found himself resting beneath Elabea's oak, a warm breeze caressing his weary face as a whisper fluttered nearby.

Chapter 34

Veiled Legacy

"Stop," Draemel ordered his prisoners.

He spurred his horse forward to a rise, nearly knocking DeMorley to the ground.

Ever since their capture, the entourage had walked in silence. Now, Draemel was animated, his senses on edge. He pulled back on the reins and listened, scanning the surrounding woods with the practiced eyes of a hunter.

"You two," he pointed his crossbow at Newcomb, who was on foot and Lassiter, who rode Paradin's horse. "Move over to that tree."

Lassiter looked a question at Newcomb, hoping for some insight into what Draemel was up to. Newcomb had no answer.

"Do as he says," Newcomb said. "All will be well."

Lassiter dismounted, and they walked to the tree as ordered.

"Now sit down and tie this around you," Draemel commanded as he tossed them a rope.

Lassiter and Newcomb sat on opposite sides of the slender tree with their backs against its trunk and wrapped the rope about themselves.

Draemel dismounted and approached. "Don't fret," he said as he tightened the last knot. "I'm not leaving you to starve; I'll return for you."

Draemel marched over to DeMorley.

"It's time. Come with me."

"Where are we going?" DeMorley squeaked, not moving a muscle. "Are you going to kill me?"

Draemel pressed the crossbow against DeMorley's wiry frame and stared into his face. DeMorley, although terrified, did not take his eyes off Draemel's cold, brown eyes.

"You snivel worse than a maiden," Draemel replied. "Now, move."

Pushing the minstrel before him, Draemel walked deeper into the woods.

"What's Draemel going to do," Lassiter asked, unable to see the men march off.

"I don't know, but I doubt he'll kill him. Draemel may be cold-blooded, but he's more interested in receiving his bounty than in killing for pleasure."

"Do you think DeMorley is guilty?"

"Of murder? No," Newcomb answered, wishing he could see Lassiter's face. "The only thing that minstrel has ever killed was a good song."

The rusk landed on Newcomb's shoulder then scampered down his side and began chewing on the rope.

"No, not now," Newcomb whispered to the rusk. "We cannot give away our identity to Draemel."

The rusk's eyes saddened, but it obeyed and climbed back on top of Newcomb's shoulder.

"Who would send out the likes of Draemel to hunt down a minstrel like DeMorley," Lassiter asked.

"A good question. The times are wicked indeed. DeMorley was perhaps just in the wrong place at the wrong time. Perhaps his life of manipulation and deception finally caught up with him."

"Do you think Draemel will kill us?"

"He's not going to do anything until he is confident there is treasure in Claire."

"Is there?"

Silence.

"Is there," Lassiter repeated.

Newcomb's thoughts were not on Lassiter's question or even on their predicament. Memories of days long past flew into his mind, as if from a whisper on the wind.

I love you as if you were my own son, Newcomb reflected, *but it did not start out that way...*

Soon after Lassiter was born, the King of Claire commissioned Newcomb to escort the babe and his mother, Anessatia, to the Isle of Lills. Newcomb had protested, of course. After all, raising a dead warrior's son was a task for women. He was a storyteller with extraordinary talents, not a nurse-maid.

But the King's mind would not be swayed. Newcomb submitted, albeit reluctantly, and they set sail for the Isle of Lills. Newcomb's heart hardened toward the boy with every rise and pitch of their ship.

Life on the Isle of Lills was comfortable and predictable, just the kind of life Newcomb abhorred. He started each day with breakfast on his terrace where he could at least savor the salty air and watch the sunrise.

When the child was of age, Anessatia would lead Lassiter by the hand and bring him to Newcomb. The storyteller taught the boy such simple tales as he might comprehend. Irritated at his lowly duties, Newcomb delivered them with an icy disposition, which infuriated Anessatia, but Newcomb dismissed her with a stern look.

Time passed, and Newcomb remained on the Isle, unsummoned by the King of Claire. He continued his passionless charge until that fateful day when Lassiter was three summers of age.

As usual after breakfast, Anessatia brought Lassiter out onto Newcomb's terrace. When she let go of his hand, he ran to Newcomb with arms wide open. The storyteller knelt to receive the boy and then it happened.

The child called him, *Father*.

That one word cut open Newcomb's hardened heart, and he understood the depth of his mission. His assignment to the Isle of Lills with Lassiter was not a punishment or a lesser mission. On the contrary, his was perhaps the greatest assignment any storyteller, or any man who called himself a man, could be given.

In an effort to make up for lost time, Newcomb scooped the boy up and drew him close. Lassiter's sweet boy-fragrance washed any obstinacy that remained far out to sea. Newcomb glanced at Anessatia and saw she was crying, rejoicing that her only son now had a father figure.

From that day forth, Newcomb was a changed man. He devoted every waking moment to nurturing Lassiter, as if he were his very own. In return, Lassiter adored him with the youthful innocence and zeal of a son.

When Lassiter was five summers of age, Newcomb instructed him in the stories of Claire as well as the tales of his true father, Hornlynn. Morning after morning they met, and like most children, Lassiter had an insatiable curiosity. He asked for every detail and nuance about his father's life, and responded to every answer with an incessant, *why?*

Newcomb answered his questions...all but one. This he kept secret, waiting for the time when the King of Claire would whisper for him to reveal it.

Newcomb's thoughts returned to the present when a whisper, like a lark's song, spoke so only he could hear.

"It is time. Tell the tale."

Wetting his lips, Newcomb swallowed and began with a question.

"Lassiter, why did you receive an invitation."

Lassiter pondered the question, journeying back in his mind to that fateful night. Unable to sleep, he had stared at the various shades of blue painted on his walls by the full moon. Opting for a view of the sea, he tossed off his cover, got out of bed, and shuffled to his window.

The breeze was gentle and the waves crested lazily, the froth silvery in the light of the moon. A brilliant flash high in the sky caught his attention; a giant being riding a flying horse and both glowing brighter than the moon.

Lassiter ducked for cover and rubbed his eyes, convinced he was in a dream. Daring another look, he raised his eyes above the window ledge. The horse hovered nearby and the phantom rider raised a massive crossbow to his shoulder.

Lassiter dropped to the floor in fear as the bolt slammed into his door. He remained motionless on the cold floor, afraid the ethereal warrior would storm through the door at any moment. When nothing happened, he peeked once more out his window. The midnight marauder was but a blur of rainbow light against the luster of the moon.

Gathering his courage, Lassiter opened his door. Embedded in its wooden surface was a crystal-clear bolt. Wrapped around the shaft was a clean, white parchment whose edges flapped in the sea breeze.

Lassiter answered Newcomb.

"I don't know why I received an invitation. Didn't everyone receive one?"

"Perhaps, but only a few had the courage to retrieve the parchment, and fewer still accepted the invitation to make the journey to Claire. Tell me, Lassiter, why did I insist upon leaving the Isle of Lills the next day?"

"You said, *It is time.*"

Newcomb paused for a moment before continuing to unfurl the story he had kept secret for so many summers.

"I think it is time you hear another story...about your father."

"Now?"

"Yes. Now."

Although Newcomb was unable to see Lassiter's face, he sensed the boy's eyes were widening with interest.

"Your father, Hornlynn, was a mighty warrior for the Only. He fell in love with your mother, Anessatia, and..."

"Old news, Newcomb. I've heard that story dozens of times. Tell me something I don't already know."

"Yes, you have heard *that* story; but not the secret story I have been entrusted to guard until now. Lassiter, you always asked for stories about your father. The secret tale I have concerns your mother."

"My mother?"

"Anessatia..." Newcomb paused, knowing that once exposed, the story could never again be hidden from the Cauldron, "is the grand-daughter of

King Culdean. Your mother was a princess, the last of the old king's bloodline. According to Allsbruthian law, your father was to serve beside her as king."

Lassiter sat silent, stunned by the secret the Cauldron coveted to know.

"Now do you understand why you were sent to live on the Isle of Lills?"

"No," Lassiter answered, his voice flat and stern.

"It was for your protection. Brairtok tried to destroy all the descendants of King Culdean, and very nearly succeeded. Your great-grandfather feared for your life, so he planned for your escape. Together with your parents, he fabricated a story that wild animals had attacked and killed both you and Anessatia. They produced evidence: clothing, ripped and covered in blood. A funeral was held for you and your mother, while we secretly set sail for the Isle of Lills. Now do you understand?"

Lassiter was silent. Newcomb continued.

"Your father was already dead, killed in battle during the Dark War. When your mother died last year, you became heir to the throne of Allsbruth."

Newcomb stopped to let Lassiter digest the news. The boy who was the true king of Allsbruth remained silent, his mind a whirlwind of questions.

"Lassiter, that is why I was commissioned to be with you from the beginning, to prepare you to rule."

"King?" he finally said, his voice rising to match his mood.

"Shh," Newcomb cautioned. "Draemel might be near. I only tell you this now because every day may be our last, and I think it only fair you should know who you truly are."

Lassiter's face lit up, a thousand questions tumbling over each other, trying to be answered first.

Newcomb continued, "Now do you understand why I have been so demanding of you? Why I get enraged when you talk about journeying to Claire in search of pretty maidens? Lassiter, you are meant for so much more. I'm convinced that the invitation is a sign from the Only that it's time to crown you...king."

"But I'm not ready to be a king. I'm not even sure if I want to be a..."

"The timing is in the hands of the Only, Lassiter. You will be ready."

"No."

Lassiter strained against the ropes.

"After all these years, you suddenly decide to tell me that my great grandfather was King Culdean; that my father was to be king; and that I'm heir to a throne in a land I've never even seen? And now what? You expect me to say, *Great news, Newcomb. While sitting here, tied to a tree, I've been wondering if I'd one day be king.*"

"You were born with this inheritance. It is in your blood. It is a gift and an honor."

"Well, I don't want any part of the gift *or* the honor," Lassiter spat. "You're a liar. First you deceived me about your identity, and now..." his voice trailed off in a fury too deep for words to express. He scowled and sat in silence, regretting the first time his mother ever winked at his father.

Newcomb sat stunned. He had hoped his story would stir Lassiter to new heights. He certainly never expected Lassiter's mood to swing to such despair. To his surprise he found himself getting angry. Lassiter's rejection of the crown, of his birthright, cut to the core of his being, and he wondered if his life's work had been in vain.

Newcomb tasted failure, and it was bitter, like poison, upon his palette. In silence they sat, the uncrowned king of Allsbruth and a disgruntled storyteller.

DeMorley stumbled through the brush while stealing glances over his shoulder at Draemel, afraid a crossbow bolt would strike him at any moment.

"Where are you taking me?" he squeaked.

"We need horses."

"And how does forcing me through these woods help accomplish that purpose?"

Draemel did not answer, but merely nudged him forward toward a clearing. Draemel pulled out his gor weapon and DeMorley's eyes widened as he recalled Draemel's savage attack against Paradin.

"Hold out your hands and don't move," Draemel ordered.

DeMorley stood frozen. He didn't move a muscle.

"Now, minstrel."

DeMorley stretched his bound hands out. His arms trembled.

"Stop moving," Draemel barked as he brought his arm back to strike.

DeMorley closed his eyes and turned his head away as Draemel brought the gor weapon slashing down. DeMorley opened his eyes, expecting to see his hands lying severed on the ground. Instead, he saw the strands of rope lying at his feet.

"You're setting me free?"

"If you wish to think of it that way," Draemel replied as he focused on gathering small sticks and tinder.

"So…" DeMorley said as he eyed a nearby thicket. "I may…run *away?*"

Draemel gave him a withering look.

"No."

Confused, DeMorley tried to rub circulation back into his wrists, which were rubbed raw from the ropes. He watched as Draemel built a fire. Sparks from flint and steel ignited the tiny dry leaves, and Draemel coaxed the flames higher by adding twigs to fuel the fire. Soon, the crackle of wood and the scent of smoke filled the crisp air.

DeMorley watched the gray smoke spiral through the trees and out into the clearing. Foreboding made his heart race.

"Is this a good idea," he asked.

Draemel ignored him and added more wood to the leaping flames.

"What I mean," DeMorley continued as he warmed his hands over the fire, "is that the smoke can be seen from a great distance and…"

"Play me a song," Draemel requested, waving away the minstrel's concerns.

"A song? Now?"

"Yes, a song. Now."

"But, what if Ebonites hear me? What if they see the smoke from your fire and… "

Draemel stared at DeMorley. The intensity in his eyes silenced the singer's objections.

"Ah. Now I understand. You're using me as bait."

Draemel cocked one eyebrow, almost in admiration for the minstrel's discernment.

"You actually *want* someone to hear my song and see the smoke so you can take their horses."

Draemel gave him a slight nod.

"Now, play me a song. A loud, happy song."

DeMorley was not sure which he feared more; being captured by a band of Ebonites, or remaining with Draemel. He swung his lute off his back, lightly plucked some strings, and made his decision.

"I said a *loud* song," Draemel barked.

DeMorley stopped.

"In a moment. I must first tune my instrument before I can sing," he quipped and enjoyed the brief moment of being in control.

Draemel grunted and tossed another piece of wood on the fire.

As he plucked the strings and twisted the tuning pegs on the lute, DeMorley asked, "Would you care for a love song? I have a true gem that I composed for…"

"I don't care. Just sing loud."

DeMorley squatted beside the fire, muttered some expletives beneath his breath, and began his song.

Convinced the minstrel could be heard far and wide, Draemel slipped into the shadows of the nearby woods.

With Draemel out of sight, DeMorley cast his eyes at a nearby thicket in the opposite direction, and pondered a quick escape. As if reading his thoughts, Draemel called from his hiding place.

"I can see you, minstrel, but I can't hear you. Now, *sing*. Or would you prefer I put this shaft through your head?"

DeMorley resumed strumming and began to sing, wondering who would come their way.

The Ebonite commander signaled for his men to halt.

"Never stop. Never stop," Paradin ordered, pressing the knife into the commander's ribs. "He might get away. He might get away."

"I thought I heard something. And I smell smoke," the commander countered.

Paradin peered around him at the thin tendril of smoke rising above the trees ahead of them. He caught an odd sound on the wind: a man's voice singing a raucous tavern song.

"A trap. A trap. Do beware. Do beware."

"That's a possibility. I'll send a scout to investigate."

With a wave of his right hand, one of his best trackers dismounted and slipped into the woods. Moments later, he returned with the news.

"It's just a minstrel singing by a fire."

"Anyone else?"

"No sir," the tracker answered as he remounted.

"A minstrel. A minstrel. What song I sing. What song I love."

"Why the excitement over a street entertainer?"

"Draemel took one. Draemel took one. Now I take. Now I take."

"We don't need the minstrel. We need… "

Paradin dug the dagger tip deeper, and the commander held his tongue.

"Where one is, another will be. Then get Draemel for me."

The commander gave the signal, and the patrol moved forward toward the minstrel's fire.

DeMorley saw them while they were still a good distance away. His mouth went dry, making it difficult to sing. He paused to swallow.

"Keep singing, minstrel." Draemel's voice floated in low tones from an unseen site.

"They're coming. Four of them."

"Silence your tongue. I have eyes. Keep playing. And sing."

DeMorley's whole body shook, causing his fingers to slip and land on different frets. The sour notes sent chills up his spine, but he played on. Chills and poor note choices were better than a crossbow bolt in his back. When he heard the clank and snort of their warhorses, his voice cracked.

The Ebonite scouting party stopped where the trees met the clearing, and one warrior dismounted and headed toward the fire.

DeMorley's fingers slipped yet again. He recovered from his mistake but kept his eyes glued on the warrior. He was so frightened that he sang lyrics from a different song and in the wrong key. The warrior marched to the fire and stomped it out with his armor-covered boot. DeMorley stopped singing.

"Get up," the scout ordered.

DeMorley sat frozen. He avoided the Ebonite's eyes, afraid his own fear-filled face would give away Draemel's trap.

What is Draemel waiting on, he wondered. *Why hasn't he killed him?*

"I said, get *up*." The scout kicked DeMorley in the side.

Slowly and precisely, DeMorley rose. If Draemel fired, he didn't want to get in the way of the target.

Nothing happened.

The Ebonite grabbed DeMorley by the arm and pushed him toward the clearing. When they arrived in front of the commander, the scout shoved DeMorley to the ground. His lute reverberated crazily from the impact.

"Where are they, minstrel," the commander demanded.

"Where are who?"

DeMorley started to stand. Knowing well the stories of the March of Reeds, he thought running away was the better means of survival. A crossbow leveled at his chest changed his mind. He sank back down to his knees.

"The ones you travel with."

"I travel alone. Would you care to hear a song? I can write one just for you..."

"Silence, fool," the scout snapped as he remounted. To his commander, he said, "He journeys alone. Let's take first blood and move on."

"Not until I'm convinced he's telling the truth. Besides, have you forgotten that lunatic? He jumped off the horse and hid, but he has my crossbow and no doubt has it pointed in this direction."

"I have a solution," one warrior said as he unsheathed his sword. "We'll kill them both. First the minstrel, then the madman."

Before his blade could fall, a crossbow bolt sank deep into his forehead and sent him flying him off his horse.

"Ambush," the commander shouted. "That shot came from the woods, not from the madman."

The commander pointed in the direction the bolt had come from, but before his men could react a large man charged them from the undergrowth, twirling a sling.

"Draemel," DeMorley exclaimed under his breath as he dove out of the way of the ensuing battle.

Draemel released his sling. The metal sphere struck the commander with a dull thud and knocked him out of the saddle. The two remaining Ebonites finally regained control of their mounts and charged.

Without breaking stride, Draemel reached into a leather pouch and retrieved another ball. He whirled his sling overhead and released the lethal sphere, striking the unprotected face of one warrior.

The last warrior raised his sword and spurred his steed to a dead gallop. Draemel grabbed one of his small axes and with a quick flick of his wrist sent it spinning through the air. The axe pierced the thick leather protecting the horse's chest. The animal stumbled and its rider crashed to the ground.

Draemel grabbed his gor weapon and leapt upon the dazed warrior. White bone slashed and jabbed. When he stopped, the warrior lay dead.

DeMorley watched, spellbound. It was the first time he had witnessed a battle.

"Are you hurt," Draemel asked the minstrel who was doubled over, emptying his stomach onto the ground. DeMorley shook his head, stood and wiped his mouth on his sleeve.

"Then grab the reins of that horse," Draemel ordered. "He'll resist you. He's been trained to remain by his master's side, even if his master is dead, but if you pull hard enough on the reins, he'll comply."

DeMorley did as commanded and watched Draemel kneel beside one of the slain Ebonites. Unsheathing a thick, sharp blade, be repositioned the Ebonite's head in order to pry out his metal sphere. DeMorley was repulsed, and feeling like he was going to get sick again, looked away.

"That's a grisly business. Why not leave those...things...where they are?"

"Do you know how much one of these costs," Draemel replied as he held up the blood-splattered orb.

DeMorley noticed the wicked, tiny spikes that encompassed the orb of death. It was a heinous weapon.

"Besides," Draemel continued as he wiped the blood off in the grass, "these are my last two."

"You only had two? What if you had missed?"

"I never miss."

"But," DeMorley pressed, "what if you had?"

Draemel's brown eyes zeroed in on DeMorley's.

"Then right now, they'd be performing a March of Reeds on us."

Draemel let out a roar of surprise mixed with pain as a crossbow bolt embedded in his upper back. Only the thick leather strap that crisscrossed his back kept it from piercing to his heart.

"Where is he?"

Draemel spun about, wild eyed.

"You told me there were only four," he said as he struggled to load his sling with his one good arm.

"There were," DeMorley yelled. "I heard them talk of another, a madman, but I thought it was a trick."

"And when were you going to tell me this," Draemel seethed through clinched teeth."

Something whizzed past DeMorley's left ear.

"You'd better get down, minstrel, if you want to keep your head."

DeMorley collapsed to the ground and peered through the tall grass for a glimpse of their invisible attacker. The whirl of Draemel's sling filled his ears, sounding like the wings of a great bird in flight.

"Show yourself and fight like a man," Draemel challenged.

A bolt zipped past his head.

"So be it. I shall come to you," Draemel roared and charged in the direction the bolt had come from.

The assailant stepped out of the shadow of the woods, compelling Draemel to stop in his tracks. His sling dropped by his side.

"Paradin?"

"So good, so good. I see, I see. Come closer, come closer, come closer to me," the madman ranted as he aimed his crossbow at Draemel.

Draemel stood frozen in shock, as if helpless to move. Paradin squeezed the crossbow's trigger.

Draemel regained his senses, and dropped to the ground. The bolt sailed harmlessly into the meadow and Draemel hopped to his feet. With a quick spin of his sling, he sent the spiked orb straight at Paradin's head.

Paradin, intoxicated with the Cauldron's fumes, leapt out of the way with inhuman strength and landed much closer to the bounty hunter.

"What's this? What's this? Draemel, Draemel missed, missed, missed."

Draemel reached for his second ball, then realized it was still embedded in a dead Ebonite. Frustrated, he threw his sling away and pulled out the sword that hung on his back.

"My blade will end you."

Draemel thrust his sword at Paradin's head, but the madman dodged his attack, laughing and taunting him with his sing-song rhyme.

"Tisk, tisk, tisk. You missed, missed, missed."

Draemel intensified his effort, but weariness and the loss of blood from his wound took their toll. He swung again and again, but only hit the cool air. Exhausted he plopped to his knees, and awaited Paradin's final stroke.

The madman's eyes glowed red. Hate consumed him as he put his foot into the the crossbow stirrup and drew it back to cock it.

"Listen. Listen. I promise you this. Paradin, Paradin, Paradin won't miss, miss, miss."

He noched his bolt and aimed it point blank at Draemel's temple. Draemel's countenance revealed neither fury, fear nor remorse. The bounty hunter had faced death before, many times. He refused to give Paradin the satisfaction of seeing him beg for mercy, or even flinch.

A peculiar sound came from behind Paradin. Without taking his aim off Draemel, the madman glanced around for the source of the disturbance, and saw DeMorley skipping across the meadow, strumming his lute and singing a bawdy drinking song.

"Stop. Stop. Stop. Or I shall kill, kill, kill."

DeMorley disregarded Paradin's mad rhyme and danced closer. He answered him within the lyrics of his song.

"You're mad, you've lost your nerve. The Cauldron black is who you serve..."

"Silence, silence, silence and I shall let you run free."

"Free to run, free to fight, free to love another night..."

"Then come closer, come closer, come closer to I. I have enough power to make both of you die."

DeMorley increased the height of his leaps and sang with greater gusto.

"Enough, enough I've changed my mind. 'Tis you who first my bolt will find."

Paradin jerked the crossbow from Draemel's temple and sent the bolt flying toward DeMorley. The minstrel's thin, prancing body was a difficult target, and the bolt sailed past. He cocked the weapon for another shot, but before he could take aim Draemel gripped his gor blade and raked it across the back of Paradin's legs. Paradin fell to the ground screaming, the crossbow tumbling from his grip.

DeMorley dropped his lute, and scooped up the crossbow and aimed it at both men.

"What are you waiting for," Draemel barked. "Shoot him. Kill him or he'll kill us both."

"No. I'm not a murderer." DeMorley tried hard to ignore Paradin's insane eyes.

"No, no, no," Paradin hissed. "Listen to me. Give me Draemel, and you shall go free."

"You fool," Draemel snapped. "He won't hesitate to take your life."

"Tie Paradin to that tree over there," DeMorley ordered with a quick wave of his weapon.

"You idiot," Draemel barked. "He escaped my knots once and he can do it again. Only this time he'll come to spill *your* blood."

"Just do it," DeMorley said, a surprising lack of fear in his voice.

Draemel yanked Paradin to his feet, the wounds from his legs leaving a crimson trail on the ground behind them. With his good arm, Draemel tied Paradin tightly to the tree.

"Fools. Fools. *Fools.* Rope cannot hold me."

"Shut up," Draemel ordered as he cracked Paradin's skull with the blunt side of his gor weapon. The madman's eyes rolled back, and his head dropped to his side in silence.

"Now," DeMorley ordered, "toss me that weapon."

The expression on Draemel's face sent shivers up and down DeMorley's spine.

"This is a big mistake, minstrel. One that you'll live to regret. If you live."

Draemel tossed the weapon at DeMorley's feet. DeMorley snatched up the cruel weapon, keeping the crossbow leveled at the bounty hunter. The two men stood staring at each other.

"Well?"

"Well what," DeMorley countered, his mouth starting to go dry.

"Well, are you going to kill me and ride away to freedom? If so, do it now. But do not miss, or it'll be the second biggest mistake of your life."

"I'm not going to kill you," DeMorley replied with a quick glance at the restrained Paradin who was regaining consciousness. "I'm going to take you, and the horses, and retrieve Newcomb and Lassiter."

An evil smile pursed Draemel's lips.

"Your feelings and loyalty will one day be your demise."

DeMorley pointed the crossbow toward one of the grazing warhorses.

"Go get the horses."

"First, get this bolt out of me."

"Do I look that stupid? I'd have to put down this crossbow, and I am not about to do that."

"Then I insist on retrieving my weapons," Draemel stated. Without waiting for DeMorley's approval, he sauntered over to the dead Ebonite and retrieved his last ball.

"Don't do anything foolish," DeMorley warned as his finger twitched on the trigger.

Draemel raised an eyebrow as he found his sling and sword and sheathed them both. If he felt threatened by the skinny minstrel with the crossbow, he didn't show it.

"Now," DeMorley ordered, "go get three horses."

Draemel complied and led the horses back. DeMorley jumped into the saddle of one of the massive animals while the bounty hunter mounted another. He gathered in the reins of a third Ebonite warhorse and tied them to his saddle horn.

"You first," DeMorley ordered.

Draemel's eyes narrowed to slits of rage. Without a word, he spurred his animal, and they galloped toward the woods.

Chapter 35

A Warrior's Battle

The early morning fog billowed thick and foreboding, shrouding everything in fantasy. Nothing appeared as it should. The Mountains of Kline surrounded them, yet were completely veiled by the mists. Giant warriors and fierce beasts loomed, only to disintegrate into towering trees or overhanging vines.

Through this haunting landscape, Romlin and Elabea rode, the cool mist dampening their faces. Unable to see clearly, they relied on their ears and the rusk's sharp instincts more than ever before.

"We're lost," Elabea whispered. The oppressive fog made speaking out loud feel unnatural.

"No, we're not," Romlin whispered back. "Look, I'll show you."

He stopped beside her and pulled out the map.

"See," he pointed. "There is Hetherlinn, and this is where we ate with the MerriNoons. This is Waelryth, and those are all the Ebonite garrisons and outposts we slipped around. That leads us to where we are now, the outlands of Ebon. Once we travel through the Forest of Ebon, we'll be in Claire."

Romlin stared at Claire's outline on the map. Most of its features within the border had already disappeared.

"But the fog?" Elabea whined, oblivious to the map's alterations. "How do you know we're traveling the correct way?"

Romlin pasted what he hoped was a reassuring smile on his face.

"Because I just do."

"But how?"

He rolled his eyes.

"I'm a hunter, and, well, I just do. It's hard to explain."

He folded the map and put it away, then spurred his horse forward. Elabea reluctantly followed.

The fog lightened long enough for Romlin to make out the Mountains of Kline on their right. The rolling hills before them beckoned them onward, toward the next line of mountains that marked the border of Claire.

The sun, rising behind them in the gloom, appeared like a soulless orb of dark orange in an endless sea of gray. Romlin strained his eyes as he studied every dark shadow to discern whether it was an adversary or simply a tree.

"Romlin," Elabea whispered as she pointed at the rusk.

It hovered over her horse's head with its hair standing on end and tail poised for battle. Romlin turned about in his saddle in search of the evil that lurked somewhere in the boggy mists.

Nothing.

The rusk grew more agitated and aggressive.

"I don't see anything through this fog," Romlin whispered as he unsheathed his sword.

"Nor I. Just listen. Maybe we can hear something."

Above their own beating hearts, above the hoot of an owl and the creak from a tree came a familiar sound from somewhere in front of them. It was not a friendly sound.

"Men talking," Romlin whispered. "Do you hear them?"

Elabea nodded as she bit her lower lip.

The voices were too faint to identify as friend or foe. Romlin searched for a place to hide, but the fog was too dense. He couldn't discern a place of safety or retreat from a broad avenue.

The sun, finally shining its bright yellow strength, started burning away the boggy mists. Like a giant veil being lifted, the fog retreated back into the cold of the forgotten night, revealing their surroundings. They found themselves in a giant valley, dotted with tall evergreens. Rising before them, its top still cloaked in mist, was a massive, dark structure sitting atop a low hill. Romlin cocked his head to the side as he tried to figure out what it was.

As the last haze of the fog dissipated, they beheld a tower made of large blocks of gray stone. It was square and became narrower in width toward its summit. Around the top was a wooden platform surrounded by a guard rail. Several men leaned against the railing, their casual voices echoing across the valley.

A smaller tower rose from the middle of the platform. It had an animal skin for a roof, and a crude wooden ladder led to its top.

"A watchtower," Romlin stammered to himself. Turning to Elabea, he half-pleaded and half-apologized with, "It wasn't on the map. I swear it."

Romlin and Elabea were clearly visible and there was no time to hide. As the fog cleared, the Ebonites atop the tower might have been surprised to see the travelers below, but their surprise did not slow their response. They snapped to attention and shouted commands to those inside.

The wind which had been calm all morning picked up to a brisk breeze and blew in the direction of the tower.

"How could I have been so careless?" Romlin murmured. "Not only do they see us, but now they have our scent. We must get out of here, *now*."

They spurred their horses into a desperate gallop and sped toward the nearest grove of evergreens. Familiar muffled barks came from the direction of the tower. They glanced back and witnessed the large wooden door at the base of the watchtower open. A pack of animals bolted out, followed by an Ebonite cavalry patrol.

"It's the same creatures that tracked us from Hetherlinn," Romlin shouted.

"Those trees won't protect us," Elabea screamed, near hysteria.

"Don't you think I *know* that?" he countered, still angry with himself for falling into such an easy trap.

He surveyed the horizon while formulating a plan.

The trees won't hide us. The mountains are too far away for us both to reach in time. But if I hold them off, there may be hope...

"Elabea, open your book and ride to the mountains. I'll hold them off and join you there."

"No," She snapped her head toward him, her eyes filled with an odd combination of dread and steel resolve. "I won't leave you."

"You must. I have to get you to Claire at all costs. I'll fight to keep you free, but my sword alone is not enough. I'll need the book's power and only you can unleash it. Now, please, do as I say."

She started to argue, but his jaw was clinched tight, and his eyes were filled with a strength she had never witnessed before.

"Go, Elabea. Now," he ordered.

Everything in her wanted to disobey. She wanted to say something, but there was too much to convey and too little time. She knew he was right.

Elabea spurred her horse forward, sparing a glance back over her shoulder. Romlin had stopped and turned to face the attacking horde. His sword was raised in front of him, ready to fight to get her safely to Claire. Her heart swelled until she felt it must burst. She was about to turn and ride to his aide when she heard the whisper.

"No, Elabea. Ride away."

"But what of Romlin?" she called out to the whisper of Claire.

"Fear not. Ride. Open the book."

Elabea obeyed. She leaned into the wind and rested her head beside the pumping neck of her horse. Her heart was heavy and she feared for Romlin's safety. Tears rolled from her eyes, though the wind whisked them away.

At full gallop, she opened the book with one hand and held it tightly against her side. The rusk was a brown blur next to her.

Romlin stood ready for the ensuing battle when a subtle whisper spoke.

"Why are you so angry?"

"This is my fault. I should have been more careful."

"Yes. It is your fault. Could it be that you are not the warrior you think you are?"

"Six beasts and four warriors approach."

"Too many; an impossible scenario. Is your blood worth this? All for a name?"

"I may die but there will be Ebonite blood flowing as well."

A second whisper entered the fray.

"Dismount," it urged.

"Dismount?"

The first whisper spoke again.

"Would a warrior of your caliber dismount his warhorse? Is that not suicide?"

"Dismount," the second whisper ordered again.

Romlin shielded his eyes and scanned the skies for clues to which whisper to trust. Within the light of the sun he found his answer: Manno Vox was poised like a viper, ready to strike at a moment's notice. Although the whisper's order still seemed illogical, Romlin began to dismount.

"Is death your destiny? Are you not deserving of more? Ride. Come. I offer life."

Romlin hesitated.

"Romlin, fight with all your strength."

"You spoke my name," Romlin said. "Only the whisper from Claire can speak my name."

His decision made, Romlin jumped to the ground.

Enraged, the first whisper spoke. Gone was its gentle tone. In its place was malice.

"So be it. Death begets death."

Romlin pulled his shield off his horse and dropped it to the ground. It hovered in mid-air and Romlin hopped on, slid his feet beneath its straps and raised his sword in preparation.

"Attack the warriors first," the true whisper ordered.

"But those animals are closer, and there are more of them."

"The sevritts obey their master's words. Kill the master and they are lost."

Romlin watched and waited for the attack to come to him.

"Do not wait," the whisper commanded. *"Fly. Take the fight to them. You are Romlin, the man-warrior."*

The words filled his muscles with soaring strength, yet his thoughts were still distracted by Elabea. He glanced over his shoulder to make sure she was safe.

"Elabea is well. Your concern is the fight before you."

Romlin shifted his weight and the shield zoomed toward his enemies while his warhorse galloped by his side. As he raced across the tall grass, he unleashed a war cry. It was the same cry that erupted from his lungs when fighting a bear or a lion in the woods of Allsbruth. Now, he fought for something more than survival. He was fighting for his love of Elabea and for a whisper from the land of Claire.

A slight shift of his weight on the shield and he swooped over the heads of the sevritts. Vicious claws slashed and scraped the bottom of his shield. Romlin's warhorse, following in his wake, thundered through the sevritts, crushing one beast's skull with its hooves.

Romlin banked and attacked from the warriors' left flank. Surprised by his aggressive move, they had little time to alter their course. Romlin's sword flashed with ferocity, the white-hot blade decapitating the first Ebonite. The next rider he sent sailing out of the saddle as his flying shield crashed into him. He swung his sword from the opposite direction and struck the third rider in the chest.

The fourth rider shouted an order to the sevritts. The beasts split into two groups, one pursuing Elabea, while the other turned on Romlin. The Ebonite grabbed his bow, noched an arrow and sent it flying toward Romlin's chest.

As if it had a mind of its own, the shield seemed to sense Romlin's peril, and angled up to deflect the arrow.

Romlin's anger boiled. He aimed his shield for the warrior and leaned forward. He hit full speed and smashed into the Ebonite before he could noch another arrow. The hapless warrior was thrown beneath Romlin's warhorse, where he was trampled into the mud.

The sevritts used the time to close the gap, and leapt at Romlin's shield, clawing at his legs. Romlin's warhorse reared on its hind legs and pawed at the beasts with its front hooves. Romlin tried to fly away, but the creatures embedded their claws into the shield and held it in place. Romlin pulled his feet free and jumped to his warhorse's saddle.

The shield shot straight up into the sky, pulling two of the sevritts with it. At its zenith, the shield flipped, catapulting the creatures to their deaths.

The warrior he had knocked off his horse had regained his senses, remounted and called for the remaining sevritt to attack. The beast leapt and sank its huge claws into the flanks of Romlin's warhorse, sending it neighing and kicking to the ground, and Romlin rolling away from its claws.

Romlin scrambled to his feet, as the beast stood on its hind legs and loosed a horrifying roar. Romlin felt a nudge upon his calves. He glanced down and was relieved to see his shield. He jumped on and it darted up just as the sevritt lunged for him. A double-handed blow from Romlin's blade separated the animal's head from its body.

While Romlin was engaged with the sevritts, the surviving Ebonite warrior raised a small horn to his lips. Three long bursts signaled reinforcements from the watchtower.

The gate at the base of the tower swung open, and another wave of sevritts and warriors raced to join the fight.

Romlin watched them come, exhaustion fueling despair.

"Go help Elabea," a whisper wafted on the breeze.

"But what about them?"

He pointed at the charging horde.

"They are no longer your concern. Go to Elabea."

Romlin turned the shield and sped across the plain, his wounded warhorse galloping close behind. He could see that she was nearing the mountains, but the sevritts were gaining ground.

"I won't get there in time."

"Sit down. Hold tight."

Romlin had learned that the whisper only spoke for his well-being, so he complied. The shield increased its speed and soon, he was flying so fast he had to turn his head sideways from the wind that ripped at his face.

When the shield returned to its normal speed, he glanced forward. He was within striking distance of the sevritts. When they caught his scent, and without an Ebonite to urge them on, they broke off their pursuit of Elabea.

Romlin moved in for the kill.

He brought his blade back and sliced through the closest sevritt's neck. The remaining two attacked but were quickly slaughtered with two quick strokes.

With all the sevritts slain, he considered flying ahead to join Elabea.

"Well done, but your task is not yet finished. Return to the watchtower. None must live to tell of your presence."

Romlin did not hesitate, but banked his shield and once more raced like the wind back toward the watchtower. He sensed something beside him. He assumed it was his warhorse, but instead found Manno Vox flying beside him.

"May I join you," the shining warrior asked in his deep, commanding voice.

"I'll be fine," Romlin replied. He did not want the Only's champion to always rescue him.

"That I know. I do not doubt your abilities. I desire the honor of fighting by your side."

Romlin smiled and nodded.

"Which do you prefer," Manno Vox asked, "man or beast?"

"I'm tired of fighting the sevritts. I prefer the Ebonites."

"So be it. The battle is yours."

The two warriors banked apart.

Manno Vox nocked his crossbow and sent a bolt flying faster than the sunlight into the skull of the lead sevritt. The remaining beasts left their masters and turned to face the Only's warrior.

Romlin swept in from the opposite direction and downed the closest Ebonite warrior. The remaining warriors turned their attacks toward Romlin. With renewed confidence and his blade more powerful than ever, Romlin began to rise to his true calling. Swift moves of his shield, followed by quick, powerful sword blows, and the battle was over.

Loud animal noises made Romlin look around. Two warhorses were up on their hind legs fighting each other. One animal struck the other on its flank with a dull, hollow thud. The magnificent animals bucked and snorted, rose once more and boxed with their front legs. Chests and heads were struck as loud snorts and whinnying filled the air.

A swift blow from a hoof caught one warhorse squarely in the head. The animal buckled to the ground. The victor whinnied, rose high onto its back legs while the other fell to the ground, dead, its service to the Ebonite empire at an end.

The victor cantered over beside Romlin and snorted as it stood by its master's side.

Romlin looked back at the watchtower and saw the remaining guard climbing the ladder to the animal skin roof.

"The tower," Romlin shouted to Manno Vox as he realized the guard's intentions, "is a great drum. He's going to sound the alarm."

Romlin was too far away to stop him, even with his speeding shield, but Manno Vox was already aiming his mighty crossbow. He squeezed the trigger. Romlin tried to follow the bolt's flight, but it was too fast and the distance too far. The Ebonite warrior raised the giant drum mallet. Before he could strike, the bolt found its mark and ripped him off the tower.

Romlin stared at Manno Vox, amazed at such an extraordinary shot.

Manno Vox reined in his mount, gave Romlin a silent, fist-to-heart salute, and disappeared into the sky with a bright flash.

Elabea, seeing the battle was won, returned to Romlin's side, the book still open in her hands. She was shocked by the carnage.

"Are you injured," she asked.

"No. Are you?"

She shook her head.

Romlin's shield, so animated during the battle, floated gently to the ground and became just a shield again. He retrieved it and secured it to the side of his horse. Remounting, they pressed on toward Claire.

Neither said a word.

Elabea studied Romlin. Her admiration for his courage and self-sacrifice had blossomed into something more, something grander and finer. He exuded a quiet confidence that had not been there before. Although she did not know what other difficulties lay ahead, she was confident of this: The boy-warrior Galadin was no more. Riding beside her was a warrior worthy of respect and honor.

His name was Romlin.

C h a p t e r 36

Tricks, Truth and Tales

Newcomb stared into the shadows of the woods. He was certain he had heard twigs snap. More cracks echoed, followed by the sound of something large brushing against low-lying tree limbs.

"Newcomb? What is it, Newcomb," Lassiter asked as he turned his head from side to side trying to see around the tree.

"It can't be," Newcomb exclaimed, as the shadows coalesced into a shape. "This is *impossible.*"

"What is?"

Lassiter pulled so hard that the ropes tore into his flesh.

"Warhorses," Newcomb answered.

"Ebonites?"

Lassiter's ropes dug deeper as he fought to get free.

"No. It's DeMorley. And he has captured..."

"Captured who," Lassiter asked as he stopped straining against the ropes.

"Draemel," Newcomb said, still not convinced he was not dreaming. "And they are riding warhorses, and Draemel has been shot in the shoulder."

"DeMorley shot him? How could a minstrel overpower someone like Draemel?"

"I suppose we both underestimated his character," Newcomb replied.

DeMorley and Draemel were close enough to hear this last exchange, and Draemel became enraged.

"He did no such thing," he railed.

"Get down and go untie them," DeMorley ordered, pointing the crossbow at Draemel's back.

Draemel cursed beneath his breath as he dismounted, walked to the tree and started to untie the knot with his good arm. Realizing the knots were too tight, he instinctively reached for his gor bone.

"What do you think you are doing," DeMorley shouted as he strained down the sight of the crossbow. His finger twitched on the trigger. "Hands away from that weapon, or I'll kill you."

Draemel stood upright and turned to address the minstrel.

"Two things," he said in a tone saturated with disdain for DeMorley. "First, the knot is too tight. I need to cut them free. Second, stop talking about killing me. We both know you are incapable of such daring."

DeMorley continued to aim the crossbow, trying desperately to appear dangerous. He scowled. He clinched his jaw. He puffed out his chest. Draemel merely cocked an eyebrow, unimpressed with his bravado.

"Very well," DeMorley shouted. "You may cut them loose. But remember, I'm watching your every move."

Draemel remained still and silent.

"Well?" DeMorley squeaked as the weight of the crossbow made his muscles twitch. "What are you waiting for?"

"I need a knife or my gor blade."

DeMorley fished out the gor weapon from his pocket and tossed it at Draemel's feet. Draemel snarled at DeMorley before picking it up and cutting the rope.

"Would one of you please tell us what happened," Newcomb asked once free of the ropes.

"It was Paradin. He's a crazed lunatic," DeMorley replied as he watched Draemel's every move. "But now is not the time for that story. Hurry to my side."

Newcomb complied.

"Here."

DeMorley passed the crossbow down to Newcomb as if it were a piece of maggot-ridden meat.

"You manage him."

He slid off his horse and staggered to a large tree where he plopped down in exhaustion.

"Paradin," Newcomb asked while aiming the crossbow on Draemel. "He was near death when we left him."

"I know." DeMorley buried his face into his hands to help relieve his pounding headache. "I thought it was a phantom, but I tell you the truth, it was Paradin."

"What about these warhorses? Where did they come from," Lassiter inquired as he came alongside his mentor and rubbed feeling back into his hands.

"It seems an Ebonite patrol rescued Paradin from death," Draemel answered as he leaned back against the tree Newcomb and Lassiter had been tied to. "Only he was different. You might say he has gone..."

"Mad," DeMorley finished as he jolted his head upright. "Stark, raving mad! Delirious. Crazy. Haunted by the dark fumes of the Cauldron. That's what he is."

"What do you mean," Newcomb asked.

"As much as I hate agreeing with the minstrel, he speaks the truth,"

Draemel answered. "Paradin had a strength, the likes of which I've never encountered and..."

"He spoke with stupid rhymes," DeMorley interrupted, wide-eyed. "His voice was pure evil, and his eyes; each one wandered freely, like a bird, as if looking for something that would never be found."

Draemel snickered.

"What's so funny?" DeMorley fired at Draemel.

"Had I known you were this frightened, I would have reacted differently."

"How?"

Draemel's eyes narrowed.

"I would have killed you."

DeMorley's mouth dropped open. His face turned a whiter shade of pale.

"Is Paradin dead," Lassiter asked.

Draemel's face filled with rage and utter contempt.

"No. You can thank our singing fool for *that.*"

"I'm an artist, not a killer. I was *not* going to murder him."

"Coward. You tied him to a tree. He'll either die of his wounds or be torn apart by wild animals. Either way, you spilled his blood."

"Enough," Newcomb commanded. "What's done is done. We need a plan of action. Another Ebonite scouting party will be sent to discover what happened to their comrades."

"What are we going to do with him," Lassiter asked pointing at Draemel.

Newcomb studied the bounty hunter, but instead of answering, he turned to DeMorley.

"Minstrel, there are questions that your story begs me ask. Why didn't you run away when you had your chance?"

DeMorley sighed. He glanced at Draemel, then back to Newcomb.

"I want my reward from Claire. I stand a better chance of getting it with help from you."

"Very well," Newcomb replied. "But that leads me to my next question: why did you bring Draemel back? You could have tied him next to Paradin."

DeMorley stared into the ground. He shook his head while he answered.

"I was unable to tie him *and* hold the crossbow. He would have jumped me. Besides," he raised his head, "if I ran while they fought, one of them would have survived to hunt me. I would rather take my chances with Draemel than with Paradin."

Newcomb gave a nod.

"So, how did you subdue Draemel and..."

"He did no such thing," Draemel interrupted. "A minstrel; outfight me? Never!"

"Then how..."

"With music," Draemel answered, embarrassed that a song, and not his might, had defeated Paradin. "This fool danced across the field singing a stupid song."

Newcomb giggled as he imagined the horrifying, yet comedic ordeal. He turned his gaze to DeMorley.

"You risked your life and battled a madman with a song?"

"As I said," DeMorley answered, trying to maintain a degree of pride, "what other option did I have? Besides, I've never fired a weapon in my life, so I did what came naturally to me."

"So you don't even know how to shoot a crossbow?" Lassiter snickered with a glance at Draemel to see his reaction to the news.

"No," DeMorley said with a wag of his head. "That's why I brought him back. Newcomb must kill him."

"Me?" Newcomb stammered. "I can't kill him."

"You can't or you won't?" DeMorley snapped.

"You know that a..." Newcomb silenced his tongue before he gave away his identity as a storyteller to Draemel. Instead, he addressed the bounty hunter.

"Throw your weapon over here. Gently."

Draemel tossed it at Newcomb's feet.

"Now your sword, and that sling."

Draemel's eyes burned, but he said nothing and complied.

"Lassiter, tie Draemel's arms together and help him mount a horse."

Lassiter's steps were timid, as if he were walking on eggshells.

Draemel held out his arms for Lassiter to tie. He draped the rope over the bounty hunter's massive arms and Draemel glared into his eyes.

"That's right, young one," Draemel whispered so only Lassiter could hear. "Make sure the knots are tight. Should I slip loose, I'll slit your snickering throat."

Lassiter swallowed a hard lump that had risen in his throat. He sensed that Draemel was not the type of man to make idle threats. He looped the rope around and double-knotted his wrists together. He made certain they were good and tight before backing away.

"We should leave him here," Lassiter warned, as he tried to settle his racing heart.

"Yes," DeMorley agreed. "Let the laws of nature settle this matter. Surely that's an acceptable notion."

Newcomb did not reply.

"He's wounded. He'll only slow us down," Lassiter pleaded. The thought of traveling beside the cold-blooded killer made his stomach turn flips.

Newcomb considered the option. Even wounded, Draemel was a dangerous foe. His strength and cunning concerned Newcomb more than his assortment of weapons. But leaving a man to die, even a killer like Draemel, was an act storytellers were not allowed to consider. It was not an act, Newcomb thought, anyone should consider, storyteller or not.

Curious, Newcomb began to read the bounty hunter's story. Darkness, pain and terror encircled his life like dark storm clouds on a prairie. These Newcomb had expected to find, but buried beneath was a hidden story. It was a gem of a tale whose facets radiated with brilliance. The revelation made Newcomb smile.

"He journeys with us," Newcomb announced.

Draemel shot Newcomb a surprised look, while Lassiter and DeMorley's mouths dropped open in shock.

Newcomb retrieved Draemel's weapons from the ground, then mounted a warhorse.

"Draemel's wound must be addressed," he said while aiming the crossbow at the bounty hunter, "but it will have to wait. We need to travel as far away as possible before another Ebonite patrol comes to investigate."

Despite his pain, Draemel mounted a warhorse. Shaking his head in disbelief, the minstrel climbed into the saddle, followed by Lassiter, a bemused look in his face; half fear, half admiration. Newcomb rode behind Draemel, who took the point. Lassiter and DeMorley followed behind. Together they cantered through the darkening woods toward the shining kingdom of Claire.

Chapter 37

The Graen Rhiau

Brairtok strode through the hallowed halls of Netniath. Marching down the dark corridor, he entered the chambers, battled against the chilling winds and bowed before the Council and the Cauldron.

"Rise," the Council instructed. "What news do you bring of the girl, Elabea?"

"We are only days away from capturing her. The vul jens are preparing a trap for the rusk as we speak."

"We desire the girl, not the rusk," the Council chided. "Even now she and the boy-warrior who guards her near the border of Claire. Will they slip through your fingers like a field mouse from a lion?"

"Never! First blood will be yours."

"The King of Claire is cunning. He will not be so easily defeated."

"The boy and Elabea race toward their own destruction. Soon they will enter the Forest of Ebon. The powers of Claire diminish within its shadows while the Cauldron's are unquenchable. They will be hunted by the graen rhiau, who will gorge themselves upon their fears."

"Perhaps. Are you familiar with the Only's story about the Forest?"

"No."

"It says, '*A day will dawn when the graen rhiau shall drink their fill. Blood will spill and tears must fall. Behold, tales will turn, for death begets life.*"

"The fool is predicting Elabea's death."

"Perhaps. But this tale concerns us. It is a riddle that even the Cauldron cannot fathom."

Brairtok's eyes narrowed and his fists tightened.

"I vow to personally feed their tattered flesh to your black flame."

"Such consumption is well anticipated, but do not underestimate our enemy. He is jealous of our power and will deceive all to gain it back."

Brairtok bowed, pounded fist to heart, turned and marched out of the hall.

Chapter 38

Escape to SriBrune

Il-Lilliad's staff leaned against a corner of his cell, and throughout the night, the feminine figurine guarded and nurtured him. Whenever she sensed his spirits dulling or listing toward doubt and self-pity, she sang him songs about Claire and the Only. As his mood lightened, her voice lifted him off the rotting straw so he could float carefree about his cell. Rainbow lights cascaded from him like an ethereal waterfall, dousing his walls with shimmering colors.

She sang stories that made him laugh and others that made him cry, but these were not tears of remorse or shame; they were tears of gratitude. They flowed from a heart that had chosen to believe, when others had considered him foolish, or even mad. He was proud of his story and humbly accepted its end that would come by the hand of a fallen storyteller.

He was still in this state of mind when he sensed another presence in the room. Surprised, Il-Lilliad opened his eyes and floated back to the ground. The flickering colors faded like so many falling stars.

Standing in his cell were two men. One he recognized, but the other was foreign to him.

"Unable to sleep," he asked TyNorai.

The chancellor's expression was stoic; unreadable.

"Oh, I see," Il-Lilliad continued, "you want to see if I've changed my mind or worse, bear witness to my execution."

"Neither," TyNorai answered, his face still as emotionless as before. "I've come to release you."

Il-Lilliad's mouth dropped open in shock. "Release me? Why?"

The chancellor paused to examine his buried feelings, and wrestle with his own past and misgivings. At last he spoke.

"I'm still not convinced of this awakening you speak of, nor of you seeing Manno Vox. But you were right about me. There is a part of my heart that desires...to see if it is true. Your words have been ringing within my head all night. I have the blood of innocent lives on my hands, and that does not sit well with me. So...I'm going to set you free. Perhaps one day, mercy and forgiveness shall be given to me as well."

Il-Lilliad sat dumbfounded upon his bed of molded straw. For perhaps the first time in his life as a storyteller, he was speechless.

TyNorai, who enjoyed witnessing his shocked expression, continued.

"However, I simply cannot let you walk out. It must appear as if you escaped. Nor can you leave following the path you took to get here. You must travel deeper into the Onderling. You must go to SriBrune."

"SriBrune?" Il-Lilliad exploded up from his bedding. "I admire your resolve to confess your wrongs, but sending me to SriBrune is simply a slow execution. If the myriad of underground rivers and passages do not keep me eternally lost, then its people will determine my fate. If the stories told in every tavern from Allsbruth to Tristan can make even the Ebonites shudder, then I fear the worst is in store for me."

"Be at peace, Il-Lilliad. You have nothing to fear, for I have not only met a SriBrunian, but I personally can vow for their outstanding character."

Il-Lilliad squinted at TyNorai, trying to discern the genuineness of his words.

"Allow me to introduce you to my personal attaché."

TyNorai rested his hand upon the short man standing beside him.

"This is Kinmin, a native of SriBrune. He journeyed here and chose to stay."

"As opposed to being executed."

TyNorai closed his eyes and nodded to acknowledge the truth of the accusation. Regaining his composure, he continued to explain the escape plan.

"You must strike me with your staff, so that it appears as if you overpowered me, then follow Kinmin. Trust him and take good care of him. He is like a son to me," TyNorai said, as he patted the small man's head.

Il-Lilliad looked Kinmin over, amazed that campfire stories and tavern tales had made the SriBrunians out to be a people of such horror and terror. From what he saw, Kinmin was the most nonthreatening, unassuming person he had ever met.

No taller than a boy of ten summers, he was thin with an oval face that held high, round cheeks. His skin was the color of tanned leather that glowed with a youthful vigor.

Il-Lilliad knelt and cocked his head to one side to get a better look at the SriBrunian. Kinmin imitated Il-Lilliad's every move, turning his head to the side as he studied the storyteller. His black eyes blinked quickly like those of a bird, and his nose was nothing more than a little bump.

"Are all SriBrunians so small," Il-Lilliad asked, scooting closer to the curious little man.

"Yes."

"With the greatest respect to his people, how could such stories of horror emerge from their land? He does not look threatening."

Il-Lilliad was mesmerized by the man and longed to reach out and touch his golden-brown skin. A brimless, brightly colored hat hid most of Kinmin's glossy-black hair, and his face was ageless. Il-Lilliad had great difficulty discerning whether the creature before him was a boy of eighteen summers or a man of thirty. His outfit was woven from a thick fabric, simple in design and loose on his small frame. His breeches were dark brown; his shirt was tan, and his vest was clay red.

"Not being what your enemy expects is perhaps one's greatest weapon," TyNorai answered. "We have protected our borders for centuries in much the same way."

"Perhaps. But he is so…"

"Childlike?"

Il-Lilliad nodded.

"Although he is nothing like the creature, something about him reminds me very much…of a rusk," Il-Lilliad stated.

"Perhaps that is why I have enjoyed his company so much. But do not be deceived as so many others have been. His abilities go far beyond that of a rusk."

To give proof of such attributes, Kinmin changed his face to that of Elabea's. Shocked at the sudden transformation, Il-Lilliad fell back against the cell wall.

TyNorai chuckled.

"How did he do that?" Il-Lilliad stammered.

"He can read your stories, just as you can his. Only he can shift light to alter his appearance into anything he desires."

"A handy ability, no doubt," Il-Lilliad said as he neared the men once more.

Kinmin's face returned to his own, or at least what Il-Lilliad assumed was his own.

"When traversing the passageways, you will greatly value his expertise," TyNorai promised. "His eyes change in size, depending on the amount of light available. Right now they are very small, almost unnoticeable, but when entering the darkness, they will become very large."

TyNorai walked to the cell door and opened it. After scanning the dim hallway to make sure it was empty, he turned and faced Il-Lilliad.

"There is not enough time to tell you all Kinmin can do. Suffice it to say he has many traits that will become endearing to you. Now, take that staff of yours and do what you must, then follow Kinmin. May the Only protect you."

Il-Lilliad retrieved his staff and contemplated how quickly circumstances could change. Only moments ago, he would have relished the thought of striking down this traitor. Now his heart felt only compassion.

"Where would you prefer it," he asked.

TyNorai pointed to a spot on the back of his head, and turned to give Il-Lilliad a better angle. Il-Lilliad cocked the staff back for the blow but hesitated. A thought came to him.

"Why not come with us?"

The chancellor shook his head.

"I still have much to sort through. Perhaps one day."

"Then my hope is this: that one day our stories can intertwine once more."

TyNorai was about to nod when the blow dropped him to his knees. Rolling to his right side, he plopped to the ground.

"And so we journey to SriBrune. Lead on, little one."

Kinmin gave a quick bow of his head and briskly led Il-Lilliad down the damp corridor toward safety and SriBrune.

Chapter 39

Tales of Nothing

Elabea and Romlin continued northward. The rolling hills and expansive vistas thrilled Elabea.

"Riding is much easier here without all the trees," she declared.

Romlin did not reply. He was too busy scanning the horizon for danger. He knew from experience that evil did not need a tree to hide behind.

"True," he answered, still focused on what lay ahead, "but that just means we're easier targets."

They crested a low hill to find the mighty River Arrgient blocking their way. Romlin scouted along the shoreline until he found a place to cross.

"See the shallow rapids," he pointed out. "It's not deep here, and the current isn't too swift. I know it's wide, but it's the only place I've seen where we can cross. Be as quiet as possible," he instructed.

Elabea noted the shimmering water and enjoyed the soothing whoosh of water. She urged her mount forward into the river, doing her best to be stealthy. Although she kept her steed's pace restrained, she had difficulty containing her own zeal. The River Arrgient signaled that they were closer to Claire, and she could feel her giddiness growing. She covered her mouth with her hand but despite her best efforts, a few laughs escaped and echoed across the water.

"Shh," Romlin warned with a scowl. "Do you want to get us killed?"

"I'm sorry," she softly replied, but he could tell by her giggles that it was not the most sincere of apologies. "I'm just so excited to be nearing Claire. Have you imagined anymore what it'll look like?"

"A little," he replied as his eyes swept the thickets on the opposite bank for danger. Instead of adding to the conversation, he remained focused on crossing the river.

"Well, what do you think," Elabea asked, thirsty for conversation.

"I still have doubts that it's even there," he answered as their horses found footing on the opposite shore.

"Haven't you seen enough to believe?"

Romlin led them into the thicket in silence. He wanted to answer her. He wanted to tell her that Claire was a beautiful land full of gardens and wonder, where all their dreams would come true. He wanted to tell her that she would be safe there, and their troubles would be a memory. He wanted to tell her all that and more...but all he could think about was the map.

All of Claire's features had vanished from the map. He feared that this meant Claire had vanished from the world, just as the Oracles claimed; that it had been destroyed in the Dark War; that the kingdom of Claire was a myth.

For Elabea's sake, he hoped the vanishing features on Digri's map was just a trick of the Cauldron; that Claire was indeed there.

"I will say," he answered as he tried his best to keep her optimistic despite his rising pessimism, "that I'm less of a skeptic."

"Well," she asked as she stroked the rusk curled up on her shoulder, "since you're more of a believer, what do you *think* Claire will look like?"

"I think..." He let his gaze wander from her face to the path before them. "I think Claire is a land full of warriors with large castles atop giant mountains. It will be the perfect place for me to become what I've dreamed of...a great warrior."

"Is that all," Elabea asked, disappointment tugging tears from the corners of her eyes.

"Yes. Why? Is there something wrong?"

She turned from him before he could see the tears.

"Well, what about the King of Claire? What about the beautiful scenery and gardens? Besides, why would there be warriors in a land that is forever at peace?"

And to herself, *What about me? What about us?*

"Ahh," he grunted. "You asked me a question, and I gave you an answer. Why must you always twist things around?"

"I don't mean to argue. It's just that the stories from the book...they're so beautiful and I wanted...I mean it has me so...excited."

And I want to share it with you, she thought.

They exited the thicket and found themselves on the western edge of the Gilden Plains. Although Romlin thought he was prepared, he was still awestruck by its enormity.

Gently rising knolls flared eastward, while tall winter grass rolled like an amber sea as far as they could see. A few trees dotted the landscape here and there while the ever-present winds greeted them with stiff resistance.

"I never dreamed it would be so vast," Romlin said. "My father often talked about how big it was, but I assumed he was making it up. He said that the Army of Ebon was so large, that they covered the entire plain."

"Maybe he's not as crazy as we all thought," Elabea said. Their eyes locked, and for a moment, they were lost in each other's gaze.

Romlin felt an indefinable urge to touch her face. His mouth lost its moisture and all he could think of was the sparkle in her eyes. Surely it hadn't been there yesterday?

Romlin's horse snorted and stamped its hoof, as if impatient to continue to journey.

With the spell broken, Romlin turned his gaze back out across the Gilden Plains. He cleared his throat, then began lecturing her on the topography of the Gilden Plains.

"Based upon the map, somewhere off to the north is the Addoli Ridge. It runs eastward and parallel to the Gilden Sea all the way to the nation of Tristan."

His tone shifted from instructive to pensive.

"About a day's ride west from Tristan's border is Min Brock."

Together, the novice storyteller and her warrior stared across the Gilden Plains to where they imagined the infamous citadel to be located. After a moment of reflection, Romlin asked the question they both had been pondering ever since leaving home.

"Will we ever be free from the tears of Min Brock?"

Elabea gazed skyward and recited one of her favorite stories from Il-Lilliad's book.

Come all who dream. Come all who hope. Drink from the rivers, from eddies so blue. Gaze from my vistas, so far and so grand. Soar through the skies on my whisper so true. Journey you must, no expense do you spare. Treasures abound in my land known as Claire.

Romlin left his troubled worries about Min Brock and flashed her a smile.

"That's my favorite story."

"Mine too. I feel like I know the King of Claire simply from all the stories the rusk has told me. It's hard to believe my dreams are coming true."

"Well, I don't wish to dash your dreams, but we still must pass through the Forest of Ebon before reaching Claire."

"It's on the border." Elabea brushed off his warning. "It can't be that difficult."

Romlin chuckled at her innocence, shaking his head.

"Elabea, it's called the *Forest of Ebon* for a reason."

"I know, but if we focus on what lies between us and Claire, we'll never get there. I can't help but dream about what lies *beyond* such places."

Their conversation was interrupted by the appearance of a rider off in the distance.

"Romlin, do you see…"

Before she could finish her sentence, she heard his sword being drawn. Even though the rider was some distance away, they could tell by his attire that he was not an Ebonite warrior.

Romlin glanced at the rusk. Despite the animal's calm demeanor, he decided to exercise extreme caution.

"Stay here with the rusk until I signal that it's safe."

Elabea did not argue and watched as Romlin cantered ahead.

The stranger did not appear to pose any real danger. Dressed as a commoner, the only weapon he carried was a dagger sheathed on his belt. Two leather bags, which Romlin assumed were full of provisions, straddled the horse's rear flanks and swung lazily in time with the animal's gait. The man's gray hair indicated he was beyond forty summers, and his short, wiry frame put Romlin at ease should the stranger try to attack.

Still, Romlin had been through too much to lower his guard. If they needed to flee, he knew it would be better to have Elabea nearby, so he signaled for her to join him. When she was safely by his side, he signaled with his sword for the stranger to stop.

"Who are you," Romlin asked.

"You're Allsbruthian," the man countered with a faint smile, "I recognize that accent."

"And you're not, judging by *your* accent. But that was not my question," Romlin replied, tightening his grip on his sword. "I'll ask you again; who are you and what is your business here?"

The stranger's curt smile faded. "Why? You're but a boy."

"Romlin thrust his sword forward. "Dare to find out if I fight like one?"

The stranger's expression didn't change, but his eyes ran up and down Romlin's blade. It seemed to fit the boy, as it if were made for him; as if the boy and the blade were of one substance.

"Tell me," the stranger asked, "what's a boy and a girl doing alone on the Gilden Plains?"

"What concern is it of yours?" Romlin replied between clinched teeth.

"None. I'm just curious. These lands are dangerous for even seasoned travelers. For two young people to stumble about out here, unchaperoned, is...well...it's very dangerous. And it's just not proper, if you know what I mean."

He glanced over his shoulder, as if someone were near, and then in a whisper added, "Besides, the Oracles forbid you to travel beyond your marker, let alone have a sword."

"We don't care," Elabea blurted, "because we're traveling to Claire."

Romlin rolled his eyes, exasperated that she once again was so quick to share secrets.

Elabea didn't seem to notice his warning glare. She continued talking as if the stranger was an old friend visiting around the communal fire at Hetherlinn.

"We have invitations to see the Only. Are you going too?" she added with a smile and eyes that twinkled.

The man laughed, a full-throated belly laugh.

"No. That I've done. That I do no more."

"What do you mean?"

Elabea's smile faded.

"I mean Claire is no more."

"How do you know?"

Romlin's misgivings about the map's disappearing features rose up in his throat and threatened to choke him.

"Because I just came from there."

The man pointed his right thumb over his shoulder.

"I don't believe you."

Elabea crossed her arms beneath her breasts and gave the stranger the same look she had given Romlin at their respite.

"Then you're a fool," the stranger replied. "Don't waste your time. Turn around and go back home where it's safe. I'm telling you the truth. There's nothing there. No Claire. No King. Nothing."

"You're making this up so you can get all the treasure for yourself," Romlin challenged.

"You think I'm lying? I left everything - my home, my family, everything - to journey to Claire in search of treasure."

"But we have special invitations," Elabea reasoned. "They're from the Only, and they have our names on them."

Elabea pulled out the parchment from her book and held it out for him to see.

The stranger was unimpressed. He fished something out of his saddlebag, and turned back around with it clutched in his hand. Elabea and Romlin stared at the pristine white parchment, with golden letters.

"I...I...don't understand," Elabea stammered, doubt clouding her eyes.

"Like I've said," the stranger declared as he shook his invitation at her. "All this way for *nothing*. So now I'm going home to Ingloid. I've lost more than just time by coming here. I put my hope once again in the stories and promises of Claire. I began to dream of what life would be like in such a land."

The stranger tucked his invitation back into the saddlebag. Though he knew it was a lie, he could not seem to dispose of the invitation, as if to throw it away would be to throw away all hope of beauty and freedom. He paused and shook his head.

"It would have been better to never have listened to such stories," bitterness dripping from his tongue. "The Oracles are true: The King of Claire is a deceiver."

Elabea, stunned by this report, shook her head.

"No," she fired at him. "You're lying. We have a map and it shows Claire is there."

"A map?"

"Yes, a map. Romlin, show him the map."

The color drained from Romlin's face. Elabea stared at him for a moment, fear starting to twist her stomach.

"Show him the map," she ordered, her tone so biting that Romlin flinched.

"Elabea," Romlin stammered, "there's something you need to understand."

She looked into his pleading eyes and was surprised to see how forlorn he looked.

"What is it," she asked.

"The map..." Romlin's voice was barely audible above the winds.

"What about the map?" she pressed.

"I only wanted to protect you."

He sheathed his sword, pulled out the map, and considered keeping it. After all, the last thing he wanted was to hurt her. He knew she would be devastated when she saw Claire's altered state. Worse, he knew she would not trust him anymore. Pain he had never felt before - the pain of disappointing someone he loved - drowned his heart in sorrow.

He stretched out his arm and handed her the map.

She jerked it from his hand and unfolded it, her eyes racing over its surface. Her face contorted at the featureless expanse that had once been Claire.

"When did this happen," she asked Romlin.

"It started twelve days ago. The landmarks from Claire have been fading ever since."

Her face clouded over, whether from anger or sadness, he could not tell.

"And you *concealed* this from me?"

Romlin closed his eyes at the accusation.

She threw the map in his face and galloped off.

"Elabea, stop," Romlin shouted as he crammed the map back inside his tunic. "I was only trying to protect you. *Elabea*."

The stranger shook his head as he watched her disappear over a knoll.

"Behold the deception of Claire. Even your best intentions have been twisted about."

He whistled and his steed lumbered forward.

"Dreams and hope. Life is but a wasteland when those perish."

"Please," Romlin pleaded as the stranger rode past, "won't you help us?"

"I tried to warn you. You refused to listen to the truth."

Romlin glared at him, but in his heart he knew the stranger was right. He spurred his warhorse in pursuit of Elabea.

"Hurry, boy," the man shouted after him. "Save her from herself. Save her from the lies of Claire. There's nothing there. Do you hear me? Nothing...*Nothing*."

Chapter 40

Defeat in Hetherlinn

Gundin was sound asleep when he felt someone shake him. Instinctively, he grabbed the dagger beneath his pillow and sprang from his bed, thrusting about with the blade. After a moment he regained his senses as his eyes focused in the dim light.

"Forgive me for awakening you," Daryess said.

She stood across the room. She knew from experience that if you were going to stir Gundin from sleep, you needed to do so quickly then retreat to a safe distance.

He mumbled something that sounded like a curse under his breath, and tried to shake the sleep from his head.

"What is it that is so important that you had to wake me up?"

"It's Quinn. You need to go to the fire. He's..."

She paused to find the best words as well as the courage to speak. Unable to muster either, she blurted out, "Gundin, you must hurry."

The urgency in her voice snapped him awake. He rested his large, reassuring hand on her petite shoulder. Without a word, he left cottage Number 7.

As soon as he stepped into the cool night air, Gundin knew something was amiss. A commotion came from the communal fire. He quickened his pace toward the fire's orange glow and recognized Quinn yelling unintelligible curses and throwing something into the flames. Large strides brought Gundin to his friend's side.

Quinn stopped his tirade and staggered as he turned to see who had drawn near. He wavered from side to side as he tried to focus his glazed eyes on Gundin's angry face.

"You're drunk," Gundin roared.

"Gundin," Quinn slurred as if meeting a long lost friend. "My friend and Hetherlinn's great warrior. Have you come to assist?"

"Who gave you wine? I thought I destroyed it all."

"Now, Gundin," Quinn said, placing a knowing finger against his nose, then wagging it in front of Gundin's face. "Did you *really* think you could outsmart me? I *always* have an extra secret hiding place...in case of emergency. Tonight, I decided was an *emergency*."

Gundin stared flabbergasted at the wooden training weapons burning in the fire.

"What are you doing?" Gundin shouted as he tried to salvage some from the flames.

"I'm *doing* what I should've been *doing* back when I wasn't *doing* what I should've been *doing*."

Quinn hurled another weapon onto the fire.

Gundin's anger churned.

"You haven't been going to the flower."

"You mean *that* flower?"

Quinn pointed a rubbery finger toward where Il-Lilliad's tulip grew. Amid the dancing shadows thrown by the fire, Gundin saw the tulip. It had been torn by its roots from the ground and stomped into the dust.

"It appears to be a wee bit… *sick*," Quinn slurred.

Gundin ground his teeth as he glared at his friend He stomped over to the pile of remaining wooden weapons.

"So you *are* going to help," Quinn said, a stupid grin splitting his face. At the top of his lungs he called out to the cottages concealed in the pre-dawn darkness, "Men and women of Hetherlinn. Gundin and I will end our misery, tonight."

Gundin grabbed a long, thick quarterstaff and marched back toward Quinn. With a mighty swing, he struck Quinn below his knees and flipped him onto the ground. Curses oozed from Quinn's dusty, drunken lips as he crawled about trying to regain his feet.

"Rise."

Gundin towered over Quinn like a mountain.

"You destroyed the flower. You deceived me with your drinking. You've betrayed us all."

Gundin swung the staff and grazed the top of Quinn's head.

"Ouch, that hurt," Quinn whined as the jolt knocked some of the intoxication from his senses. "Stop. You'll kill me."

"Not yet, I won't. You haven't suffered enough."

Gundin marched back to the pile of weapons and pulled out a similar staff and tossed it at Quinn's feet.

"Pick it up," Gundin commanded.

Quinn squinted at Gundin while rubbing his sore head.

"You desire to spar," he asked.

"I desire to do much more than that. Pick it up. *Now*."

Quinn picked up the quarterstaff, pushed himself up from the dirt, and faced his friend on wobbly legs.

"I get it," Quinn said, his sarcasm thick. "You want to see…who the real man is."

Gundin struck without warning.

Crack.

The blow knocked the quarterstaff out of Quinn's hands. Quinn stared at it lying at his feet with a puzzled expression on his face.

"Perhaps I miscalculated your intentions," he mumbled.

"Pick it up. Defend yourself."

Quinn picked up his quarterstaff. He gripped it with the same anger that had started his fall into self-destruction and faced Gundin. Even in his inebriated state he was a dangerous foe.

The men slowly circled each other, their weapons ready to strike. Quinn swung first. Gundin easily blocked the blow.

"Why, Quinn? Why?"

"Why?" Quinn answered, his tone at once sober, yet full of despair. "Because all is hopeless. Nothing is changing. Not you; not me."

"You know that's not true," Gundin replied with a quick strike on Quinn's buttocks.

Quinn yelped as he tried to massage his stinging rear while maintaining his defensive posture.

"With the passing of every day, our men get stronger," Gundin continued. "Linwith and Il-Lilliad should be nearing their destinations and..."

"And we still battle the demons of Min Brock," Quinn shouted as he launched a quick strike to Gundin's left side.

"Well placed," Gundin said with a smile, unaffected by the blow. "Perhaps you'll become a great leader after all."

"I don't want to lead. I've done that already. I'm through believing empty stories about the Only, told by forgotten storytellers."

Gundin's smile retreated and his anger flared up again. He whirled his quarterstaff overhead, then brought it down and smacked Quinn's right foot.

Quinn danced about holding his foot and staff. Curses rolled from his drunken lips.

"Empty stories?" Gundin shouted as his eyes drilled into Quinn's inebriated face. "I find it hard to believe that someone of your caliber considers Claire's stories *empty*."

A quick spinning move and he struck Quinn's good leg, sending him crashing to the ground with a thud.

Quinn lay still, and did not move.

"Quinn?"

Gundin wondered if his friend was seriously wounded. As he bent down to examine him, Quinn rolled over and brought his staff up into Gundin's chin. Dazed by the blow, Gundin stumbled backward. Quinn jumped to his feet.

"Do you still have your daydreams," Quinn asked as he twirled the quarterstaff between his hands. He no longer appeared a hapless drunk.

"Yes, but they're not as strong as before."

"So tell me, what has changed?"

"The change is like the seasons," Gundin answered. He reflected on his frequent visit to the tulip. "Slowly the changes come, almost unnoticeable, until one day you realize something different is upon you."

Quinn, amazed at his friend's poetic and philosophic expression, lowered his guard. "Where did you learn such eloquence?"

"Where do you think? From my time bowing before the tulip."

Gundin struck like a snake, and since Quinn was unprepared, the blow caught him squarely in the stomach. Quinn doubled over and dropped to his knees.

Gundin leaned upon his staff and watched Quinn gasping and moaning beside the fire.

"I'm but a simple man, Quinn, and lack the mind of a great leader like you. But even I know a great mystery when I encounter one."

"What are you talking about?" Quinn wheezed, still clutching his stomach and trying to regain his breath."

"The whisper."

Quinn shot Gundin an inquisitive look. Gundin continued his explanation.

"On my first trips to the flower, I heard nothing but the ramblings in my own head. For weeks it was that way. I felt foolish. I considered quitting, but then I heard a whisper, just like I heard when we were boys and climbed the oak."

Quinn pulled away from his gaze and stared into the burning flames.

"Sometimes," Gundin said, his voice rich with excitement, "the noises in my own head and the Cauldron's drone would drown it out, but I would strain to listen, and although sometimes faint, it was there...every day...faithfully.

"Those sweet mornings beside the tulip freed me from my lapses into madness. I awoke eager to spend time with the flower, and the whisper, desperate to become someone of significance once more. Now that I think about it, it was as if they longed to know me more than I desired them."

Gundin chuckled at the thought.

"Imagine. The King of Claire seeking me, the local madman."

Gundin's laugh faded and his expression grew serious once more.

"Be honest with me, Quinn. You at least owe me that. Did you hear the whisper too, or have I gone completely mad?"

Quinn followed the flame's twisting tongues as they spiraled up into the dark sky. He gave Gundin a solemn, embarrassed nod.

"I knew it," Gundin shouted with a wide grin and eyes brimming with life. "The whisper *is* real. I'm *not* losing my mind. Tell me, what did it say?"

"Simply, *Delight. My delight.*"

"Yes. I heard the same words."

Gundin dropped to a knee, grasped Quinn by his shoulders and turned him so he could look into his face.

"I believe I know what that means. It's even clear to a simpleton like me. Could it be, Quinn, that we're a delight to the King of Claire?"

"Impossible," Quinn wailed, throwing his gaze back into the flames. "We betrayed everyone that day at Min Brock. He'll never delight in failures like us."

Gundin glanced at the desecrated flower.

"All I know is every day, I need to hear the whisper and breathe the tulip's aroma. Without them, I'll slip back into madness."

Gundin stood and walked over to the uprooted tulip, caressing its trampled petals.

Quinn pushed himself up, still clutching his stomach, and came alongside him. As they stared at the flower, shame swept over Quinn like fire across a sun-parched grassy field.

"What have I done," he asked to no one in particular. "My recklessness has destroyed your hope...our hope."

Gundin draped an arm over Quinn's shoulders.

"My friend, what's done is done. We must leave the horrors of Min Brock in the past and journey forward."

"How? The Cauldron's power is too great. Even now, the vapors taunt us. Without the flower we're doomed."

"The Only will not forsake us. We've journeyed this far. Let's not allow this defeat to determine our future."

Quinn's expression remained stoic.

"How could the King of Claire delight in me? I've failed in battle, I've failed at home..."

A vision of Elabea invaded his mind.

Oh, how I miss her. Her eyes always radiated love to me, but I was too consumed with my pain to notice...to care.

Overcome by his failures, Quinn sank to his knees. Quietly, secretly, his heart cried out for the one thing he longed for but knew he did not deserve - mercy.

The vision of Elabea was so vivid that it fanned his remnant hope into flame. At that moment he grasped the unexplainable depths the whisper from Claire was offering.

"Could it be that the Only delights in me as I do Elabea? Is it possible that my little girl will bring hope to us all...despite all the wrong I've done?"

Tears - marking the countless summers of self-loathing and shame - pooled in Quinn's eye. They rolled down his cheeks and landed on one of the tulip's petals.

Quinn lifted his face and met Gundin's eyes. Quinn held his next words close, knowing that once they were released, the Cauldron would hear, and hunt them both.

What he was about to say was not only a violation of the Oracles, but a declaration of war. Still, the vision of Elabea and the echo from the whisper, *Delight. My delight*, gave him the courage to speak the words.

"We must rise up against the odds we now face and fight, not just for our honor or personal glory, but for the sake of our children. With the power of the King of Claire, and your help, I swear to lead the fight."

Gundin's eyes lit up.

"A fight?" He pulled Quinn up from the dirt. "I *love* a good fight."

He swatted Quinn on the back in jovial camaraderie, which was hard enough to knock a smaller man off his feet.

The two men once again prepared for battle, but unlike before, they understood that the fate of one determined the destiny of the other. So it came to be that a drunk and a dreamer, bound together by their failure at Min Brock, began their journey anew. Only this time, a whisper and a tulip led the way.

The two men, brothers in arms, headed back to their respective cottages. When their doors closed, with only the dying communal fire as witness, something astonishing happened.

Quinn's tear on the tulip shimmered. Almost as if it had a life of its own, the tear drop moved, and gaining momentum rolled down the tulip's petal, clearing away the dust to reveal a vibrant red path. The flower's lingering scent, refreshed by a single human tear, battled through the Cauldron's vapors and flew in a flash back to Claire.

A gentle rain washed the filth from the tulip like a mother wiping dirt from her child's face. Roots quaked as they found life once more, and slipped deep into the mud to drink the rainwater. The tulip rose upright as the rain danced about the flower of hope. And a whisper, like a lark in spring, fell upon its petals.

"Delight. My delight."

Chapter 41

Blind Eyes Behold

Elabea galloped up the knoll and away from Romlin with wild abandon born of desperation. She heard him crying after her, pleading for her to stop, but his betrayal had wounded her too deeply.

She refused to cry. She refused to acknowledge his calls. Instead, she set her jaw in determination and rode to find the truth on her own.

Her rusk darted about, frantic to get her attention, willing her to open the book, but she ignored its efforts.

Racing down the knoll's opposite side, the stranger's words echoed in her mind.

"I'm telling you the truth, there's nothing there. No Claire. No King. Nothing."

"He was lying. He *had* to be," she shouted to no one. "If there's no Claire, no Only, then my life is…"

On the distant horizon she saw a woodland full of tall trees and dark shadows. Romlin had warned her about the Forest of Ebon. He told her how dangerous it was. She almost paused, but a doubt wormed its way into her thoughts.

Romlin lied about the map. Why should I trust what he said about the forest?

She dug her heels into the warhorse's flanks and urged it faster. As she galloped, a thunderhead of memories swirled amidst questions about Claire; about the Only; abut Il-Lilliad; about…Romlin. At the heart of the storm was the Ingloid's nagging taunt.

There's nothing there. No Claire. No King. Nothing.

Elabea was enraged, but confused. She pulled back hard on the reins, and her warhorse ripped open the ground in order to a stop so suddenly. Seeking counsel from the rusk, she flipped open the book and he flitted near her face.

"Is the stranger's tale true?"

"Claire is not what it appears to be," the rusk replied, willing her to understand.

"No more riddles. Is it *true?*"

The rusk gazed into her troubled face.

She has suffered so much betrayal, it thought. *First her father, now*

Romlin. Will she have the courage to trust again? Will she become a great storyteller, or have my efforts been in vain?

Finally, he answered.

"Some see it, some do not."

She slammed the book shut and violently spurred her horse.

The Forest of Ebon loomed, but despite its ominous darkness, she raced ahead at full speed. She spied a path and plunged into the woods. The gentle rise became a steep incline. Massive, ancient conifers guarded the way, their thick branches forming a foreboding canopy high overhead.

Her horse, near exhaustion from the run, frothed heavily and glistened with sweat. Elabea, normally very attentive to her animal's needs, became irritated at his weariness, obsessed with getting to Claire no matter the cost.

"Faster," she chided with a slap of the reins across its neck. "Don't slow down."

But the terrain was too steep and the animal too exhausted to comply. Frustrated, she slid off and continued on foot.

The rusk flew ahead of her, alarmed at her desperate flight. Over small ledges she climbed, using any handhold to propel herself upward. Amidst her desperate climb, she heard Romlin call from far below.

"Elabea."

His voice echoed through the forest. She ignored it.

The rusk hovered in front of her, his fur standing on end. Evil hunted Elabea stealthily like a panther in the shadows.

Elabea glanced up the hill in time to see a shadow dart out of a deeper shade. She stopped and looked around. More figures moved among the trees. At times they looked human with faces drenched in shadow. One hovered nearby. She recognized its face.

"Mithe, the old widow from Hetherlinn," she breathed. "What is she doing here?"

The shadow that had been Mithe shifted into a different shape, flapping about in the cold breeze like a sail of black cloth. With no warning, it shot overhead and disappeared into the gloom.

Whispers filled the forest around her. Some she recognized. Others she did not. They writhed about her like a pit full of snakes, charming and hissing, moaning and laughing.

The rusk stayed in front of her, his tail ready for battle. She opened the book.

"Rusk, what have I done?"

"A dangerous thing is what you have done."

"I'm sorry, but Romlin lied to me, and now I question..."

"Now is not the time, Elabea. The graen rhiau long to feast upon your fears."

"Graen rhiau? Can you stop them?"

"My venom is useless. They are but shadows, fear lords from the Dark Flame."

"What am I to do?"

"Keep the book open. They long to drink from your essence. Do not listen to them. They are not real. No matter what you see or hear remember this: *they are not real.*"

The rusk heard something new in a different part of the forest.

"Elabea, I sense an even greater danger approaching. I must attack it while you battle here. Read a story, and in time, the fear lords will depart."

With that, the rusk darted off.

Romlin found her exhausted mount desperately licking a wet rock for water. He called her name. *Elabea* echoed eerily in the dark forest. There was no answer. He dismounted, untied his shield and carried it on his back.

He found her trail marked in the brown pine needles of the forest floor and charged up the steep embankment after her. With each stride, he called her name.

"Elabea. *Elabea.*"

He feared their noisy plunge into the Forest of Ebon would attract any nearby Ebonite patrol. The thought of Elabea being captured, perhaps being subjected to a March of Reeds made him push himself even harder.

The higher he climbed, the easier her trail was to read, and it told a tale of frantic desperation. Romlin's self-loathing expanded.

This is all my fault. I should have shown her the map. Maybe I can make this right again. Maybe...

He gritted his teeth and he continued upward.

The rusk swooped through the trees, racing toward the other danger, flying near the treetops to avoid detection.

It hated leaving Elabea alone with the graen rhiau, but knew that Romlin was close behind. What concerned him most was her trust and dreams. They hung by a thin thread of hope.

It flew faster, sensing its nemesis was close at hand. He zipped around a massive pine and flew into the trap.

"What's this?" a dark voiced hailed from the nearby shadows. "Why it's the rusk that murdered my brother," the vul jen declared.

The rusk stopped and hovered as it planned its next move.

"And I shall destroy you as I destroyed him," it taunted the vul jen, hoping to buy time.

"But what of me," a second voice asked.

The rusk spun about and spied another vul jen hiding in the shadows.

"Even a great rusk such as you cannot destroy two vengeful brothers."

"By the power of the Only, I will fight to whatever end lies before me, but know this: Today, at least one of you will die. The question is: which one?"

"Such arrogance," a third voice floated out of the woods. "You are so full of your own confidence that you can't count. What will you do with three vul jens? The Only doesn't live in *our* woods and Elabea's precious book isn't here, either."

The rusk now realized the extent of the dangerous trap he had fallen into. The vul jens held the advantage, perched higher and surrounding him from three angles. He considered escaping back to Elabea, but the vul jens would follow his trail and attack her as well. Knowing he needed help, he whispered to the Only, Manno Vox and even Romlin.

"What's this?" a vul jen taunted. "The mighty rusk is frightened?"

The rusk finished his call and faced his nemesis.

"Fear? Fright?" Those are the kindred spirits of the Cauldron, and you know them well. Come what may to me, Elabea will live. She *will* become a great storyteller."

"Enough babble. Brothers, it's time for revenge."

Before the vul jens could take to wing, a warm breeze swept down from a distant summit. The vul jens gagged on Claire's sweet breeze, while the rusk was invigorated and prepared to fight.

The vapors of the Cauldron flourished in the forest and also caught the scent from their enemy's homeland. In retaliation, the vapors attacked the rusk with its whisper.

"Death begets death."

"I do not fear your tale."

"True, but I can read your story. There is one thing you do fear."

The rusk tried in vain to hide his emotions, but the Cauldron was too cunning.

"You fear that Elabea will discover the truth about Claire, and that her demise will mean your life was meaningless."

The Cauldron penetrated the secret room of the rusk's heart and peered into his dream: to escort Elabea into Claire and bow together before the Only's throne.

"*Such pathetic dreams,*" the whisper mocked.

The rusk did not answer. It knew that deep within the Forest of Ebon, surrounded by a powerful enemy, such dreams might not come to pass. Despite his heavy heart, he refused to give up hope.

With what it knew might be its last words, the rusk shouted out a battle cry. That cry darted through the Forest of Ebon, carried by the winds of Claire, and fought and clawed through the vapors of the Cauldron. The cry grew in intensity as it rushed across the Gilden Plains, a thunderstorm of conviction, then rocketed into the sky. There, it pierced the invisible river high overhead and exploded with such force, that the words echoed throughout all the nations.

"He lives. *The King of Claire lives.*"

The Cauldron, who habitually gorged upon the river, unwittingly drew the declaration into its chilled halls. When the Only's name ricocheted within its flames, the Cauldron burned with rage.

"*End their story,* it screeched. *Now!*"

Filled with the power from the Dark Flame, the vul jens launched their attack. Dark violet streaks fell from black shadows. Brown swirls intertwined with purple and twisted about in aerial combat to the death.

Elabea cowered in the darkness as the graen rhiau attacked. A shadow raced straight for her. Its attack was so swift that she was unable to get out of the way. When it struck, it passed through her, and she was left feeling deeply chilled.

"*Why persist?*" the graen rhiau whispered within her mind.

The whisper sounded exactly like her mother's voice. She caught the whiff of breakfast porridge. She wondered if her mother was missing her too. Homesickness washed over her like an ocean wave.

The rusk's warning whispered in her mind, and she fought against her feelings. She opened the book, flipped through its pages and desperately looked for a story to counter her grief.

"*My daughter, why push me away? You have endured so much pain. Please, come back home.*"

"You're not my mother," she shouted into the dark woods.

"*Of course I am. Who else would I be? Come home and play in your meadow. I'll make you some breakfast porridge. I miss you.*"

Elabea felt light-headed and weak as images of home danced across her imagination. Her mother's voice was so alluring, and the thought of a good night's sleep in her own bed was so inviting, that she began to question her convictions.

I miss you too, Elabea voiced in her thoughts.

"Of course you do, so won't you hurry home, my daughter?"

As she pondered the request, Elabea remembered her desire to see if Claire existed and felt conflicted on what to do. She slid her hand inside her pocket and found her invitation. As she stroked the golden letters of her name, she remembered a conversation she had with Il-Lilliad back in his cave.

He warned me that whispers from Ebon could never say my name, she recalled.

To her mother's whisper she said, *If you're truly my mother, then speak my name.*

Will you trust the words from a storyteller or your mother? After all, look at all you assumed to be trustworthy: that boy, the map, the promise. Perhaps those are the lies, my daughter.

Now convinced the whisper was a counterfeit, Elabea pulled her hand from her pocket and flipped through the pages of the book for a familiar story. She turned a page and her eyes widened as she recognized the etchings. In a last ditch effort of belief she recited it from memory.

"Invisible vapors from flames so dark. Shadows and whispers from endless nights. Riddles and questions that never quite spark. Depart from my child, my one true delight."

The graen rhiau hissed. Unable to overpower such a potent tale, it darted back into the shadows.

Elabea recognized a nearing shape.

"Romlin," she exclaimed. "Thank goodness it's you. The graen rhiau are attacking."

"Don't worry," he said from the shadows. "We'll fight them together."

"Hurry. They're getting ready to attack again."

"I didn't mean to deceive you earlier with the map."

"I know, you only meant to protect me from the truth."

Relieved that he would join the fight, she closed the book. "I simply want to discover the truth myself."

His shadow drew near.

"Can we ever know the truth," he asked.

"Yes. Of course we can know the truth. Either Claire is there or it's not."

The shadow stopped.

"And what if it's not?"

"Then my life…"

"Is hopelessly lost."

The tone of his voice sent a chill through her. She gripped the book tighter.

"Romlin, why did you say that?"

The shadow crept forward. She poked her finger into the book's pages.

"Romlin?"

She stepped away from him.

The shade charged. She opened the book just as it struck. Her entire body felt achy and weak. A foul taste clung to her tongue and the graen rhiau tormented her from within.

"Romlin is dead. He has been killed by Ebonite warriors."

"No," she stammered.

The graen rhiau delighted that she attacked with her own words and not a story. It drank from her fears.

"First blood. Caused by your foolish, girlish ways."

"He's a great warrior."

Visions of Romlin being struck down by Ebonites shadowed her thoughts.

"Witness the vision. He was a great warrior. Now he is a dead warrior. Death begets death."

Elabea weakened. The graen rhiau grew bolder and riddled her with questions.

"Truth? You desire truth?"

"Yes."

"The truth is you have been betrayed, deceived, and left to die alone in my forest of darkest shades. The boy warrior is dead. The map has faded. And why? Because there is no Claire."

"Not true," she whispered, trying to shake the map's featureless images from her mind, desperate for the true Romlin to appear, longing to be home in her meadow, nested high in her oak.

"Where is he, then? Where is Manno Vox? The Only? Your fears betray you. They flow from your pathetic heart like eternal springs."

Elabea dropped to her knees, exhausted, defeated. She closed the book.

"First blood."

Romlin stopped his ascent and listened. The sound came again, only now it was closer.

It was the cry of a girl.

Elabea.

He pushed himself upward, her anguished cries urging him onward.

He found her kneeling on the forest floor. Despite the mountain's cold air, sweat poured off her, soaking her garments as if she had been caught in a sudden rainstorm. Her eyes were closed, and her body swayed eerily about. Clutched to her side was the book. It was closed.

Shadows slithered toward him.

"Elabea, what's wrong," he asked while keeping an eye on the approaching shadows and wondering where the rusk had gone.

When Elabea heard his voice, her eyes blinked open. She was pale, shivering and appeared to be in extreme pain.

"Where's the rusk?"

She opened her mouth and tried to tell him all she was going through and everything that had happened, but all that came out of her mouth were a few guttural tones.

Romlin touched her arm. Icy cold. He met her pleading eyes and followed her gaze to the book.

Of course, he realized as he snatched up the book. He opened it and set it before her eyes. In a moment color flushed her face, and warmth chased the chill from her flesh.

Renewed by the book's power, Elabea recited the story before her, although in a strained voice.

"Invisible vapors from flames so dark. Shadows and whispers from endless nights. Riddles and questions that never quite spark. Depart from my child, my one true delight."

A black fog seeped out of her and floated overhead. Its sweet, sickly scent wafted about them.

Romlin, shocked to see the graen rhiau so close, fell back gagging at the nauseating aroma.

Reenergized, Elabea rose and stood between Romlin and the graen rhiau, repeating the tale with greater zeal.

The graen rhiau flapped wildly about and hurled coarse whispers in an attempt to frighten her from finishing. Elabea would not back down. She repeated the story, only this time, with all the passion of her heart.

"Invisible vapors from flames so dark. Shadows and whispers from endless nights. Riddles and questions that never quite spark. Depart from my child, my *one true delight*."

Hissing and wailing filled the air. The sweet, nauseating aroma tried to envelope her, but the future storyteller stood her ground. With one dark flash, the graen rhiau were gone, disappearing into the deeper shadows of the forest.

Elabea knelt beside Romlin. She started to reach for him, but memories of the shadow-Romlin made her draw back. Courage overcame fear and she stretched out her hand and touched his cheek. Feeling warm skin instead of cold shadow, she sighed in relief.

"It really *is* you. A moment ago, I saw you, and yet it was not you, and I..."

"Where's the rusk?" Romlin interrupted.

Despite the unanswered questions they both had, he knew that now was not the time for such conversations. Danger still lurked in the perilous woods.

"He heard another danger and flew off," Elabea answered.

"Which way did he go?"

She was about to answer when they heard the rusk's battle cry echo all about.

"He lives. *The King of Claire lives.*"

"The rusk. He's in danger. All because of me." Tears welled up in her eyes. "What have I done? What have I done?"

"Elabea, I heard his call, too," Romlin said as he unsheathed his sword.

"But how," she asked as she wiped her eyes. "I'm the only one who can hear him talk."

"Maybe this is another trick of the forest," Romlin warned.

"We can't wait here," Elabea argued. "He might need our help."

Romlin nodded.

"Come on. His cry came from over there."

They charged through the black forest, wondering if they had heard the rusk, or if the graen rhiau were deceiving them with false whispers.

Up ahead they could hear animals snarling and tree limbs cracking. They increased their speed.

At the top of the slight incline they witnessed the aerial combat between the vul jens and the rusk. The battle was so intense, all they could see were streaks of purple and brown.

One of the vul jens spotted Elabea.

"Not only will you die today," it said to the rusk, "but you will get the pleasure of knowing that your deepest fear will be realized."

The Cauldron joined the assault.

"The end of the story is near, rusk. Elabea is ours."

"Run, Elabea," the rusk cried as he fought. "Run to Claire. Hurry."

"My dear rusk," the Cauldron challenged aloud for all to hear, *"you*

desire her to see the truth? You are indeed desperate."

"Yes, I desire her to discover the truth," the rusk shouted back. "The Only will not let her fail."

"*The Only is but a breeze in my forest of shades. His power is impotent. This story will end today.*"

Romlin held his sword poised to strike, but the battle was so swift that he was afraid of hitting the rusk.

A horrific scream filled the air and one vul jen fell dead to the ground.

The two remaining vul jens intensified their attacks. One caught the rusk in its sharp talons and dangled him overhead, while the second ascended to prepare for a death dive.

Romlin pulled off his shield and dropped it hoping it would fly.

It plopped onto the forest floor.

He spun around to check on Elabea. She held the book closed and stared up at the rusk who twisted and fought to free himself from the vul jen's grip.

"Elabea, I can't fight until you open the book."

Tears filled her eyes as she mumbled, "This is all my fault."

"Elabea," Romlin snapped. "*Now.*"

She nodded and flipped the book open.

The shield came to life and hovered. Romlin jumped on and zoomed toward the fray.

"*The book. The stories,*" the Cauldron raged. "*Now is the time to destroy them all. End the story forever.*"

The rusk stopped struggling and gazed down into Elabea's teary eyes. Empowered by the book and the breeze from Claire, he whispered into her mind.

"*Be strong. Be true. You are my delight, and you always will be, my Elabea.*"

Elabea shook her head.

"No," she cried up to him. "This can't be happening."

A page from her book fluttered against her arm and inspired a new idea.

"I can save you. I can tell a story."

Her mind scrambled to recall a story the rusk had told her along the journey. She frantically flipped through the pages, digging for a tale to aid the animal she loved so much.

A vul jen shrieked.

Elabea gasped and looked up in time to see the vul jen strike.

When she saw the rusk's body fall limp and lifeless, she screamed and dropped to her knees.

"Nothing can keep you from entering her dreamworld," the Cauldron roared to the vul jens. *"Destroy the boy. Destroy Elabea with her own dreams. The Only's story is about to end."*

Romlin reached the vul jen that had held the rusk, and with one swift blow, split the creature in two with his glowing blade. He banked sharply and pursued the surviving brother. The vul jen swooped around the trees as Romlin followed his every move.

He's faster than I thought, Romlin observed, *and I'm getting further away from Elabea. I must return to her.*

Abandoning the pursuit, Romlin returned to the battlefield and landed gently beside her.

Elabea clutched the rusk to her chest, rocking back and forth, sobbing and moaning. She sensed Romlin's presence and looked longingly into his face.

"This is all my fault. I couldn't think clearly. The Cauldron's whisper…the drone…I couldn't recite a story."

Emotions swelled in Romlin. He longed to comfort her, but still felt responsible for hiding the map's truth from her.

The Cauldron's whisper pounced on his indecisiveness.

"Yes, you are right to reason as you do, for had you shared the map's deceitful nature with her, would she have darted off so recklessly? Would the rusk be dead?"

Shame rolled over Romlin like a tidal wave. He wanted to drop to his knees and pull her close, tell her he was sorry for keeping the truth from her, and that the rusk's death was as much his fault as hers. Instead, he remained as still as a statue.

Off in the distance, a whisper snickered.

Romlin's shield rose into the air of its own accord, and as if to alert its master, nudged him in the calves. Romlin was still too lost in his own misery to notice until a foreign sound stirred him from his introspection - the clatter of armor and Ebonite voices coming their way.

"Elabea, we must go," he said as tenderly as he could. "They're coming."

Elabea, lost in her pain, continued to rock. Romlin glanced back down the hill and located their enemy. The warriors were rapidly gaining ground.

"Elabea," he said with more urgency as he offered her his hand. "You must leave him. We must hurry."

Oblivious to the danger, Elabea continued to mourn.

The snickering whisper rose to a full-throated laugh. It taunted them from every direction.

If we don't leave now, Romlin reasoned, *we'll die.*

He realized that she was not going to move or let go of the rusk, so he sheathed his sword and gathered her into his arms.

The shield positioned itself behind him, and he plopped down with her in his lap. As she continued to moan and rock in his arms, he maneuvered the shield to where the book lay open. Leaning over, he grabbed it, and together they sped toward the summit.

He glanced over his shoulder and was relieved to see the Ebonites falling behind. Facing forward, Romlin focused on their flight. He attempted to pry her fingers from the rusk, but her grip was too strong. He wrapped his arms around her and whispered in her ear.

"All is well, Elabea. Soon we'll be in Claire."

Romlin scanned the woods for any threat, whether from graen rhiau, vul jens or Ebonite warriors. The woods were void of enemies, and he was about to relax, when the whisper stopped laughing and declared...

"*Upon a map blind eyes behold what was becomes no more...* "

Romlin pushed aside both the whisper and his doubts and concentrated on the path ahead. The woods were becoming brighter.

"Elabea, the trees are thinning. We're almost there."

Claire's warm breeze gently caressed their faces. Romlin breathed deeply. The invigorating aromas from the mysterious land filled him with excitement. Perhaps he had been wrong about everything. After all, the rusk's last words were that the King of Claire was alive. Maybe the disappearing map was a trick of the Cauldron after all.

"Look, we're going to make it. Can you smell the air; the flowers?"

The shield cleared the last of the trees and settled gently down on the summit. Romlin jumped off and ran to a jutting precipice. The sight stole his breath. As far as he could see in any direction was orange and tan sand.

Claire was nothing but a desert.

GLOSSARY

Characters

Anessatia: Lassiter's mother; grand-daughter of King Culdean.

Areall: Elabea's mother; married to Quinn.

Brairtok: Lord/king of Ebon.

Council: Dark lords of the Cauldron; seers and overseers of Ebon's power.

Culdean: King Simeion's oldest son; heir to the throne.

Daryess: Galadin's mother; married to Gundin.

DeMorley: Minstrel who joins Newcomb and Lassiter to Claire.

Digri: Jolly, short chef of MerriNoon.

Draemel: Bounty hunter in pursuit of DeMorley.

Elabea: Journeys to Claire with Galadin.

Friarlinn: King Simeion's youngest son; murders his brother to become king.

Galadin: Elabea's friend; superb huntsman; assists her on her trek to Claire.

Gundin: Great warrior; father of Galadin; married to Daryess.

Hinnmith: Ebonite commander.

Hornlynn: Lassiter's father; married to Anessatia; died in the Dark War.

Il-Lilliad: One of the last storytellers; survived the March of Reeds massacre.

King of Claire: Enigmatic ruler of Claire; also known as the Only.

King Simeion: Once great king of Allsbruth.

Kinmin: Tiny, dark skinned SriBrunian; escorts Il-Lilliad to SriBrune.

Lassiter: Hornlynn and Anessatia's son; mentored by Newcomb.

Linwith: Quinn's older brother.

Manno Vox: One of the Only's mighty warriors.

Mithe: Old widow of Hetherlinn.

Newcomb: Lassiter's mentor; storyteller.

Paradin: Draemel's partner.

Phinnton: Hetherlinn boy; mother sang about the *Singing Stones of Addoli*.

Quinn: Great leader of Allsbruth; Elabea's father; married to Areall.

Romlin: Galadin's new name given to him by Manno Vox.

Rittmar: Bee-like creature; chancellor for the nation of Bal-Malin.

TyNorai: Chancellor of Aggellon; former storyteller of the Only.

Countries, Places & Cities

Addoli Ridge: Mountain separating the Gilden Sea from the Gilden Plains.

Aggellons: A timeless nation in the Onderling.

Allsbruth: Beautiful, tranquil land; home of Elabea/Galadin.

Bal-Malin: Island nation inhabited by insect-like creatures and worms.

Cauldron: Perpetual fires of Ebon; housed in the citadel of Netniath.

Cave of Freers: Lair of the four vul jens; located in mountains of Ebon.

Claire: Nation reportedly destroyed in the Dark War; home to storytellers.

Ebon: Victors of the Dark War.

Ferra: Nation due east of Allsbruth; Torrens Bay is on its southern coast.

Gilden Plains: Enormous grassy plain; home to Min Brock.

Gilden Sea: Northern sea where the island of Bal-Malin is located.

Hetherlinn: Village in Allsbruth; home to Elabea and Galadin.

Hoitt: Fishing village in Ingloid; Draemel's home.

Ingloid: Nation east of the Gilden Plains.

Isle of Lills: Island in the Sea of Illsbruth; Lassiter was mentored by Newcomb.

Isle of Rythe: "Island of the cursed" off the east coast of Ebon.

Kise: Capital city of Ebon; home to the Cauldron.

MerriNoons: Digri's country; noted as excellent chefs.

Min Brock: Once great citadel of Allsbruth; turning point in the Dark War.

Netniath: Citadel for the Cauldron; located in the city of Kise.

Onderling: Underground world; home to Aggellon and SriBrune.

Pillar of Addoli: Monolith beside the Addoli Ridge.

River Arrgient: Main tributary west of the Gilden Plains.

Torrens Bay: Southern port town of Ferra; exciting yet corrupt.

Tristan: Nation noted for mining ore and forging weapons.

Sea of Illsbruth: Southern sea; home to karshe and the Isle of Lills.

SriBrune: Kinmin's homeland; located within the Onderling.

Valley of Clouds: Near Waelryth; home to ryators.

Vorak: Brairtok's castle in Kise.

Waelryth: Passage created by the Cauldron to invade Allsbruth.

Creatures

Bangaleers: Crab-like creatures of Waelryth; latch upon their victim's face.
Fea dracas: "Little dragons" that live in the hollow of trees.
Gors: Large, hairy scavengers.
Karshe: Silver-plated dragons in the Sea of Illsbruth.
La-zeer: Predator from the Gilden Sea.
Rusk: Small animal that defends storytellers; very poisonous tail.
Ryators: Giant, translucent dragons that live in the Valley of Clouds.
Sevritt: Large, swift Ebonite tracker.
Vul jen: Large, dark, dreamstalker; favorite prey is storytellers.
Worms: Mysterious creatures that live on Bal-Malin.